ELIZABETH
LOWELL

D E A T H

IS

FOREVER

(Originally published as
The Diamond Tiger)

AVON BOOKS
An Imprint of HarperCollinsPublishers

Death Is Forever was originally published as *The Diamond Tiger* in 1992 and reissued in 1999 by HarperCollins.

This is a work of fiction. Names, characters, places, and incidents are products of the author's imagination or are used fictitiously and are not to be construed as real. Any resemblance to actual events, locales, organizations, or persons, living or dead, is entirely coincidental.

AVON BOOKS
An Imprint of HarperCollins*Publishers*
10 East 53rd Street
New York, New York 10022-5299

Copyright © 1992, 2004 by Two of a Kind, Inc.
ISBN: 0-06-051109-5
www.avonbooks.com

First Avon Books paperback printing: June 1992; December 2004
First HarperTorch paperback printing: February 1997

Avon Trademark Reg. U.S. Pat. Off. and in Other Countries, Marca Registrada, Hecho en U.S.A.
HarperCollins® is a registered trademark of HarperCollins Publishers Inc.

Printed in the U.S.A.

10 9 8 7 6 5 4 3 2 1

*For
Jessica Aird,
my source down under*

*And for
Evan,
for all the usual reasons,
plus love*

Prologue

**Western Australia
1989**

Abe Windsor better be dead or I'll bloody well kill him myself.

Jason Street's thought was both promise and prayer. He'd had plenty of time for both in the ten hours since the call had come in from his spy at Crazy Abe's station in Western Australia. Street had spent every minute of the time since then trying to get to the desolate station and the Sleeping Dog Mines. Four hours on a chartered flight from Perth followed by endless black hours behind the wheel of the battered Toyota Land Cruiser, pushing the vehicle at reckless speeds over dirt tracks, racing toward one of the most isolated areas on the continent.

It wasn't the brutal drive that fed Street's fury. It was the fear that more than a decade of his patience and cunning had gone up the spout, wiped out by a savage old man's insanity.

Above the land the Southern Cross faded from the sky, slowly overwhelmed by the yellow violence of the rising sun. The daybreak temperature along the southeastern edge of the Kimberley Plateau was 87 degrees Fahrenheit. As the sun rose, so did the temperature. The brutal torrent of light revealed clumps of grasslike spinifex and stunted gum trees, red dust and occasional outcroppings of stone. And over all was the sun, always the sun, the only true inhabitant of Western Australia.

Stones ricocheted like pistol shots off the undercarriage of the straining vehicle. Lurching, skidding, bucking, the Toyota fought its way over a road that existed more in the driver's mind than on the dry surface of the land itself.

Street had no doubt of his course. He'd spent ten years going to and from Crazy Abe's station, trying to tease and wheedle and cozen the old man's secret out of him. After all those years Street was certain of only one thing—if Crazy Abe's secret was still within the reach of pain, Street would have it before the Southern Cross rose above Australia again.

In an explosion of dust, the Toyota shot over the top of a low rise. Ahead lay Abe's meager station. The old man's possessions were spread out like wreckage across several acres of flat, barren land. There was a ramshackle tin-roof house, a few sun-scoured outbuildings, tractors consumed by rust and misuse, broken mining equipment, discarded four-wheel-drive trucks, and the remains of a World War II RAAF Dakota that had crashed within sight of the station a few months before V-J Day.

Suddenly a glistening, noisy, and very modern helicopter leaped into the sky just beyond the house's tin roof. Street stood on the brakes, bringing the Toyota to a shuddering stop. When the helicopter banked and passed overhead with its red belly beacon flashing, he searched for identifying marks. He expected to see the shield of the Western Australia State Police, the insignia of the Australian Defense Forces, or even the logo of the Flying Doctor Service.

The sleek sides of the helicopter were blank, anonymous as an egg. The owners were no more interested in advertising their presence at Abe Windsor's station than was Street himself.

Furious and fearful at the same time, he slammed his fist against the steering wheel. Then he rammed the Toyota into gear and drove headlong down the hill. As the vehicle skidded to a stop in the loose red earth near Abe's shack, he rolled out and dropped to the dirt, a cocked semiautomatic pistol in his hand. Moving with the precision of a commando, he slid from the cover of the vehicle to the shelter of a rusty stamp mill and from there to the protection of a corner of the house.

He risked a quick glimpse through a dirty window. A single paraffin lamp guttered in the big room of the station house. A barefoot corpse lay beneath a tattered piece of canvas on the long table in the center of the room. The only thing moving was the outback's customary plague of flies.

Cursing through clenched jaws, Street discarded caution and used his heavy boot like a battering ram. The upper hinge of the door popped out of the casement, the latch broke, and the door swung open drunkenly.

The smell of old death rolled out into the sultry yard.

Street looked at the room over the barrel of his pistol.

Nothing looked back.

Gagging at the smell, he walked to the table and flipped up one corner of the tarp, setting off a cloud of flies. Judging by the condition of the corpse, Abe Windsor had been dead for some time. Even allowing for the heat and humidity of the October buildup toward the "wet," Street guessed the old man had been dead for at least three days, maybe more. But there was no doubt that it was Abe Windsor who lay beneath the tarp. The heavy ridge of scar on his left wrist had resisted decay better than the softer flesh around it.

Street turned away with an exclamation of disgust and

glanced at the room without a lot of hope. He doubted that the occupants of the helicopter had left behind anything except flies. But he might have surprised them before they'd finished searching everything on the station.

Grimacing, breathing carefully through his mouth, Street turned back to the corpse. He pulled the dirty undershirt open and looked for the worn velvet pouch that Abe had always worn around his skinny neck.

The pouch was gone.

With a seething curse, Street went to the unpainted wooden shelf next to Abe Windsor's rocking chair. The battered tin box was missing too.

"So you went for your last walk in the bush, did you, you old wanker?" Street said savagely to the corpse. "Did you take that bloody box with you like always? Did your secret die out there in the bush with you? And who in hell was watching you besides me?"

There was no answer but death's hideous grin. For an instant Street was sure the old man was still alive, still mocking him.

"You knew what I was after the whole time, didn't you? Christ, but you loved stuffing me around. Sod you, old man. You're dead and I'm not."

Tiny sounds came from beyond the kitchen door as decaying floorboards shifted.

Someone was headed out of the house.

Street spun and dashed through the doorway into the gloomy kitchen. He was quick enough to catch a flicker of movement as a dark-clad figure slipped through the back door. Sounds came again, the soft, rapid thud of bare feet fleeing over sun-baked earth.

Street leaped to the open door and tripped a quick shot. The bullet caught the fleeing man a few feet before he reached the corner of an outbuilding. He jerked and sprawled facedown in the dirt.

Cautiously Street approached the man and checked for weapons. Nothing. He stood and rolled the man over with one booted foot. Chu, Abe's cook, squinted up at Street through eyes that swam with pain. Street pointed the gun at a spot between the cook's eyes.

"Where's the box, you thieving Chink?"

Chu hissed through his teeth, his face contorted with pain, and said nothing.

"Listen up." Street ground down on Chu's wounded shoulder with the flat sole of his boot. "Where's the box and the velvet sack?"

Chu groaned and said something in Chinese, a plea or a curse or both at once.

Street bore down harder with his foot. From the corner of his eye he caught a hint of movement as someone lunged toward him from the cover of the outbuilding. Reflexively Street's head turned toward the new attacker.

The instant Street's attention was divided, Chu doubled up and aimed a kick at the Australian's crotch.

The two prongs of the attack were so swift and so well-coordinated that Street knew immediately he'd fallen into a trap laid by professionals. His own reaction was equally quick and deadly. He fired point blank at Chu and at the same time twisted so the cook's kick was off the mark.

In the split second before the heavy bullet struck, Chu's heel thudded harmlessly into Street's muscular thigh. Street continued the twisting motion, throwing himself off to the side and bringing his gun to bear on the remaining attacker. As Street hit the ground, he triggered two shots at the second attacker. Both shots missed, but Street's action avoided a head-high kick that would have smashed his skull.

The attacker flew past Street, who was still in the midst of his defensive roll. When Street landed on his belly, he twisted again and calmly shot the attacker twice in the back. Something about the single exclamation of pain and the fall told Street that the attacker was a woman, and that she was dead before she hit the ground.

Even as the information registered in his brain, he was rolling again, anticipating another attacker. He came to his feet in a crouch, his back to a wall and his pistol covering the entire station yard.

Fifty meters away a flock of pale cockatoos, startled by the shots, called noisily among the stunted trees. After a few moments the cockatoos settled back onto their perches, leaving the silence of death to spread unbroken over Abe Windsor's station. All that moved were the flies, as though the searing October sunlight had wings.

Quickly Street checked the bodies of the two people he'd just killed. No sign of the tin box or the velvet bag. He went over the bodies again, hoping to discover who had sent them and why.

Neither Chu nor the Chinese woman carried anything that might identify them: no papers, no clothing labels, no weapons.

Frowning, Street sat on his haunches and studied the two dead bodies. Chu had been at the station for years now, but Street had never noticed the calluses on the cook's hands and feet. They belonged to a highly trained fighter, not to a simple scut worker. The woman's hands were similarly hardened. The two Chinese had worked as a team, a team that had been prepared to kill or die.

Now they were dead and Street was no closer to knowing who they'd worked for than he was to Crazy Abe's diamond mine.

Street spat on the red earth, then turned his back on the bodies. There was little chance that anything of value remained, but after a decade of watching the mousehole, he wouldn't let frustration make him overlook any chance at all. It was just possible that the box containing the old man's doggerel and his will were still hidden on the station.

The stench in the house hadn't changed.

Street went through the place with the practiced motions of a man who had searched those same rooms many, many times before. As always, nothing new turned up. Nor did the tin box. Wiping dirt and sweat from his eyes, he went to stand over the corpse of the old man who had evaded him in death as he had in life.

"Ten years of 'Chunder from Down Under,'" Street snarled, his voice low in his throat. "Ten years of your stink and your sly laughter. To hell with you, Abe Windsor. And to hell with whoever inherits the Sleeping Dog Mines."

1

**Northern Territory, Australia
October**

"Two people died getting this to me."

Cole Blackburn looked at the small worn velvet bag in Chen Wing's hand and asked, "Was it worth it?"

"You tell me."

With a swift motion Wing emptied the contents of the bag onto the ebony surface of his desk. Light rippled and shifted as nine translucent stones tumbled over one another with tiny crystalline sounds. The first impression was of large, very roughly made marbles that had been chipped and pitted by use. Nine of the thirteen stones were colorless. Three were pink. One was the intense green of a deep river pool.

Cole's hand closed over the green marble. It was as big as the tip of his thumb and surprisingly heavy for its size. He rubbed it between his fingers. The surface had an almost slippery feel, as though it had been burnished with precious oils. He turned the stone until he found a flat, cleanly chipped face. He bathed it with his breath.

No moisture collected on the smooth green surface.

Excitement stabbed through Cole. Without a word he walked to a liquor cart that stood against a nearby wall. He picked up a heavy leaded crystal glass and glanced at Wing, who nodded. Cole brought the green stone down the side of the glass in a single swift stroke.

The stone scratched the glass easily and deeply. The stone itself wasn't marked.

At random Cole picked up other stones from the desk and drew them down the crystal surface. New scratches formed. The stones themselves remained untouched. He pulled a well-worn jeweler's loupe from his pocket, angled the desk light to his satisfaction, picked up the deep green stone, and examined it.

The sensation was like falling into a pool of intense emerald light. Yet this was not an emerald. Even uncut and unpolished, the stone held and dispersed light in ways that only a diamond could. It shimmered between his fingers with each tiny movement of his hand. Light flowed and glanced among the irregularities in the stone's surface and gathered in its luminous depths. There were no fractures and only two very minute flaws, both irrelevant to the diamond's value. They lay just below the surface, where they would be cut and polished out of existence.

Cole looked at several more stones before he put his loupe back in his pocket and said, "White paper."

Wing opened a desk drawer, extracted a pure white sheet of Pacific Traders Ltd. letterhead, and slid it across the desk. Cole pulled a small chamois bag from his pocket and removed a rough diamond that he knew was of perfect color. Uncut and unpolished, the stone had a natural octahedral shape. It looked almost manmade next to the worn, irregular stones from Wing's bag.

Cole spaced the diamonds across the surface of the paper. One of the stones changed color subtly, becoming more coral than pink. The other pinks deepened to a lovely clear rose. Most of the white stones took on a blue sheen that exactly matched Cole's diamond. One or two showed a very faint yellow cast to their white, a color shift that only an expert eye would have detected or cared about.

And the green stone burned more vividly still, an emerald flame against snow.

Cole lowered the loupe and studied the green diamond with both eyes again. It still glimmered with an internal fire that was both hot and cold.

Years before, in Tunisia, he'd seen a stone that was nearly the equal of this one. The smuggler who owned the rough claimed it had come from Venezuela. Cole didn't believe it. But before he could raise enough cash to buy the truth, someone had sealed the smuggler's lips by cutting his throat. The smuggler's death hadn't shocked Cole. When it came to diamonds, a man's life was valuable only to himself, and his death could easily profit any number of people.

What did surprise Cole was that these diamonds had cost only two lives. He'd never seen a handful of diamonds to equal the ones resting on the white paper, drawing their color from the peculiar circumstances of their birth rather than reflecting their surroundings.

Cole picked up his own exemplar diamond, put it away, and examined the dark velvet bag that lay collapsed across the desk's ebony surface. The velvet was old, so old that the passage of time and the hard surfaces of the diamonds inside had worn the cloth to near-transparency in places. The velvet didn't care. It was dead.

But the stones weren't dead, not in the same way. They

shimmered with light and time and man's insatiable hunger for the rare and valuable.

"What do you want from me?" Cole asked, watching the diamonds with brooding gray eyes.

For a moment Wing thought the question was directed at the stones. Though he'd known Cole for many years, the Hong Kong businessman didn't claim to understand or predict the American prospector's complex mind.

"Are they diamonds?" Wing asked.

"Yes."

"No chance of deception?"

Cole shrugged. The motion made light move over him. Raw black silk gleamed in his sport coat. His hair was the exact color and luster of the silk. His skin had been weathered in the wild places of the world. Fine lines radiated out from his eyes, legacy of a life spent squinting into the light of a desert sun or the flare of a miner's lamp. Above his left temple a scattering of silver showed in his thick hair. He looked older than his thirty-four years. By every measure that mattered, he was.

"There's always a chance of deception," Cole said. "But if these were made by a man, he'll be the ruin of every miner and diamond mine in the world."

Wing smiled.

"If you're worried," Cole said, "I can find someone in Darwin with a thermal inertia tester. Nobody's beat that test, not yet."

This time it was Wing who shrugged. "Unless you brought an instrument with you, there's no time. These stones must be on their way in a few hours."

"Where are they going?"

"America."

"Where did they come from?"

"Kimberley."

Cole was silent. When he spoke, his voice was neutral. "South Africa's deposits are pretty well played out."

"Not Kimberley, Africa. The Kimberley Plateau, here in Australia."

Wing smiled as though enjoying the chance to show that he understood the difference between the two Kimberleys. It was a common enough mistake. People automatically linked diamonds with Africa, despite the fact that the biggest diamond mine in the world, the Argyle, was in the remote tropical deserts of the state of Western Australia.

Cole smiled in return, but there was little humor in the hard curve of his mouth. "Did the Chen family invest in the Argyle mine on the basis of these stones?"

"I didn't say Argyle, only Kimberley."

Swiftly Cole thought through the possible implications. If those stones came from the Argyle, the cartel that controlled the world's supply of diamonds had made a major new discovery and had become a little richer in the process.

But if the stones were from some new source, the diamond game had a new player and all hell was about to break loose.

Either way, life would become very interesting for the man holding that handful of bright diamond markers in the coming international shoving match.

"Kimberley, Australia," Cole said, pinning Wing with gray eyes that were as clear as glacier ice. "Is that where the stones were found?"

For the first time Wing hesitated. "They came to me from there, but as to where they were originally found . . ." He turned his narrow hands palm up.

"Are there more?"

"This is all that came to me," Wing said carefully.

Cole walked to the window and looked out over the

palms that framed the front lawn of the government casino in Darwin, Northern Territory, Australia, fifteen hundred miles from the Kimberley Plateau. The hard tropical sun and humidity-hazed sky made the Timor Sea look like spun aluminum.

The sun's heat radiated through the double panes of glass in the window close to Cole. In the background came the vague hum of machinery as the casino's air conditioning filtered out tobacco smoke from the gaming rooms below and at the same time cooled the steamy, overbearing heat of tropical October. It was high spring down under. The buildup had already begun.

Buildup, the season when animals died and men went crazy.

Tropical Australia in October was one of the few places on earth Cole found unlivable. For some reason the heat and humidity in the eucalyptus and acacia scrublands affected him more than the same conditions in Venezuela or Brazil.

But inside the Darwin casino, man's machinery kept the tropics at bay, delivering high-tech air that had neither the savor nor the character of any climate or country. If not for the Aboriginal drawings on the wall, the room could have been located anywhere from Hong Kong to Johannesburg, London to Los Angeles, Tel Aviv to Bombay. The furnishings were a fusion of Western woods and Eastern artistic traditions. The clothes combined Eastern fabrics with Italian design flair.

"Were these diamonds mined in the Kimberley?" Cole asked, being blunt because there was no longer anything to gain from circumspection.

"I hoped you could tell me."

Cole's eyes narrowed beneath black eyebrows. Wing wasn't usually evasive, not when he wanted something.

But then Wing didn't usually walk around with a major fortune in uncut diamonds in his pocket. He and his family were too pragmatic to dabble in a commodity whose market price was controlled by a well-entrenched cartel. The Chens usually stuck to mining and refining metallic ores whose names were familiar only to space scientists and weapons makers.

"I can't tell you positively where the diamonds came from," Cole said, "but I can tell you they *didn't* come from the Argyle."

"The stones speak to you?" Wing asked skeptically.

Cole simply looked at the other man.

"How can you be so certain?" Wing demanded. "Argyle has pink diamonds."

"The Argyle mine is a bort hole filled almost entirely with industrial diamonds. Sure, there are pinks in the place, but these pinks are darker, cleaner, and a hell of a lot bigger than anything the Australians have admitted to finding. It takes the patience of an Indian stone polisher to make jewelry out of Argyle's junk."

Wing stirred the diamonds with his fingertip. Light pooled and gleamed as though the stones were wet. "Are you saying these aren't Australian diamonds?"

"No. Just that they're not from the Argyle itself. Hell, Wing, there are seventy different companies working the Kimberley Plateau. Nobody has found much but industrial-grade goods." Cole paused before adding, "At least that's what ConMin has been putting out."

Wing grunted, his skepticism matching Cole's. Con-Min told the world what it wanted the world to hear about diamonds, period. Real intelligence was hard to come by, which was why Wing had called in Cole. "What else do the stones tell you?"

"They're alluvial."

"Explain, please."

"They've been out of the mother pipe a long, long time, washed out by erosion."

"Is that bad?"

Cole shook his head. "Jesus, you still don't know shit from schist, do you?"

"You didn't disparage my questions when we were partners."

"When we were partners you didn't bait me with a handful of fantastic rough," Cole shot back. "These diamonds are the cream of some old, eroded diamond pipe. The flawed goods and small stuff have been destroyed by time. The stones that survived all had the corners rounded off their natural crystalline shape."

"That's good?" Wing asked dubiously.

"When it comes to cutting time, yes. Stones dug fresh and sharp from a pipe lose half their weight in cutting and polishing. These alluvial stones will lose no more than twenty percent between the rough state and some spoiled lady's finger."

"Then these stones are at least thirty percent more valuable than nonalluvial rough diamonds of an equal weight?" Wing asked quickly.

Cole smiled. Wing didn't need to know much about diamonds to keep a balance sheet in his head. That was one of the reasons Cole trusted his former partner. He knew what motivated Chen Wing.

Profit.

"When you take into account color and size as well," Cole said, "you've got at least a million dollars wholesale sitting on your desk, as is. Cut and polished, those stones are worth one hell of a lot more."

"How much more?"

"Depends on how badly someone wants them. The fancies—"

"Fancies?" Wing interrupted.

"Colored diamonds. They're bloody rare, and a true green is the rarest of them all. Wherever that lot came from, it's God's own jewel box."

"Are there mines like that?"

"In Australia? Not that I know of."

"Are there such mines anywhere?" Wing demanded impatiently.

"Ever hear of Namaqualand? Southwest coast of Africa, just below the mouth of the Orange River?" Cole asked.

Wing shook his head.

"About sixty years ago a geologist called Hans Merensky was prospecting on Crown holdings there. He came across some diamonds lying together on top of the ground, neat as eggs in a quail's nest."

Though he said nothing, Wing sat straighter in his chair and leaned closer to Cole.

"Everywhere Merensky looked he found more diamonds," Cole said. "Soon he couldn't hold them all in his hand. Most of them were too big to fit down the neck of his canteen. He had to store them in candy tins."

With a soft grunt Wing looked at the small handful of diamonds on his desk and imagined the sensation of making an even bigger find.

"Yeah," Cole said in a low voice. "That's how I felt when I first heard the story. Every diamond hunter lies awake at night and dreams of how it would feel to find a jewel box like that."

"Jewel box. You're serious, then?"

"Jewel box, diamond trap, concentrated gem gravels— call it what you will. It's a place where time and water and gravity have done the heavy work of mining for you. They've worn away the softer rock, carried away the dross, and concentrated the diamonds."

"I don't understand."

Cole curbed his impatience. "Diamonds are heavier and far harder than most minerals, so they sink in quiet parts of river bends, collect behind boulders or in tree roots, or get caught in gravel. Gold does the same thing for the same reason. It's heavy. Most of the big diamond finds started with men looking for placer gold."

"What happened to Merensky?"

"He filled a half-dozen candy tins full of diamonds, diamonds as big as eighty carats. Gem quality, all of them. He sold out his claim for one million pounds, which in those days was a king's ransom."

"To whom did he sell?"

"Guess," Cole said sardonically.

Wing grimaced and hissed a word through his teeth. "Shit."

"That may be your opinion, but stockholders think quite highly of ConMin."

"Do you think these are cartel diamonds?" Wing said, glancing at the stones on the desk.

"No."

"So quick? No doubts?"

"You would have lost more than two people getting the likes of these away from the diamond cartel," Cole said flatly.

"But the cartel would be interested in them?"

"If those stones are all from the same spot, and that place is a new strike, the cartel would move heaven and earth and take on hell to grab control of the find. Archimedes said he could move the world with a lever long enough. The mine that yielded those stones is a lever that long."

Wing grunted. "What else can you tell me about these stones? Anything, no matter how small."

"Just that the stones don't 'feel' like African diamonds. The colors aren't right. Too much pink. No Cape yellow at all. Several of those whites are twinned crystals, macles. Australia is known for macles. The green diamond isn't likely for Africa at all. Brazil, maybe, but that green is both more intense and yet more fiery than the Dresden diamond, which is the best of the Brazilian greens."

Wing touched the green diamond with new appreciation.

"All in all," Cole said, "if that's a representative sampling from some prospector's cache, I doubt that it was found in Africa. ConMin's only other significant source of diamonds is the Soviet Union, and the Soviets aren't noted for gem goods, much less for blue-whites. Their goods have a very slight greenish tinge."

"Then this lot could have come from somewhere in Australia?"

"Possibly. The Ellendale find had green gem-quality diamonds. Nothing as big or as deeply colored as that, of course, or presumably the Australian government would have developed Ellendale rather than Argyle."

"What you're saying is that it's possible these stones came from a single strike in Australia?"

A glance at Wing's face told Cole that he could no longer trust Wing, because there was more involved in these diamonds than profit. He'd seen Wing in quest of profit before. There was nothing of the cheerful entrepreneur about the other man right now. He was intent, dedicated, and predatory down to the tips of his immaculately manicured hands.

"How badly do you need to know?" Cole asked calmly.

"Not me. Us. You and me."

Cole's expression hardened. "We aren't partners any more. We sold BlackWing Resources Ltd. to your uncle five years ago."

"I think it would be wise for us to become partners again," Wing said, reaching into another drawer and pulling out a sheaf of papers. "This is a partnership agreement very similar to the one we signed when we created BlackWing."

Cole glanced at the papers but made no move to take them. "I read too slowly," he lied softly. "So translate the jargon into common English. But don't go all Mandarin and lawyerly on me, or I'll walk right out that door and catch the first plane back to Brazil."

Without hesitation Wing set the papers down on the desk. The fingertips of his right hand moved almost caressingly over the expensive, textured sheets. When he spoke, it was slowly, a man choosing each word with care.

"Ten years ago we formed BlackWing Resources on the basis of your geological brilliance and my financial abilities. It was a good match, a profitable one, because each of us brought different strengths to the deal."

"It also worked because you hired geologists to check my work and I hired accountants to check yours," Cole pointed out blandly.

Wing smiled. "There was intelligence in our partnership, at least as much intelligence as trust. The Chen family needs your intelligence again. We need you."

"For what?"

"We believe that you may be a part owner of the deposit that yielded these stones."

The air conditioning made the only sound in the room for several long moments while Cole studied Wing.

"I've bought, sold, and swapped a lot of diamond claims in my life," Cole said finally. "Are you trying to tell me I've overlooked something this good?"

"Sign this partnership agreement and I'll answer your

questions. But unless and until you sign, not one more word."

Wing gathered the rough diamonds and began to return them one by one to the worn velvet bag. Cole watched until the green diamond vanished.

Then he picked up the papers and began to read.

2

Alaska

The polestar shimmered above tundra, river, and mountains alike, providing a brilliant center for the night to circle in icy splendor. Moonlight brushed the river with silver. The illumination was ghostly and cold as snow. A black wind from an undiscovered tomorrow rushed down the long valley, whispering of ancient glaciers and a coming midnight that knew no dawn.

That was what Erin Shane Windsor hoped to capture, the delicacy and chill of eternity drawn in moonlight upon a river surface that was slowly turning to ice.

Unaware of the cold and isolation of the vast Alaskan landscape, Erin made a final adjustment on her camera and stepped back from the tripod. She tripped the shutter with fingers that no longer could feel the texture of the bulb release. The shutter opened and closed reluctantly, stiff with cold. As insurance, she exposed several more frames of film. The long, silk-on-silk sound of the camera mechanism was loud against the arctic silence.

After the last exposure, she immediately went to work on a new combination of settings. When she fumbled the settings a second time, she swore softly, sending out her breath in a plume of glittering silver moisture. She had only moments to capture the shot she wanted. Right now the moon was at just the right angle to illuminate three of the river's sinuous curves and to suggest similar curves in the folds of the mountains themselves.

But the world was turning and the wind was pushing clouds into a single mass. Each passing second changed the most important element in the entire image—light.

Erin's watch cheeped a warning.

She ignored it. The sound was only the first of several mechanical reminders she'd programmed into the watch. When she was shooting pictures, no other reality existed for her. Her ability to concentrate was a double-edged gift, putting her at odds with a civilization that required time to be divided and subdivided into portions that had no meaning beyond urban landscapes.

"Dammit, hands, settle down," she muttered as her numb fingers made slow work of resetting the camera's finicky time and exposure mechanisms.

The watch cheeped again.

Even as she shut out the sound, part of her mind reluctantly understood that there was a world beyond her camera lens. And in that other world she had a plane to catch to civilization, the very civilization she'd avoided for seven years.

Like the geese and shorebirds she photographed on the tundra, and like the whales she photographed from skin boats, she was southward bound. Unlike the birds and whales, she was heading toward days divided into hours divided into minutes divided into seconds, with no time off for good behavior, world without end, amen.

She squeezed the bulb release, advanced the film, then squeezed again, listening as the shutter delicately framed instants of time that transcended clocks and heartbeats.

Rapt, patient, shivering with a cold she didn't feel, she worked over the camera again, compelled by the black and silver starkness of the landscape, photographing her farewell to a land she loved.

There was a mythic quality to the arctic that had attracted her on first sight. That quality was reflected in the "uncivilized" lives of the Eskimo and Aleut subsistence hunters she'd met and lived among. She'd gone with men in skin boats through shifting leads in pack ice, hunting whales. Out in the frail boats she'd learned that primitive man feared, loved, and revered his prey.

Modern man simply killed with high-tech weapons, risking nothing of himself and therefore learning nothing of himself or his prey, of life or death or transcendence. She had known those kinds of men, too. Modern men.

She would rather freeze to death in the arctic than live as they did.

Her watch's warnings came at shorter intervals until they became constant, reminding Erin of the urgency of the telegram that had been read to her over the shortwave radio that morning.

You must return immediately stop family emergency stop instructions to follow stop james rosen esq.

"Shut up," she muttered. "Just . . . shut . . . up."

She jabbed a numb index finger at the alarm button on her watch, silencing it. But she knew it was too late. Her concentration had been ruined, because she couldn't turn off James Rosen Esquire as easily as she'd silenced her watch.

You must return immediately stop

Erin shoved aside the demand. She'd ignored civilization for seven years. She could ignore it for seven more minutes. She would have ignored the summons forever if she hadn't realized that her own arctic cycle was ending.

But it was.

She hadn't taken all possible pictures of the arctic, but she'd taken all the images that were necessary for her own needs. The violence that had driven her into the wilderness seven years ago had faded to a whisper. She wasn't the same person she'd been then.

The answers she'd found in Alaska no longer fit the questions she was asking herself.

Jeffrey will be ecstatic, Erin thought, wishing the idea gave her greater comfort.

Jeffrey Fisher, her New York editor, didn't understand the part of her life she spent in the wilderness. Nor did he understand the restlessness that sent her out to places where others rarely went. He loved her photographic technique, her artist's eye, but he was forever trying to get her to do "civilized" photography—English farmhouses and French vineyards, ancient Greek statues and modern Mediterranean resorts.

At first she'd tried to make Fisher understand why she didn't want his European assignments. She'd tried to explain to him that while civilization removed the grueling lows of physical deprivation, it also leveled off the psychic highs of survival.

Fisher hadn't understood. Her preferred world of stark Pacific Rim landscapes and remote cultures was simply too distant from Manhattan, and too different in ways both obvious and subtle, for him to understand. The East Coast looked east, toward Europe and the past. The West Coast looked west, toward the undeveloped Pacific Rim and the future.

Unfortunately she'd run out of internal and external excuses for not accepting the European assignments, for not shooting farmhouses and wine cellars and sterling silver by candlelight. She'd made herself clear her schedule so that no one would be left hanging if she was gone for several months or even a year. She'd done everything but work up enthusiasm for shooting European set pieces when she would rather shoot almost anything else.

She'd been to the Continent many times. She'd been more depressed than impressed. Part of it was simply that her former fiancé had been European, or at least had claimed to be.

Family emergency stop

Part of it was that she associated Europe with her father's work, diplomacy and secrets and treachery, the kind of betrayal that scarred its survivors for life.

Assuming there were any survivors to scar.

Instructions to follow stop

Instructions, but no truth. Man had invented civilization in order to escape natural truth and had invented time in order to more carefully package human lies.

Family emergency

Motionless, Erin stood surrounded by brilliant silver light and radiant natural silence, eternity condensed into a shimmering unity that had a sweeping disregard for human concepts such as truth and lies, life and death, fair and unfair.

You must return

Life wasn't fair or unfair; it was simply unexpected. Sometimes life's surprises were breathtakingly beautiful, like the arctic. Sometimes they were breathtakingly cruel, like Hans. But surprises were always the raw material of life, and she had chosen to live.

Erin silenced her wristwatch alarm for the last time and began packing up her equipment for the long trip to Los Angeles.

3

Antwerp

"How long ago did the two Chinese assassins die?"

The voice, slightly distorted by the satellite link and the scrambler, had a dry Etonian disdain. Hugo van Luik was a stocky Dutchman with a full head of white hair, but he sounded like a whingeing Pom to an Australian ear.

There was the sound of a bottle gurgling at the other end of the line. Van Luik could imagine Jason Street swilling beer from an oversized can.

"Twelve hours," Street said, "maybe a bit more."

"Why was your report delayed?"

"You want me spilling our business on open phone lines, do you?" Street shot back. "This is bloody Australia, remember. Anybody with a receiver can listen in on two-way radios. I buried the chokies, took the place apart, and then got back here to Perth before I called."

Van Luik was grateful to be ten thousand miles away from the country and the man he detested yet was never free of. Van Luik's office on the fifth floor of the gray, anonymous office building on Pelikanstraat, the main street of Antwerp's diamond trade, might as well have been in hell for all the comfort it gave him.

He closed his eyes against the blinding pain of a growing headache. At the moment he was alone in his office, so he allowed himself the luxury of slumping. He felt like he was impaled on a giant fishhook. Nausea twisted in his stomach, then slowly subsided. He drew a deep, grateful breath. He was a powerful man, both physically and in his profession, but he paid the price of power. Lately that price seemed to grow every day.

"Very well," van Luik said. "To summarize, the holographic will, the velvet sack, and the tin box were gone by the time you arrived. A decade's work—wasted."

"Too bloody right. You should have let me open Abe Windsor up my own way. He'd have spilled his secret soon enough."

"Perhaps. But more probably a man his age would have died under torture and left the secret to his heir. At the time, the risks seemed too great."

"Not now, mate. Now they look bloody small."

"Your hindsight is superlative."

No reply came from the other end of the line, unless another gurgle of beer could be called a comment. Street loathed the precise Dutchman whose power was hidden behind the bland, meaningless title of Director of Special Operations, Diamond Sales Division. But even while Street loathed van Luik, he feared him.

"Very well," van Luik said. "Now go back over it from the beginning."

It was his favorite tactic with a hardhead like Jason Street. Repetition reinforced the subordinate role and at the same time exposed little inconsistencies that suggested information withheld or lies told.

Street knew the drill as well as van Luik did. The Australian took another long swallow of beer and belched into the telephone. "Not much to tell, really. Abe had been drinking for a few days. Full as a boot, he was. Nothing different there. About three days ago he went crook, grabbed a shovel, and took off into the bush, screaming something about digging his own grave."

"Was that unusual?"

"Hell no, mate. Happens once a month, like a woman bleeding. Only this time Abe was telling the truth. He must have died out there in the bush. His body looked like he'd been slow-roasted on a spit. Dead as tinned fish and three times the smell."

Van Luik felt nausea welling up again, though not because of Street's words. Death and corruption were matters of indifference to the Dutchman. It was helplessness that made him feel sick.

"How did Windsor's body get back to the station?" van Luik asked.

"The chokies must have found him."

"Chokies?"

"Chinks, slants, slopeheads, Chinamen," Street said impatiently. Van Luik spoke four languages but couldn't—or wouldn't—remember the Australian slang Street always used. "They trucked him back."

"How do you know that? Did your informant at the station tell you?"

"Sarah? She'd already gone walkabout with her bronze-wing brats. She was drinking with Abe, same as usual, and passed out. When she sobered up and he still wasn't back, she called me, then headed for the back of beyond."

"Why?"

"She knew I'd kill her if Abe was dead."

"Then how do you know the Chinese found Windsor?"

"There were no new tracks going into the station. The

cook must have called in the chopper when Abe didn't come back. Or else he followed Abe and staked him out in the sun for a yak about missing mines."

Van Luik let his silence reach halfway around the world.

Street kept talking. "The bloody cook had to be a tout, same as Sarah. Lots of people knew Abe had some nice stones in the sack. Wasn't just us on to him."

Van Luik massaged the bridge of his nose. "Go on."

"It must have been the chokies that found Abe out in the bush, brought him back, then ransacked the station, which means Abe didn't talk before he died."

"I profoundly hope so. Unfortunately the 'chokies' knew enough to take the tin box as well as the diamonds, didn't they?"

Jason Street took a swig of beer and said nothing. He'd been hoping van Luik wouldn't realize the implications of the missing box so quickly.

"Didn't they?" Van Luik's repeated question had an edge to it.

"Right, they took the bloody box."

"So we must assume they are at least as well informed as we are. They must realize that the contents of the bag are worth only a fraction of what the contents of the box may ultimately be worth."

The encrypted satellite channel hummed invitingly, waiting for Street to agree with the obvious.

"I suppose," the Australian said reluctantly.

Van Luik looked out across the wet, gray rooftops that housed the most skillful diamond cutters and the most ruthless gemstone brokers in the world. Sometimes he could relieve the pain by resting his eyes on distant vistas. And sometimes he simply had to endure.

He closed his eyes and endured, trying to think beyond the blinding instants of pain that measured his heartbeats in the blood vessels behind his eyes. Jason Street had come to ConMin with the highest recommendations ten years ago, when he had been barely thirty. Nothing had happened since then to make van Luik doubt Street's abilities or his ultimate loyalties.

Until now. Now something was wrong. Street was temporizing, lying, or withholding some crucial bit of information. Van Luik couldn't tell whether the Australian was lying to avoid ConMin's wrath or for some other, less obvious reason.

"Were you able to get any information on the helicopter?" van Luik asked softly.

"I checked every charter operator in Western Australia and the Northern Territory. No luck. No trace of a flight plan in the air traffic control system, either. Must have been privately owned."

"Find that helicopter." Van Luik almost gagged with the sudden blinding agony his outburst triggered. He breathed shallowly through his mouth for a moment. When he spoke again, his voice was controlled and calm. "We must find out who has the poetry and the stones."

"I'm working on it, mate."

Van Luik shifted the phone to his left hand and massaged his right temple with long, well-manicured fingers. Light flashed from the little finger of his right hand, where he wore a five-carat, emerald-cut, D flawless diamond. The stone was pavé set in matte-finish platinum. It was the only jewelry van Luik wore or needed to wear. In Antwerp the stone was a calling card, instantly identifying him as a fellow of the international diamond brotherhood.

"You have, of course, a copy of 'Chunder from Down Under'?" van Luik asked.

"Sarah checked it a week before Abe died. It hadn't been changed since the last time I sent a copy to you."

"I don't suppose she was able to copy the will,

though?" Van Luik's tone was quiet, almost accusing. When Street didn't answer, the Dutchman added, "Did she even manage to look at it?"

Street drew a deep breath and prepared to tell van Luik what he already knew. "Abe left 'Chunder' on his bedside table, but his will was his own bloody little secret, and he kept it even closer than the stones around his neck."

Van Luik grunted. He opened the file on the desk in front of him and glanced through a sheaf of photographs. They were grainy prints, blown up from the tiny negatives of a Minox camera, page after page of spidery, old-fashioned handwriting on rough, lined tablet paper. Meaningless ramblings or a dead man's cleverly disguised clues to a missing diamond mine. The truth of the poetry was still elusive.

"You have a copy with you," van Luik said.

It was a statement, not a question. Street bit back a savage retort and said only, "Yes."

"Begin."

"Rack off, van Luik. We've been around this course so many times that—"

"Begin," van Luik interrupted coldly.

There was a silence, followed by the subtle rustling of paper as Street shuffled through pages of Crazy Abe's oddly lucid handwriting.

"Any particular verse strike your fancy?" Street asked in a goading tone. He knew that "Chunder" offended van Luik in more ways than his inability to pierce its central secret.

"The fourth verse this time, I think."

"Right." Street began reading aloud, his voice uninflected. " 'Find it if you can,/If you dare to go/Where the dark swan floats/Over a dead sea's bones,/Where men are Percys and Lady Janes are stone.' " When he finished reading, Street waited.

So did van Luik.

With a muttered curse, Street began explaining lines he'd read and explained so many times he no longer really saw them. "The first line—"

"Is self-explanatory," van Luik cut in. "So is the second. Begin with the third."

"Right. Black swans are all over the outback, like koalas used to be all over the east coast. He could be talking about a strike near a billabong."

"Explain."

"A billabong is a deep river pool that becomes a waterhole in the dry season when the shallow parts of the river dry up," Street said mechanically.

"Go on."

Street's hand tightened on the telephone. Of all van Luik's quirks, the one of making someone repeat the same information over and over again was the most irritating. It was also the most effective in preventing lies, a fact Street understood and had put to use for himself with his own subordinates.

"Abe could have made a strike near a billabong, except that there aren't any waterholes on his mineral leases or on his station that are big enough to be called a billabong," Street said in a monotone. "The only reliable year-round water is the well at his station house."

Van Luik made a curt sound that could have meant anything. Street knew it was a signal to keep talking.

"That leaves the bloody 'dead sea's bones,'" Street continued tonelessly. "Since we don't have a billabong for the swans to swim in, it's no shocker that we don't have any waterholes sitting on top of a marine fossil bed to point the way to the mine."

"Go on."

Street smiled thinly. He suspected that van Luik found sex distasteful. Abe hadn't. The only time he wasn't stuck in a woman was when he drank too much beer and brewer's wilt took him down.

"So Abe tells us to find the mine if we dare to go 'Where men are Percys and Lady Janes are stone,'" Street said, drawing it out. "Aussies call their cock their Percy. Guess what a Lady Jane is?"

Van Luik grunted. He didn't have to guess. He'd heard it all before, many times.

"So Abe is telling us to go where men have a cock and women have a stone pussy," Street said succinctly. "Welcome to the outback. That narrows the mine's location down to a few thousand square miles of uninhabited country."

When van Luik would have spoken, Street talked right over him.

"In the next verse, an 'amber river' must be beer, right?" Street said. "You drink enough of it and you'll 'piss a yellow sea.' Then there's—"

"Go to the next verse," van Luik interrupted.

"Right. 'Crawl into my bed and onto my Percy,/Bridget and Ingrid, Diana and Mercy,/Kewpie and Daisy and Kelly,/Rooting and hooting about love./Mistresses of lies,/Damn their hot cries.'" Street took a breath and continued sarcastically, "We've already decoded Percy, which leaves us with the other names. They aren't cities, towns, settlements, crossroads, tracks, paths, stations, or any other bloody thing but Aussie slang for pussy."

Van Luik made a sound of disgust.

"Rooting is screwing," Street continued relentlessly. "Now maybe the old bastard saw mining as a sexual experience or maybe he didn't. Either way, that verse has sweet fuck-all to tell us about where he found his bloody diamonds."

"Go to the ninth verse," van Luik said.

"You go to it. I've had enough."

"Begin with the fourth line."

Street gripped the phone so hard his hand ached, while he reminded himself that now was not the time to lose his temper. Even though it hadn't been his fault, the secret to the Sleeping Dog Mines had slipped through his fingers. If going over "Chunder" one more time was the only punishment he got, he'd be lucky.

" 'Stone womb giving me hope,/Secrets blacker than death/And truth it's death to speak.' " Street waited, but van Luik said nothing. " 'Stone womb' is a mine, right? Didn't we decide that—oh, six, seven years ago, when he changed 'woman' to 'womb'?"

Van Luik ignored the sarcasm. "Yes. Go on."

"Wombs, women, and mines are dark places, and telling where his mine was would have been the death of Crazy Abe, and he bloody well knew it."

" 'But I will speak to you,/Listen to me, child of rue.' "

Street said nothing, too surprised by the reversal of roles, van Luik reading the doggerel they both had come to loathe.

" 'Let secrets sleep/Waiting for the offspring of deceit./While 'roos and rutting gins/Leap on the ground above,/A handful of old candy tins/Rattle around below.' "

Silence stretched over the communications link as an unhappy certainty grew in Street. "He's talking about an heir, isn't he? Not just any poor sod that happens to be reading 'Chunder,' but his own bloody heir."

"I am afraid you are correct. 'Child of rue' can no longer be understood to be a comment on the general unhappiness of mankind."

"Bloody hell," Street snarled. "What could his heir find in that blurter's poetry that we can't?"

The ache between van Luik's eyes grew greater with each heartbeat. It would have been so much easier if there had been some unmistakable hint of treachery on Street's part, some tangible proof of unreliability from the man on the other end of the line. But there wasn't, which meant that some unknown and therefore utterly unpredictable force was at work to upset the fragile balance of ConMin's Diamond Sales Division, a balance Hugo van Luik had spent his life trying to maintain, a balance that had been achieved at the cost of so many principles and ideals and lives.

Van Luik pictured the Australian scene in his mind, wondering whether Abe Windsor had finally babbled the secrets of his mine to the spinifex as he lay dying. A useless speculation in any case, for the spinifex had neither ears to hear nor mouths to communicate. All van Luik had was the fact that Jason Street had been told about a holographic will and had been shown sheet after sheet of manic poetry; and that, when drunk, Abelard Windsor would talk about diamonds as green as billabongs shaded by gum trees, diamonds as pink as a white girl's nipples, diamonds the color and clarity of distilled water.

Futilely, fiercely, van Luik wished that he'd been able to turn Street loose years ago to use his quick, cruel skills. Street would have opened up the old man like a sturgeon, spilling the glistening caviar of truth. Or better yet, if possible, a swift death, a death that would have killed the secret of the mine as well. . . . But neither idea had been approved by van Luik's superiors.

Now it was too late.

"No one can prove the mine exists," van Luik said softly, not even aware that he was speaking aloud. "He was, after all, quite mad."

"Dream on, mate," Street retorted. "The mine exists. They called him Crazy Abe and he might have been, but not like that. Diamonds were his children, his women, his country, and his god. I've heard a lot of lies in my day and bloody little truth. Hearing Abe talk about diamonds was like being a priest in the confessional. The truth, no matter how wild. I never got my hands on the stones in the bag, but I'd bet my life they were real."

Silence stretched into a sigh. "The sixteenth verse. Read it."

This time Street didn't argue. Before he'd only feared that Abe Windsor would leave the secret of the diamond mine to someone other than his friend Jason Street. Now Street was certain. He'd sworn the poetry had nothing new to teach him.

He'd been wrong.

" 'It can be yours, all of it./Say goodbye to mallee root,/Say g'day to my queen,/Go a yard for each year of deceit,/Turn around once—see it?/Stupid merkin./Can't find shit in a loo, can you?' "

Van Luik waited.

"Mallee root is rhyming slang for prostitute," Street said tiredly, finding nothing new in the line. "There's no map or local name like it on any of Abe's properties or claims. As for his 'queen,' it's probably his mine, right?"

Van Luik grunted.

"As for the rest, until you know where to stand and how long Abe was deceived, the words are useless. Same for 'Take a map of Tasmania,/Find the little man in the boat./Go on, row on.' The map of Tasmania is slang for pussy, and the little man in the boat is—"

"Yes, yes, yes," van Luik cut in impatiently. "Knowing that Abe is talking to his heir doesn't suggest any new interpretations to you?"

Street hesitated, then sighed. "Not a hope, mate. Not a bloody hope. But I doubt the chokies will have any better luck making sense out of the poem than we have. They were probably looking for maps or ore samples, anything that would point them in the right direction. It's a big station, and Abe had mineral claims in other places as well."

"But it must mean something to someone," van Luik said harshly. "Windsor's heir might be able to decipher it. That's the possibility we must guard against now."

"Do you know who the heir is?"

"Not yet. We should know soon."

"Find out," Street said. "I'll take care of him. No worries, mate. With the heir dead and the mines abandoned, the government will let the claims lapse. I'll file new ones, you'll underwrite a real search, and the mine will eventually be found and controlled by us. No worries."

"Even with the claims in hand, you'll be no closer to finding the mine than you are right now."

"No worries. I'll find the bloody thing. All I need is time and money for equipment."

Van Luik smiled weakly. If only it was that easy. But it wasn't. Nothing about the Sleeping Dog Mines had been easy. Nothing at all. Since the instant of their discovery, the diamonds had been both a siren call and a threat of death.

The siren call had proved false. The threat could prove to be all too real.

"We will consider your solution," van Luik said.

"Don't consider too long. This operation is balls-up enough as it is."

The line hummed, telling Street that van Luik had disconnected.

4

Darwin
Chen Wing's office

Despite the dense legal language, Cole Blackburn only had to read the partnership contract once. He had a nearly perfect memory. It was a quirk of mind that had sometimes helped him and more often had brought him pain. Too many things had happened to him that he would rather forget.

The agreement itself was quite clear. The contract allowed Cole to purchase half interest in BlackWing Resources for the sum of one dollar U.S. In return, he would agree to sign over to BlackWing his interests in any Australian mining claims or patents he held. At the moment, that amounted to zero claims and patents. BlackWing had been worth $10 million U.S. five years ago, when Cole had sold his half to the Chen family. Since then, the value of the company had at least doubled.

Beneath all the legal bells and whistles, Cole was being offered $10 million in equity for the investment of a dollar, plus mining claims and patents he didn't hold. The contract itself was fully executed except for his own signature. Everything was clear except the reason for the offer.

That was why Cole had spent the past nineteen minutes reading between the contract's lines. Granted, circumstances surrounding the dissolution of his partnership with Wing had been unusual. The family of Chen had paid Cole $5 million partly to soothe him for the loss of a lover who was their daughter, Wing's sister. But now the shrewd clan that controlled a sizeable portion of Hong Kong and Macao seemed to be offering him twice that much for no reason he could see.

It made him nervous.

He was no lawyer, but he was sophisticated enough to see that there were no loopholes, no tricks built into the partnership agreement, no obvious or subtle way for the Chen family to recoup from Cole Blackburn the missing $9,999,999.

Without signing, he dropped the document back on the desk. "It's too early for Christmas."

Wing shrugged. "It's not a gift. The present geologists at BlackWing are either too inexperienced or too corrupt to find what we want."

"And what's that?"

"Diamond mines," Wing said succinctly.

"Why do you want them? You've got a half-dozen Pacific Basin holdings that pay better returns than the average diamond mine."

Wing rubbed his palms together thoughtfully, then shook his head. "Have you looked at oil prices lately? At gold? At copper? Iron? Uranium? They are, as you Americans say, in the toilet." He smiled slightly. It had been a long time since he had used American slang.

"Diamonds have had their own problems," Cole said. "What cost sixty-two thousand dollars American per carat in 1980 costs about twenty thousand at the moment."

"Yes, but take a slightly longer view and you'll find that in 1974 the same diamond cost only forty-three hundred dollars per carat. Trust me, my friend. I have done my research carefully. Diamonds are the only commodity to have increased in real value over the last fifty years."

"Thanks to the cartel."

Wing sighed. "They're bloody geniuses, aren't they? At meetings of the UN, countries argue and do nothing. At meetings of Consolidated Minerals, Inc., countries agree and make money. ConMin is the only monopoly in history that has channeled rather than set free the inherent greediness of man. Prices rise, but slowly. Long-term stability, not short-term profits. ConMin has an almost Chinese appreciation of time."

"And power."

"That too," Wing agreed softly. "That most of all."

"So the Chen family wants a diamond prospector who owes nothing to the diamond cartel."

Wing was momentarily startled. He'd seen Cole only infrequently in the five years since his sister Lai had broken her engagement to the American. In that time, Wing had forgotten that Cole's mind was as quick as his well-conditioned body.

"Yes, that is precisely what we want," Wing admitted.

Cole leaned back in the sleek leather chair and listened to his own instincts. He was used to operating on them at times and in places where more than money was at stake. His instincts had urged him to come to Darwin on the strength of Wing's cryptic phone call.

Instincts . . . or sheer restlessness.

Whichever was speaking, Cole was ready to listen. He still didn't know precisely what Wing wanted. More accurately, Cole didn't know what the Chen family wanted. But he did know that touching the luminous green diamond had made him feel more alive than he'd felt in years.

Listening carefully to his inner silence, waiting to hear the whisper of instincts telling him to avoid an unseen trap, Cole waited for another minute. He heard nothing but the quickened beating of his own heart. He'd found diamonds and diamond mines all over the world. He had made and lost small fortunes, and large ones as well, but he'd never found the equal of Wing's green diamond.

Now he was being offered the chance to find a whole mine full of them, God's own jewel box.

Cole pulled a pen from his pocket and signed his name on the contract and its copies with quick, slashing strokes. Saying nothing, he folded one contract and put it in his breast pocket. Then he pulled a dollar bill from his wallet, clipped the bill to the remaining contracts, and flipped the papers back across the ebony desk.

"All right, partner," Cole said. "Tell me about this diamond mine you want me to find."

Wing's smile was amused. "The Chen family didn't hire you merely because you're a brilliant prospector, although you are. We brought you into this because you have a verbal promise from Abelard Windsor of a fifty-percent interest in Sleeping Dog Mines Ltd. as a full repayment of gambling debts incurred by him during a night of playing Two Up."

For an instant Cole was too surprised to say anything.

Wing allowed his small smile of triumph to spread into a grin. It was the first time he had ever seen Cole off-balance.

"That was twelve years ago," Cole said. "Christ, I didn't even know you then."

Wing made a dismissing motion with his hand. "Did Mr. Windsor ever pay off that debt?"

Cole made a sound too harsh to be called laughter. "There were times Crazy Abe couldn't remember from one day to the next what happened. He was just too drunk. I was a long way from sober myself. So was everybody else at the station."

"Do you have an IOU?"

"Old Abe wasn't that crazy," Cole said dryly. "Besides, it wasn't serious gambling. We were just killing time in a station shack, waiting out the first storm of the wet."

"This was found at the station," Wing said.

He drew a frayed, worn piece of paper from the center desk drawer. He handled the paper very carefully, holding it by the corner as though to avoid smudging it . . . or leaving fingerprints.

Cole leaned forward and read the faded writing.

*I owe Cole Blackburn half of Sleeping Dog Mines
Because I lost at 2-up one too many times!*

Abe Windsor's signature and the date were written across the bottom of the sheet in a fine, formal Victorian hand.

"The Chen family has taken the liberty of having two handwriting experts certify this document, so you need not fear embarrassment on that score," Wing said calmly. "Even without the note, it is a legitimate gambling debt. With the note, the debt will be promptly recognized by the Australian government when you press your claim."

"But I won't." Cole's voice was soft and final. "Crazy Abe is sly and mean as a snake in the blind, but he's never screwed me. He fed me, gave me a place to sleep out of the rain, and as much beer as I could swim in." Cole's voice changed, becoming more matter-of-fact. "I've seen Sleeping Dog One. That hole is never going to produce anything but bort. And if the old man has found a jewel box in one of the other Dogs, he's welcome to it. I sure as hell won't try to screw him out of a lifetime strike in the name of a gambling debt I never took seriously."

"Crazy Abe doesn't need his mines anymore. His body was discovered in the bush yesterday."

Cole looked away for a moment. When he looked back, his eyes were the color of winter rain. "God grant a quiet rest to that unhappy old bastard. Going walkabout with him was like stepping back in time, a century at least, sometimes more like ten centuries. Despite his Continental education, he was a real primitive."

"So I gather from reading his poetry. There is much of it, and all of it is bad."

Wing produced a battered tin box from the belly drawer of his desk. Inside lay several documents and a supply of rough paper waiting to be filled with future poetry. He picked up one of the documents and scanned it quickly, frowning.

Cole smiled crookedly. "He wrote poetry by the yard. Which one is that?"

"Something called 'Chunder from Down Under.' I am told that the late Mr. Windsor regarded this particular piece of doggerel as a kind of rhyming treasure map, a guide that would lead his heir to the diamond deposit."

"What?"

"The key to locating the lost mine is hidden somewhere in this swamp of rhyme and memory," Wing said, handing the sheets across the desk.

Silently Cole scanned the closely packed lines, reading at random.

> *While 'roos and rutting gins*
> *Leap on the ground above,*
> *A handful of old candy tins*
> *Rattle around below.*

"The 'candy tins' is an interesting, er, metaphor, but as a treasure map it leaves a lot to the imagination," Cole said.

"There's more of it," Wing said, trying and failing to

keep the hope from his voice. "But I fear it is all . . . difficult."

"Or simply insane. They didn't call him Crazy Abe because they couldn't think of another name. That old man didn't just march to his own drummer, he had his own bloody band."

Wing sighed. "We suspected as much. We were rather hoping the poetry would mean something special to you."

"And if I find this mine, under the contract I just signed, half of my interest is yours, as co-owner of BlackWing Resources Ltd. In short, the Chen family thinks I'm going to find Crazy Abe's jewel box for you."

Wing nodded once.

"Then you just lost a ten-million-dollar gamble," Cole said calmly. "The jewel box may exist, but it sure as hell wasn't in Sleeping Dog One. That's a pipe mine, not a placer pocket. Dog One's diamonds haven't been washed out of the lamproite. Getting them out is a hammer-and-blast job, and then you have to crush the lot to get to the diamonds. You'll get sharp-edged junk. Ninety-five percent of it is bort."

Wing didn't look impressed.

Cole made an impatient noise. His new partner just didn't understand the difference between the extraordinary, exquisite stones in that worn velvet bag and the largely worthless crap that Crazy Abe had gouged from his Sleeping Dog Mines. Like most people, to Wing diamonds were diamonds—the emperor of gems, the most valuable stone on earth.

"Wing, the biggest diamond Abe ever got out of Dog One was maybe fourteen carats, flawed, fractured, and the color and clarity of bad coffee."

Wing didn't move.

Cole leaned forward. "You aren't listening to me." He

pulled the contract out of his breast pocket and tossed the document on the desk. "Rip it up, and while you're at it, burn that forged IOU. I'm not interested in screwing the Chen family out of ten million dollars."

"We consider it an investment."

"In bort?" Cole asked sardonically.

"In the future."

Cole realized that Wing was utterly serious, which meant that the Chen family was willing to spend millions on a long shot. There could be only one reason for a gamble of that magnitude.

Someone believed there was a high-grade placer diamond mine on one of Abe's claims.

"What makes you think I can find that mine after the Chen family and all its resources have failed?" Cole asked.

"What makes you think we have failed?"

Cole's expression was both cynical and amused. "You wouldn't be calling me in if you had a chance in hell of success on your own. We were partners, but we never were million-dollar buddies. I know you. You know me. Cut the bullshit and tell me what's going on."

"Mr. Windsor's heir is a girl. A woman."

"There's a big difference between a girl and a woman," Cole said dryly.

"Only to an American." Wing shrugged. "To me she is a female manqué."

"Lacking what?"

"A man."

"Haven't you heard? A modern woman needs a man like a snake needs ice skates."

Wing laughed softly. "She isn't one of those cold females who want only power. She was engaged once. Presumably, her appetites are normal, if rather suppressed at the moment."

"What happened?"

"Officially the man decided he wasn't ready for marriage."

"Unofficially?"

"He was a spy, a Soviet intelligence agent who tried to use the girl to gain access to secret information. Her father and brother are American intelligence agents. All that was almost seven years ago. She was twenty at the time. She has stayed away from men since."

"Smart woman."

"There are lessons to be learned from the past." Wing hesitated, then added delicately, "This young female may have learned caution too well. The same might be said of you."

Cole's mouth flattened into a thin line. He and Wing both understood that the remark referred to Chen Lai, Wing's sister, a woman of exquisite form and infinite betrayal.

"I learned long ago that diamonds are more enduring than women," Cole said.

"And more alluring?"

Cole shrugged.

"If a woman was all that stood between you and 'God's own jewel box,' what then?" Wing asked.

For a moment Cole thought about the shimmering green diamond. There was an extraordinary rarity and beauty to the stone that transcended whatever dollar value man might put on it.

Without waiting for an answer, Wing reached into his breast pocket and withdrew a palm-sized picture. He slid the glossy color photo past the diamonds.

Cole glanced at the picture the way a poker player looks at his last card—with a single, comprehensive, expressionless glance.

The woman in the picture had long, shiny, mahogany hair. Where the sun struck it, deep auburn fire burned. Her skin was neither brown nor pale, having instead a golden cast that suggested time spent outdoors in active movement rather than lying oiled and passive on a beach. Her mouth was well defined, full, and smiling. Her eyes were a luminous shade of green that made Cole think of the diamond.

Then he thought of what Wing had said about a girl and a woman manqué.

"Manqué? I don't think so," Cole said. "This is quite a woman. Look at the subtle tension in her expression, a kind of elemental animal wariness watching from the depths of her eyes. There is innocence, too, an untouched quality, a gut honesty left over from a time before language came with its structure of truths and lies."

Wing's eyebrows rose. "It's a good portrait, but not that good."

"I know her," Cole said simply.

"What? How?"

"I've never met her, but I know her work. I recognize her from the jacket photo on her book, *Arctic Odyssey*. On the book, her last name is given as Shane, not Windsor."

"Erin Shane Windsor," Wing said. "She is the great-niece of Abelard Windsor."

For a moment Cole was very still, remembering some of the woman's photos and at the same time hearing in his mind the eerie harmonics of wolves on the frozen tundra. The voices of wolves sang a truth known only to wild animals and restless men. And to a few women. Very few. Erin Shane Windsor was one of them. He'd sensed it in her photographs. It had caught him, held him, shaken him.

Discovering *Arctic Odyssey* had been one of the few pleasures in Cole's recent life. Even in memory, the intense sensuality revealed in the photographs remained vivid, textures of ice and sunlight and velvet shades of color that cried out to be touched. He'd been struck by something else in the photos, as well. The photographer had an unflinching appreciation of the balance of death and life, darkness and sun, ice and heat. The photographs had been powerful rather than sentimental, intelligent rather than pleasant. They had spoken to him on a level that bypassed civilization and language and lies.

"Don't bet ten million bucks that I'll be able to seduce Erin Shane Windsor," Cole said. "Her photos suggest that she's neither stupid nor naïve, and a woman this attractive isn't likely to be bored."

"Whether you seduce her or not is your choice. Your job will be to keep her from getting killed while she unravels Crazy Abe's secret or until you find the mine yourself. After that, Miss Windsor no longer matters. Only the mine itself is important. That must be protected at all costs."

"Even at the cost of Erin Windsor's life?"

"Her life. Yours. My own. Next to that mine, nothing else is important. Nothing."

Cole gave Wing a measuring look. Those words sounded less like the owlish graduate of Harvard than like Chen Li-tsao, Wing's uncle. Chen the Elder was a breathtaking pragmatist who used, rather than valued, human life. But Wing hadn't been like that. He'd always seemed more gentle, softened by his Western education—as Cole had heard Uncle Li complain more than once.

Wing had changed in the past five years.

"The Chen family has been working on this a long time, haven't you?" Cole asked slowly.

"Ever since we became certain the Brits were going to abandon Hong Kong to mainland ideologues. One of my uncles has been living with Abelard Windsor for longer than you have known him."

Cole rummaged through his visual memories. "The

cook. The one Abe always called 'the bloody ugly chink.' The cook was there the night we got drunk. That's how you found out about the gambling debt."

Wing didn't say a word.

Silently Cole let new understanding crystallize around the new facts.

"I'll be damned," he said softly, looking at Wing with new appreciation. "You're going to buck the diamond cartel. I knew the Chen family was ambitious, but I didn't think they were ready to take on the world."

"Not the world. Simply Consolidated Minerals, Inc."

"No difference, Wing. A cartel that can hold Uncle Sam and the Soviets by the same short hairs can squeeze the nuts off a Hong Kong clan."

"And the reason the cartel has such power is diamonds," Wing said coolly. "In their implication for the balance of international power, diamonds are as pivotal right now as the atomic device that was exploded at Alamogordo almost a half century ago. But unlike a bomb, diamonds are subtle. Leverage rather than annihilation."

Cole smiled thinly. "The waterhole theory of power. It's not what you own but what you control."

Surprised, Wing said, "Exactly. Diplomacy rather than war. Indirection rather than attack. Diamonds give control without causing national enmity, for who can hate the emperor that is neither heard nor seen nor named?"

"I can name it—the diamond tiger. Be careful, Wing. You could fall off and get eaten."

"Or I could ride and be ruler."

"That's always the lure, isn't it?"

"You should know. You have ridden before."

"Not really," Cole said, shrugging. "Not the way you mean. I don't give a damn for international power games."

"But you have played them in the past, and you have played very, very well."

"Only until I figured out how to get people to leave me alone," Cole said.

Wing smiled faintly. "Only Americans believe they are free. It gives them a certain, ah, piquancy."

Ignoring the other man, Cole looked at the photo of Erin Shane Windsor. Before he'd been asked to choose, Cole would have said without hesitation that Crazy Abe's placer diamond mine was worth whatever it took to own it. But now Cole was being asked to make the choice, and the answer was as unexpected as the green diamond had been.

The life of a woman who was able to create *Arctic Odyssey* was worth more than God's own jewel box.

But only to Cole. If Erin Shane Windsor was to survive being Crazy Abe's heir, she would need all the help she could get.

Cole knew the Chen family. If he turned down Uncle Li's offer, the clan would forge a new IOU, using it as bait for the next prospector on their list, a prospector who probably wouldn't appreciate wilderness photographs of the sort that could put a man in touch with his own soul.

Without a word Cole took the IOU and the picture of Erin from the desk. He put the two pieces of paper in his pocket, careful not to look at the photo again. He didn't want to sense the innocence that lay as deeply within Erin Shane Windsor as her wariness. Whether she knew it or not, a place had been reserved for her aboard the diamond tiger, where there was only one rule: Don't fall off, or you'll be eaten bones and all.

And the innocent were always the first to fall.

"All right, Wing. Tell Uncle Li he has his man."

5

Los Angeles
A day later

Cole's Qantas flight had been forced to land from the west because the Santa Ana wind was sweeping over the Los Angeles basin. Now, four hours later, the wind finally was dying. The San Gabriel Mountains at the east edge of the basin were still clear and stark, but the smog that had been pushed out to sea was beginning to filter back into the high-rise canyons of the city center. Pollution turned the late-afternoon sky an unappetizing shade of orange.

He tried to rub the fatigue of two trans-Pacific airplane flights from his neck as he studied the central city from his thirty-eighth-floor window. The queen city of the Pacific Rim was spread around him like an architect's drawing. Close by were the international headquarters of half the money-center banks of the Southwest, plus buildings wearing the logos of the most powerful of the Seven Sisters. Unlike the diamond cartel, the rulers of the world oil trade were welcome to operate in the United States.

That had always amused Cole. The two cartels operated the same illegal way. The only difference between them was that oil was an essential and diamonds were a luxury.

Just beyond the tall buildings, in a four-block stretch along Hill Street, the Jewelry Mart lay, a mixture of aging business buildings and gleaming new high-rises. The Jewelry Mart was second only to Manhattan in importance in the gold and gemstone trade.

The handful of diamonds in Cole's briefcase would be like a grenade thrown into the midst of these diamantaires.

Smiling at that prospect, he closed the long metal window blinds to shut out the distractions of the city. He reached for the coffee mug he'd kept filling from the BlackWing office's bottomless electric coffeepot. Ignoring the heat and bitterness of the liquid, he swallowed a mouthful and then another one, hoping that caffeine would help him focus. He felt faintly disoriented, as though he'd left part of his mind somewhere over the empty Pacific.

One by one he began rolling up the maps that he'd spread on the broad hardwood table. Carefully he returned each map to its own cardboard tube and placed them in the storage rack. The maps belonged to Black-Wing's L.A. headquarters. He'd spent most of the last two hours poring over the best Western Australia maps BlackWing could offer, looking for some hint of a suggestion, searching for the faintest of clues to point the way to the source of Crazy Abe Windsor's diamond mine.

Cole might as well have taken a nap. BlackWing's maps were designed to locate metallic ore claims—iron or nickel, uranium or gold. They didn't give him many of the fine geological details that he needed to find diamonds.

He glanced at his watch, but what caught his eye was the copy of *Arctic Odyssey* that lay open on the desk. He'd turned to the book repeatedly in the past twenty-four hours, as though it would somehow help him understand the woman he was about to meet. The photograph that most haunted him covered two pages. It showed dawn and tundra, ice and nesting geese. "Uncertain Spring" could have been a trite portrayal of seasonal regeneration, but it wasn't. Instead, the photo showed an arctic dawn where life hung on by a bloody fingernail.

Slowly Cole ran his fingertips over the picture, as though he could feel as well as see it. The photo captured a freezing summer dawn. In the background, seen through low streamers of windblown snow, more ghostly shapes than living flesh, adult geese put their heads to the screaming wind as they flattened themselves protectively over their nests.

In the foreground of the picture, beneath a transparent shroud of ice, lay a gosling that would never feel the warmth of the rising sun. The small creature's death was agonizing, as was the beauty of the new day and the determination of the adult geese to save their remaining offspring.

Looking at "Uncertain Spring," Cole knew that Erin Windsor had discovered the frailty, even the absurdity, of life.

He only hoped she had learned something about the value of life as well, her own included. If she had, she would be happy to take BlackWing's offer—three million dollars for her interest in an Australian diamond mine that might not even exist.

Brooding over the photo, he wondered if Erin Windsor would recognize the danger of being owner of a unique diamond mine whose output ConMin couldn't control or bury with the contents of their huge London vault. Certainly Matthew Windsor would know the danger to his daughter. Any professional intelligence analyst would be able to calculate the danger down to the last bit of money, adrenaline, and blood.

Cole hoped that, at twenty-seven, Erin would still listen to her father's advice. If she did, she'd be satisfied with BlackWing's offer. If not, there would be hell to pay.

And Erin would be the one paying it.

He glanced again at his Rolex, then at the battered tin box with its burden of priceless gems and worthless poetry. He slipped the tin box into a briefcase secured with a combination lock and fitted with a steel handcuff. With a wry smile he clicked the cuff into place around his left wrist, knowing that he was more the briefcase's prisoner than vice versa. Then he went out of the office, locking the door behind him.

The thirty-eighth floor of the BlackWing Building contained the executive suites. The building was expensive and discreet, like BlackWing itself. Cole took the elevator down to street level and reentered the push and pull of the everyday world in downtown Los Angeles. The other offices in the building were vomiting their nightly portion of commuters. Clerks and craftsmen and brokers crowded the lobby.

Cole and the chained briefcase didn't attract any attention. Besides BlackWing, the building housed dozens of gemstone wholesalers and jewelry dealers. Men of a dozen nationalities and all races came and went frequently, carrying similar briefcases. It was another sign of the care Chen Li-tsao had exercised positioning BlackWing for its assault on the diamond tiger.

A black Mercedes limousine waited at the curb. Its driver leaned against the gleaming front fender, waiting with a look of professional indifference on his face. When Cole emerged from the building, the driver straightened and moved to open the rear door of the limo.

"Good afternoon, Mr. Blackburn. Still going to Beverly Hills?"

"Yes."

The driver was young, athletic, Chinese, and had hands calloused by martial arts. He spoke with a relaxed southern California accent. Cole knew without looking at the driver's license that one of the man's names would be Chen. A branch of the Chen family had been established in America since 1847.

The driver ignored the Santa Monica Freeway, where afternoon traffic was already starting to congeal. Keeping to the surface streets, the limousine reached Beverly Hills in twenty minutes. The lights were just starting to come up in the high-rises along Wilshire Boulevard and the boutiques of Rodeo Drive when the limousine pulled under the awning of the Beverly Wilshire Hotel and stopped. A uniformed bellman opened the back door.

"I could be awhile," Cole said to the driver.

"I'm yours for the duration. I'll be here whenever you're ready."

Cole didn't doubt it. The Chens would keep an eye on their ten-million-dollar gamble.

6

Beverly Hills
Late afternoon

At one corner of the Beverly Wilshire's crowded lobby, Erin Windsor lounged unhappily in a brocaded armchair, watching the jet-setters and the Hollywood groupies pouring into the stately hotel. She would have preferred some place less grand than the Beverly Wilshire, and some location less ostentatious than Beverly Hills, but the law firm had booked the suite. Apparently they hoped to impress her.

What a waste of time, she thought.

Even though she'd decided to leave the arctic, she still found civilized pretensions more boring than amusing and more irritating than either.

To help the time pass, she tried to imagine herself as the owner of a remote ranch in Australia. Although she was fascinated by the Pacific Rim, she'd never visited Australia. Now James Rosen, the family lawyer who owned a lucrative practice in Century City, had informed her that she was the owner of a "station" and a set of mineral claims. All this a gift from a man named Abelard Windsor, a great-uncle she hadn't even known existed.

Rosen had been able to show her the location of the Windsor holdings on maps and had even managed to dredge up some travel-guide photos of the state of Western Australia. The photos made it clear that the Kimberley Plateau wasn't a lush, friendly kind of place. It was home to a rack-of-bones breed of beef cattle called Kimberley shorthorns, and to exotic animals that included kangaroos, long-tailed birds of prey called kites, and highly poisonous snakes called mulgas.

Erin had been fascinated. The primitive landscape appealed to her, especially because she was on the edge of condemning herself to an indeterminate sentence in very civilized Europe.

Other than the fact of the bequest, Rosen's information had been sketchy. When he'd gotten tired of her questions, he'd told her that Cole Blackburn, the courier who was delivering Abelard Windsor's will, would answer all her questions.

Idly Erin scanned the crowd again, wondering what Cole would look like. All Rosen knew about Cole was that he was a geologist who represented the law firm involved in the administration of the Windsor estate. The law firm was well known in Australia and in Hong Kong. When pressed, Rosen admitted that the situation was unusual but hardly a cause for alarm. The law firm had excellent credentials.

Even so, Erin had chosen a vantage point screened by the crowds in the lobby so that she might be able to pick Cole out before he spotted her. Her decision wasn't entirely conscious. She always arranged encounters with male strangers, so that she wasn't taken by surprise. Part of the reason was her natural reserve. Part was a caution learned at the slicing edge of a knife.

The lobby was full of travelers with luggage and business types with expensive leather briefcases. Many of the

men were tanned and appeared wealthy, but none of them
stood around looking from face to passing face, hoping to
find someone they had never met in the hotel lobby.

For a moment Erin thought the casually dressed, long-
haired blond male with the oversized leather rucksack
might be Cole. The man had the tanned, outdoorsy look
that field geologists in Alaska had. He was handsome,
with fine features and a gentle smile, and it all added up to
a quiet modern male who understated his masculinity. He
was the sort of man Erin found herself with much of the
time when she was in the world of New York and Europe.

The young man had been standing near the reception
desk for a few minutes, scanning the crowd, waiting for
someone. Erin was about to leave her blind and introduce
herself when a dazzling middle-aged woman in evening
clothes threw herself into the young man's arms. Erin
saw little television in Alaska, but she immediately recognized the woman as the bitch star of an enormously pop-
ular weekly series. In person, she looked at least a decade
older than her escort.

The couple chatted for a moment, then walked arm in
arm toward the lobby bar where a party was already under way. Erin thought the actress clung to the young man
in a peculiarly possessive way, displaying him like a
woman leading a small dog in a show. If the young man
disliked it, he kept it under wraps.

Lapdogs aren't noted for their teeth.

Erin's wry thought didn't show on her face. As the
couple passed, she realized that the young man's tan was
salon perfect, not a squint line on his whole smooth face.
The leather rucksack was also an affectation. No bulges
or scuffs marred its expensive lines. He walked like a
man used to getting in and out of taxis.

As soon as the couple vanished, Erin's eye was caught
by a striking slash of darkness in the midst of all the glit-

ter and gilt—a black-haired man in a black silk jacket and open-collared white shirt. His skin had been changed by sun and weather rather than by carefully applied artificial light. He walked with the unconscious grace of a healthy animal. A black leather case was handcuffed to his wrist.

He was looking right at her.

For an instant Erin's pulse accelerated with a purely female response. Then her elemental awareness gave way to an irritation that was close to anger and even closer to fear. This easy-walking man with his knowing eyes and his powerful body was exactly the sort of man she'd learned at such cost not to trust. He was a predator. Like her father. Like her brother.

Like Hans.

Because she knew she was reacting irrationally, Erin fought to cover her response to the tall stranger. The man was nothing more to her than a business appointment, a courier, an errand boy.

He walked to the place where she sat screened by foliage from the bustle of the lobby. Screened, but obviously not hidden. Not from Cole Blackburn.

There was no hesitation in Cole's stride when Erin came to her feet and stood waiting for him. He'd had no trouble picking her out of the crowd. Her natural auburn hair burned like a campfire amid the pale candles of the rinsed, bleached, and dyed jet-set women. She was dressed in a black cotton blouse and slacks that had the relaxed appearance of clothes just taken from a suitcase. The contrast of black cloth with red hair and pale, smooth skin was arresting, but Cole would have bet good money that the clothes had been chosen for their ability to travel rather than for how they looked.

Erin nodded as though to confirm that she was his appointment. Then she walked toward him and Cole cursed silently, feeling like he'd just walked into an ambush.

The still photo of Erin had told only a tiny portion of the truth. There was a quality to her movements that put Cole's body on full sexual alert. He'd felt nothing like it since Chen Lai, with her black eyes and golden skin and hidden laughter. Chen Lai, the honeyed snare he'd barely escaped intact, because he'd given Lai more of himself than he should have, mistaking simple lust for the complex emotion of love. It was a mistake he would never make again.

As they approached each other, Cole studied Erin, looking for some sign that she was conscious of the elemental sexuality in her movements. If she was, she didn't show it. There were no sidelong looks to see how the men around her were reacting. There was no careful polish of the female surface—no artful makeup, no gleaming-red nails, no tousled hair or undone buttons.

Lai's sexuality had been calculated to the last fraction. Erin's wasn't, which only increased its allure. And her eyes were the same incredible green of the diamond that men had died for in the past and would doubtless die for in the future.

The idea made Cole smile crookedly. He'd seen men die for much less tangible, much less beautiful things than a diamond that was the color of every summer God ever made. Ideology, theology, philosophy—none of them could be cut and polished and set to shimmering and dreaming in shades of green on a man's palm.

"Erin Windsor? I'm Cole Blackburn."

Her eyes widened as she realized how big he was, like an oak taking root in front of her.

Cole was used to the reaction. He kept his hand extended until she recovered enough to take it.

"Mr. Blackburn," Erin said, releasing his hand immediately. "I was expecting someone—er, different. Mr. Rosen, my lawyer, called you a courier."

"I've been called worse. Is there a place where we can talk privately?"

"Is it necessary to be private?"

He shrugged. "Not to me. I just thought you'd like to be alone when I hand more than a million dollars in rough diamonds to you."

"You're joking," she said, startled.

"Do I look like a stand-up comic?" He lifted the hand that held the briefcase, showing her the chain and handcuff that leashed it to him. "You can see the diamonds right here if you prefer, but I'd advise less witnesses."

Erin made her decision quickly, on the basis of survival instincts she'd developed in the arctic. Considering who and what Cole Blackburn was, the risk involved in being alone with him in her hotel room was less than taking possession of a fortune in rough diamonds in a very public lobby.

"My room is on the ninth floor," she said, turning and walking toward the elevators.

Cole followed, telling himself he was past the age to get aroused by something as trivial as the arc of a woman's hips. His body silently, violently, disagreed.

The elevator doors thumped softly closed, shutting out the hushed seething of the lobby. Erin gave the machine a destination. Instantly it began to rise.

"What did your lawyer tell you?" Cole asked.

"That he'd been contacted by a highly reputable international law firm, which informed him that I was the sole heir of a great-uncle whose name I'd never heard. I was told that a Mr. Cole Blackburn would arrive at five P.M. in the lobby of the Beverly Wilshire. He would deliver the will and answer all my questions."

"Your lawyer was half right."

"Which half?"

"I'll give you the will. But you'll have more questions than I'll have answers."

"How can you be sure?"

"Any woman who can take a picture like 'Uncertain Spring' asks the kind of questions that have no answers."

Surprise showed clearly in her green eyes. "You called me Windsor. How did you know I'm Erin Shane?"

"The photo on the jacket of *Arctic Odyssey*."

The elevator stopped and the doors whisked aside. Erin looked warily at Cole, as though changing her mind about taking him to her room.

"Your first instinct was correct," he said matter-of-factly. "I'm not going to touch you unless you extend a platinum invitation." The elevator door started to close automatically. Cole caught it with his big hand and held it open, looking directly at Erin as he added, "And you're not in the business of extending invitations, are you?"

"No. Are you always this blunt?"

"It saves time. You have about four seconds before the elevator door starts buzzing. Your room, my limousine, or some neutral third choice?"

Erin looked at the man whose gray eyes were as clear as ice and infinitely more alive. She had the feeling of being pressed to make a decision whose consequences were totally unknown.

A few years ago she would have refused all choices and gone back to the known dangers of the arctic, but a few years ago she hadn't been restless, feeling as though something vital was missing from her life, from herself.

A year ago she would have been frightened by a man like Cole. Now she wasn't, not entirely. The realization gave her a heady sensation of being freed from a cage of her own making.

It was like watching dawn after a long arctic night.

"My room," she said, walking past him.

When they were inside she closed the door, tossed her purse on a nearby chair, and turned toward him. He looked at her for a long moment, then bent and worked over the combination lock on the briefcase until it opened. Using a key that had been left inside the briefcase, he unlocked the heavy steel cuff. A moment later he pulled out a tin box, removed a worn velvet bag, and handed the box over to Erin.

"Abe's will was holographic," Cole said, "written in his own hand without benefit of lawyers. It's pretty simple. It leaves everything he owned to you. Most of the rest of the papers are covered with doggerel."

Erin blinked. "Poetry?"

"Not as far as I'm concerned."

She smiled slightly. "Not much good, huh?"

"I don't want to prejudice you," he said, returning her almost hidden smile. "You might like it. After all, some people like goanna charred whole in a campfire."

"Goanna?"

"Lizard."

Erin's smile widened. "You'd be amazed at some of the things I ate in the arctic."

She took the will and began to read it, frowning over the spidery, faded writing.

I, Abelard Jackson Windsor, being of sound mind and body, do hereby bequeath all my worldly possessions and mining claims to Erin Shane Windsor, who is the daughter of Matthew McQueen Windsor, who is the legal son of my brother, Nathan Joseph Windsor.

With the exception of thirteen rough diamonds and the papers in this box, all my possessions and claims are to be held in trust for Erin Shane Windsor until (1) she has been physically present on the

*Windsor station for a minimum of eleven months
of every year for five years or (2) until she finds
the mine these diamonds came from, whichever occurs sooner.*

*In the event that neither (1) nor (2) occurs, my
possessions are to be given to charity (with the exception of the thirteen diamonds, which in any
case belong to Erin Shane Windsor), and my mining claims are to be forfeited.*

Signed Abelard Jackson Windsor
Witnessed by Father Michael Conroy

*Erin: Trust no man who deals with ConMin,
He'll sell your soul for a handful of tin.*

*Your heritage is a jewel box
Kept beneath stone locks.
Poetry will show the ties.
Goodbye, my Queen of Lies.*

And I am the King.

Erin read the document again, then gave Cole an odd
look.

"Questions?" he said.

"ConMin? Is that what I think it is?"

"Consolidated Minerals, Inc."

"Diamonds," she said tersely. Her gaze went to Cole's
briefcase for a moment.

"That's the most famous aspect of ConMin's holdings," he said. "But diamonds are only part of it. ConMin
also deals in everything from iron ore to rare earth ele-
ments. Their specialty is strategic minerals. ConMin is

the most powerful, most lucrative, and most discreet cartel on the planet."

Erin flipped through the poetry quickly, then returned to the will and read aloud, " 'Trust no man who deals with ConMin,/He'll sell your soul for a handful of tin.' "

Cole didn't react.

"Are you employed by ConMin?" she asked.

"No. I don't like working for anyone."

She considered that for a few seconds, then smiled slightly. It was a point of view she shared. "Is that why Abe sent you?"

"Your great-uncle didn't send me. I haven't seen him in years."

Silence, then the sound of papers being shifted while Erin scanned the sheets of doggerel again.

"Are you a lawyer?" she asked without glancing up from the papers.

"I'm a diamond prospector. Do you know anything about diamonds, Ms. Windsor?"

"They're hard, they're expensive, and they're rare."

"And some of them are extraordinary," he said softly. "Some of them are well worth killing for."

She measured him for a long moment. "Are my great-uncle's diamonds extraordinary?"

"All the stones I saw of his were bort, which is the lowest grade of industrial diamond, which is the lowest grade of diamond, period."

"Worthless?"

"Not quite. But nothing to make my pulse leap, either."

Wryly, she wondered just what it would take to disturb this very controlled stranger. "Then my great-uncle's diamonds aren't extraordinary at all, are they?"

"Hold out your hand."

"What?"

"Hold out your hand."

"Why?"

"Just do it, Ms. Windsor."

"Go to hell, Mr. Blackburn."

His expression didn't change.

Erin had the feeling she'd been tested in some way she didn't understand. She had no sense of whether she'd passed or failed or would be tested again.

Moving with a deftness surprising in such a big man, Cole opened the worn velvet bag and poured the contents out on his own palm. Erin watched while light slid and shimmered over the marble-size objects, as though they were wet or oiled. Most of the stones were colorless. Several were a deep, lovely pink. One was a green so pure it looked like condensed, concentrated light.

Automatically she reached for the green stone, then stopped, looking up at Cole's eyes. For the first time she realized that his eyes weren't a colorless gray. Tiny shards of pale blue and green and silver radiated out from the pupils in a subtle display of color that was hypnotic.

"Hold out your hand," he said softly.

This time she didn't hesitate.

Cupping Erin's smaller hand in his own, Cole poured the stones into her waiting palm. They made muted crystal sounds when they moved against one another.

"These can't be diamonds," she said, her mouth dry.

"Uncut, unpolished, extraordinary. They're diamonds. And they're yours, for better or for worse."

Silently she picked up diamonds at random, as though to assure herself of their reality. She held up first one, then another, toward the overhead light. The stones were transparent. They drew light the way a magnet draws iron.

"They're vsi or vvsi, or flawless," Cole said.

"What?"

"Very small imperfection or very, very small imperfection."

"I wasn't looking for flaws. It's just . . . *the colors*. My God, I didn't know that colors like this existed short of rainbows and lasers. So pure. So damned pure."

"You should look in your mirror more often," he said.

"What?"

"The green diamond is a dead match for your eyes."

Her head snapped up at the personal comment. Suddenly she realized she was standing very close to a man she didn't know, his hand was cupped beneath hers, and his breath was mixing with hers in an intimacy that should have terrified her. For the space of one shared breath, two, three, she waited for fear to spread through her body, a fear that had been brutally beaten into her seven years ago.

Her pulse raced, but not from fear. It came from an elemental female response to being close to a man she found very attractive. The realization that she was once again capable of a sexual response to a man went through her mind like sunrise through night, changing everything it touched.

"Which of Abe's mines did those diamonds come from?" she asked, her voice low, almost husky.

"I don't know."

"Are there more like these?"

"I don't know."

"Does anyone?"

"I don't know."

Erin looked at the powerful, impassive stranger who was still standing close to her. "What do you know, Mr. Blackburn?"

"That I prefer to be called Cole."

She retreated across the room, opened the curtains, and looked out over the glittering city that was condensing from the darkened sky.

"What do you know about the source of these diamonds, Cole Blackburn?"

"They're probably Australian, but not from any known mine. They've been out of the mother pipe a long, long time. The green diamond is unique. The pinks are superb. All but one of the whites is of the first water." He paused, then added calmly, "I also know that if you keep your inheritance, you'll have to give up standing in front of windows."

Swiftly she turned to face him. "What does that mean?"

"Ask your father."

"My father is a difficult man to reach. You're right here. I'm asking you."

"If I tell you," Cole said, "you'll have a thousand doubts and questions to match. If your father tells you, you'll believe him. That will save time."

"It would be even quicker if you tell me right now."

"Whoever owns the Sleeping Dog Mines is a deer at the beginning of hell's own hunting season," Cole said.

"Why?"

"The colored diamonds are unique. ConMin has nothing like them in its vaults."

"So?"

"If there's a mine full of stones like yours, ConMin has to control that mine's output or lose its monopoly. Monopoly is power. Right now ConMin has enough power to cut deals with First World nations, to control Second World nations as often as not, and to buy Third World nations outright. The Sleeping Dog Mines threaten ConMin's power," Cole said, "which threatens the entrenched interests of various nations who have a stake in the diamond tiger. When you ride that tiger, the only rule is survival. ConMin has ridden for more than a century."

Erin looked at the gleaming, shimmering stones. "You make my legacy sound more like a curse than a gift."

"It is." Cole looked at his watch. "Call your father. The first thing he'll want to do is have the diamonds appraised. Make very certain that the appraiser does not have ConMin connections, or the appraisal will be worse than useless. I'd give you the name of a reliable appraiser, but then your father would assume conspiracy."

"You must know my father quite well."

"I've never met him, but I've dealt with men like him. I'm one myself."

"CIA?" she asked coolly.

"No. Survivor."

When Cole looked up from his watch, Erin froze. His intensity was as real as the diamonds she held. He was wholly focused on her in the same way that she focused on her photography when she worked. At that instant she was the only thing in the world that existed for Cole Blackburn. To be the focus of such scrutiny was both unnerving and exhilarating.

"You don't like taking orders," Cole said in a soft voice, "and I don't like giving them. But I know what the stakes are. You don't. At least two people died getting those stones into your hands. I'm betting that you're intelligent enough not to defy me for no better reason than temper. If I'm wrong, I'll survive. You won't. You have a choice. Trust your father, trust me, or trust God that the next stranger coming through that door doesn't have a gun in one hand and a revised version of Crazy Abe's will in the other."

"I'll think about it."

"You do that, Erin Shane Windsor. Think very hard. And while you're at it, think about 'Uncertain Spring' and the gosling that froze to death in an unexpected blizzard."

For a slashing instant she remembered the cruel, beautiful dawn when she'd discovered the gosling lying rigid beneath a glittering shroud. She'd wept at seeing the tiny body encased in ice.

And then she'd taken out her camera to catch the brutal perfection of a time and a place and a dawn that owed nothing to man.

"Life has always defined death, and death, life," Cole said, watching her intently. "Anyone who understands that as clearly as you do should be able to decide how much a diamond mine that might not exist is worth—but whether or not the mine exists, owning it could cost your life. When you understand that, you'll sell your inheritance to someone who knows the territory."

"Someone like you?"

"Yes."

"What would you pay me for a mine that might not exist?"

"More than you need. Less than your life is worth." He turned and walked to the door, opened it. "I'll call you at the end of the week. If you want to reach me before then, call BlackWing. The number is in the tin box with the rest of your legacy."

The door closed, leaving Erin alone with a handful of extraordinary diamonds.

7

Los Angeles

For a long time Erin stood motionless, staring at the rough diamonds in her palm, absorbing a reality she'd never known before, watching light shift and shimmer through their mysterious crystal cores. Curious, she touched the tip of her tongue to the green stone. It was cool, clean, faintly salty. She tasted her own skin for comparison. Less salt. She tasted one of the colorless diamonds. No taste at all.

He held this stone, not the others.

She could see him cradling the green diamond in his palm, smoothing his thumb over it, watching the heart of summer shimmer and glow in his hand.

The salt I tasted came from his skin.

A strange shimmer of awareness shot through the pit of her stomach. What unnerved her even more was that she wanted to taste the stone again.

I tasted him.

Erin shoved the stones back into the worn velvet bag as though she'd been burned. Restlessly she picked up the first sheet of poetry and began to look for clues to the location of a diamond mine that might or might not exist. She scanned the sheets quickly, then more slowly, frowning.

When she was finished, she read the sheets again, shaking her head. None of it made sense. Although diamonds were mentioned several times, drinking, pissing, and screwing were mentioned much more often. There was no mention of a mine at all.

Muttering about crazy old men, Erin stuffed the pages back into the tin box and picked up the will again. When she finished reading it, and its warning, she felt no more at ease. Remembering her conversation with Cole Blackburn wasn't any comfort either.

Whoever owns the Sleeping Dog Mines is a deer at the beginning of hell's own hunting season.

You make my legacy sound more like a curse than a gift.

It is. Trust your father, trust me, or trust God that the next stranger through that door doesn't have a gun in one hand and a revised version of Crazy Abe's will in the other.

The words echoed uneasily in Erin's mind as she stood in the silent room. Mysteries were her father's meat and wine. He lived in a world where every act was examined, cut into thin sections, put under an electron-scanning microscope, with the results argued at the highest levels of government. It was a world where every man had more than one shadow, where names changed more often than Paris fashions, where betrayal was the only thing that could be trusted.

Her father's world.

Her brother Phil's world.

Her ex-fiancé's world.

Erin's head moved in an abrupt, negative gesture that sent streamers of hair sliding across her cheek. Automatically she brushed the strands aside. Just as automatically she brushed aside memories that had nothing new to teach her. Treachery existed. Betrayal existed. She accepted that.

But she no longer existed for them.

Seven years ago she'd been a victim in an undeclared war. She wasn't a victim any more. She'd learned to defend her body with techniques both ancient and modern. She'd learned to defend her mind by discovering other worlds, incredible worlds, places where ice was alive and mountains radiated light, places where people laughed and shared their last bite of food with a hungry stranger, places where death existed, yes, but as a natural extension of life processes rather than as a premeditated act of perversion and political power.

Perhaps there was even a place out there where the incredible green stone was real, a place where the restlessness in her body would be stilled, a place where she could trust men again.

And if not all men, then at least one.

"That's the question, isn't it?" Erin asked herself softly. "You can't answer that question alone. What's important is the future, not the past."

The phone felt cool in Erin's hand, smooth, an impossibly perfect surface against her sensitive skin. It was the thing she found most startling about civilization, all rough surfaces smoothed into a beguiling perfection. A false perfection, because beneath the surface terrible things seethed, waiting to explode into life. The primitive world was exactly opposite, its rough surfaces concealing a serenity of emotion that was beguiling . . . and also, in its own beautiful way, false.

Primitive and civilized shared one central truth: Death always waited for the unwary, the unlucky, or the unwise.

But life also waited, a fire burning beneath ice.

Erin punched in the telephone number that remained the same no matter where her father happened to be stationed at any given time. When the phone was answered, she spoke quietly, clearly, and hung up.

Then she sat on the bed, stared at the handful of stones that could be diamonds or glass, and waited for Matthew Windsor to be summoned by his beeper to return his daughter's call.

8

Beverly Hills

People don't walk up to you and hand you a million bucks in a tin box. Not in the real world. Not even in the Beverly Wilshire Hotel. It's just flashy glass, baby. Next time this Blackburn guy calls he'll be selling you a map to the mine.

Matthew Windsor's cool, faintly impatient voice echoed in Erin's ears as she stared at the phone she'd just hung up. She hissed out a curse. Part of her agreed with her father. Another part of her believed that the stones were real, because Cole Blackburn was real.

All too real.

She turned away from the phone but couldn't stop thinking about the conversation. After a few more verbal pats on the head, her father had agreed to make "discreet inquiries around D.C." for Erin. When—and if—he had anything interesting, he would call.

She hadn't argued. As a senior officer of the Central Intelligence Agency, her father had access to every database in the government, from the FBI to the U.S. Geological Survey.

She was still running the conversation through her mind when the phone rang. The instant she picked up the receiver, her father began speaking in a clipped voice.

"Describe Cole Blackburn," Windsor said.

"Big," Erin said, running through a kaleidoscope of impressions in her mind. "Even bigger than Phil. Not fat. Hard. Caucasian. American accent. Intelligent. Confident. Moves well. Black hair. Gray eyes. Well-defined mouth, off-center smile. Faint scar along left jawline. Random scars on his hands. Big hands, by the way. Long fingers. No rings. Expensive clothes but not fancy. There's nothing fancy about the man. In all, I suspect he'd make a bad enemy."

Windsor grunted. "You've got a good eye. That's Blackburn to a T."

"I'm a photographer, remember? I make my living looking at things." She waited. Only silence came over the line. "What's going on, Dad? Is Cole Blackburn a con man?"

"I can't go into it on the phone, baby."

Anger flashed through Erin. Part of it sprang from her loathing of the world she'd run from for seven years, but most of her anger came from even older memories of being shut out of the enigmatic world of spy and counterspy that consumed so much of her father's life.

"Did Blackburn show you any identification?" Windsor continued.

"Just himself. To a T, I believe you said. Should I believe what he told me?"

"Baby, I can't—"

"Yes or no," she cut in. "One word."

"It's not that easy. I'll be in L.A. tomorrow. We can talk about it then."

Erin looked at the phone as though it had grown fur. "You're coming to L.A.?"

"Don't sound so shocked. I haven't seen you for almost a year." His voice changed, becoming harder. "Just to make sure I don't miss you, stay put in the hotel room. Have room service take care of the food. Rest up. Do you hear me, baby?"

"Yes," she said, understanding that Windsor didn't want her to leave the room. "But I don't like it."

"I'm not wild about it myself," he said flatly.

There was a three-beat pause before she said, "All right. I'll be here when you get here."

"In your room."

"In my room," she said between clenched teeth.

There was the sound of air rushing, as though Windsor had let out a relieved sigh. "Thanks. It means a lot to me. I love you, baby."

Before she could answer, her father was gone. Throughout her life, he'd told her many times that he loved her, but for the past seven years he hadn't waited to find out if she loved him in return.

Slowly Erin hung up the phone and wandered restlessly around the room, turning on lights against the darkness beyond the closed drapes, wondering why her father had insisted she stay in the room.

Maybe he'll tell me tomorrow.

Maybe not.

Matthew Windsor had spent his entire life in the forest of mirrors that nation-states created to mislead one another. Discretion was as natural as his heartbeat. Most of his life had been lived in places he couldn't admit to having been, not to his wife or his daughter, perhaps not even to the son who had also become an officer of the CIA.

She understood the necessities of her father's work, but she resented his job deeply, not only because of what it had done to her but also because of what it had done to the intelligent, thoughtful, loving man she knew her father to be. Secret wars meant secret lives, and secret lives made human trust impossible.

Erin wanted to trust her father, just as she wanted to trust the rest of the world. But trusting everyone wasn't a very bright way to live and could be a very painful way to die. She'd been lucky once.

Next time she might not live to learn.

9

Beverly Hills
One day later

Late-afternoon light burned through the west-facing windows of the hotel suite. As the shafts of sunlight flowed across the rosewood tabletop, thirteen rough crystals shimmered to life. Erin Windsor stood very near the table, bent over her camera equipment, totally focused on the stones. She was consumed by the pure colors, entranced in a dazzling new world seen through the extreme close-up lens of her camera.

She'd spent the day totally focused on the mysterious, breathtaking crystals, waiting for her father. More than once she'd despaired of capturing the subtle play of light and the violently pure colors, the flashing glitter and fathomless shadows, the tiny rainbows chained among the curved hollows that high magnification revealed on the surface of the stones. When she turned the diamonds just so, light fragmented across the table. When she turned the stones another way, light glowed from within like flame burning within ice. When she turned them yet another way, light pooled and shimmered as though the crystals were alive, breathing.

"Are you really diamonds?" she muttered in a combination of frustration and curiosity.

The afternoon light changed, deepened, becoming a golden torrent. The crystals burst into flame.

For an instant Erin froze over her camera, transfixed by the changed stones. They were a song sung in silence, inhuman in their beauty, the translucent tears of a rainbow god.

Suddenly she didn't care if the crystals were diamond or YAG, zircon or quartz. She worked like a woman possessed, triggering the camera, shifting stones, composing shots, reloading film, driven by the stones' savage beauty and her own equally savage need to capture the instant when crystal and light became lovers, each transforming the other.

Not until the light was spent within the crystals and the stones slept once more did Erin straighten and move away from the camera. Unconsciously she put her hands in the small of her back and stretched, relieving the tension of hours bent over the arrangement of lens and bellows and tripod. She felt exhausted and exhilarated at once, an explorer returning from an undiscovered land, her mind full of new visions and yet hungry for more.

Reluctantly she turned away from the stones and looked at her watch, wondering if she should set up some fixed-light shots or if her father would arrive soon, bringing with him unanswered questions from a past she didn't want to discuss. Maybe he would have answers for her future instead, answers she could listen to without feeling angry and betrayed.

Someone knocked on the door twice. "Baby? It's me. Open up."

"On my way."

At first the security locks and latches defeated Erin.

Then she got the sequence correct and opened the door. Her father stood in the hallway, as tall and handsome as ever, dressed in the charcoal business suit, white shirt, and silk tie that was the male uniform in the world of business and diplomacy.

"I wouldn't mind a hug if you wouldn't," Windsor said, his mouth smiling and his eyes very serious.

There was no hesitation before Erin stepped forward and wrapped her arms around her father. He closed his eyes and hugged her in return, lifting her off her feet with the embrace.

"Hugs don't bother you anymore, do they?" he asked very softly.

For an instant, she looked surprised. Then she realized it was true. She no longer panicked at being held by a powerful man.

"I hadn't thought about it, but you're right."

"That's why you're leaving the arctic, isn't it? You're finally over that schleimscheiber Hans. Thank God, baby."

Before she could say anything, Windsor released her and stepped back. A woman moved from the shadows, where she had been waiting patiently.

"Hello, Erin Shane Windsor. I'm Nan Faulkner."

Startled, Erin took the blunt, broad hand that was being held out to her. The fingers were as firm as they were dark. Like the woman herself, the handshake was no-nonsense, controlled, and short. The business suit she wore had a narrow skirt and was a darker shade of gray than Windsor's. She didn't wear a tie. She was a solid presence, buxom and broad without being fat. A thin black cigarillo smoked in her left hand. The same hand held a black box with a single gauge on the surface and a wand plugged into the side.

Windsor was the last one through the door. He secured the various locks without a fumble.

Faulkner took one look at the stones shimmering on the table and said, "Holy Christ."

In a controlled rush, she went to the table. She threw her smoking cigarillo in Erin's half-empty coffee cup, swept open the curtains to take advantage of the falling light, and switched on the black box. In rapid succession she touched the tip of the wand to stone after stone, beginning with the smallest and working her way up to the biggest.

"Jesus," she muttered as stone after stone registered in the diamond range of thermal resistance. Then she touched the green stone. It, too, registered in the diamond range. "Sweet. Jesus. Christ."

After she touched every stone, Faulkner shut off the machine and pulled a loupe from her coat pocket. She scanned each stone before she turned to Windsor.

"All but one of the white ones are of the first water, D, O+, River, Finest White, Blanc Exceptionnel, call it what you will," she said. "They are the most pluperfect bastards I've ever had the privilege of seeing."

"Shit," Windsor muttered.

"The colors might be irradiated," Faulkner continued, "but I doubt it. Radiation is too easy to pick up on. It's used to cover flaws or off-colors, but these babies don't have any problems worth mentioning, much less trying to hide. I'm a betting woman, and I'm betting these are high-ticket fancies."

Windsor said something savage beneath his breath. Then, "How bad is it?"

"Couldn't be worse. Next to these colored stones, hen's teeth are as common as sand in the Sahara."

"I don't understand," Erin said.

Faulkner set aside all the diamonds except the green one. "Take an average diamond mine. Only twenty percent of what's found is gem-quality goods. Less than one percent of the gem-quality stones will be over one carat after they've been cut and polished. In other words, less than two-tenths of one percent of a diamond mine's entire output ends up bigger than a carat of gem goods. Of those, only a goddam small percentage of that is D flawless."

Erin blinked and looked at the diamonds. They were a lot bigger than a carat.

"I'm too old to be a top color sorter any more," Faulkner continued, "but I'd bet my firstborn that all but one of those whites is a D. D or not, the bastards will be flawless when they're cut. Rare diamonds. Very, very goddamn rare."

Windsor grunted.

"Yeah," Faulkner said. "But that's not the worst of it. When it comes to fancies, you have to invent another word for rare. That's what makes this pile of stones so dangerous. If they were just big and flawless, ConMin would still be able to beat you into line with Namibia's stones. But Namibia has nothing like these. Nobody does. That green is absolutely singular."

After a moment of silence, Faulkner turned away from the beautiful, dangerous stones and looked at Windsor. "We should have brought a couple of marines. This is worse than anybody thought. And," she smiled coldly, "better, too. I've waited a long, long time to get van Luik where the hair is short."

"Are you the agency's resident diamond expert?" Erin asked.

Faulkner hesitated, then shrugged. "Matt says you can be trusted. I hope he's right. At the moment I'm a government consultant to the biggest American jewelry trade association. The job requires that I work with a company that can't operate directly in America because monopolies are illegal here."

Erin felt the floor shift beneath her feet as she was

drawn back into the forest of mirrors that was international power politics. Her father's world.

Seven years ago that world had nearly destroyed her.

"Have you had them certified?" Faulkner asked, gesturing to the diamonds.

Erin shook her head. "Dad said to stay put. I did."

Faulkner smiled at Windsor. "You were right."

"Now that we've established that I'm a good little girl," Erin said coolly, "tell me why it matters."

"The diamond world is wired together like a power grid," Faulkner said. "You walk into the GIA out in Santa Monica or into some little appraiser's office down on Hill Street with these stones and you'd generate a surge that would register in London and Antwerp in a matter of hours. ConMin uses computers to keep track of every important piece of rough in the world, even the ones they don't own themselves. And believe me, these are important pieces of rough."

"I'm getting that message. Why does the agency care?"

Faulkner's eyes narrowed. "Diamonds are a big cash item in the economies of a dozen nations around the world. You'd be surprised what countries will do for American dollars or Japanese yen, especially countries whose ideologies are based on Karl Marx rather than Adam Smith. When my predecessor left, he told me the world revolves on a diamond pivot. It's not always true, but it's true often enough to put the fear of God into a heathen like me."

"That's why I want you to let me handle it for you, baby," Windsor said. "I don't want you hurt again."

Erin looked at her father. For the first time she noticed the lines in his face, the heavy splash of silver in his formerly dark hair, and the circles beneath his eyes. He looked tired and uncomfortable, as though caught between his impulses as a father and his duty as a sworn officer of an intelligence service.

"Did the diamonds come with a note or a map," Windsor asked, "or a claim register or a bill of sale, anything to indicate their origin?"

"Everything came in an old tin box that had no markings," Erin said.

"Delivered by this Blackburn?" Faulkner asked.

Erin nodded. "He told me to have the diamonds appraised by someone not connected to ConMin." She glanced at Nan Faulkner. "I'm not sure you meet those requirements exactly, but at least I know your first allegiance isn't to the diamond cartel."

"Did Blackburn tell you anything else about the diamonds?" Windsor asked.

"Only that they'd belonged to Abe and that two people had died to see that I got my legacy. He told me that I would die, too, if I wasn't very careful. Then he told me to call you."

"I owe him a big favor," Windsor said. "So do you. He probably saved your life. Let me handle your legacy for you."

"I couldn't, even if I wanted to, which I don't."

"Why?" Faulkner asked.

"The terms of the will require that I live on the station for five years to gain final title, or until the mine is found, whichever comes first."

"No amount of money is worth getting killed for," Windsor said.

"It isn't the money," Erin said. "In fact, there's no guarantee I'll find a single diamond. Apparently Abe was the only one who knew where the diamond mine was, and he didn't talk before he died. He didn't leave a map, either."

Windsor refused to be drawn away from his main point. "If you're not after money, why are you going to Australia?"

"It's a whole new continent," she said simply. "A whole new world. I want to smell it, taste it, see it, photograph it, live it."

"That's the point, baby. You could die there instead of living."

"I was told the same thing about the arctic." She tried to avoid a shouting match by changing the subject. "Do you know much about Abelard Windsor?"

Her father shook his head. "Dad never mentioned him."

"His own brother?"

"Things happen, Erin. Things that tear families apart." *Things like Hans Schmidt, foreign agent.*

But neither father nor daughter spoke the thought aloud.

Erin got up, took the tin box from her oversize purse, and pulled out the sheaf of papers. "Until I knew the stones were real, I didn't know if the whole inheritance was an elaborate hoax. Frankly, after reading 'Chunder from Down Under,' I thought Great-uncle Abe might have concocted the whole thing in some Australian psycho ward. Here. Read this. Clues to finding the mine are supposed to be in it."

For several minutes the only sound in the room was that of dried, rough paper rustling as Windsor scanned a sheet rapidly, then passed it to Faulkner. He glanced up after the fifth sheet.

"Is it all the same?" he asked.

"Different words," Erin said, "but the same."

He grunted, shuffled through the remaining pages, then took the first page from Faulkner again.

"It doesn't improve with rereading," Erin said dryly. "I've read it and read it and read it, using all the tricks and tools I learned as an English major at the university."

"And?" Windsor asked.

"I didn't find any meanings but the obvious one. The hero eats raw croc liver, drinks, talks about black swans, drinks, pees, drinks, apparently screws everything that moves and some things that don't, eats more raw croc, pees. And he drinks. Did I mention that?"

"It could be a code or cipher of some type," Faulkner said. "Would you mind if we copied it and sent it to Washington for analysis?"

"An Australian might be more helpful than a code expert," Erin said. "Do you know what 'chunder' is? Poetic thunder, maybe?"

"Never heard of it," Windsor said. "My parents might have been Australian, but they never talked about their life before America."

"That's kind of odd, isn't it?" Erin asked.

Windsor shrugged. "Runs in the family, like chasing after a diamond mine that might not exist but could kill you anyway."

The daughter's shrug was an exact match of the father's.

"Shit, baby. Why are you really doing this? What does Australia have that you don't have here? A crazy old man's mythical diamond mine? Is that what you want from life?"

"It's not a bad start," she retorted. Then she sighed and tried to put into words something she'd sensed about herself but never pinned down. "After *Arctic Odyssey*, there just hasn't been another project I wanted to do. I found some peace in the arctic, but I don't believe anymore that it's my future. Maybe Australia is. Maybe it isn't. I won't know until I go there."

"What about here in America?"

"I don't think I'd see you any less if I live in Australia than I've seen you while I was living off and on in the arctic."

"Baby—"

"That's just it," Erin interrupted calmly. "I'm not a baby. I've been making my own decisions for seven years."

Windsor closed his eyes for an instant, then opened them again, focusing on his daughter, the image of the woman he'd loved and lost when a drunk driver failed to hold his lane at ninety miles an hour.

"It's all yours, Nan," he said finally. "I told you she wouldn't turn it over to me."

Windsor went to stand by the window, his back to the room, clearly separating himself from whatever happened next.

"I have a child myself," Faulkner said, lighting up a thin cigarillo. "If he were in this kind of fix, I'd be standing by the window and letting your father explain the facts of life. A good man, your father. But he's personally involved, so he's not calling the shots for the agency on this one. I am."

Motionless, Erin waited while Faulkner drew on her cigarillo and blew out a streamer of smoke.

"Let's build a couple of scenarios," Faulkner said. "If we assume Abe was simply crazy and had nothing more on his station than cow shit and flies, there's no problem. You go to Australia, and then you stay there or come home. No big deal. Right?"

Erin nodded.

"A pretty scenario," Faulkner said, staring out the window. "It would be nice if it was true. But I've got a gut certainty it isn't."

"Why? Just because you and my father have chosen to live in a world of conspiracies and betrayals and lies doesn't mean that my world has to be that way."

"Until you became Abe's heir, you had the choice," Faulkner said calmly. "Now you don't. Consider this scenario. Maybe the diamonds are real but not from Australia. Maybe they were stolen from Namibia by dissidents who used them to purchase arms."

"Then how did Abe get them?"

"Does it matter? The normal route for submarine goods—smuggled diamonds—is to European or American cutting centers via Egypt. Maybe some of Abe's old prospector buddies were smugglers. Maybe they preyed on the smugglers or knew those who did. Maybe Abe was a smuggler himself. What do you think, Matt?"

"I hope to hell he was, because it would mean there's not much danger for Erin in Australia. Smugglers certainly wouldn't approach her to buy or sell or hold their goods. Smuggled goods would also answer the question of why Erin was warned off ConMin. ConMin, after all, would be the legal owners of those diamonds."

Erin didn't like what she was hearing, but there was a logic to it that she was too intelligent to dismiss.

"But that scenario still leaves open the question of Abe's 'jewel box,'" Windsor continued. "Was it simply a cache for stolen Namibian gems? If so, then Erin is in some danger if she goes to Australia, because other people—smugglers—will know about the cache."

"Your father's right," Faulkner said, turning back to Erin. "The danger to you could be finessed if Abe was just a smuggler, a channel. You could go to Australia with a cadre of expert bodyguards and stage a determined, very public search of the station premises. You wouldn't find jack. You'd leave to take photographs of the outback and then fade from the picture. Nobody would ever bother you again."

A long plume of smoke rose from Faulkner's full, beautiful lips.

"Here's another scenario," Faulkner said. "Assume Abe was crazy like a fox. Assume he really had God's own diamond mine hidden somewhere on his station. A mine that could yield tens or even hundreds of pounds of diamonds like that handful on the table."

Faulkner watched Erin's instant disbelief followed by speculation and then by unhappy realization.

"That's right," Faulkner said, nodding. "You're talking about the kind of money that goes beyond wealth to become power. Raw political power. The kind of power that people, corporations, and nations kill for."

"I don't want that," Erin said instantly.

"What you want and what you get ain't the same thing," Faulkner said sardonically. "Scenario number four. Do you have any idea how many new gem-quality diamond mines have come into production in the past fifty years?"

"No."

"I do," Faulkner said. "I did a survey that's locked in a vault in Virginia right now. New mines have entered production in the Soviet Union, in Australia, and in a few African republics that can be brought to heel by the cartel. The Soviets had to invent some polite ideological fictions, but they fell right into bed with ConMin because ConMin controlled the world outlet for their stones. Australia did the same. But only a handful of mines have been discovered, maybe a new one every decade."

"Not surprising," Erin said. "Diamonds are rare."

"That's what ConMin tells us every chance it gets," Faulkner retorted. "The diamond cartel has hundreds of geologists exploring all over the world. They're the cream of the diamond geologists, the expert elite. They have never—repeat, never—found a diamond mine. Not once. The only new mines in the last fifty years were found by prospectors who didn't get paid by ConMin, prospectors who were working over ground that ConMin geologists had already thoroughly explored. Does that suggest anything to you?"

"Either ConMin's geologists are very bad, ConMin's luck is incredibly bad, or ConMin doesn't want to find new mines," Erin said.

"Fast, brief, and right on target. Too bad you hate your daddy's profession," Faulkner said. "I could use you, but only if you use your damned brain. Think about anonymous diamonds and warnings, ConMin, and Crazy Abe's jewel box. The diamond cartel has its hand in any new mine, anywhere in the world, that's capable of producing significant amounts of gem-quality rough diamonds. That monopoly has political as well as economic ramifications."

"The diamond pivot again?" Erin muttered, not wanting to believe, but finding less and less justification for doubt.

"You got it," Faulkner said. "The balance of power is just that—a balancing act. When something is that delicately poised, it doesn't take much to rock the boat. At the moment, there's nothing the U.S. would like better than to get control of a diamond mine that would give us more leverage within the cartel. So would a great many other nations."

"Do you understand now?" Windsor asked quietly. "If Crazy Abe had a diamond mine, whoever owns it will find himself a moving target. I don't think you have the skill to survive. I do. Let me handle your inheritance, baby."

Silently Erin went to the window. Without consciously remembering Cole's warning, she stood to one side, able to see out without being seen. The lights of the city were like a lake lapping against the base of black mountains.

"You'd both like Cole Blackburn," Erin said finally. "He wants me out of the game too. I'm supposed to see him tomorrow, to give him my answer to his offer to buy out my inheritance."

"How much is he offering?"

"Three million dollars."

"That plus those thirteen diamonds would make you rich," Windsor said quickly. "You'd never have to do a thing you didn't want to do. How much money do you need, anyway?"

"If you need more than three million," Faulkner put in smoothly, "I know investors who would top Blackburn's offer. We'd all be a lot more comfortable with American investors than with a loose cannon like him."

The room was quiet for a moment. Erin looked at the stones on the table. Even in the dim room, fugitive light shimmered through them like whispered secrets, vanishing as she looked, reappearing along unexpected curves, then vanishing once more. The crystals fascinated her as nothing ever had, not even arctic ice.

"Thank you, but no," Erin said softly. "I'm keeping my inheritance. Every last undiscovered bit of it."

10

Cole Blackburn sat with his feet on the map table, staring out over the city of Los Angeles to the darkness that was the Pacific Ocean twelve miles beyond. He was trying to interest himself in the task of plotting a new run of computer data onto the LandSat maps of Western Australia, which were spread on the flat table. No matter how he told himself he should do it, he just wasn't interested.

Crazy Abe had been a dinosaur. He hadn't belonged to the modern age, so his secrets weren't likely to yield to modern methods.

On the other hand, there was little else for Cole to do but look at satellite maps until Erin allowed herself to be bought out. *If* she allowed herself to be bought out. If not, he might have to resort to the IOU Wing had thoughtfully provided.

Cole didn't like that idea, because it would mean that Erin was staying in the game. Far safer to buy her out and be done with it.

He glanced at his watch. He had an hour to kill before Erin and her father came to BlackWing for a meeting.

Matthew Windsor's sudden appearance wasn't surprising, but it was a complicating factor. Cole hoped that Windsor would tell his daughter to sell out rather than buck the diamond tiger.

At the same time, Cole knew that Windsor was CIA, and the CIA had a vital interest in the diamond cartel. Corporations, clans, and government institutions were all alike in one way. Each required complete loyalty, the sacrifice of children, wives, and private lives to the greater glory of the collective. As a matter of principle, independent men or women had to be seduced, intimidated, bought, or removed. Independence was an enemy to Consolidated Minerals, to the Central Intelligence Agency, and to the Chen family.

If Matthew Windsor was a devoted CIA officer, he would think nothing of using his daughter's inheritance as a stalking horse for American interests. If he was a truly amoral player, he would use his daughter without telling her.

Darkness was turning the windows on the thirty-eighth floor into partial mirrors. The city beyond was still there, but reflections from the room flickered across the face of the glass each time Cole moved.

And even when he didn't.

His conscious mind was still registering that fact as he spun away from the desk and came to his feet in a single motion. A knife blade gleamed in his hand as he went swiftly, silently to the door joining the two rooms of the office suite.

"Impressive," a voice said from the next room, "but a pistol has more range. I'm Matthew Windsor, by the way. I can prove it if you don't mind letting me reach into my pocket."

Cole looked at the tall, solidly built man in a dark suit who was waiting in the doorway that led to the hall. The man wore an expression of well-chilled competence. He also had eyes the same shape and color as his daughter's.

"You're early," Cole said, returning the knife to its wrist sheath with an easy movement.

"Nobody knows I'm here. I'd like to keep it that way."

A tongue of adrenaline licked through Cole, quickening his whole body. "What did you do with the guard?"

"Don't worry. I didn't stuff anybody in a closet. The floor guard at the elevator was very polite. He's getting a cold glass of water so I can take my heart medicine."

"I'll see to it he's retrained. Maybe we can find a job for him in the infirmary." Cole gestured toward the hall door. "After you."

"Cautious man."

"I want to live long enough to take heart medicine."

Windsor laughed softly and went back out into the hall.

Cole locked the door and jerked his thumb to the right. "That way. Conference room is the fifth one on the left."

Windsor glanced around as they walked past suite after suite of offices. He stopped in front of the fifth door on the left, tried the handle, and stepped back. "It's locked."

"That didn't bother you before," Cole pointed out, unlocking the door.

When he flipped on the lights, jarrah wood paneling from Australia glowed in shades of cream and rust.

Windsor turned to Cole. "If I knew who owned you, I'd know whether to ignore you or take you out of the game."

Cole didn't comfort himself by thinking that Windsor was bluffing. Beneath that graying hair was a hard body and a mind that had twenty more years of nasty tricks to draw on than Cole Blackburn did.

"Nobody owns me," Cole said. "I like it that way. That's the way it's going to stay."

"No one is that independent."

"Who's talking, Windsor? The spook or Erin's father?"

"Let's start with the spook," Windsor said. "The spook sees all kinds of red flags in the files marked Cole Blackburn. You're a killer, for one thing. You have anything to say about that?"

"Which incident bothers you?"

"Start with the eighteen-year-old killer, the one who went into the marines instead of going to jail for murdering a man."

Cole walked to a leather chair at one end of the conference table and sat down, wondering why Windsor was trying to get under his skin—and why it was working.

"It was manslaughter, not murder," Cole said. "A bar fight that went sour."

"Dead is dead."

"As for the marines, it used to be a fairly common sentence where I came from."

"So you went into the marines, forward recon," Windsor said coldly. "Good outfit for killers."

"Cut the crap. You're not the one to ride me over spilled blood. You've sent plenty of men over the fence."

"Some men like to spill blood. Some men are indifferent to it. Which are you?" Windsor asked.

"Neither."

After a moment Windsor nodded. "Let's fill in some gaps in your file. How did you make the jump from recon marine to geologist without going to college in between?"

There was silence while Cole decided whether to answer the question. In the end he shrugged and answered because it didn't matter. "My gunnery sergeant served in a dozen countries. He learned all he could about gems and geology in every place he was stationed. He talked about it to anyone who would listen. I was the only one. He bought me my first Brunton compass and nursed me through basic geology texts. He was a hell of a man."

Windsor nodded again. "Marcel Arthur Knudsen, right?"

For the first time, Cole looked surprised. "So that's what the M stood for. He never told me."

"He never tells anyone, if he can help it."

"How well do you know him?"

"I know people who know him," Windsor said. "There are still people in the Pentagon who think he was God's topkick. But you've done a lot of traveling since the sarge knew you. For instance, Zaire."

"Yeah, I was there." Cole smiled thinly. "How much did it cost you boys to bail Thompson out of that jail in Kinshasa?"

"The agency wasn't as amused as you are. If the political police had found out who Thompson really was, he'd have been executed. Your little stunt nearly killed him."

Cole's smile changed, becoming as cold as his eyes. "You're breaking my heart. Thompson tried to get me killed. Damn near managed it. If he tries it again, I'll put him in the ground any way I can."

Windsor grunted. "You're even-handed, I will say. You gave the same treatment to the KGB agent in Cairo in . . . 1982, was it?"

"Was Schmelling really KGB? I thought maybe he was just a particularly filthy dealer in submarine goods."

"Full colonel in the Overseas Directorate," Windsor said.

"If I'd known that, he would have ended up another one of those bodies you seem so worried about."

"That would have been unfortunate. He was doubled, working for us at the same time. Hell, Schmelling was more valuable than Thompson ever thought of being."

"Not to me. He was about as much use as my Brazilian partner."

"The one you killed?"

"The one who stuck a knife in my back, missed anything vital, and lived to regret it."

"But not for long," Windsor said dryly.

"Two months. Long enough."

"Think you're hell on wheels, don't you?"

Slowly Cole shook his head. "I'm just a man who likes to be left alone. That annoys some people. A lot. They start crowding, and I don't like being crowded, and things go from sugar to shit real fast. So why are you crowding me, Windsor? Does the CIA want me to get out of its picture? Has the agency decided to preempt Erin's inheritance?"

"I don't know. All I know is that I don't like a lot of what I saw in your file. You're lethal and you're unreliable. Nobody has ever figured out how to control you, except maybe that sour old gunnery sergeant in the marine corps. I'd just as soon you didn't come anywhere near my daughter."

"I'm not lining up to be your son-in-law. I'm just trying to buy Crazy Abe's mineral claims."

Windsor hesitated, drew a deep breath, and let it out. "That's the problem, Blackburn. I don't think Erin is going to sell. She won't take help or direction from me, and she won't divest herself in favor of investors put forth by the agency. She's got the bit in her teeth and there's bugger-all I can do about it."

For an instant Cole wasn't sure whether to swear or cheer. He'd guessed that Erin was a woman who answered to herself and for herself, a person who chose her restraints as carefully as he did. But even while the maverick in Cole cheered a kindred spirit, the pragmatist in him swore quiet, unhappy oaths. Erin's love of freedom could cost her life.

Not to mention Cole Blackburn's.

"Shit," he said, his eyes narrowed against a combination of anger and admiration that surprised him.

"Yeah," Windsor agreed. "Shit. My daughter is lovely, talented, and bright, but she knows zip about bucking nations and corporations. As a matter of fact, up to now she has structured her life with total privacy in mind."

"Do you blame her?"

"No. There are times I'd like to retire from the world myself. But I didn't inherit the Sleeping Dog Mines. Erin did. If she won't sell her inheritance, she'll have to live with the real world."

"Or die with it."

"I'd like to avoid that. What about you?"

"I think the woman who created *Arctic Odyssey* is worth more than her weight in fancy diamonds."

There was a moment of startled silence before Windsor laughed. "They were right. You're a real loose cannon."

"Who is 'they'?" Cole asked dryly. "The spooks you work for?"

"Among others." Windsor hesitated before continuing. "I've been with the CIA for thirty-two years. I've had to do some hard things in that time, but I'm proud of my agency, of my record, and of my country."

Cole made a neutral sound.

"This is the first time in my entire career that I've put my own interests and those of my family ahead of the agency's," Windsor said simply.

Cole sensed that the other man was telling the truth. But Cole also understood that Windsor was a trained, experienced, and skillful operator of covert schemes.

"That's very uplifting," Cole said blandly. "But you're forgetting I know what you do for a living."

The other man smiled grimly. "I spent a long night last night, reading and rereading your file. In some ways, the important ones, we're a lot alike. You've never betrayed a friend or forgotten an enemy. I want Erin to be your friend. I want you to help her even if she won't sell you Abe's claims. In return I'll do everything I can to help you. I won't betray the agency, but I'll cut every corner I can as long as I can—information, logistical support, whatever you want. When the time comes that Erin is ready to move on to something else, I'll guarantee you the inside track on the sale of her claims. Just keep her alive."

"I'll do what I can."

For an instant Windsor was furious. Then he looked at Cole's pale crystalline eyes and realized he meant every word: He would do what he could.

"All right," Windsor said softly. "But there are a few things I still don't understand about you."

"Do they matter?"

"They might. How did you get hold of Abe's will?"

Cole shook his head.

"That's what I thought," Windsor said coldly. "How can a man who prizes his independence so goddamn much belong to one of the most ruthless tongs in Asia?"

"Easy. I don't belong to the family of Chen."

"Do they know that?"

"Not my problem," Cole said calmly.

"It will be if you make the mistake of thinking Erin's interests in this are identical to the Chen family's."

"I don't give a damn about Uncle Li's interests."

After a moment Windsor nodded curtly. "Good. That saves me the trouble of taking you out of the game and finding someone else to look for Erin's diamonds, someone I'd control. There are a half-dozen good geologists in the agency."

"Baker is the only one who could find brown shit on a white tablecloth," Cole said, "and he's on loan from Con-

Min. If the CIA ever really wants to find a diamond mine, give me a call."

Windsor smiled. "I just did, didn't I?"

The door opened and closed and Cole was alone in the conference room. He took a long breath, let it out soundlessly, and wondered how a much younger Erin had found the guts to go against her old man.

11

Beverly Hills

Erin was on her way out of the hotel room when the phone rang. She answered, expecting either her father or Nan Faulkner, who had quietly insisted on coming to the meeting with Cole Blackburn. The faintly hollow sound of the connection told Erin the call was long distance even before she heard the voice of Jeffrey Fisher, her New York editor. He was her age and one of the hottest young stars in the field of art publishing. He was also so excited he could hardly speak.

"How do you do it?" Fisher demanded. "You're a witch, aren't you? You cast spells on people from your den up there beyond the Arctic Circle. That's it. You're a sorceress. I used to think I was the only one haunted by your aloofness, but I can see you own the whole world. They're dying to beat a path to your door and cover you with wealth and glory."

"Jeff, what in the name of God are you babbling about? Slow down."

"Slow down? No way, can't do it, no reason to do it, and you'll be as wild as I am when you hear what just happened. It's the chance of a lifetime. It's a book that will make you the most famous photographer in the world. It's fantastic, it's incredible. It's . . ." His voice died as he searched for the word he wanted.

"Spit it out. It's . . . ?"

"Diamonds," he said in a hushed voice.

A chill moved over Erin. "What?"

"Diamonds. You've just been invited to do a definitive—no, make that *the* definitive—book about the most glamorous thing on the face of the earth."

"Invited?" She cleared her throat. "Really? By whom? When?"

"By the people who own all the diamonds in the world, that's who. Consolidated Minerals, the company that controls the output of every diamond mine worth mentioning. ConMin has decided to cooperate in the most extensive and expensive photographic study of their product ever undertaken. They want one and only one photographer to do it. Erin Shane. Apparently somebody saw your work in *Arctic Odyssey* and said, 'If she can do that for frozen water, think what she can do for real ice.'"

Erin closed her eyes and thought about coincidences. Nothing she told herself made her stomach stop sinking.

Fisher caught onto the fact that Erin wasn't nearly as excited as he was. "Hey, kid, listen up," he said. "You've been out in the cold too long. It's frozen your brain. Harry Conner went nuts for the idea, especially because ConMin would be underwriting the project. He's talking a solid advance—middle six figures at least, maybe more. If you play your cards right, your agent might be able to get it to seven figures, all to the left of the zero. That would be for world rights, of course."

Erin made a sound that could have meant anything from joy to despair. "Jeff?"

"Yeah, I know, it's just too—"

"When did they call?" she asked, interrupting ruthlessly.

"Who?"

"ConMin."

"I got the first call about an hour ago, some guy with a Dutch name, Hugh van Louk or something like that. He and Harry are thrashing out the details now."

"I see."

"No, you don't, or you'd be over the moon the same way I am," Fisher retorted. "Remember that book you wanted to do years ago? Well, this is it. *Diamonds, Grit to Glitz.* This time ConMin will let you into a London sight. This time anything you want from them is yours, and they'll pay you a queen's ransom in the bargain. The timing is perfect for you. It will mean delaying your European book, but I didn't get the feeling you were exactly tearing down doors in your eagerness to do that one."

She forced herself to listen for a few minutes longer, and even managed a question or two. Then she looked at her watch and knew she'd run out of time. "Sorry, Jeff, my cab is waiting. I'll call back as soon as I can."

She hung up, grabbed her purse, and headed for the lobby. A cab appeared as soon as she stepped through the glass doors. She gave terse directions and settled back for the short ride.

She wanted to believe that her inheritance and ConMin's sudden interest were a coincidence. *Nice try. Doesn't fly.* Which left her with an unhappy question. *How did ConMin find out so fast?*

Maybe her father would know. Or Cole.

Neither possibility made her feel good. She arrived at the BlackWing Building ready to push and push hard to get answers. Cole met her as she got off the elevator. As she looked at him, she realized they both were wearing the same clothes they had worn yesterday. Both shirts showed signs of having been put through a hotel's laundry-room wringer, telling Erin that she and Cole traveled the same way—light. The thought was oddly reassuring.

Neither of them said a word until they were inside Cole's office.

"Is my father here yet?" she asked.

"The guard hasn't called up for him," Cole said, neither lying nor telling the whole truth. His eyes narrowed as he noted the stark lines of tension around her eyes and mouth. "What's wrong?"

"I won't know until I get a few answers."

Before Cole could say anything, the phone rang. He picked it up, listened, and hung up. "Your father is on his way up now. There's a woman with him."

"Nan Faulkner. She has something to do with diamonds."

A few minutes later the guard returned with Matthew Windsor and Nan Faulkner in tow. Impassively the men introduced themselves and shook hands before taking seats in the conference room. Faulkner sat. Erin didn't. She turned and looked at the three other people.

"Which one of the players benefits if the fact that I'm Abe's heir gets out?" Erin asked.

"What do you mean?" Faulkner asked.

"Just what I said. Who benefits? The agency? Con-Min? Cole? Me?"

"ConMin," Cole said.

Faulkner and Windsor looked at each other. "ConMin," Faulkner agreed.

Erin turned to Cole. "They're offering me a million. How much did they pay you?"

"Not a cent."

"Erin, what the hell is this about?" Windsor demanded.

She answered without looking away from Cole. "Con-Min called my publisher and offered me the kind of access that most photographers would kill for. Just because

I'm brilliant, they said, just because I'm the only button pusher in the universe capable of producing images for a definitive—no, *the* definitive—book on diamonds. ConMin is so thrilled with the idea that they're hinting they would underwrite a million bucks in advance."

"Christ Jesus," Windsor muttered.

"I doubt that he had anything to do with it," Cole said. "Who called you?"

"Jeff Fisher, my editor. Harry Conner, the publisher, is hammering out the details right now. Old Harry is over the moon, and Jeff thinks he's finally going to make publishing history."

"What do you think?" Cole asked.

Erin made a dismissing gesture. "The idea's a good one. I tried to interest Jeff in doing a grit-to-glitz book on diamonds five years ago. He couldn't get me in the door at ConMin. Nothing personal. They'd turned down every other photographer and publisher in New York. Company policy." She took a deep breath. "So why did they change their minds?"

"Easy," Cole said. "They know you're Abe's heir."

"Brilliant, Mr. Watson," Erin retorted. "Of the four of us in the know, who the hell tipped ConMin?"

Nan Faulkner's chuckle was soft, almost inaudible. Erin shot her a narrow look.

"Matt, you worry too much about your little girl," Faulkner said. "She's smart enough to come in out of the rain. The good news is that the leak didn't come from the agency. Matt and I are the only ones who know, and we aren't talking."

"It didn't come from me, either," Cole said.

"Prove it," Faulkner said coldly.

He shrugged. "I knew where Erin was. ConMin had to waste at least two days trying to contact Erin through her publisher, which means ConMin didn't know where she was. If they did, they would have skipped the middleman and made their offer in person. In addition, I want to buy the mineral rights Erin inherited. So does ConMin. I wouldn't give them a handful of spit."

Erin thought it over for a moment, then nodded. "All right. Then who did?"

"I don't know." Cole looked at Faulkner, then looked back at Erin. "Who made the approach?"

"A man named Hugh van Louk, or something like that."

Faulkner's breath hissed out. "That's Hugo van Luik, ConMin's number-one badass. Director of Special Operations for DSD—that's Diamond Sales Division—and a half-dozen ambiguous titles, all of which boil down to one job—troubleshooter. When the cartel has trouble, he shoots it dead."

"You know him?" Erin asked curiously.

"I butt heads with him every fifth Monday, all year round. As a matter of fact, I'm flying to London from here."

Cole looked at Windsor. "How long has Ms. Faulkner worked for ConMin?"

"Never, babe," Faulkner shot back. "I represent the U.S. diamond industry's interests at the advisory level. There are a shitload of people in the business who'd like to have ConMin's seat on the diamond tiger. We just haven't quite figured out how to pull it off."

"Every fifth Monday," Erin said, remembering her research for the diamond book her editor hadn't been able to sell to Harry Conner five years ago. "The sights, right?"

Faulkner's sharply penciled eyebrows rose. "Right." She struck a match and held it to the tip of a narrow cigarillo. "Ten times a year, always on Mondays, the world diamond industry assembles in London and receives its marching orders from DSD in the form of allotments of rough." She blew out a pungent stream of smoke. "At my end, on the advisory level, the producer countries are informed of DSD's needs, how much rough they will buy. At the other end, the cutters and brokers—there used to be three hundred; now there are only a hundred and fifty—are shown the goods and quoted a price."

"Tell her about the negotiations," Cole said ironically.

"What negotiations?" Faulkner asked.

"That's what I meant." Cole looked at Erin. "There aren't any negotiations. It's all take it or leave it, on both sides. The diamond producers are told what ConMin's Diamond Sales Division will buy and how much they'll pay, and the cutters and brokers are told how much rough they'll buy and at what price. If they agree, they pay cash. If they decline more than once, they're never invited to a sight again, which is about the same as being cut out of the diamond business in its entirety."

"If that's how ConMin does business," Erin said, "they'd be smart to keep it a secret instead of inviting me to do a book about them."

Faulkner dismissed the suggestion with a wave of her hand. "They're so powerful they don't have to apologize or hide. As long as they stay outside the United States, beyond the reach of the Sherman Antitrust Act, ConMin can do business any way it wants."

"Sounds like OPEC," Erin said.

"Close," Faulkner said, nodding. "ConMin is just as high-handed as OPEC ever thought of being. The difference is that the world can get by without diamonds a hell of a lot longer than it can get by without oil. We had no choice but to break OPEC. The diamond cartel is a different matter. Diamonds are a luxury, not a necessity, or we'd have busted ConMin as fast as we cracked Sheikh

Yamani's brainchild. There would have been no other choice."

"If ConMin is that powerful, why are they bothering with this charade about the book?" Erin asked.

"Deniability," Faulkner said. "The folks who run Con-Min are powerful, not stupid. If you were Tiffany Anyone instead of Matt's daughter, I suspect you'd have died before you got a chance to count old Abe's diamonds. But you're Matt's daughter, so ConMin has to use titty-fingers. They aren't preventing discovery of a new diamond deposit, they're sponsoring an art project. They aren't threatening your little ass, they're offering to put it in mink-lined luxury."

Erin wasn't impressed.

Faulkner sucked hard on the dark cigarillo.

"Hell, babe, by the time they're done wining and dining and waving money," Faulkner continued, "you'll hand over the mineral rights and kiss their corporate cheeks for caring. You don't know there's a mine out there, right?"

Erin nodded.

"And even if there is, there's no guarantee you'll find it," Faulkner concluded. "So ConMin comes into the game with a sure million and a career-making book versus whatever Blackburn is offering."

"Three million," Cole said.

"Presuming you're good for it," Faulkner said scornfully. "I'd get a Dun and Bradstreet, a Standard and Poor's and every other kind of check on this character. He looks like trouble to me, even if his suit coat is silk and fits him like a lover." She waved her cigarillo at Erin. "Let ConMin romance you around a little. What can it hurt? It will give your daddy and me time to get a team into Crazy Abe's station and vet the place for you." She pinned Erin with a dark glance. "What about it? It makes everybody happy, except maybe Blackburn."

The silence in the room was so complete that Erin could hear the distant sound of a jet plane lifting from LAX. She looked at her father and then at Nan Faulkner. Their motives were clear and understandable. She looked at Cole, who was as mysterious as the diamonds he'd brought to her. Then she looked back at her father.

"Is Cole ConMin's man?"

"I can't be certain," Windsor said.

"Best estimate," Erin said coolly, using language her father understood.

"He's not ConMin's."

"Is Cole a diamond prospector?" Erin asked.

"Yes," Windsor said.

"A good one?"

Windsor nodded.

For a moment there was silence while Erin reviewed the options that had been outlined by her father. She still didn't like any of them.

So she chose none of them.

She reached into her purse, pulled out the worn bag, opened it gently, and shook out the stones onto her palm. She admired their shifting, mysterious light for a moment, then returned all but the deep green stone to the velvet prison. Silently she looked from the diamond to the man who had handled the stone long enough to leave his taste on its time-polished surface.

"I won't sell you the mineral rights," she said to Cole, "but I'll give you one half the output of any diamond mine that you—"

"Erin, for the love of—" began Windsor.

"—help me discover on my claims," she continued relentlessly, ignoring her father's interruption. "Nobody will make you a better offer, because nobody will be willing to give up half the mine and the power it represents. To seal the bargain, I'll give you this."

She held out the green diamond, letting it shimmer and glisten on her palm.

Cole whistled softly through his teeth. His eyes focused on Erin with an intensity that was almost tangible. " 'Help you discover,' " Cole repeated. "That means you're coming with me."

She nodded. "The will requires it."

"How good are you at taking orders?"

Windsor's hard laughter was all the answer anyone needed.

"Yeah, that's what I figured," Cole said. "That's not good enough, Erin. There will be times and places where I'll give orders and I'll give them once because there won't be time for explanations."

"I can live with that."

Cole smiled slightly. "Then pack for London."

"Why?"

"It will make ConMin feel better." Cole didn't say that it would make Faulkner and the agency feel better, too. "If they think they're going to co-opt you, they won't be as eager to reach for more drastic measures."

Erin didn't like it, and it showed, but she said, "All right."

"Second order. We're roommates from now until the mine is discovered or you sell out your interest, whichever comes first."

Silence stretched and stretched while Erin measured the big man who was watching her with eyes as hard and beautiful as the diamonds he loved.

"Do it," Windsor said to his daughter. "If you're going to be so stupid as to go through with this, you'll need someone like Blackburn around."

"Suite-mates," Erin corrected, her voice clipped.

"Only if the connecting door stays open," Cole said. "All the time, Erin. Every damned minute."

She nodded curtly and without warning flipped Cole the stone. He caught it, his hand moving so quickly it was a blur.

"Done," Cole said.

Faulkner slanted Cole a bleak, furious look. "*Mazel und broche,* babe. I hope you step on your cock."

12

Los Angeles

Erin sat in the window seat of her new hotel room, watching darkness descend on the Los Angeles basin. She sensed the crowded streets and sidewalks around her like a heavy weight. The hotel suite, with its two bedrooms and comfortable sitting area, was easily twice as big as her other room. She still felt confined.

She wasn't used to sharing her living space with another human being, especially one as large and plainly masculine as Cole Blackburn. His presence in the other half of the suite was both a lure and an irritant.

Abruptly Erin stood up, giving in to her restlessness. She paced the room without seeing the luxurious fabrics with their Jacobean design or the indigo richness of the carpet. Pacing wasn't enough. She felt like she'd been caged inside buildings forever. What she wanted was the vast, isolated sweep of the arctic. She would settle for the Pacific Ocean's far horizon.

When Erin appeared in the open door of Cole's bedroom, he looked up from the desk, where he'd been working over the maps he'd brought from BlackWing.

"Could we . . . ?" Erin began, only to have her voice fade.

The husky contralto of her voice made Cole's body quicken. She sounded like a woman with a little loving on her mind, yet she was standing in the doorway like she was poised to flee at the first sign of masculine interest. It had been that way from the beginning, conflicting signals that kept him aware of her all the time.

Not that he needed any help keeping her on his own internal radar. His body had decided after one look that it wanted to get as close as it could to Erin Shane Windsor. If it hadn't been for her obvious nervousness at having to share a suite with him, he would have sent out some signals of his own. But he didn't. She wasn't acting like a woman who wanted a man.

Yet she was looking at him as though she wanted him.

"Could we . . . ?" Cole asked.

"I need to get out. To walk. On the beach. I know it's dark, I know you'll tell me it's not safe, but I have to get out and I'm going to. With or without you."

There was no mistaking the staccato urgency in Erin's voice. For an instant Cole ticked off the possibilities. If he'd been certain that danger was imminent, he would have tied Erin to her bed. But he wasn't certain. ConMin was a business, not a government or a criminal clan. ConMin would try to co-opt Erin before they tried to kill her.

And he had to admit that her presence was giving him cabin fever. If he stayed in the hotel room with Erin while she was putting out all those restless signals, he'd have a hell of a time keeping his hands in his pockets. Making a pass at her wouldn't be smart. If she wanted him, she would have to hand out a clear invitation.

She hadn't even come close to that yet.

"I could use some fresh air myself," Cole said.

"Three minutes," Erin said instantly.

She headed back into her room, moving fast.

A bit less than three minutes later, she reappeared just as Cole was grabbing a black windbreaker from the closet. Without waiting for him, she headed toward the hallway door.

"Erin, wait!"

She didn't even pause.

Cole crossed the room in a silent rush. Just as she opened the door a few inches, his hands shot over her shoulders and pinned the door. She made a choked sound. His powerful arms were braced on either side of her. He was all around her, surrounding her.

Trapping her.

Erin froze, remembering another time, another door, another big man trapping her. Memories welled up in a choking black tide, threatening her control.

"What the hell are you thinking of?" Cole demanded. "You don't just open a door and walk through like a—"

With an incoherent cry Erin turned and attacked, the side of her palm slashing toward his throat. He barely blocked the blow in time. He deflected her knee with his thigh even as her head slammed into his jaw. Off balance, reluctant to hurt her, he went in low, scissoring her feet out from under her, pulling her down until she was flat on the rug beneath him.

Silently, savagely, Erin struggled, using everything she'd learned in the past seven years.

Nothing worked.

Cole countered the blows with his greater strength and skill, keeping her from hurting either one of them. She was wasting her strength. She went completely still and waited for him to mistake her submission for defeat.

He looked at the green eyes so close to his and felt ice move beneath his skin.

"Erin, listen to me, I'm not going to hurt you, but I

can't let you walk blithely into a hallway until I check it out. I'm not going to hurt you, honey. I'm on your side."

He repeated the words again and again while Erin watched him with feral eyes. Gradually what he was saying sank through fear to the intelligence beneath.

"I understand," she whispered. "You can let go of me now."

"Not a chance," Cole said instantly, his voice no longer soothing. "Not until you tell me why you were doing your best to kill me a minute ago."

"I'm sorry. I . . . panicked."

"I noticed. Why?"

Erin's voice died as she realized that Cole was holding her helpless, his body heavy over hers. She should be terrified, but she wasn't. More than his soothing words, more than anything he could have said, his restraint calmed her.

She'd attacked him. He'd done nothing more than defend himself. Even now, despite the blood oozing from a cut on his lip and the bruise on his chin where she had butted him, he was being careful of her.

"You didn't hurt me," she whispered. "You aren't hurting me now."

The wonder in her voice startled him, but before he could ask what she meant, she was trying to explain.

"When you slammed the door it was like Hans all over again, going to the door and he caught me and then he let go and I ran and he caught me and it happened over and over. . . ."

"Hans?" Cole asked softly, but there was nothing soft about his eyes.

She shook her head slowly.

"Talk to me, Erin. We're going to be living in each other's pockets. I don't want to step on a land mine again."

She closed her eyes. He was right.

"Hans was my fiancé seven years ago. He was as big as you. As strong. Oh, God, he was so strong." She shuddered, then went on in an odd, flat voice. "I found him going through my father's wall safe, photographing every bit of paper. I turned around to run, but it was too late. He was so quick. Like you."

Cole waited, his pupils dilated almost as much as hers.

"When I tried to scream, Hans hit me in the throat," she whispered. "Then he hit my shoulders. I couldn't scream, I could barely breathe, my arms were numb, my fingers wouldn't work. Then he let me run to the door again but I couldn't open it, couldn't move my arms, couldn't make my fingers close. When he got tired of my kicking he dislocated my knees.

"Then I couldn't move, I could only feel and see, and whenever I closed my eyes he hurt me." Erin's voice dried up and then resumed again, terrible in its lack of emotion.

Cole listened despite the overwhelming need to make her stop talking. He didn't want to hear her low voice describing just how much of a blood sport sex had been to her fiancé.

Even as Cole locked his jaw against the bile rising in his throat, he wondered at his own primitive response. He'd heard worse, seen worse, the kind of savagery that was labeled inhuman because sane people didn't want to believe how low humanity could sink.

Cole knew he shouldn't be surprised, shouldn't be appalled, and he certainly shouldn't be enraged at what had been done to Erin.

But he was.

As he listened he clenched his teeth against the turmoil of emotions ripping through him, a combination of despair and killing rage the likes of which he hadn't felt since Lai had casually aborted his child and married another man on the command of her family.

Slowly Erin's words faded into silence. She realized that Cole had long since rolled onto his side, removing his weight from her, touching her only in the slow sweep of his hand over her hair while she talked. She looked at his eyes and saw both rage and a sadness that made tears burn against her eyelids. Without stopping to think, she curled against him, needing the reassurance of his warmth, wondering if he ever needed reassurance in the same way.

"Are you all right?" he asked finally.

She nodded. "I thought I'd forgotten. But I hadn't. Not really. I feel better now. Lighter. Kind of floating." She rubbed her cheek against his chest and let out a long sigh. "Thank you for being . . . gentle."

"You're the first one who ever accused me of that," Cole said, smiling oddly.

After a moment Erin looked up and saw a drop of blood slowly welling from Cole's lower lip. She touched the small cut with her fingertips. "I'm sorry."

"No problem."

Her fingertips slid down beneath his chin, sensing the slight raised area where her head had bruised him.

"Here too," she said. "I hurt you."

He tried to subdue his elemental response to her touch. She frowned as she looked at the bruise. She touched him even more gently, almost caressingly. He closed his eyes and told himself she didn't know what she was doing.

"I'm sorry, I wasn't thinking," she said, lifting her fingertips as the tension in his body communicated itself to her. "It must hurt to have me touch it."

He made a sound that could have been a throttled laugh or an equally throttled curse.

"It doesn't hurt. It feels good. Too damn good," he said bluntly.

"What?"

"Your fingers. My skin. I like the combination. What about you?"

Her hand hesitated, then resumed touching him. Silently she admitted that she was caressing him rather than looking for signs of injury.

Very slowly Cole resumed stroking her hair. After a time his fingertips traced the shadows beneath her cheekbones and the outline of her mouth. She made an odd sound and looked up at him. His eyes were closed and his expression was intent, focused on the sensations coming from his fingertips while he traced again the curve of her lips.

"You're smiling," he said without opening his eyes.

"It tickles."

"Does it?" He ran his fingertip across her full lower lip again. "Is that why you're holding your breath?" He felt her body tighten as he bent down to her. "Don't panic, honey," he whispered against her mouth. "This won't hurt, I promise. I won't even hold you. I just want to know if you taste half as good as you fight. Okay?"

Surprised, caught off balance by the combination of humor and hunger in Cole's voice, Erin waited for fear to claim her.

Nothing happened except a delicate, intriguing brush of warmth against her lips when Cole exhaled. A spear of sensation went from her breastbone to her knees, making her shiver.

"Frightened?" he whispered.

"I . . ."

He waited.

"After Hans . . ." she said, then took a deep breath.

"Afterward, the psychiatrists told me that virgins who had been brutalized the way I'd been nearly always became whores or nuns. I haven't let a man get close to me in seven years. I don't know if I can even now. I might panic again."

"I'll risk it if you will."

"Will you . . . be gentle?"

"What do you think?"

She looked into the gray eyes that were only inches away and wondered how she had ever thought they were cold.

"Yes," she whispered.

The tip of Cole's tongue slowly traced the sensitive skin at the edge of her upper lip. At the first touch, she made a small sound. The gliding caress was unexpected, exquisite, unlike anything she'd ever known from a man. Slowly her body relaxed and softened, lifting subtly toward Cole, wanting more of his warmth. He repeated the gentle touch, tracing her whole mouth, enjoying the chaste caress with an intensity that surprised him.

When Erin felt the tip of his tongue along her lower lip, she shivered and instinctively closed her eyes, wanting to focus only on the sensations radiating through her from his touch. When he slowly outlined her lips again and yet again, lingering to probe the sensitive corners of her smile, everything shifted around her, fear vanishing, nothing existing but the warm caress.

Even when she felt the resilient heat of his biceps beneath her palms, she didn't realize that she had reached out and was holding on to him.

"Cole . . ."

"Yes, like that," he said, his tongue sliding between her open lips, touching the tip of her tongue with his own. "Let me taste you. Just a taste, honey. That's all. I won't hurt you. You know that, don't you?"

As he spoke he caressed her mouth again and again, not holding her, not forcing her, touching her with nothing but the tip of his tongue and the warmth of his breath.

And because it was the only way Cole permitted himself to touch her, his senses narrowed down to the tip of his tongue. He felt the heat and textures of her mouth with a sensual intensity that was as new to him as it was to her. The vividness of the experience intrigued him. He traced her tongue again, dipping into the heat and softness underneath, tasting her as he had never tasted a woman in his life, savoring and caressing until he felt like every nerve ending in his body was concentrated in the tip of his tongue.

Finally Cole forced himself to stop. He eased away and came to his feet in a lithe motion, not trusting himself to stay close to Erin any longer without trying to mold her to the hungry length of his body. He wasn't used to kissing a woman and not having her. The experience was as new to him as discovering the astonishing sensitivity of his own tongue.

Her eyes opened slowly. Her palms felt cool without his heat to warm them. So did her lips, her mouth, her tongue.

"Cole?" she asked huskily.

"Time for that walk, honey."

She looked at the big hand he was holding out to her. When she took it, he pulled her to her feet and slowly, deeply, interlaced their fingers. His palm was warm and hard. The inner surfaces of his fingers were smooth and hot. She caught her breath at the sensations shivering up her arm when he flexed his hand.

When he would have let go of her, she protested. "Wait."

Cole froze.

Erin touched the cut on his lip with a fingertip that

trembled very slightly. When she traced the edge of his mouth, the rasp of his stubble was pronounced, underlining the surprising smoothness of his lips. While the silence lengthened she traced his black eyebrows, his cheekbones, his chin, and then his lips again. He closed his eyes, permitting the gentle, exploratory torture for as long as he could trust himself.

"No more," Cole said finally.

Erin saw the pale blaze of his eyes as they opened and automatically stepped back. He didn't release her hand.

"I'm sorry," she said quickly. "I thought you liked it."

"That's the problem. I like it way too much." He looked at her, making no effort to disguise the elemental hunger he felt. "I wanted you the first time I saw you. Nothing that's happened since has changed my mind. But I've never kissed a woman without having her, even when I was fourteen, and—"

"Fourteen?" Erin interrupted. Then, as realization hit, *"Never?"*

"She was nineteen and she knew exactly what she was doing. So did I, after she was through." Cole smiled and put his finger under Erin's chin, closing her parted lips. "Don't look so shocked, honey. Where I came from, I was a slow starter, but I caught on real quick. I didn't want to marry so I didn't go looking for the kind of girl who kissed and said no. The girls I went out with didn't know the word no. Dinner, a movie, and the backseat of a car."

"The movie, no doubt, was optional?"

Cole smiled crookedly and flexed his hand again, rubbing his palm over Erin's, drawing her closer to him without meaning to. "Most of the time, so was the dinner," he admitted.

"Are you bragging or complaining?"

"Neither," he said, bringing Erin's hand up to his lips

once more. Very gently he caught her index finger between his teeth, tasted her, and released her quickly. "I'm trying to explain that in some ways I'm as new to this kind of playing as you are. Or did you see a lot of bad drive-in movies through steamy windows when you were a teenager?"

She tried to laugh, but her breath was too thick in her throat. "No. I was thirteen until I turned nineteen. Gawky and shy and plain. Phil, my brother, didn't help. I had a terrible crush on a boy who was three years older, a senior. When he asked me out, Phil called the guy and told him that if he so much as kissed me he'd be history. Saturday came and the guy didn't show up. I found out later that he had a thing for virgins. Kept a regular scorecard."

"Funny how different men are. I never was interested in a virgin until you."

Erin closed her eyes. "Not so funny after all. I'm not a virgin."

"You've never given yourself to a man," Cole said matter-of-factly. "That makes you a virgin in my book." He released her hand. "Stay put while I make sure it's safe to take a ride."

13

Pacific Coast Highway

Cole drove erratically, first slow, then too fast. It was deliberate. He studied traffic in mirrors, looking for cars that matched his speed.

"Well?" Erin asked when she couldn't stand it any more.

"Nobody yet."

They turned off the highway and cruised several empty parking lots. No one took the bait. Finally he decided it was safe and parked at Will Rogers State Beach.

Eager to be outside, she reached for the car door. Then she stopped and looked over at Cole. He was still studying the rear and sideview mirrors. Despite her impatience to be out on the beach with nothing in front of her but seven thousand miles of water, she didn't open the door.

"You're a fast learner," he said approvingly.

"Pain is a great teacher."

"I'm sorry. I tried not to hurt you."

"You didn't hurt me," she said quickly. "That was why I stopped fighting. I expected to be hurt and I wasn't. You're damned heavy, though."

He smiled slightly. "Next time I'll let you be on top."

She gave him a startled sideways look and then the kind of almost-shy smile that told him the thought intrigued her.

"Two choices, honey," he said. "Go for a walk or take a remedial course in window steaming."

She smiled sadly and looked away. "Don't tempt me."

"Why not?"

For a moment the car was silent. She turned around to face the man who had taught her more about sensual pleasure in a few minutes than she'd learned in her entire life. More importantly, he'd taught her the nature of the restlessness that had driven her from the arctic. The discovery of her own sexuality was as unexpected as Cole's gentleness had been.

"I'm interested in what you're offering," she said, "but I don't know how much and I won't until it happens. Or doesn't happen. That's not fair to you."

"If life was fair, someone would have gutted Hans before he had his first wet dream."

Erin stared. Though Cole's tone was casual, his eyes were like hammered silver.

"But life isn't fair," he said. "Only damned unexpected. Back in that hotel room you taught me something new about pleasure, and I would have sworn that was impossible. We could die before we take our next breath, or we could live to teach each other something else new about ourselves. So I'll take what comes and not worry too much about what doesn't. How about you?"

"I—I don't know."

"Think about it. And while you do, think about this. A man who can't control himself belongs to anyone who can. I don't belong to anyone but myself. We could be dead naked and you could be all over me like a hot rain, but if you changed your mind, I'd get up and get dressed and that would be the end of it." Cole's ice-pale glance went from mirror to mirror as he spoke. "While you think about that, let's walk. We've both been caged up more than we're used to."

Erin waited until he came around and opened her car door. Caution, not old-fashioned etiquette. When he laced his fingers through hers once more, she found herself smiling. He saw the pale gleam of her teeth in the moonlight and smiled in return.

"You really like being outside, don't you?" he said.

"Yes, but that's not why I'm smiling. I feel about sixteen again, holding hands beneath the cool moonlight." She gave him a sideways look. "I suppose you were about six when you started walking out with girls."

He laughed softly. "Enjoy it. When we get to Australia, you won't even want to stand close to another person, moon or no moon."

"Why?"

"Too bloody hot. The Kimberley is in the upper part of the continent. The tropical part."

"Tropical? The pictures I've seen of the Kimberley look more like desert."

"Oh, it's dry all right. Most of the year. Then the buildup begins, and great rivers of clouds pour in from the Indian Ocean. You sweat and the sweat just stays on your skin, making you hotter than ever, because sweat can't evaporate into air that's already saturated. The body can't cool itself, and the sunlight is a razor slicing into your skin. The temperature goes way over a hundred, and the humidity gets right up to the point of rain and then it sticks there and sticks there until men literally crack up and go berserk."

She made a sound of disbelief.

"It's true, honey. The Aussies even have a name for that kind of madness. They call it going troppo. I've come close a few times myself. It taught me something. I avoid the buildup now."

"You make it sound irresistible."

"Oh, that's not the worst of it," he said, taking a deep breath of the cool, brine-scented air. "When the wet finally comes, the country is swamp. For months at a time you can't travel except by plane."

"What about four-wheel-drive?"

"Not unless it floats."

"No bridges?"

"Only on the one major highway," Cole said. "When the wet is really on, those bridges are under water a lot of the time. They're built low and with removable railings so that trash doesn't get caught and create a dam. Even so, they wash out a lot." He looked over at Erin. "That's what ConMin is trying to do by offering to fly you all over the world to photograph diamond mines. ConMin knows that if you don't get into Crazy Abe's claim in the next few weeks, you'll have a hell of a time getting in at all until summer dries things out. I should be in the Kimberley right now, prospecting before the temperature goes to a hundred and twenty and the air is too wet to breathe."

"Then we shouldn't go to London at all."

"It will keep Faulkner and van Luik off our backs while Wing sets up things on the other end."

"Wing?"

"My partner."

"Oh. That's right. BlackWing. Dad said something about that."

"Yeah, I'll just bet he did." Cole looked down at Erin. "Don't worry, honey. If your mine can be found, I'll find it for you."

"Yes. Dad said that too."

Cole walked in silence for a time before he stopped and very gently pulled Erin toward him. When there was no resistance on her part, he bent and brushed his lips over hers.

"Don't go to Australia. You'll be safer with your father. He may have gray hair, but he's one tough bastard."

She started to object, only to be distracted by the gliding caress of Cole's tongue over her lips and the warmth of his breath as he spoke urgently.

"The climate and the land have killed men who were much stronger and more experienced than you are," Cole said simply. "The Kimberley Plateau is no place for a white woman."

"People told me the same thing about the arctic." Curious, she tasted his chin as she'd once tasted the green diamond. "Salty. Male. Warm. You taste good, Cole."

His breath came in with a ripping sound. Swiftly he caged her face between his hands. "Woman, you do love to take risks, don't you?"

"Risks?" She looked up at him with eyes made dark and mysterious by moonlight. "How so?"

"I could make you stay home. I could crowd you sexually until you turned and ran for cover."

Erin went very still, searching the hot silver gleam of Cole's eyes. Then she sighed and smiled almost sadly. "Yesterday you could have, when I didn't know you. But not today. Today I found out that you're a hard man but not a cruel one. You're not at all like Hans."

"There's a world full of people who would disagree with you," Cole said flatly.

"I'm not one of them. I'm the woman you had laid out like a lamb for slaughter, but all you did was stroke my hair while I cried, and then you kissed me so gently I felt like crying all over again. I was certain I'd never trust a man after Hans. I was wrong." She touched Cole's mouth with her fingertips. "It's too late to make me afraid of you. I'm going to Australia, and I'm going to be with you every step of the way."

Cole told himself that he was sorry he couldn't intimidate Erin, sorry that she stood so trustingly in his arms, leaning against him, her breath a warmth rushing over his skin.

He told himself, but he didn't believe any of it.

For a long time he simply held her, listening to the surf and wishing he'd exaggerated the difficulty of living and working in the Kimberley.

But he hadn't exaggerated. The buildup was a corrosive time, fraying men's tempers to the point of violence and beyond. The wet wasn't much better. When the wet arrived, it would wash the land right back into the Stone Age, where the most simple things were difficult. Even survival.

Especially survival.

14

"I've been attending funerals." Chen Wing's voice was thinned by more than the satellite relay joining him to Cole. "They have an unsettling effect."

Cole smiled grimly. "You didn't expect to make war on ConMin without suffering a few casualties, did you?"

Wing didn't reply for a moment. Then he changed the subject. "Have you made any progress?"

"Directly, none."

Wing muttered a quiet curse in Cantonese.

"Relax," Cole said. "At this stage, that's the best news you could hope for. I've spent most of the last three days examining maps from the BlackWing files."

"And?"

"Nothing. That's good news. If I could find Windsor's jewel box in a few hours using existing maps, so could any other geologist, including the ones on your staff. You told me they reported finding nothing, correct?"

"Yes."

"They probably weren't lying, because the maps told them nothing. The other possibility is that the maps told the story but your geologists withheld it to sell it to someone else. If so, I didn't find what they were selling."

"If you haven't found it, they didn't. You're the best. You always have been. Lucky in mines, unlucky in love."

"Number one, that isn't how the saying goes," Cole said. "Number two, my love life is none of your damned business."

There was a brief silence, followed by a sigh. "I'm sorry," Wing said, his tone soft, almost whispering. "Funerals have an unfortunate effect on my common sense. One of those funerals was that of my second cousin and brother-in-law, Chen Zeong-Li."

Images flooded through Cole's memory, images of the passionate black-eyed woman who was Wing's sister, the woman who in the end had loved her family and power more than she had loved any man, including Cole Blackburn.

"Zeong was a decent man," Cole said finally. "I'm sorry to hear he's dead."

"Are you? There was a time when you would have killed Zeong and danced on his grave."

Cole didn't say anything.

"If you choose to resume the relationship with Chen Lai," Wing continued, "this time the Chen family would not intervene."

This time.

The words echoed in Cole's mind, reminding him of things he would rather have forgotten. Shortly after he'd signed the original BlackWing agreement, Lai had dumped him because the family of Chen disapproved of a non-Chinese husband. A secret lover was tolerated while Cole advanced the Chen family's mineral business, but when it came to marriage and children it was more important to consolidate blood and business ties in Kowloon.

Now Zeong-Li was dead, Lai was widowed, and the family of Chen was offering Cole the very woman they once had forbidden him.

"No, thanks," Cole said calmly. "A smart man only wipes his ass with poison ivy once."

From the other end of the line came a charged silence, followed by the sound of harsh, humorless laughter. "You haven't changed."

"Hard to harder, half smart to half smarter. That's a change, Wing. It's the only change that matters. I've survived."

"What will you need at Abe's station?"

Without a pause Cole accepted the change of subject. "I'll need a helicopter to do photo, radar, magnetic, and scintillometric studies of Abe's claims. Ideally the information from the last two should be recorded on separate transparencies, laid over the first two, and then integrated with information that I'm putting on the topo and geological maps, but I won't have time to handle all the integration and programming myself."

"We have a mainframe here," Wing said.

"I don't like that. It increases the chances of a leak."

Wing said nothing.

Cole shrugged and accepted what wasn't going to change. "Can you set up a ground station at Windsor's place—modem, satellite link, and graphic printers to handle the output from your end?"

There was a pause. "I'll need several days."

"You'll get it. What about the inputting on your end?"

"I'll do it myself."

"Then I'll transmit data as fast as I get it. Set up a secure file in BlackWing's main computer, code access 'chunder.' "

"Chunder," Wing repeated. "Within an hour you can

have a printout under that name from any Chen business computer anywhere in the world."

"Good," Cole said. "What about the rest of the transparencies I'll need? Who will do them?"

"My people."

"Be damn sure you trust them."

"They are of the family of Chen, and they won't know the location of the scraps of land they're working on. They will have only a grid to work from. I am the only one who knows the latitudes and longitudes."

Cole laughed quietly. He understood Wing's kind of trust, the kind that was weighed and measured. "That leaves us with just one problem—the helicopter. I put the names of nearby mining exploration outfits through the computer."

"I saw the printout."

"Then you know all of them are tied to ConMin in one way or another. The only way we'll have a chance against the cartel is if we keep them off balance, wondering what's going to happen next. That means working fast and as quietly as possible. If we have to go to New South Wales or the Nullarbor for the chopper, the logistics of fuel supply will be impossible. If we get one closer to home, ConMin will have a direct pipeline into our operation. Take your pick, Wing."

"I did. I reran data and selected the five companies that are least indebted to ConMin. Several of those are also indebted to Pacific Enterprises, Inc., Pan-Asian Resources Ltd., or Pacific Rim Development and Resources Ltd."

Cole recognized all three firms. They were powerful forces in trade among the countries that circled the Pacific Ocean. Apparently all were under control of the Chen family to a greater or lesser degree. "What's your best pick? Pan-Asian Resources?" he said.

"We have enjoyed amicable relations with them for years, yes," Wing admitted.

"Which of the Australian firms do they control?"

"Control? None. We are simply in an advisory capacity."

"Yeah. ConMin does a lot of that too."

Wing ignored him. "Metalworks and Mines Ltd. is my first choice for a helicopter, with Western Australia Iron and Gold Surveyors second. I will make inquiries immediately."

"What if neither one comes through for you?"

"I can say with great certainty that Metalworks will have a helicopter available for short-term lease. Do you need a pilot?"

"I'll fly it myself. What about that list of survey equipment I faxed you?"

"Everything you need will be at the station when you get there," Wing said.

"Someone to set it up and guard it would be nice. I'm a miner, not an electronics expert, and I'll be away from the buildings most of the time."

"Noted. Anything else?"

"Maybe some of the amenities of life. Abe's idea of furniture was a dirt floor."

"Noted. Will you require a single bed or a double?"

Cole broke the link without answering. Immediately he put in Matthew Windsor's number.

It was time to find out what Erin's father was willing to do for his daughter.

15

Darwin, Australia
A day later

"For this I packed my cameras and clothes and sent them to London without me?" Erin asked, disgusted.

"No," Cole said, without looking up from his maps. "You did that to make ConMin think they had you coming to heel nicely. Confuse, mislead, and misdirect. It's the only way to survive."

"One more run through 'Chunder' and I won't care if I survive."

With that, Erin tossed aside the sheets of Abe's doggerel. She'd been sitting in the window seat of their Darwin hotel, studying the poem and looking out at the lush tropical landscaping. Her body swung between sleepiness and an irritable kind of restlessness, which was her own personal version of jet lag. She'd be better as soon as she slept, but it was only five o'clock. She had to stay awake for a few more hours. Reading "Chunder" wouldn't help her.

Cole glanced up from the desk in the living area of the suite. Transparent topographic and geological maps of Australia were spread across the hotel desk in front of him, along with maps showing the distribution of active and reserve mineral claims in Western Australia and the Northern Territory. On top of those maps lay transparencies of the Kimberley Plateau and of Western Australia. A compass, ruler, pencil, and a lined notepad were within reach. The pad was covered with cryptic notes.

He didn't really expect to find the answer to the Sleeping Dog Mines in the maps, but they gave him something to think about besides Erin's warm tongue and husky voice approving of his taste. He looked at the sheets of paper she'd tossed aside.

"Did you know that Chunder is Aussie slang for vomit?" he said.

"Lovely," she said. "Old Great-uncle Abe was a real literary light, wasn't he?"

A slight smile was Cole's only response. *Chunder* was the most elegant of the slang contained in Abe's doggerel. If Erin had any idea of the meaning of the words she'd been reading aloud, Cole suspected she would have blushed to the soles of her feet. Abe had been a randy bastard right up to the day he died.

"What time is it?" she asked, yawning suddenly.

"Same as it was the last time you asked—too soon to go to bed. You'd wake up a couple hours before dawn."

"Damn. I'm finally feeling sleepy."

"Fight it."

Muttering, she went and stood next to him, looking over his shoulder at the maps.

"Help me stay awake. Explain some more of these maps to me." She braced herself with a hand on his shoulder as she leaned closer. "This time I'll try not to yawn in your ear."

"Sit down before you fall down," he said, gently pulling her onto his lap.

Instantly she tensed.

Ignoring her rigid body, Cole began pointing out features on the nearest map.

As he talked, Erin gradually began to relax, trusting her weight to the muscular support of his thighs and chest, feeling the heat of his body sink into hers.

Though Cole savored each small softening of her body against his, he kept talking as though nothing but the maps mattered.

"I understand topographic maps," she said finally, "but what is this one?"

As she leaned forward to point, she shifted in his lap. The pressure of her hips against his groin made his breathing thicken. With a silent curse at his unruly body, he concentrated on the transparency she was pointing to. The clear plastic was four feet by four feet, exactly the scale of the topographic map and covered by seemingly random patterns of rainbow colors.

Deliberately Cole reached around Erin with both arms and slid the transparency over the topographic map. The motion also brushed his biceps against her breasts. The contact made her gasp. Her breath unraveled suddenly, but she didn't withdraw. His arms moved again, caressing and freeing in the same motion. While he spoke, he traced lines with a calloused fingertip.

"The blue lines are sandstone," he said. "There's a lot of it in the Kimberley. The brown crosshatches are limestone. The yellow diagonals are volcanic rocks. The pink dots are water deposits. The white dots are wind deposits. It makes a difference to us, because usually only water deposits contain diamonds."

As Erin grew accustomed to looking both at and through the transparency, she could see how the water deposits almost always coincided with rivers or beaches or low spots on the topographic map. But there were a few places where pink dots appeared without any sign of rivers or lakes or ocean.

"Is this a water deposit?" she asked. "There's no sign of water anywhere close."

Cole looked at the slender finger with its clean, unpolished nail. When he saw where she was pointing, he gave her full marks for quickness.

"That's what geologists call a paleo-floodplain, a place where a flooding river used to overflow and leave silt and stones behind. The river is long since gone, but the characteristic deposits of a floodplain are still there."

"Does that mean diamonds could be there?"

"If the ancient river flowed through diamond-bearing rock, yes."

"Did it?"

"Probably not. It didn't flow through any volcanic rocks."

She frowned. "I didn't know the Kimberley Plateau had volcanoes."

"It does, but they're real ancient. They've been eroded flat and sometimes even down beyond that, to the magma chamber itself. Nothing is left but the barest bones of what once was an awesome piece of living nature. When you're digging for diamonds, you're digging up a grave."

"Lovely thought," she said beneath her breath.

Cole reached for another transparency and drew it onto the top of the stacked maps. This time Erin didn't flinch when his arms brushed the sides of her breasts.

"Since nothing volcanic shows on the surface," he said, keeping his arms around her, "we have to look down below."

"How?"

"This map outlines stations, mining claims, and mineral reserves in the Kimberley. The stations are green, active claims and reserves are red, lapsed claims and reserves are blue."

She made a sound of dismay as she saw the network of overlapping lines. "There's nothing left of the Kimberley. Somebody's been over every inch of it already."

"They've staked out claims and then abandoned them."

"Because there was nothing there," she said unhappily.

His arms tightened, shifting her subtly on his lap, allowing him to brush his lips against her soft hair. "I don't need virgin land to find pay dirt, because most men are no damn good at what they do."

The warmth of Cole's breath against her neck made Erin shiver. It was pleasure rather than fear that rippled over her skin, pleasure that made her lean more fully against him.

He smiled, caressed her again, and went on speaking in a deep, slow voice, as though he had nothing more on his mind than maps.

"Most of Abe's claims were worked over in the 1920s by men looking for gold. When they didn't find anything worthwhile, they abandoned the claims. Since then no one has been there except an occasional jackeroo or a walkabout Aborigine."

She stared at the piled maps, seeing lines and designs and colors and more lines and designs. And no answers at all.

"The problem isn't that the plateau is too well known," Cole said, pulling another transparency out and lining it up with the underlying maps, caressing Erin with every motion, every breath. "The problem is that we don't know nearly enough."

She tried to speak, but couldn't. His strength, his heat, his very breath surrounded her.

Yet all she could think about was getting closer.

"This transparency shows what kind of plants grow,"

he said, allowing his lips to linger against her neck. "Plants change with elevation, rainfall, and soil. They can tell you whether limestone or sandstone or volcanic rock is underneath the soil."

He moved another transparency onto the pile. He took a lot of time stacking it, for each movement of his arms caressed another soft curve of Erin's body.

"This shows roads, trails, dams, airstrips, towns, houses, windmills, microwave relays, and whatever else man has added to the landscape. Look at it, honey. Look at it real carefully."

As he spoke, he released her from his touch. She stared at the final transparency, trying to gather thoughts scattered by the unexpected splinters of pleasure that had pierced her with every brush of his body against hers. Gradually she realized that the final map had the least marks of any map on the pile.

Man had touched Western Australia only lightly, and the Kimberley barely at all.

"In that pile is everything we know about the Kimberley," Cole said. "Put your hand over a part of the map. Any part."

Puzzled, she did as he asked.

"You have a few thousand square miles under your hand," he said. "Lift it and tell me what we know about that piece of land."

She moved her hand aside, looking at the transparency and then at the key that ran down the side.

"No paved roads," she said. "One graded road, and a few station roads that are little better than wild-animal trails. Five station houses." She leaned closer. "Three of them are abandoned. A handful of windmills." She leaned forward even further, looking through the top map to the one just beneath. Again she looked at the color key on the map's margin. "Lowland grasses, spinifex, scrub gum."

Cole lifted the top two transparencies, letting her see the ones underneath more easily.

"Parts of three stations," she continued. "About seven mineral claims sort of in a line." She bent lower. "The claims run along a river," she said, reading through to the topographic map. "Well, some of the year it's a river. The rest of the time it's dry. Dashed lines, right?"

"Right. Go on."

Frowning, she went on to the next map. "The land is nearly flat. Sand and sandstone. No permanent water."

"What else?"

There was a long silence while she sifted through the maps again. Finally she looked up at him. "That's it."

"Think about it, Erin. Thousands of square miles, and you've summed up man's knowledge of it in less than three minutes."

She made a startled sound.

"You could call the station owners pioneers and you wouldn't be wrong," he said. "The twentieth century is only a rumor out in the Kimberley. Western Australia is a different place, a different land, a different time. Civilization is whatever you can carry in on your back."

After a moment she asked, "How old was Abe?"

"Had to be eighty, at least, when he died."

"What was his health like?"

"He could walk most men into the ground. He could drink the rest right under, including me."

She frowned. "Then there's no place on Abe's cattle station or on his claims that he was too old to prospect?"

"Doubt it. Not when I knew him, anyway. And he discovered his jewel box before I knew him."

"All right, what about Sleeping Dog One, Sleeping

Dog Two, and all the rest?" she asked. "What makes you so certain those mines are worthless?"

"I've been in Dog One. It's a pipe mine, pure and simple, and not much of one at that. Nearly all bort. The diamonds in that tin box came from a placer mine with a high percentage of gem-quality stones."

"What's bort?"

"Industrial diamonds," he said, "useful only for abrasives or drill bits."

"No gemstones at all?" she asked.

"Nothing like your diamonds. His were all sharp edges, flaws, and yellow to brown."

"Are all Abe's mines like that?"

Cole smiled at the disappointment in Erin's voice. "I'm afraid so, honey. Not one of them is located on or near a modern river course, either, which means the Dog mines just aren't a likely source of placer diamonds."

With a gloomy expression she looked at the maps. "What did you mean, *modern* rivers? What other kind of river is there?"

Absently Cole's fingertips smoothed over the paper as he thought about the passage of time over the face of the land, time transforming everything it touched, wearing down old mountains and building new ones.

"Paleo-rivers," he said finally. "Old as the hills. Older."

"I don't understand."

"The Kimberley Plateau has spent a billion and a half years above sea level. That makes it the oldest land surface on earth. Almost every bit of the rest of the Australian continent—and the other continents too—have been recycled top to bottom in one way or another in the last billion and a half years. Not the Kimberley."

Cole leaned away from Erin for a moment, pulled a big opaque map of Australia from the bottom of the pile, and spread it out on top.

"Look here," he said. "Australia is the flattest inhabited continent on earth. The driest, too. The Kimberley Plateau is about the only thing west of Ayers Rock that's high enough to make a decent hill anywhere else in the world."

She made a startled sound and looked at the map again.

"In the center of Australia," he said, "the land is so flat that rain collects in circles like dew on a gigantic picnic table." His long index finger traced the shallow rise of the Kimberley Plateau. "This area stayed high and dry, but the rest of Australia, the flat center and the even flatter southwest, have been underwater more than above. There are huge limestone and sandstone beds covering those areas to prove it."

When Cole looked up he found that Erin was focused on the map with an intensity and intelligence that was almost tangible.

"At the edge of the Kimberley the land rumples a bit," he continued. "The locals call them mountains. Anyone else would call them hills. They're what's left of a limestone reef that was buried and then resurrected by erosion."

" 'A dead sea's bones,' " she quoted softly, remembering a phrase from Abe's poetry.

Cole's eyes narrowed. He pushed the continental map aside and pulled out the map of the Kimberley Plateau. He traced the line of the Napier Range and the other limestone ranges that ring the Kimberley today, as the living reefs once ringed the Kimberley long ago. Seven of Crazy Abe's claims straddled limestone outcroppings. Three of them were within the boundaries of the station itself. None was near a Dog mine.

"Cole?" she asked, sensing his intensity.

Instead of answering, he grabbed another map, this one showing major modern watercourses. There were no year-round rivers, but in the wet more rain came down than even the parched, porous land could absorb. The result was a series of on-again, off-again "rivers" that were little more than flood channels several miles wide.

She watched while his intent, nearly silver eyes measured distances and catalogued possibilities. The speed and decisiveness of his work suggested an intelligence that was as impressive as his physical strength.

Watching him, she had to admit just how drawn she was to him—and never more so than now, when the intelligence and discipline in him were real enough to touch.

Don't even think about being his lover.

She wasn't the kind of person who did anything by halves. If she gave herself to him physically, it would be impossible not to give the rest of herself as well. There was no guarantee he wanted anything more than her body. It was a recipe for disaster.

Yet the lure of him sank into her more deeply each moment she was with him.

Without warning, Cole looked up and caught Erin's luminous green eyes admiring him. When she realized it, she looked away hastily.

"Well?" she asked, gesturing to the map.

He shrugged. "About two-thirds of Australia can lay claim to being the burial ground of a dead sea's bones."

"Oh," she said, disappointed.

"On the other hand, when it comes to checking existing claims, I'll concentrate on the areas with limestone outcroppings first."

A smile transformed her face. "Then I helped?"

He grinned. "I hope so. We've got a hell of a lot of land to cover any way you look at it."

"Is there a river?"

"Not the way you mean it. There were paleo-rivers, though. They drained into the shallow sea where reefs formed. There were beaches, too, maybe like Namibia's beaches, where every time you dig down to the oyster line you come up with diamonds running out of both hands."

"Where are the old rivers on Abe's claims?"

"I never saw any sign of them," Cole said, "but they're there. They have to be."

"Because of the diamonds?"

"No. Because the Kimberley Plateau has always been there, and a sea was usually there, and water always runs down to the sea."

Unconsciously, she worried her lower lip with her teeth, something she often did when nervous or thinking hard. "What about your maps? Do they show old rivers?"

"No. The only maps I can get my hands on are of the tectonic sort. They're useless if you're looking for something that's smaller than a hundred square miles."

"How big are diamond pipes?"

"Most of them are only a few hundred square acres on the surface. A lot of them are smaller. A few are huge."

"Talk about a needle in a haystack . . ."

"I'd settle for that," he said sardonically. "If it was a needle, I'd whistle up an industrial-strength magnet and suck that baby out in nothing flat."

His eyes went back to the maps. Instantly he was absorbed, pursuing some line of thought Erin could only guess at. She watched him openly, wishing her cameras were lying on the table instead of on the chair next to her bed. Though she rarely did portraits, preferring the timeless beauty of wilderness to the transient faces of humanity, she wanted to photograph Cole. Like the land, there was more to him than his harsh exterior.

16

London

Hugo van Luik passed down the long hallway like a ghost. The lush green wool carpeting, the tapestries, and the heavy curtains soaked up every sound his steps made. A closed-circuit television camera mounted on the wood-paneled wall tracked his progress. Depending on the time of month, this office was the repository of anywhere between two and three billion dollars in rough diamonds.

When he reached the heavy, hand-carved wooden door at the far end of the hall, he stopped and tapped a four-digit code into the security key pad. The lock retracted, allowing him to push the door open and pass into the next long hallway to the next electronic locks, until finally he was inside the conference room.

Although meetings of the "steering committee" of the Diamond Sales Division of Consolidated Minerals were "unofficial," "advisory," and never publicized, such gatherings were crucial to the economic expectations and requirements of the nations that attended. Individual diamond sight-holders always made their needs known to the DSD through formal channels, but what happened in this room today would determine how—or whether—those needs would be met. To an extent startling to outsiders, DSD enhanced or diminished the economic health of nations.

Van Luik checked his own watch. Given a choice, he would have put this meeting off for five weeks, until the next sight. By then the monsoon season would have started in Western Australia and the matter of Abelard Windsor's dangerous bequest would be moot for another six months. But putting off the meeting wasn't possible.

Abruptly he turned to the majordomo who was hovering by the half-open door.

"Send them in."

The representative from Israel strode in first. Moshe Aram was lean, wiry, and fit. He was a member of the Israeli secret service, Mossad. The diamond trade was too crucial to Israel's economy to be left in the hands of diamantaires or politicians. That was how the troubles had begun back in the 1970s.

The United States representative, Nan Faulkner, followed on Aram's heels. Faulkner sat down, poured herself a glass of ice water, drank it, and poured another. Then she lit a cigarillo and balanced it on the lip of a heavy crystal ashtray that had been put at her place.

Van Luik nodded at the woman but said nothing. Although Faulkner was an old hand at DSD meetings, van Luik always maintained his distance from her, believing her to be a political token rather than a real player in the game of international power.

He went to his own chair at the head of the table and watched calmly while the others took their places. There was little polite talk. Each person was there to ensure that his country's interests in the diamond trade were presented to the diamond cartel.

The Soviet representative, Boris Yarakov, looked unusually surly. Attar Singh, India's representative to the cartel, was as politic as Yarakov was boorish. Singh had no choice but to be accommodating. India no longer produced diamonds, so it no longer commanded the attention it once had. What India brought to ConMin and DSD was a bottomless well of cheap labor willing to spend its hours and its eyesight on the task of shaping and polishing diamonds so tiny they would once have been sold for industrial use at a quarter the price of polished goods.

The Continental diamond trade was represented by Nathaniel Feinberg. As with India, the Continental interests were cutters and polishers rather than producers of rough diamonds. They had less power in the diamond cartel than the owners of the gem-producing diamond mines themselves. Those mines were the treasure and bane of the diamond cartel's existence: There were more than enough mines to fill the world demand for gems.

Australia had used its own geologists, rather than ConMin's, to explore the vast Kimberley Plateau. The Argyle diamond mine had been the result. Because the remote Argyle strike was monstrously expensive to develop, Australia sought outside capital. Once the banks learned that Australia wasn't a member of the diamond cartel and thus had no guaranteed market for the Argyle's output, development money dried up.

The power games hadn't stopped there. India, unhappy with the cartel, had offered to guarantee a market for Argyle's melee diamonds. The banks were approached again, guaranteed market in hand. Before the loan went through, the Indian government was privately informed that DSD would undercut India's markets by flooding them with below-cost stones of the same size, quality, and cut as India would produce from the Australian mine. DSD and ConMin were rich enough to absorb the losses indefinitely.

India wasn't.

No single diamond-producing country could survive a pissing contest with the contents of DSD's London vaults. India withdrew its offer to finance the development of the Argyle mine, and Australia did what every other individual or nation with a diamond mine had done.

Australia cut a deal with ConMin.

Ian McLaren was Australia's representative to DSD. He watched van Luik warily, and with good reason. ConMin had a long memory.

Van Luik opened the Moroccan leather folder in front of him, signaling that the session was open. Immediately everyone began passing single sheets of paper to the head of the table. Each month the mining countries put forth a projected production figure, and each month the cutters and polishers stated their expected needs for raw material. It was up to van Luik to reconcile those two sides of the diamond equation.

He collected the "prayers" of each cartel member, but the papers were a formality. The same figures had been faxed to van Luik the previous day. In any case, the prayers were useless. He'd known for the past week how the next three months' output of DSD diamonds would be distributed.

Swiftly van Luik lined up sheets from producers opposite those from buyers and compared amounts with the agenda in his head. There would be some very unhappy people leaving the building today. It wouldn't be the first time, and van Luik wasn't fool enough to believe it would be the last.

"Mr. McLaren," van Luik said abruptly, "DSD can't at this time provide a guaranteed market for the undeveloped Ellendale pipes. As you know, the gem content of Ellendale was very high for a pipe mine. Somewhere in the neighborhood of sixty to eighty percent, was it not?"

"Yes, but—"

"Are you not aware," van Luik interrupted, "that the market has barely recovered from the disaster of 1980? This most definitely is not the time to bring a new gem mine into production."

"Then could we anticipate a price increase on our industrial diamonds?" McLaren asked curtly.

"Regretfully, no. If the price of industrial diamonds goes much higher, Japan would be tempted to begin mass-producing them in their labs, and then Australia would be left with a hugely expensive, hugely unprofitable mine and no way to repay the cost of its development."

"But—"

"I will be at the Argyle mine shortly to discuss long-range planning for its product. Be assured Australia's interests are DSD's interests as well. For the moment, the last thing either of our interests need is one more gem diamond mine."

Without waiting for a response, van Luik slipped McLaren's prayer to the bottom of the stack and addressed the problems created by the next sheet in line.

"Mr. Singh, you will receive two-thirds of the melees you requested," van Luik said.

"My cutters would be most grateful if a greater proportion of our sights were made up of larger rather than smaller melees, which are the dregs of the diamond trade."

"You have the only workers capable of turning a profit on the smaller melees," van Luik said. "However, if India would like its allotment reduced, DSD will do so. China has made inquiry about the melee trade recently. We told them our entire output of rough was allocated at present. Naturally we assured them that we would keep their interest in mind, should the situation change."

Singh's face went very dark beneath his stark white

turban. Yet when he spoke, his voice was flat and calm. "India has no objection to the kind or quantity of diamonds it will receive in the next three months from DSD."

"Excellent. Your cooperation will be remembered. Mr. Feinberg, your associates' requests will be met in full."

Feinberg nodded.

"Mr. Yarakov, the market for larger gems is just recovering from the disastrous speculation of 1980 and 1981," van Luik said. "We regret that we can handle no more of your output."

Yarakov looked angry but didn't open his mouth.

Van Luik paused, obviously expecting an argument. When none came, he went on to the next prayer. "Mr. Aram, your requests are unreasonable. If we allocated you that many melees, India and the Soviet Union would have little work for their own polishers."

Van Luik's dry, soft voice carried easily through the big room, because none of the people moved or muttered among themselves. Even Moshe Aram was quiet. In the 1970s, Israel had cut eighty percent of all melees. But in the early 1980s, Israel had been instrumental in the diamond speculation that had nearly broken DSD's hold on the diamond market. ConMin hadn't forgotten. Or forgiven. The cartel had cancelled the valuable sight invitations of 150 diamantaires, thereby gutting the diamond industry in Tel Aviv.

Soviet and Indian markets now received the majority of the melees.

"You will receive thirty-seven point six percent of your melee request," van Luik continued. "The Soviet Union will receive eighty-nine point eight percent of its request. Those amounts will be evenly divided among the next three sights in London. How you divide it among your diamantaires is, as always, a matter of your own discretion."

"You have punished us long enough," Aram said roughly. "We have done as you wished. We have altered our banking regulations and raised the margin requirements on sight boxes. Our cutters can no longer speculate. What more do you want from us, that we tear down Ramat Gan? What gives you the right to bleed the economy of a small, struggling, democratic nation and send our lifeblood to men who persecute Jews in the Soviet Union?"

"DSD trades in diamonds, not ideologies," van Luik said neutrally, shifting Israel's prayer to the bottom of the pile as he spoke. "You may, of course, ask for an increase in your allotment at this group's next advisory meeting."

"But—"

"The neutrality of DSD is well known," Nan Faulkner said dryly, cutting off another angry eruption from Aram. "Somehow, both sides in World War Two managed to get their hands on industrial diamonds. Nothing has changed since then."

Faulkner stubbed out her cigarillo and gave van Luik a level look.

"It's also well known that what happens in these advisory meetings has a ripple effect that goes far beyond the diamond market," she said. "You may not consider ideology, but each government represented at this table does. If the Israeli cut stands, I'll be forced to recommend that our American sight-holders substantially lower their requests."

Van Luik was surprised, but he didn't show it. "You may naturally do as you wish. However, in your country the sight-holders are also free to go against your recommendations. In that case DSD would naturally cater to the requests of its most immediate market—your retail jewelers."

Faulkner's smile was as cold as the glass of ice water

she drained before answering. "Yeah, that's the problem with a real democracy," she said, lighting another cigarillo. "But I tell you, it wouldn't take much effort to raise the taxes on diamonds at each stage—imported rough, loose polished stones, and finally set stones. In a year or two, diamond jewelry would go up in price, say, sixty percent in the American marketplace. Luxuries are just that, babe. Luxuries. If they get too pricey, people go without."

Van Luik opened his mouth.

Faulkner was quicker. "As for the sentimental trade," she continued, "lots of Americans would follow Princess Di's example and have colored gems in their engagement rings, especially if the jewelry manufacturers launched a campaign based on treating your loved one like royalty. At the same time, there might be a grass-roots political movement to boycott apartheid's diamonds."

"No aspect of Consolidated Minerals, Inc., has ever supported apartheid," van Luik said flatly, "and that most definitely includes DSD."

"Tough shit, babe. People associate diamonds and the diamond cartel with South Africa. Within five years at most, fifty percent of your American market would dry up. Maybe even seventy-five percent."

Faulkner smoked her cigarillo and said no more. She didn't have to. U.S. sales accounted for more than a third of all gem transactions in the world—the most profitable third.

"There is always Japan," van Luik pointed out.

"There sure is," Faulkner agreed, her voice hearty as she picked up the pitcher of ice water and began to pour. "The U.S. led them into buying diamond engagement rings. We can lead them right out again. That leaves you with half your former world market, which means that every country at this table just took a fifty percent cut in pay. Hardly worth it just to yank Israel's chain one more time, is it?"

"Remember, Ms. Faulkner, Consolidated Minerals controls more than diamonds."

"Which is the only reason there hasn't been a grass-roots campaign against diamonds in the U.S. before now," Faulkner shot back, setting down the water pitcher with a thump. "You need our diamond markets, and we need your strategic minerals. So let's cut the bullshit and find a more generous compromise than you've suggested so far."

Van Luik could count his heartbeats in the stabbing pain behind his eyes. He'd warned his superiors that the United States might be difficult if ConMin squeezed Israel too hard. No one had listened.

Now they would have to.

"Perhaps the loss of jobs and foreign exchange in Israel could be compensated for in another way," van Luik said, looking toward Singh.

"Forget it," Faulkner said. "Israel doesn't need any favors at India's expense. Why not take it out of the Bear's thick hide? The Soviet share of the melee market has gone up by about ten percent every six months for the last nine years."

Yarakov turned on Faulkner and spoke before van Luik could. "As a result of recent political changes in our country, the Soviet Union has employment and foreign exchange problems of its own. Your country supports glasnost in the world press, but we still have to pay for American wheat with American dollars."

"Take your restructuring even further," Aram suggested in a hard voice. "Incorporate your farms. Then you'd be up to your ass in wheat, just like America."

"Gentlemen," van Luik said sharply, pinching the bridge of his nose, "I believe the basis for compromise exists. Russia will continue cutting an increasing propor- tion of the larger melees, because the Soviet Union does a better job than anyone else for the same money."

Aram looked unhappy but kept silent. What van Luik said was the truth, no matter how distasteful.

"The Soviet Union will guarantee a good price on melees for Israel's artisans to fashion into jewelry," van Luik continued, giving Yarakov an unflinching stare. "In turn, Israel will agree to train a number of Soviet crafts- men in the art of creating luxury jewelry." He turned to- ward Nan Faulkner. "Does that seem a satisfactory compromise?"

"Ask Moshe. It's his country," Faulkner said, blowing out a pale stream of smoke. "The United States would have no objection so long as the net result doesn't hurt Is- rael's position within world economies."

Van Luik nodded and felt a tremor of relief. Faulkner was the key. Her tacit acceptance of the compromise meant that markets rather than ideologies would rule again today.

"Mr. Aram?" Van Luik turned toward the Israeli.

"We would require a twenty-year noncompetition agreement," Aram said sharply. "We taught the Russians how to cut melees and look what happened. They're run- ning us out of the market."

"Five years," Yarakov said, looking at his blunt hands rather than at Aram.

"Fifteen."

"Five."

"Thir—"

"Five!" Yarakov interrupted impatiently. "That is my final offer."

"That might be your final offer, babe, but can you kill a deal like this without Moscow's approval?" Faulkner asked. She tipped her glass of water from side to side, making the ice inside click softly. When Yarakov was silent, Faulkner turned to Aram. "How does twelve sound to you?"

Though Faulkner's voice was casual, there was nothing casual about her suggestion, and Aram knew it. He hesitated, then nodded. Yarakov didn't look happy either, but he nodded also, sealing the agreement.

"Ms. Faulkner, your requests are disappointingly modest," van Luik continued.

"So is the market."

"We disagree. DSD studies indicate an increasing demand for luxury jewelry worldwide. We have added twenty percent to your request. We are confident that the American market will be able to absorb it, particularly with the new advertising campaign American jewelers will be launching soon."

Faulkner knocked the ash from her cigarillo and looked skeptical.

"The theme of the campaign," van Luik said, "is 'The time to show her is now. Give a diamond as important as your love.' The stress will be on mounted diamonds in excess of one carat."

Faulkner shook her head, making the high-quality diamond studs in her earlobes glitter. "It will take time for such a campaign to have an effect. Meanwhile, we'll have expensive diamond jewelry up the gazoo. Give us a year's grace."

Van Luik made a note on the paper in front of him. "Three months' grace, Ms. Faulkner. If your sightholders don't like the contents of their parcels, they may, as always, refuse them."

Faulkner stubbed out her cigarillo and said nothing.

"Are we in agreement?" van Luik asked, looking around the table. There was no dissent. "*Mazel und broche.*"

There was a muttered chorus of "*Mazel und broche.*"

Even Nan Faulkner said the traditional words before she shoved back her chair and stalked out of the room, mentally preparing her report for the Secretary of Defense. She was certain of one thing. She would conclude with a bitter truth: Another gem diamond mine was definitely needed.

A mine controlled by the United States, not ConMin.

17

Darwin, Australia

Erin looked up from the remnants of her dinner as Cole approached her. A busy restaurant hummed around her. She barely noticed it. She was watching his lithe walk with an unconscious intensity. It was the same way she listened to his words, looked at his eyes, breathed the air that had touched him. . . .

Last night she'd fallen asleep in his lap with the hard proof of his arousal against her hip. This morning she'd awakened fully dressed and alone in the bed. The intense sexuality that was as much a part of Cole as his intelligence was fully controlled.

The realization still rippled through Erin's mind at odd moments, rearranging everything in its wake, leaving a feeling that was both peaceful and shimmering with anticipation.

Yet even as the feeling radiated through her, she knew she was reading too much into Cole's restraint. He wanted her, and he was smart enough to know that pushing her sexually would guarantee that he didn't get her.

She was edging toward wanting him, and she was smart enough to know the emotional risks involved.

Cole Blackburn didn't strike her as the kind of man who would let himself be vulnerable to love. She wasn't the kind to give herself to a man without loving him.

"Ready?" he asked, holding out his hand.

She stood and slid her hand into his. "Did you get them?"

"They're strapped to my waist. I got a room at a different hotel and left our stuff in it."

"My camera bag?" she asked.

He smiled slightly. "It's safe in the room. And no, you can't take pictures yet. No one watching you with a camera would mistake you for a tourist."

She sighed.

He squeezed her hand. "We'll rent a car using the new passports and leave tomorrow morning. Once we're out of the city you can take all the pictures you want."

"That's a rash promise. I'm going to hold you to it."

Laughing, they walked out of the restaurant hand in hand, looking like a couple having a relaxed night on the town. Outside it was warm, humid, and smelled like a city built in a greenhouse.

As they strolled beyond the circle of illumination thrown by a streetlight, they all but disappeared. He was wearing lightweight cotton slacks, shirt, and shoes. All black. Erin was wearing the same. Cole had insisted on dark colors at night and khaki during the day. Since he'd bought everything—including the nylon duffels they were using as luggage—she hadn't complained. All she had of her former baggage was a single camera bag and the diamonds belted around her waist beneath her clothes.

A breeze stirred vaguely, bringing the scent of the sea.

"Now will you let me go see the Indian Ocean?" she asked.

"Timor Sea, actually."

"Sold."

He laughed softly and looked down at the woman who walked so gracefully by his side. She'd been different since she'd fallen asleep in his lap. Her relaxation with him and her gentle verbal teasing only increased his desire. So did the frank approval in her eyes when she watched him.

"Come on," he said. "There's a way down to the sea over here."

He led her to an unlighted, zigzagging walkway that tunneled down through lush growth to the nearby water. They were only a few feet from the coarse sand beach when he stopped short, muscled her against the trunk of a tree, and pinned her in place with his body as though they were lovers too impatient to wait for privacy.

After a reflexive instant of fear at being manhandled, Erin relaxed. Cole's predatory attention wasn't on her. It was on the path behind them that led back up to Darwin's sidewalks.

"I thought I heard somebody behind us," he said very softly against her ear.

With each breath Erin took, the strength and weight of his body broke over her, sending her heart racing. Only a small part of her response was the residue of old terror. Most of it was new desire.

There was just enough light from the waxing moon for her to see the strong tendons in his neck, the black beard stubble that was a shadow beneath his skin, and the deep, steady beat of life in his throat. The pressure of his body was impersonal rather than sexual, protective rather than seductive. She told herself it was better that way.

She lied.

"Come on," he said in a voice that was barely a thread of sound. "Farther down the beach there's another way back up to the sidewalk."

Their shoes made a thick, gritty sound in the coarse sand. To their right the sea lapped, rather than broke, over the beach. Clouds with blurred edges ran like buttermilk over the sky, soaking up moon and stars until nothing remained but a vague haze and a dissolving ripple of moonlight on the water. Where trees overhung the sand, intense shadow flowed out. The densities of light and shadow fascinated Erin. They weren't like any combination of dark and bright that she'd ever seen.

"Wait here," Cole said softly. "If you see anyone or anything move ahead of you, yell my name and come running back to me."

"Where are you going?"

The only answer was the whisper of steel being drawn from the leather sheath he wore at his wrist. Like another shade of darkness he glided back the way they had come. She stared into the night intently, trying to see where Cole had gone.

Hands shot out of the darkness, grabbing her.

Before she had a chance to panic, she was following the self-defense routines that had been drilled into her until they were as much a part of her as her memories of Hans.

The man holding Erin made a triumphant sound that ended in a grunt of pain as her heel connected with his kneecap. He spun aside, hanging on to her with only one hand, grabbing his knee with the other.

She screamed a warning to Cole as she tried to break her attacker's wrist with the edge of her palm, but he yanked her off balance as he fell. She went down as she'd been trained to do, loosely, rolling instantly to her feet, poised to run, for escape was always the best defense.

The man's hand shot out and wrapped around her ankle. She kicked him in the face. He bellowed in pain.

Suddenly men were swarming all over her, grabbing at her hands and feet. She used everything she'd ever learned, knowing even as she fought that there were too many men for her to win, that they were too strong, and, worse, some of them were trained in unarmed combat. She'd taken her captor by surprise when she'd defended herself effectively.

The other men had seen what had happened to their friend. They were overwhelming her by sheer weight. Silently, savagely, she fought back. She'd promised herself seven years ago that she would kill or die before any man raped her again.

Suddenly she took a blow to the diaphragm that literally paralyzed her, driving the breath from her body. She barely heard one of her assailants give a high scream of pain in the instant before he reeled away from her and slumped unconscious into the sand. There was another flurry of motion as a man was lifted up and flung away. He landed hard and lay gasping for air.

The three remaining men abandoned Erin and looked around frantically, trying to find the invisible attacker.

"Run!" Cole ordered.

For an instant she didn't recognize his voice. There was a flatness in it that she had never heard before. She sensed motion to her left and turned her head.

"Damn it, run!"

Cole looked huge in the nebulous light. His hands and his body made sinuous, almost hypnotic motions as he waited for the men to attack him. With each continuous motion he shifted balance smoothly, always poised to attack or defend in any direction, never giving away his intentions. The knife he held had the dull shine of mercury. Slowly he backed away, trying to draw the men from Erin, who hadn't gotten up.

The men rushed Cole in a ragged line.

Erin saw the sudden gleam of steel blades as two of the men drew knives. She tried to call out, to warn Cole, but there wasn't any air left in her body. She fought against herself as she'd fought against the men, trying to drag air back into her lungs so that she could do more than lie helpless on the cold sand.

Cole watched the oncoming men, picking the order of his targets with the cool precision of a man who was used to being on the wrong end of the fighting odds. He had two advantages. The first was that he didn't have to worry about injuring a friend by mistake. The second was that the men would expect him to defend himself rather than attack them.

The two men holding knives came eagerly forward, keeping just enough distance between them so that Cole could fight only one at a time. He'd already chosen his target—the bigger of the two, the man who moved and held himself like a fighter.

Cole feinted toward the smaller man, then pivoted and leaped toward the bigger one. Cole's left hand slapped aside the knife. Simultaneously the edge of his right hand delivered a chopping blow to the man's throat. The attacker went down, choking, a threat no more.

Using the momentum of his turn, Cole lashed out with a high, powerful kick to the smaller man's head. There was a thick sound as he connected. The smaller attacker went facedown in the sand and stayed there.

One man remained standing. Two others had staggered back to their feet and were closing in again.

"Erin!" Cole said.

She tried to answer but couldn't. She still couldn't breathe, much less speak.

"Erin."

Only silence answered.

Cole looked at the three attackers who were still standing. "You're dead men."

With an inarticulate sound one of the three reached inside his windbreaker and drew out a long, oddly shaped gun.

Swiftly Cole bent, straightened, and turned in a blur of motion, sending sand hurtling into the man's eyes as the two unarmed men leaped forward. Cole rolled with the attack, taking the blows in order to get in close and finish off at least one of the attackers before the gunman got his vision back.

Erin struggled to her knees with wrenching sobs as breath slowly trickled into her lungs. She saw Cole go down beneath the two men and heard the man with the gun cursing in a heavy Cockney accent. He was on his knees, clawing at his eyes and swearing, temporarily blinded. She hadn't the strength to stand, so she did the only thing she could. She crawled closer, gathered a double handful of sand and flung it in the man's face.

His frantically moving fingers ground the new sand into his eyes. Screaming curses, he came to his feet, flailing around with the gun.

Even as Erin thought of making a grab for the gun she knew she was still too weak. She dug out more handfuls of sand and threw them into the man's face. Grunts and curses came from the darkness beyond, followed by the unmistakable sound of a breaking bone. In the sudden silence the metallic click of the gun being cocked was like thunder.

"Get down!"

At Cole's command Erin flattened out, rolled over and over, and then hugged the ground as the blinded man began firing wildly, shooting in the direction the sand had been coming from. She'd expected shattering noise from the gun. All that came were thick spitting sounds.

Cole had also thrown himself to one side, knowing that the next bullets would be aimed in the direction that his shout had come from. Instants later two bullets kicked sand where he'd been, proving that while the gunman was temporarily blind, he wasn't deaf or stupid.

Erin lay utterly motionless, trying not to breathe, knowing that any sound she made would send a bullet in her direction. Because it was so quiet, she thought that Cole was also hiding by not moving. Then she caught a suggestion of motion from the corner of her eye. She turned her head very carefully. It took all her self-control not to cry out at what she saw.

Slowly, relentlessly, timing his movements so that they were covered by the faint lapping of the waves, Cole was easing closer to the gunman.

Fear washed coldly through Erin. If Cole made one mistake he would be shot down before he could do anything to prevent it. It was the same for her in this lethal game of blindman's buff. Only if they were motionless would they be safe. Yet only if they moved could they ultimately survive.

The gunman wouldn't stay blind for more than a few moments.

She dug her fingers further into the coarse sand, gathering grains to fling into the gunman's eyes. She looked from the gunman to Cole, measuring the distance yet to be covered.

Cole's head moved once in an emphatic negative gesture. He'd seen her hands clenching in the sand. He didn't want her to move suddenly, calling down bullets on herself before she had any chance to get away.

Silently Cole slid closer to the gunman, who was between him and Erin. If Cole threw his knife or hit the attacker with a flying tackle, there was a very good chance that the man would topple, gun blazing, right onto Erin.

To prevent that Cole had to be within arm's reach of the man, so close that the sound of the waves no longer offered any cover for his movements, so close he couldn't even breathe without warning the gunman of his presence.

Erin's hands closed in the sand with such force that her fingers ached. Slowly she began gathering herself with a series of small movements.

Cole's heart hesitated, then slammed hard as more adrenaline pumped through him. If the gunman sensed Erin's movement he would turn and shoot before Cole could do anything. If she would just lie still, she'd be safe. But she wasn't lying still. She was trying to get close enough to fling more sand into the man's eyes.

The gunman had his back partially to her, and his head was turning. He was poised to spin in any direction, his breathing ruthlessly controlled, listening like a cat at a mouse hole. The silenced gun wove from side to side, covering as wide a field of fire as possible.

Erin saw the glitter of moonlight in the man's eyes as he turned toward the water. Cole was silhouetted against the pale gleam of the sea, a target too big to miss even with blurred vision.

She threw sand and rolled aside in the same violent motion.

The gunman spun toward her, firing before he could see a target. The bullet hit the sand, spraying grit. The gunman whirled back around toward the sea, warned of an attack more by instinct than by any noise Cole made. The gun spat again.

Cole grunted just before the base of his palm smashed against the man's nose with a driving upward blow. The gunman's head snapped backward, and blood poured blackly in the moonlight. The man crumpled without a sound to the sand.

"Erin! Are you all right?"

"Yes. Just shaken."

"Watch the pathway we came down."

Cole picked up the gun and checked the load with a few swift motions before he sheathed his knife. Methodically he began inspecting the other four men for signs of consciousness.

"Anyone coming?" he asked Erin as he bent over the first man and made a swift, hard motion with his right hand. The man didn't move in response.

"No. W-what are you doing?"

"Making sure they're not faking it."

Cole's method was ruthless and effective—stiffened fingers driven into the groin. No conscious man could take it without a reflexive whimper and a convulsive movement to protect himself.

Numbly Erin watched. She was trembling in the aftermath of adrenaline, but she felt almost unnaturally calm. She'd been through sudden violence before, survived it, and adjusted to the reality that she would never again expect the world to be a safe place.

This time the violence had been much easier to bear. She'd managed to defend herself. She'd fought and she hadn't even been injured. Her mind was safe, too. She no longer had any naïve belief in personal safety to be wrenched away by the attack. It was all old news. Later she might cry and shake, but not now. Now she was emotionally numb.

Surviving.

The fourth man groaned and curled up at Cole's blow. Erin flinched.

"Still clear?" Cole asked her.

"Yes. Shouldn't we get the police?"

"That would put us out of commission as effectively as these men tried to."

Cole yanked the fourth man into a sitting position. "If

you can hear me, open your eyes or you'll get another shot to the balls."

The man's eyes opened.

"Who was the target, me or the girl?" Cole asked.

The man didn't answer.

Cole's hand moved once, hard. The man made an odd sound and jerked convulsively.

"Who was the target?" Cole repeated.

"You," the man groaned.

Relief went through Cole. He couldn't expect to protect Erin for long from outright assassination attempts. Mayhem was different. Especially if it was aimed at him.

He turned and threw the pistol into the sea. "A hit?"

The man made a hoarse sound. "Just a kneecapping."

Erin's breath came in harshly as she realized that the point of the attack had been to permanently maim Cole.

"Who hired you?" Cole asked.

"Don't know."

Cole believed him. It was typical of thugs not to know any more than the name of the target and how to get to him. Cole pressed his thumbs into the man's neck until the carotid arteries closed down. Unconsciousness swiftly followed. Cole opened his hands, releasing the man.

"Anyone else coming?" Cole asked.

"No."

"We'll go up the other way just the same. There was somebody back on the first path, but he didn't get in the fight."

"Why?"

"He may be calling the cops. Let's go."

Cole got to his feet and bent to help Erin up. His normally smooth motions were marred by a slight hitch at every other step. She thought she saw the slick gleam of blood on the dark fabric above his left knee, on the inside of his thigh.

"Are you hurt?"

He grunted.

"Cole," Erin said urgently.

"He didn't kneecap me, thanks to you. I'll only limp for a day or two instead of the rest of my life."

"But—"

"Later. Shock is a good anesthetic, but it wears off fast. By then, I want us to be in a safe place."

"Is there one?"

He turned away without answering, which told her more than she wanted to know.

18

Darwin

"I still think you should let me take you to a doctor," Erin said unhappily.

Cole walked into the hotel room, saying nothing. His leg ached and was bleeding, but he knew the wound itself was little more than a burn. All he needed was some help cleaning and bandaging his thigh.

She shut and locked the door behind her. The hotel room was small and modestly furnished. Her old camera bag and new duffel were on the bed, as was Cole's new duffel.

"Let me help you to . . ." Her glance went to his thigh. "My God!"

"Don't go all soft and useless on me now," he said. "It's just blood."

Moisture shone darkly against his slacks. If the cloth had been any color but black, he couldn't have concealed the fact that he was wounded. As she watched in horror, a bright scarlet rivulet slid from beneath his cuff onto his shoe.

"Unless you're planning to leave tracks all over the

carpet, you'd better go into the bathroom," she said in a voice that was too high and thin.

He walked unevenly to the bathroom, lowered the toilet lid, and sat down to remove his shoes and socks. Silently she sank to her knees in front of him, pushed his hands away, and began pulling off his shoes. Blood dripped onto her fingers. She made a low sound of distress and tried to work faster.

"Relax, honey," he said. "It's not serious."

"Just a scratch, right?" she shot back, angry because he was hurt and there was nothing she could do to change that. "I've got news for you, big man. Scratches don't bleed this much."

"Blood isn't spurting with each heartbeat, so the bullet didn't get anything important. As for the mess—hell, it's not like you don't see blood regularly."

"I only hunted whales once."

"I was talking about your period."

Erin gave Cole a glittering look. He smiled. She let out a pent-up breath and shook her head.

"Has anyone ever told you that you're impossible?" she asked, bending over his feet once more.

"Nope. Want to be the first?"

She made a sound that could have been exasperation or amusement, but her hands were much steadier now. Cole was right. She saw blood every month, like clockwork.

By the time Erin had his shoes and socks off, Cole had unbuttoned his shirt and tossed it beyond reach of the blood that was sticking to everything. With quick motions he unzipped his slacks and began removing them. At the scrape of cloth over the wound, his breath hissed between his teeth.

"You're hurting yourself," she said. "I'll cut off the pant leg."

"No. I don't want to waste time shopping again. I'll have to wear these pants on the airplane."

She looked up. "Does that mean we're going back to California?"

"No. We're going to Derby. With luck, they'll waste their time looking for us between Darwin and Abe's station while we come in from the other side. Get a pillow-case, honey. I'll rip it up for bandages."

"I've got a first-aid kit in my camera bag."

By the time she got back to the bathroom, Cole was standing in his jockey shorts, one hip propped against the washbasin as he tried to examine the red slash across his muscular inner thigh. To Erin's adrenaline-heightened senses, the naked strength of his body was suddenly, violently attractive. She remembered the terrible feeling of rage and helplessness she'd known when she went down beneath the attackers. Then she'd heard Cole's voice promising vengeance for her hurt, and she'd known— really *known*—that this time she wasn't fighting alone. This time a man was going to use his strength to help her rather than to brutalize her.

Cole turned toward her. As he moved, light fell across him at a different angle, creating new shadows and highlights. For a crazy moment she wanted to grab her camera and catch the supple strength and masculine textures of his body. He was . . . beautiful.

The thought stunned her.

"Sit down," she said huskily. "Let me help you."

His eyes narrowed at the change in her voice, a softness where before there had been only the clipped irritation and anger of an adrenaline backlash. Now she was looking at him like she'd never seen him before, her extraordinary green eyes clear and wide, approving of him with an intensity that made his heart pound heavily.

Silently he sat down on the toilet seat.

She rinsed out a washcloth in cold water before she bent over him. The enforced intimacy of the contact made her feel weak. She tried to think of Cole as a man who needed help rather than as a powerful, nearly naked warrior whose thighs she was kneeling between. Then she saw his wound and forgot about what he was or wasn't wearing.

"It always looks worse than it is," Cole said, seeing the pallor of Erin's cheeks.

"But the blood—"

"I saw your pictures of the whale hunt. You had to be ankle deep in blood to get those shots."

She remembered shooting roll after roll of film and then being violently ill. Afterward she'd reloaded her camera and gone back to work.

"I threw up all over the place," she said as she pressed a cold cloth against the wound, stopping the slow oozing of blood.

"You do and you clean it up, honey. Blackburn's First Rule of Housekeeping."

Glancing up, she saw his amused gray eyes and wondered how she had ever thought they were bleak or cold.

"Right," she said. "No throwing up. Besides, you're smaller than a whale. Barely."

She caught the flash of his smile as she bent over him once more.

"Hurt?" she asked, increasing the pressure.

"What do you think?"

Her smile turned upside down. "It hurts."

The back of his index finger brushed lightly down her cheek. "I've felt a lot worse." His breath came in as she shifted the cloth. "I've felt better, too," he admitted wryly. "Burns are the worst for pain."

The pronounced tendency to tremble, which was the result of adrenaline and anxiety, faded from Erin's hands as she worked. While Cole held the compress in place, she started cleaning up the muscular length of his leg.

"Well, no one can say you aren't a red-blooded American male," she muttered as she rinsed out the washcloth for the fifth time. "Hairy, too."

He laughed.

She tried to smile, but it didn't work. Soon she would have to clean the wound itself. No matter how gentle she was, it would hurt him.

"Just what I thought," he said, lifting the compress to check. "Shallow and messy. No big deal."

"How can you tell?" she asked through clenched teeth. "You can't even see all of it."

"I know how it feels when something cuts muscle and grates on bone. This didn't. But if it bothers you that much, I'll get in the shower and clean it up myself."

She paused in the act of turning on the hot water in the sink and looked at Cole. The bathroom light poured over him, outlining every ridge of muscle, sinew, and bone. He literally filled the alcove where the toilet was.

"There's no way something could draw blood on you and not cut muscle," she said, wringing out a hand towel in the hot water with quick, angry motions, hating what she would have to do next.

"You slap that over my thigh and I'll turn you over my knee," he warned.

"Try it, big man, and you'll end up on the floor."

"Feeling feisty, are you?"

Her hands paused. He was right. The knowledge that she had come through violence intact was fizzing slowly through her, dissolving through years of fear, changing them, changing her. Part of her felt she could take on any man and throw him ten times out of ten. Common sense told her she was insane even to think about it. She let out a long sigh.

"First time on the winning side?" he asked.

She nodded.

He smiled crookedly. "Don't let it go to your head. If a hit had been ordered, we'd be facedown in the sand. You should have run like hell when I told you to."

Shaking her head in silent disagreement, she knelt between his powerful legs. Her hair gleamed in shades of mahogany and copper and gold as she moved. His breath came out in a rush as the warm towel draped tenderly over the wound. Her hands worked slowly, gently, carefully, cleaning the angry furrow.

"I mean it, honey. You should have run," he said quietly, stroking her gleaming hair with his hand. "It's the first rule of self-defense."

"You should have taken your own advice."

"It didn't apply to me. I wasn't defending myself."

Her breath came in. "I know. You were defending me."

Beneath his palm her head turned. He felt the warm touch of her kiss against his hand in the instant before she rose to rinse the towel under the faucet once more.

She wanted to thank Cole for defending her but didn't know what to say that wouldn't sound hopelessly naïve and foolish. He'd fought for her when she'd been helpless. She didn't have any words to tell him how much that meant to her. She was still discovering it herself. But she was certain about one thing.

She couldn't have left Cole Blackburn to die while she ran away unhurt.

She knelt once more and went back to cleaning the wound. Hot tears gathered at the back of her eyes when his breath hissed out and he began cursing in a low voice.

"I'm sorry," she whispered, hating the knowledge that she was hurting him. As gently as possible she blotted the wound, trying to see how deep it was and if any cloth from his slacks was imbedded in his flesh. "Can you turn more to the left?"

Cole's leg bent. He braced his foot against the washbasin and wondered if Erin had the slightest idea what it was doing to him to feel her hair slide against his uninjured thigh, to feel her hands on his bare leg as she steadied herself, to feel her breath against his naked, sensitive skin. At least her unintentional seduction was taking his mind off the bruised, burning pain radiating from the shallow wound. He'd been lucky as hell to get away with such a minor injury and he knew it.

"How's that?" he asked, shifting until light fell directly on his inner thigh.

"Good."

She put her hand on Cole's thigh to hold him in place. With an effort she forced herself to concentrate on his wound as though she was looking through a camera lens. She bent closer, peering at the scarlet furrow. No matter how she turned, a shadow still fell across the wound, concealing its depth.

Caged between his legs, she shifted awkwardly, almost leaning against his torso in order to see from a different angle. The motion sent first her shoulder and then her hair sliding across his groin.

A shaft of desire went through Cole, tensing his whole body.

"Does that hurt?" she asked anxiously.

"Not . . . quite."

His voice was thick and his eyes were focused on her hair, not on her hands. He wondered if silk or satin or fire came in that particular color. Her hair felt like all three when it slid down over his skin, the strands cool and silky, yet somehow warm at the same time.

"Lift a bit higher if you can," she said, pressing gently with both hands against his thigh. "That's good." She looked at the wound and let out a long sigh of relief. "You're right. It isn't serious. It must hurt, though."

Cole didn't bother to deny it. "Have any bandages in that kit?"

"In your size? I doubt it," she said dryly, starting to get to her feet.

"Stay put, honey," he said, holding her gently in place against his body. "I can reach it."

When he leaned forward, he all but surrounded Erin. She felt the supple power of his leg beneath her hands, felt the soft abrasion of his body hair against her wrists, and sensed the living, quintessentially masculine heat brushing against her arm. Sensations shivered from her breastbone to her knees, shortening her breath. Carefully she drew in air, telling herself that she must be mistaken. She couldn't have felt what she thought she'd felt.

Cole couldn't be aroused.

A tube of antibiotic ointment appeared at Erin's eye level. She took it, carefully blotted the wound again, and began smoothing ointment over raw flesh. Cole hissed a string of words in a foreign language. She didn't ask for a translation.

With each light brush of Erin's fingers against his body, Cole's pulse leaped. The burning of the wound didn't compare to the way she set fire to his blood. Because there was nothing he could do about either fire, he kept cursing in the kind of Portuguese used in the diamond fields of Brazil, blasphemies that could etch steel.

As he cursed, he told himself it was a simple case of the oldest aphrodisiac of all—adrenaline. He'd felt it before, the aftermath of ambush, the vivid, almost overwhelming rush when he knew that he'd survived, and then the sexual hunger that was his body's way of celebrating being alive. If Erin had been any other woman he would have pulled her onto his lap, burying himself in her until he came with a violence that equaled his arousal.

But Erin wasn't any other woman. She'd been raped and brutalized to the point that she might never invite a man into the hot, sleek depths of her body.

Grimly Cole tried not to think about the delicate hands that felt so tantalizing on his skin. Like Erin's breath, warm and sweet. Like the scent of her. Like her breasts brushing against his leg when she bent even closer, trying to reach the back of his thigh. The soft resilience of her flesh was a brand against his naked skin. He flinched and swore, wondering why this one woman among all women aroused him to the point of pain.

"Whatever happened to the strong, silent type?" she muttered unhappily, biting her lower lip.

"Do you believe in the Easter Bunny too?" He hissed another curse between his teeth.

By the time Erin was finished, her lip had tooth marks in it, but there was almost no fresh bleeding along the wound. Two square bandage pads appeared at her eye level.

"Don't believe the advertising on the wrapper," she said. "These stick just like the old kind."

As she shifted position to put the first bandage in place, she brushed intimately against Cole. He drew in his breath hard. She froze against him, thinking she had somehow hurt him again.

"You should put the bandages on yourself," she said unhappily. "I'm too clumsy. I don't want to hurt you any more."

Cole looked down at the woman curled between his legs, her eyes haunted and yet so beautiful it came as a shock of pleasure each time she looked at him.

"You're not a bit clumsy." He dropped the bandages into her lap. "And I like having your hands on me."

Her head snapped up.

"How about you, Erin?" he asked, watching her intently. "Do you like having your hands on me?"

"I don't like hurting you." Tears filled her eyes, magnifying their beauty. "I'm sorry, Cole. I really don't mean to hurt you."

His fingertips brushed the length of her right cheekbone. "Such a tender little thing to be so brave."

"I'm not brave. I was so scared I was shaking."

"What do you think courage is, honey? It's being scared and getting the job done anyway. The rest of it is just bells and whistles. Useless."

Calloused fingertips caught the tears that trembled on the edge of release. He brought his hand to his lips, tasting the clear, diamond-bright drops.

"Salty and very, very sweet. Nobody has ever cried for me, Erin. Not one person on earth."

She closed her eyes, unable to bear the intensity in his. When she opened them again, it was to concentrate on Cole's wound. She smoothed the bandages over his leg, trying not to hurt him. It wasn't easy. Her concentration kept splintering over his words and the fact that she was kneeling between the legs of a man who was nearly naked and fully aroused, yet wasn't touching her in any way.

But what really ruined her concentration was that she wasn't afraid. She should have been terrified by his strength and his arousal. She wasn't. She was restless, nervous, jumpy, and alert, but she wasn't afraid.

"That should do it," she said in a husky voice.

Hurriedly she stood and walked into the bedroom. She didn't hear Cole get up, didn't hear him follow her, but she sensed that he had. His hands settled on her shoulders and squeezed lightly.

"Thanks." His voice changed, becoming harder. "But honey, the next time I tell you to run, *you damn well better run*."

"I couldn't have run even if I'd wanted to," she said,

exasperated and angry. "That bastard hit me so hard I couldn't breathe for—"

"He hit you?" Big hands spun Erin around, stopping her words. "Where?"

"Here," she said, pointing just below her breastbone.

Without a word he began unbuttoning her blouse.

"Cole! What do you think you're doing!" she said, pushing at his hands.

"Hold still."

It was the same flat voice that Cole had used on the attackers. She obeyed instantly, but it was from surprise rather than fear. With a feeling of disbelief she watched her blouse separate beneath his deft fingers. She opened her mouth but no words came.

"Does this hurt?" he asked impersonally.

She felt the exquisitely gentle probing of his fingertips along her ribs. Odd shivers of response marched over her skin, leaving a wake of goose bumps.

"Does it hurt?" he asked again, looking into her shocked eyes.

Her mouth opened but she couldn't even take a breath. She shook her head in a negative.

"This?"

Warm, slightly rough fingertips moved along her ribs to her breastbone.

"A little," she whispered.

She saw him frown and felt the pressure of his fingertips increase.

"Now?"

"That hurts a little more, but still not much."

She watched Cole's face as he touched her. His eyelashes were very thick, very black, making his eyes appear like clear crystal touched with tiny shards of blue and green. The intense black of his hair was reflected in the heavy shadow of beard darkening his tan skin.

"Take a deep breath," he said.

She breathed in.

"Again. Deeper." Cole watched her face closely but saw no sign of real pain. Her ribs rose reassuringly beneath his hands, telling him she was able to fill her lungs in a normal way. "Does it hurt now?"

"Some, but not enough to interfere with breathing. Really. I've been hurt much worse tripping over camera equipment."

He smiled slightly and kept probing. "Ribs?"

She shook her head.

"Here?"

"Ouch!"

"That's what I thought. Your ribs are okay but you took a shot to the diaphragm." His fingertips traced the beginnings of a bruise. "You're going to be wearing a rainbow for a few days." He turned her around so that her back was to him. "You hurt anywhere else?" he continued, running his hands over her slowly. "Spine? Kidneys?"

"No."

"Sure?" he asked, kneading Erin's lower back gently, searching for any signs of soreness, any flinching away from his light, probing touches.

"I'm sure."

"Let me know if that changes."

Cole turned Erin around and calmly began buttoning her blouse once more, trying very hard not to notice the taut swell of her breasts beneath her bra and the soft heat of her skin. When his hands were between her breasts, she took a swift, involuntary breath. Unavoidably his hands brushed against her.

She felt the accidental touch and held her breath, waiting for him to take advantage of the moment. She knew he wanted her. He couldn't hide his arousal while standing in front of her wearing jockey shorts that were becoming less concealing with every one of his heartbeats.

Without a pause, he kept buttoning her shirt.

She closed her eyes and told herself that she was relieved, not disappointed. Cole's past might have been as shadowed as a midnight jungle, but his deepest instincts were honorable. He would protect rather than brutalize. Yet there was no doubt that he could, and would, fight with disciplined savagery if he had to.

That's the key, she realized. *Discipline.*

More than any man she'd ever known—even her father—Cole was in control of his mind, of his body, of his instincts, of himself. The certainty of his self-control raced through her, more heady than wine, leaving a curious heat in its wake.

"Be sure to tell me if you start hurting," he said again, turning away. "I'm going to wash out my slacks."

"Cole?"

Her voice dried up as she watched him turn toward her once more. He was so much bigger than she was, so much stronger, nearly naked, and his eyes were burning as he watched her.

"You better lie down, honey. You look a little strung out."

For the space of one breath, two, Erin didn't answer.

Then she went to the bed and lay down. As she closed her eyes, the sound of running water came from the bathroom.

19

Darwin

Using the bathtub faucet Cole repeatedly rinsed blood from his slacks. When the water running through the pants came out clear rather than red or pink, he wrung out the slacks, rolled them up in a towel and squeezed, blotting up water. A snap of his wrist shook the cloth out. He tossed the slacks over the shower rack to dry, picked up his shirt, and put it on.

He took a lot of time, long enough for his fierce arousal to subside.

When he came out of the bathroom, Erin was lying wide-eyed on the bed, staring at the ceiling.

"Does your diaphragm hurt?" he asked. "Is it keeping you awake?"

She wondered how to tell him that she wasn't closing her eyes because every time she did she saw an image of him, his chest naked except for a black wedge of hair that tapered to a line and vanished behind the white of his underwear.

"Erin?"

"Every time I close my eyes I see . . ." Her voice died.

"The fight?" he asked.

She shook her head. "You."

The corner of his mouth turned down. "And that scares you."

"Not . . . quite."

Cole didn't miss her exact imitation of his earlier words. He crossed the room and stood by the bed, watching her. "Are you trying to tell me something?" he asked.

Her head turned toward him, revealing brilliant green eyes and a smile that hovered on the edge of turning upside down. "I liked you better without the shirt."

"Did you? I got the feeling it made you uneasy as hell."

"There's rather a lot of you," she said, watching him through thick, lowered lashes.

"You noticed," he said dryly.

When Erin realized where she was looking, she blushed to the roots of her hair. "You're making this hard for me."

"No. That's what you're doing to me. Again."

"I noticed," she muttered.

He laughed, surprised as always by her combination of wariness and humor. The laugh ended as his breath came in with a soft, ripping sound. Erin's hand was on his leg, her fingertips light against his skin as she traced the edge of the bandage.

"That's dangerous territory, honey."

"It's all I can reach from here."

"If I get any closer, I'll be in bed with you. Is that what you want?"

"I . . ." Her voice died. She swallowed and tried again. "I don't know. All I know is I like touching you. I like looking at you. I like it when you hold me. I like it when you kiss me. I like the taste of your skin. I like the feel of your hands on me." She looked at him in unconscious appeal. "I want you more than I ever thought I'd want any man. Is that enough?"

"It's a hell of a start," he said in a low voice. "Move over, honey. Let's find out what else you like."

Wondering if she'd made the right choice, she moved over. She felt the mattress give deeply as his weight settled on it. Torn between fear and desire, she closed her eyes and waited for him to pull her into his arms.

When he didn't, she opened her eyes. He was unbuttoning his shirt and watching her with an intensity that made her breath shorten.

"Cole?"

"Whatever you want," he said simply, throwing the shirt aside. "But you have to tell me, Erin. I won't take a chance on guessing wrong and frightening you."

She gave an odd laugh. "Some of the things I want with you already frighten me."

He smiled slowly. "Sounds interesting. Should we begin with them or save them for last?"

"I think . . . a kiss."

As she spoke, she looked at his mouth with an unconscious hunger that made Cole as hot as a physical caress. Desire wedged in his throat, in his gut, ripping at him. With a silent curse, he hoped that his self-control was as good as he'd always thought it was.

Deliberately he lay on his back, laced his fingers together, and put his hands behind his head. "Then why don't you come here and kiss me?" he said.

Surprised, she hesitated. Even after Cole's statement about not frightening her, somehow she'd expected him to quickly take the lead. That he hadn't both reassured and tantalized her, for as he lay on his back there was no doubt of his own arousal.

Slowly she turned onto her side and bent down to

Cole's mouth. The kiss was gentle, almost chaste, until she ran the tip of her tongue along his lips. The taste of him was even better than she remembered, hotter. The feel of his tongue caressing her own made streamers of sensation uncurl in the pit of her stomach.

She didn't know how long she kissed him before both of them were breathing quickly and she was making small sounds at the back of her throat with each deep, slow stroke of his tongue. At every breath, every heart-beat, she joined her mouth more deeply with his, lured by the hot pleasures of his kiss. Slowly her hands began to explore his arms, from his strong wrists to the hard swell of biceps and shoulders to the surprising, exquisite soft-ness of the hair beneath his arms.

For long moments she savored that unexpected silki-ness. Then her fingers moved on, exploring. She threaded through the intriguing fur on his chest, stroking and kneading the flesh beneath, silently telling him just how much she enjoyed his masculine textures and strength, and drawing a nearly soundless groan of plea-sure from him when her fingers skimmed the flat disks of his nipples.

"Did you like that?" she asked, touching his nipples again, feeling them change as they drew into tight beads.

"I'm not sure," he said in a low voice. "Why don't you try it five or ten more times?"

For an instant Erin didn't understand. Then she did, and laughed. "You're teasing me."

"I would have sworn it was the other way around," he said. "But I'll forgive you if—"

Cole's voice broke as her hands skimmed down to the elastic band of his underwear. And stopped. When she re-versed direction and went stroking back up his chest, he had to bite back words of disappointment. Slowly she bent and tasted first his neck, then the middle line of his body to his breastbone. With great care she closed her teeth over a sleek swell of muscle. His breath broke again and she smiled.

"I like that," she said. "I like knowing I can affect you."

"Then run your hands a little farther down and watch the fireworks," he offered, smiling despite the need that made his whole body clench.

Her laughter was like soft flames licking against his stomach. For a few moments there was only the sound of skin sliding over skin and his quickening breaths as she stroked his chest.

"Cole," she whispered against his neck, "would you touch me too?"

He unlocked fingers that ached from the pressure he'd used to keep from reaching for the soft temptation of her body.

"Where?" he asked huskily.

She made a puzzled sound against his skin.

"Where do you want to be touched?" Cole felt the heat of Erin's blush where her cheek lay against his chest. He smiled. "Good. That's one of the places I'm dying to touch."

But he teased her first, caressing the hollows beneath her slanting cheekbones, fitting the warmth of her neck into the hard curve of his palm, massaging her arms from shoulders to fingertips until her eyes closed and his name came from her lips in a sigh of pleasure. He kept stroking her until she began to twist in slow motion against his hand, wanting him to touch the breasts whose nipples were growing hard with her own arousal.

"Cole, please," she said, her voice husky.

"Please, what?"

Instead of answering, she took his hand and drew it

over one breast. The first instant of contact made her shiver. Instinctively she moved against him, trying to ease the sensual ache as her nipple hardened in a rush.

Cole felt the change in her, saw it, and the force of his own response made his hand shake. Slender fingers closed over his, but not to push him away. Slowly she pressed him closer and yet closer, moving against his hard palm.

"Do you like that?" he asked, trying to make his voice gentle, and failing. His tone was like his body, too hard, too hot, too obviously aroused.

"Yes, but . . ."

He set his jaw and lifted his hand, freeing her. Immediately her arms moved as though to shield her breasts if he changed his mind.

"It's all right," he said.

Then he realized that Erin wasn't withdrawing. She was trying to unbutton her blouse, but her hands were trembling too much. A wave of desire clenched his body, shaking him with its intensity. He took her hands, brushed his lips over them, and smoothed her fingers against his chest.

"Let me," he said.

"I'm sorry," she whispered, "I don't know what's wrong. I'm shaking, but I'm not scared. Really I'm not."

"Look at my hands."

She looked, saw the fine tremor in his fingers, and made a sound of surprise.

"Yeah, it shocked me too," he said. "I've never wanted a woman until my hands shook."

Her eyes widened. She glanced back to his face and saw that he was watching her, half expecting her to panic.

"Should that make me nervous?" she asked.

"Why not?" he muttered. "It scares the hell out of me."

Deliberately Erin glanced down the length of his torso.

"Um, I don't know how to put this, but that doesn't look like fright."

Cole laughed and the claws of hunger loosened in his groin. His fingers eased between the warm folds of her blouse, pushing aside the dark cloth until he could see the smooth rise of her breasts beneath a rose-colored bra.

"Should I stop now?" he asked, sliding a fingertip beneath the edge of the bra, skimming the rising and falling of her breasts. "Or do you want me to touch you the way you touched me?"

Before courage deserted her, Erin reached up and undid the front fastening of her bra.

For the space of two breaths Cole simply looked at her and counted the pulse hammering in his body. Her breasts were more beautiful than he had expected, full and high, and her nipples were flushed deep rose with desire. Her skin was flushed as well, bringing into stark relief the fine white lines of old scars.

Understanding hit, bringing him under control in a freezing rush. *"He used a knife on you."*

It took her a moment to figure out what Cole meant.

"I forgot about the scars," she said. "They're much less ugly than they used to be, but I understand if you don't want to—"

Erin's voice broke as the tip of Cole's tongue traced first one scar, then another, then another, touching her so gently that tears gathered and overflowed. His words were another kind of caress, a glittering fire licking over her mind and body, telling her that she was beautiful, softness and heat, sweetness and hunger, a sensual fire burning all the way to his soul.

The restraint and unexpected tenderness of his caresses unraveled her. She forgot the past, forgot the future, forgot everything but the exquisite sensations radiating through her body with each touch of Cole's hands, his body, his mouth, until she was breathless and whimpering softly, twisting against him in slow motion.

Cole felt her response in the heat of her skin, tasted it in the fine mist he licked from between her breasts, heard it in the soft, broken cries that were his name. Her sensuality was as unexpected as it was uninhibited. Blood hammered through him so fiercely he could barely breathe. He bent to her breasts once more, tugging on a hard peak with his mouth while his hand slid down her body, undoing her clothes, pushing them to her knees, then returning to find the softness and heat that had been hidden beneath cloth.

When his hand curled possessively around her tangled thatch of hair, Erin went rigid.

Instantly Cole retreated. Then her sultry response spilled over his fingers. A wild answering heat swept through him, making him groan with the knowledge that it was pleasure, not fear, that had tightened her body. He moved his hand again, rubbing his palm over her sensitive flesh, and was answered with another passionate shudder. Unable to stop himself, he slid one finger between soft folds of skin and caressed even softer, hotter flesh.

"Cole." Her husky voice was barely recognizable.

"I'm right here," he said, teasing the hard peaks of her breasts with his tongue while his finger slowly withdrew from her body, only to return even more deeply. "Do you want me to stop?"

She laughed a little wildly. Then her breath broke in a cry of surprise as pleasure burst, sending heat shimmering through her. Instinctively she moved, seeking more of his touch, needing it with a force she neither understood nor questioned.

"Is that yes or no?" he asked, biting her nipple with exquisite care.

Another shudder of pleasure ripped through her, taking her voice. "Yes," she managed finally. "I mean no."

Erin's eyes opened. Their smoldering color was more beautiful than anything Cole had ever seen, even the green diamond she'd given him.

"Don't stop," she said.

"Does that mean I can finish undressing you?" he asked, his voice as caressing as his hand.

She looked down the length of her own body to the dark masculine hand nestled between her legs. She made an odd sound, not quite laughter and not quite embarrassment.

"All I'm really wearing is you," she said. "I should be embarrassed, but I . . . like it."

Cole set his jaw against the force of his own response. Erin's honesty and sensuality kept taking him by surprise, stripping away his control with every hot word, every hungry movement, her eyes a green fire burning through him. He tried to be gentle as he took off the rest of their clothes, but he knew he was moving too quickly, almost clumsy with the violence of his own need. He saw her head turn slightly and knew the exact instant she saw that he was as naked as she was, lying on his back, unable to hide the extent of his arousal.

Closing his eyes, Cole prayed he wouldn't have to find out if he could keep the promise he had made to her: *We could be dead naked and you could be all over me like a hot rain, but if you changed your mind I'd get up and get dressed and that would be the end of it.*

"Cole?"

His eyes opened. "Frightened?"

Slowly she shook her head.

"Sure?"

She nodded.

"Then what is it, honey?"

Unable to bear his intent look, Erin bent and brushed

her mouth over his shoulder while she asked her question. "Is it all right if I touch you?"

"Any time, anywhere, any way you want."

Her hand slid hesitantly down his body. "Even here?"

His breath broke. "Especially there."

Her fingertips were cool, uncertain, and incendiary as they traced the hot, unfamiliar textures of his desire.

"I can feel your heartbeat," she whispered, curling her hand around him.

He shuddered and groaned.

"I'm sorry," she said instantly, withdrawing.

"Do it again and I'll forgive you." His breath came in with a ripping sound as her hand returned to his hard, aching flesh. "Yes, like that. Just . . . like . . . that."

In an agony of pleasure, he pressed rhythmically against her hand, once, twice, three times before he managed to bring himself under control again.

"There's another way to tease each other," he said finally, his voice low and almost rough. "A way we'll both enjoy." He saw her expression and smiled. "I said tease, not ease. I won't take you, honey. You'll have to give yourself to me every inch of the way. Do you believe me?"

When she nodded, he lifted her and settled her astride his hips. Her breath broke as she felt him lying between her legs, pressing against her without entering her, sending streamers of sensation coursing through her with each small movement of their bodies. When he rocked her hips gently, sliding her over his hard flesh, a low ripple of sound came from her lips. He rocked her again and fought not to lose control.

He released her hips but the rocking didn't stop, for she couldn't stop, her breathing rapid and broken, her body shaking, urgent, driven.

"Cole," she whispered, reaching for him, trying to

complete the union she'd never expected to want, much less *need*, until she was wild with it. "Help me!"

His hand moved, covering hers, guiding her. "Like this," he said, pulling her mouth down to his. "Like this."

Their mouths and bodies joined at the same time. A low sound of pleasure came from Erin as she settled over him, feeling him fill her slowly, never taking before she could give, until finally she could get no closer and he could get no deeper. She tried to speak, to tell Cole how incredible the sensation was, but when she lifted her mouth from his, the motion tightened her around him even more.

Words burned into silence as she moved again, deliberately measuring herself and him at the same time, pleasuring both of them, feeling the world slide away with each motion, each breath, until Cole made an anguished sound and went rigid beneath her. She felt the intimate pulses of his release deep inside her and shivered in return, balanced on the brink of something elemental, unknowable.

Then his hand moved, searching through her sensual heat, finding the focus of her need. He stroked the satin nub, caressing her until her eyes went wide with surprise. Intense pleasure burst through her, drawing a ripple of sounds from her lips as her body convulsed delicately around him. He drank the sounds with a kiss and held her until they could both breathe evenly again.

And even then he held her, for he had tasted the salt of tears as well as passion on her lips.

"Honey?" Cole asked, kissing Erin with a gentleness that was at odds with his harsh voice. "Did I hurt you?"

She shook her head.

"You're crying."

"Am I?" Her hand moved to her cheek. She took a shivering breath. "I am." With a sigh she smoothed her cheek against his chest before burying her face against his neck. "I'm happy, Cole. I never expected to be. Not this way. I never expected to fall in love after Hans. Then I met you."

Cole's hand hesitated as it stroked down the elegant line of her spine. "Don't mistake what we have as lovers for love. You can get hurt that way. I don't want to hurt you, Erin."

For an instant her eyes closed. She hadn't expected Cole to return her love, but she'd hoped.

"I believe you," she said, letting out a long, shaking breath. "Unfortunately, I'm not a halfway kind of person. But don't worry. I'm not expecting any deathless promises from you. That doesn't mean I won't try to trip you and beat you to the floor from time to time."

He laughed in surprise and brushed a kiss over her hair. "I'll look forward to it."

Erin touched his hot skin with the tip of her tongue, tasting him almost secretly. Then she gave a long, shuddering sigh and relaxed against him. With her next breath she was asleep.

The trust in the utter relaxation of her body sank into Cole, sliding past defenses he didn't even know he had, shaking him as deeply as passion had. For a long time he lay quietly, smoothing his hand over Erin's hair and back, thinking of the past and the unknown future.

But most of all he thought about how he would keep Erin alive when ConMin got serious about canceling her ticket to ride on the diamond tiger.

20

Amsterdam

Hugo van Luik sat in the half-light of his study, holding the phone in one hand and trying to think. But it was hard to think while Jason Street poured Australian slang into one ear, the night poured silence into the other, and painkillers blurred everything.

Frowning, van Luik stared through the open door to the bedroom across the hall. Limned by light from the street, his wife stirred and rolled over in bed. Her hair was a pale silver glow in the darkness. If she was awake, she hadn't called out to him. Thirty-eight years of marriage had taught her to leave her husband's business to him. If the problem that loomed in the middle of the night took five minutes or five days, she rarely commented. Or perhaps she simply didn't notice.

Van Luik sighed soundlessly. Once he'd relished alarms and intrusions at odd hours. They were proof of his importance to the plans of corporations and nations. Now he regarded the job at hand—that of bringing the elusive Cole Blackburn to bay—as one more hoop to jump through. Van Luik was tired of hoops and trials of strength. He simply wanted it done.

Finished.

"Are they still in Darwin?" Street asked across the thousands of miles.

"They checked out of the hotel before the men found them. No one checked into any other Darwin hotels under the names of Blackburn or Windsor. No one rented a vehicle under those names. And we believe Blackburn might be wounded."

"Gunshot?"

"Yes," van Luik said.

"Then he'll avoid doctors."

"We are assuming the two are still in Darwin."

"Maybe," Street said. "And maybe they're using false papers. Her father would be able to get them anything along that line they wanted."

"Agreed. I have asked McLaren to enlist his contacts in ASIO. They will use photos to assist the search."

"McLaren, eh? Was he the wanker who hired the girls Blackburn chewed up?" Street asked sardonically.

"Mr. Blackburn is a formidable brawler, from all accounts."

"What do you expect them to say, that he fought like an old woman?"

Van Luik bit back a curse as pain stabbed. "Next time, you will take care of the matter yourself."

"With pleasure, mate. But first we have to find the bastard."

"What is the best way for him to reach the Windsor station?"

"There're only two ways. You rent a plane and fly in or you rent a Jeep and drive. I'll bet on the Jeep. He'll need it at the station anyway."

"What about a bus?"

"To the station? Not a chance. It's way off the only highway."

"Could he walk there?" van Luik asked.

"Not this time of year, mate. He'd be dead of heat-stroke before a day, and the tart would pack it in after a few hours. Tell McLaren to shut down Darwin's rentals. I'll take care of Derby."

"Derby?"

"It's the only other place in northwestern Australia you can rent a Jeep. This isn't bloody London."

Silence, followed by a single word. "Street?"

"What."

"Find them. Make certain they discover nothing before the monsoon makes it impossible to prospect. Failing that, destroy the mine."

"What if it's the size of bloody Argyle?"

"We think not. We have reason to believe it is a pothole placer deposit of the sort that could be destroyed quite easily."

"What makes you think so?"

Van Luik grimaced and counted his heartbeats in the violent pain behind his eyes. "You have your faults, Mr. Street, but geological incompetence isn't one of them. Do you really believe Abelard Windsor could have hidden something the size of Namibia's beach deposits from you for the past ten years?"

"Not a chance, mate. Not a bloody one."

Grimly van Luik pursued the main point. "The wet may be enough of a delay for our purposes. Many things can change in the span of five months. Important things. Things that are crucial to maintaining the balance of power within the cartel. Keep Blackburn off the station."

"That could be real tricky, mate. Accidents happen. I might end up killing the girl trying to stop him."

"What is the English saying, beggars cannot be

choosers?" Van Luik pinched his nose. "Whatever happens, make certain it looks like an accident. If you end up killing her, it would be far better if the body disappeared. I will be waiting for your call."

Street started to speak, heard the click as the connection was broken, then hung up hard. After a moment he dialed another number, waited, and spoke again.

"G'day, luv. You got any Yanks asking after your Rover?"

"No Yanks, just a Canadian pair wanting to see Windjana."

Street hesitated. "Canadian?"

"Right."

"Man and a woman?"

"That's right. Name's Markham."

"When did they make their reservation? Last month?"

"Called from Perth a few hours ago. They're catching the Ansett flight. Why?"

Street thought quickly. He could assume it was simple coincidence that a pair of Canadians got a sudden urge to see Western Australia's bleak outback wilderness. He could assume it was simple coincidence that Windjana Gorge was in the direction of Abe's station. He could assume Blackburn and Erin were still hiding out in Darwin, nursing a wound.

Street could assume all those things, but he'd be a fool not to at least get a look at the couple.

"Luv," he said, "I'd really like them delayed. Say until tomorrow morning."

"What's in it for me?"

"Eight inches of the best you'll ever get."

"Cocky bastard, aren't you?"

"You should know."

"When you going to pay up?" she asked, laughing.

"I'll be there before dark."

"I'll be waiting."

Street hung up smiling and feeling an anticipatory ache in his crotch. Nora was the prettiest single girl in Derby, which meant that she was only as plain as a termite mound rather than as ugly as a burned stump. But she had her oddities in bed, which put most men off. Not Street. He found her inventiveness stimulating.

Whistling softly, he began packing a small rucksack, hoping Cole Blackburn—if it was him—chose the overland route instead of flying in. There were very few roads between Derby and Crazy Abe's station.

Jason Street knew every foot of them.

21

Derby

Derby had the feel of a town on the downhill slide from exhaustion to extinction. The buildings perched unevenly on stilts, as though the wide plain at the edge of the ocean flooded regularly. Although Derby's street was wide enough for multiple lanes of traffic in both directions, only one lane in each direction was paved. The parkway between the lanes was planted with grass and baoboab trees, with their huge trunks and spindly branches that resembled roots. The patchy asphalt was soft from the heat. No cars, trucks, or buses were moving. The climate sapped people of everything but the ability to sweat.

Darwin had been hot, air-conditioned, and modern. Derby was hot and primitive.

Cole and Erin had been waiting eighteen hours for a vehicle that had been promised seventeen hours ago. When the Rover finally appeared, it was as unimpressive as the town itself. The vehicle looked like what it was—a well-used, shambling, rattling sort of reliable wreck, filled with junkyard odds and ends, toolboxes and tarps, spare tires and jacks, metal mesh, and God knew what else, all of it stored in cabinets held shut by nails stuck through hasps. A railed cargo platform ran the length of the top. The fenders were loose, but the steel mesh that separated cargo from passengers was securely fastened and strong enough to hold back a bull.

Even though Cole had waited a long time for the Rover, he still insisted on giving it a thorough vetting before they left town. Between Derby and Fitzroy Crossing several hundred kilometers down the Great Northern Highway, there were no towns, no settlements, no service stations, no crossroads, no tow trucks—nothing but the spinifex, gum, and wattle wastes of Western Australia.

Erin stood in the miserable shade cast by the overhang of a tin roof and watched Cole check out the Rover's engine. If his wound bothered him, he didn't show it. Nor had he shown it that morning, when he had awakened her with kisses and touches that had melted her until their bodies were joined in an intense pleasure that made pain impossible.

Smiling at the memory, she ignored the sweat that gathered beneath her sleeveless, scooped-neck T-shirt and trickled down toward the shorts that had already begun to turn an unappetizing shade of brown. Despite Derby's incredible humidity, the air was thick with a rust-colored dust. Flies descended in the pause between gusts of sultry wind. Automatically she waved the persistent insects away from her face.

Cole did the same as he bent over the Rover's grimy engine. The gesture was known as the "outback salute."

The heat kept taking Erin by surprise. Now she knew why Cole had insisted on having shorts, tank tops, bikini

underwear, and thong shoes for the car. The only conces-
sions to Western dress were socks and sturdy walking
shoes.

The floppy cabbage-leaf cloth hat Erin wore, her
nearly black sunglasses, and the crisp nylon travel bag at
her feet were all new. Even the Canadian passport in the
bag was new, at least to her, although it had a well-used
look about it. Cole had produced it, along with one for
himself, after they'd arrived in Perth. Mr. and Mrs.
Daniel Markham of Nanaimo, British Columbia.

There had even been a well-worn gold wedding ring
for Erin to wear. It was inscribed with her mother's name.
The realization that she was wearing her mother's wedding ring unsettled Erin. Family photos had arrived with
the passports, photos of Erin's grandmother, Bridget Mc-
Queen Windsor. When Erin first had seen the photos,
passports, and ring, she'd wondered if Nan Faulkner
knew what Matthew Windsor had done, or if her father
was putting his lifelong career at risk in order to make up
for the misjudgment of seven years ago.

There had been no answer to that question, simply a
note from her father that had said:

*This is all I could find of my father's life in Aus-
tralia. Be careful, Erin. I love you.*

Dad

The gold ring smoldered in the tropical light, reminding Erin of the photos tucked within her nylon bag, photos that she hadn't really looked at. She leaned over into
the sun, rummaged in the duffel, retrieved the envelope,
and stood upright in the shade again.

She went quickly through the photos, then more slowly.

They dated from the time when both Windsor brothers were young and exploring Australia's wild outback together. The black-and-white images showed a land that was sparse, spare, bleak. Yet the men were always smiling, especially when Miss Bridget McQueen was in the photo.

One picture in particular held Erin's interest, a photo of the young Bridget wearing an old-style dress and standing on a rocky rise with thin, peculiar trees and strangely shaped rocks all around. Bridget was radiant, mischievous, and impudent as she looked up from beneath long lashes at the invisible man who was taking her picture. Off to one side was a man with dense, straight eyebrows, unkempt hair, and a look of raw longing on his face as he watched the young woman whose unbound hair lifted on the breeze.

On the back of the photo was written *Some love for silver, some love for gold, / We love for the heat that never runs cold.* The writing was even, elegant, and old-fashioned. Perhaps bad poetry and careful script had run in the Windsor family.

"That's it," Cole said, slamming down the Rover's hood. "Let's hit the road."

Erin stuffed the pictures back into their envelope and put it in her camera case. As she bent over, her head poked beyond shade into sunlight.

The heat was suffocating. She had to force herself to drag the thick air into her lungs. It felt like she was sucking oxygen through layers of used sauna towels.

And this was spring, not summer.

Erin tried to imagine what Derby would feel like under the full weight of a summer sun. She couldn't. The heat would be unbearable, unspeakable.

The interior of the Rover seat was as hot as it was

dusty. The engine fired quickly on the first try. Erin sat and sweated.

"You were right," she said.

"About what?"

"Sweating. It doesn't help."

Cole smiled a bit grimly. "I'd rather have been wrong. I hate this bloody place during buildup."

As the Rover began moving, the steady flow of air from the open windows helped to cool Erin. After fifteen minutes the heat and humidity no longer seemed remarkable or shocking to her, simply exhausting. Derby disappeared in the side mirror, a sorry group of low buildings strewn across the flat landscape like God's afterthought.

The alien quality of the land was more subtle in its impact than the heat, but ultimately more powerful. To Erin, accustomed to Alaska and California, the area around Derby was like being on another planet. The land was utterly flat as far as the eye could see. No mountains rose in the heat-hazed distance, no hills, not even hummocks. The trees were few and stunted. If grass grew at all, it grew in sparse clumps. The iron-red soil showed through the spare veneer of plants.

Slowly she became captive to the alien land, absorbing its shapes and textures, its heat and humidity and flatness, the strangeness that was both subtle and overwhelming.

Cole's restless glance flicked to the rearview mirror. The heat haze made it impossible to be certain, but he thought there was a vehicle behind them. As no side roads had come in, the other car must have come from Derby. He frowned, looked in the side-view mirror, and picked up the speed so subtly that the average driver wouldn't notice and would gradually be left behind.

Scattered termite mounds began to appear, sometimes thickly, sometimes not. There was no obvious reason for difference between many and few. Most of the mounds were knee-high spikes that looked like the air roots of mangrove trees. The bigger mounds were six feet or more tall and wide at the base. The great dry blobs of reddish earth looked for all the world as though miniature castles had been built of rust-colored wax, only to have the punishing weight of tropical sunlight warp the wax until nothing remained but the slumped ruins of the original design.

The air simmered with heat and moisture. To the right and to the left of the Rover, the sky was a heat-misted blue. Directly behind was a distinct river of clouds of every color, from white to blue-black. As it moved, the river widened until it resembled a huge, barely opened fan laid across the empty sky. And still the clouds came on, churned out by an invisible source.

"There aren't any mountains or storms, so where are the clouds coming from?" Erin asked finally.

"The Indian Ocean."

Absently she plucked at the tank top that had become a damp, faithful shadow over her body from neck to waist.

Cole caught the motion from the corner of his eye and turned for a better look. She'd taken his advice and kept her clothes to a minimum. That minimum didn't include a bra. The damp cotton top clung to the full curves of her breasts and peaked unmistakably over her nipples. The temptation to slide his fingers between cloth and skin was so sharp that he looked away.

More sensed than seen beneath the brilliant sunlight, lightning danced behind the Rover. No rumble of thunder followed.

"I thought this was the dry season," she said after a time, looking over her shoulder.

"It is."

"Then why is it raining?"

"It isn't."

She blew a wisp of hair out of her eyes with unnecessary force. "Not here." She waved a hand over her shoulder. "Back there."

"Just a tease. When the wet comes to stay, clouds and lightning go from horizon to horizon and the rain comes down like high-mountain thunder."

"A tease." She sighed and pulled at her damp, clinging tank top.

"Don't do that. It's too hot to think about what I'm thinking about."

She gave him a sideways look and a remembering kind of smile.

"Quit distracting me and get familiar with the country," he said, handing a map to her.

But he was smiling too.

She opened the map against the sixty-mile-an-hour wind coming through the open windows. Holding the paper across her knees, she matched the map with the landscape of sparse trees and thin grasslands that flashed by on either side.

Finding where they were on the map was easy. The Great Northern Highway was the superhighway of Western Australia, linking Darwin and Perth through almost five thousand kilometers of uninhabited land. The road was only one lane wide. It was better than the only other road that penetrated the interior of the vast western state.

Out beyond Derby the road divided. The Gibb River Road went north. The Great Northern Highway went east. Once that basic choice was made by a motorist, there was nowhere to go but forward or back. There weren't any other through roads. The Gibb was also one lane wide, but that lane was dirt. It ran north, up onto the

Kimberley Plateau, where it dead-ended. There was nothing but scattered stations and mineral claims from one end of the Gibb River Road to the other.

When the time came to make the choice, Cole turned onto the Gibb River Road. Dust began to boil up from the tires.

"I thought Abe's station was closer to the Great Northern Highway," Erin said.

"It is. But we're tourists going to Windjana, remember?" What he didn't add was that it was a lot easier to spot a tail on a dusty road than on a paved surface.

She went back to studying the map. Every thirty to fifty kilometers, the map showed spur roads taking off from or merging with the two highways.

"What are these dirt roads named?" she asked. "I haven't seen any signs, and there aren't any numbers on the map."

"They don't have names or numbers. Most of them dead-end out at some station or mine."

A boil of dust ahead caught her eye. Gradually a car appeared in the emptiness ahead of them. It was the first vehicle they had seen since Derby. She held her breath as the two cars rushed headlong at each other on the single-lane road.

Two vehicles hurtled forward, each driver holding the single lane until the last possible moment. Neither one slowed in the least. A glance at the speedometer told Erin that the closing speed of the two vehicles was at least 120 miles per hour. At some unseen but mutually understood signal, each driver turned his left-hand wheels out on the shoulder, making room for the cars to pass with inches to spare.

As the vehicles raced by, each driver lifted his right index finger from the steering wheel in recognition.

At first Erin thought it was all sheer luck that no one was killed. By the third time an oncoming car roared past in a boil of dust, she realized that she was participating in a bizarre Aussie ritual.

"This has to be the world's longest-running game of Chicken," she said distinctly.

He smiled, touched her cheek with his fingertip. His smile faded as he glanced in the mirrors, then concentrated on the road in front again.

"Why is the roll bar on the front bumper?" she asked after a time of silence.

"It's called a bull bar out here and a 'roo bar in the rest of the outback. Most outback vehicles have one."

"Why?"

"Cheaper than fenders," he said. "A bull bar also keeps whatever you hit from getting under the wheels and flipping you over."

"What can you hit besides termite mounds?"

He tilted his head toward a handful of rust-colored, bony cows grazing in the limited shade of the stunted trees. "Kimberley shorthorns."

"They're hardly bigger than mule deer," she said.

"They're big enough to kill you, and they're not the only thing running around. This country isn't fenced. Everything roams—kangaroos, feral donkeys and horses, bush bulls. Any one of them could be big enough to get in underneath the front wheels of a Rover."

"Does that happen often?"

"If you drive these roads at night, sooner or later you'll hit something big enough to matter." His eyes narrowed as he looked in the side-view mirror. "That's why a short-barreled shotgun is part of my outback equipment. You can't be certain of killing an animal outright in a collision. Especially a bush bull."

She looked at the cattle again. They were slat-thin,

pony-size, and ragged. "Is one of those a bull?"

"Probably, but that's not what a bush bull is. A bush bull is a feral water buffalo."

She looked dubiously at the sandy, dusty country. "*Water* buffalo?"

"Up around Darwin they get at least sixty inches of rain a year. Most of it comes in a four-month stretch. Monsoon season. It gets plenty wet then."

"Fifteen inches a month?"

"More in January. Less in other wet months. That's when all the dotted lines on that map turn into huge muddy rivers and every little crease in the land runs liquid." He watched the rearview mirror for three seconds and then forced his attention back to the road ahead. "The fords are impassable in the wet, and the few bridges that have been built are under water. The unsealed roads and station tracks are useless."

"With all that water, why aren't there dams to ensure a year-round water supply?" she asked. "Then they could at least irrigate hay to feed those poor cattle."

"This is the wrong kind of country for dams. Too flat. Even if you could build a huge reservoir, the soil is too porous. The water would just soak in and vanish."

As he spoke, he glanced into the side mirror and accelerated gradually, hoping Erin wouldn't notice.

"Look at the map again," he said to distract her. "The Fitzroy and the Lennard aren't really rivers in the usual sense. They're floodplain channels that are dry until the wet begins. The rest of the time they're chains of year-round waterholes that you could throw a rock across without straining your arm."

She gave him a startled look.

"It's true," he said. "The Kimberley's savannah landscape is deceptive. You go through a gallon of water a day just sitting in the shade, if you can find any to sit in. This place will kill you almost as fast as a classic Saharan dune landscape. Maybe faster, because it's so hard to believe what's happening. But I believe it. This climate will grind you into dust."

Erin turned and looked out at the empty land racing by. She tried to imagine inches of rain pouring down week after week for four months.

"What happens to all the water?" she asked finally.

Frowning, Cole checked his mirrors again, holding the inside mirror with his hand to reduce vibration. The clarified reflection left no doubt.

Someone was back there, keeping pace.

He pressed down on the accelerator harder and kept talking, not wanting Erin to get frightened. "Some of the water evaporates. Most of it just sinks in and slowly percolates to the sea through rock formations that hold water like a sponge. Limestone is one. Sandstone is another."

She remembered the BlackWing maps she had stared at for hours. "Weren't those blue crosshatches on your map limestone?"

He nodded, glanced in the rear and side mirrors, and saw no change in the relative positions of the two vehicles. The vague dust cloud far behind them had speeded up shortly after he had. Gently he eased off on the accelerator, slowing undetectably.

"Windjana Gorge is an ancient reef," he said. "The Oscar Range is marine limestone. Old, old reefs, and the fossils to prove it."

"But no water?"

"Sometimes you get springs and seeps where the limestone beds have been fractured. The water that flows up is fresh and probably thousands of years old."

"What if there aren't any springs? Does that mean the limestone doesn't hold water?"

"Not necessarily. When conditions on land are right,

water dissolves passages in the limestone and all the runoff water goes straight underground. Eventually you can have rivers slowly flowing through solid rock. That's how you get cave systems like Carlsbad Caverns in New Mexico."

"Do you think something like Carlsbad exists in the Kimberley, just waiting to be discovered like Abe's diamonds?"

Cole heard the excitement in Erin's voice and tried not to smile. "The odds are against it. Caves are short-lived. Most of them don't last any more than six million years."

"Is that all? Gosh, maybe we'd better drive faster."

He glanced at the deadpan innocence of Erin's expression and smiled despite the sticky heat and the persistent vehicle behind them. "In human terms, caves last forever, but they're only mayflies compared to diamonds. Those rocks wrapped around your waist might well be the oldest things on earth."

"What?" she asked, startled.

"It's a long story." He glanced into the mirrors.

"This is a long road," she said, smiling.

Her smile made him wish that they were anywhere else, so long as it was safe. Because it wasn't safe now. The vehicle behind them had shifted speed every time Cole had. Whoever was back there didn't want to catch up or pass.

It might be that the traveler had unconsciously paced himself against the car ahead, or it might be something a lot less innocent. Either way, innocent or not, they were trapped. There was only one road for the next thirty klicks, and both vehicles were stuck with it.

He stared into the mirror, then glanced quickly at Erin, afraid that she'd notice his growing distraction. He didn't want to tell her about the tail unless he had to. Adrenaline would exhaust her even faster than the brutal climate.

The terrain began to pitch up very subtly. Experience told him that about ten minutes ahead there would be long, rolling creases in the land. Then the road would fork. The spur would go to Windjana Gorge. The Gibb River Road would head on toward the King Leopold Ranges and an eventual dead end at the tiny settlement of Gibb River. Nearly all the Gibb traffic was to stations along the way.

No locals went to Windjana in the buildup. Nor were there any tourists in Derby. He and Erin were so unusual that they'd been stared at on the street. Which meant that if the dust cloud turned off at Gibb, everything was fine. If the dust cloud followed the Rover to Windjana, everything was fucked.

"Cole?"

He glanced away from the mirror. "Hmm?"

"How do diamonds get into volcanoes?"

"We used to think diamonds crystallized out of molten rock as it cooled," he said. His voice was calm, revealing none of the tension rising in him as he drove toward the Windjana spur. "But the inside of a volcano is damned hot. Diamonds would melt there like chips of ice in fresh coffee."

He paused and glanced aside to see if she was looking in her side-view mirror. She wasn't. She was watching him, her beautiful green eyes wide and intent, unaware of anything else . . . including the dust cloud following them.

The first highway sign in fifty miles appeared just as the dirt road divided. The Gibb River Road continued straight ahead. The right fork led to Windjana Gorge and Tunnel Creek national parks.

Cole turned right.

"Not too long ago," he continued, "a bright lab boy

looked at the dark specks caught inside a diamond and wondered what they really were."

"I thought they were carbon," she said. "You know, little bits of stuff that hadn't quite made the grade to diamond."

"That's what everyone assumed. Then someone *looked*. The stuff is pyrope, which is a special kind of garnet. You can tell how old pyrope is by measuring its radioactivity. The diamond the lab boy was looking at had come from a kimberlite pipe that was a hundred and thirty million years old. The diamond and its garnet flaw should have been the same age as the pipe. Instead, they were *billions* of years old."

"But then how did the diamonds get into the pipe? Wasn't the magma hot enough to melt diamonds after all?"

"No one knows. My own private guess is that there's a diamond zone somewhere, way down in the earth, past the point where steel pipe bends and melts and rock flows like wax left out in the sun, down where the pressure and temperature are so great that diamonds were squeezed out as the planet itself cooled more than four billion years ago."

Unconsciously Erin's hand went to the cloth belt beneath her shirt where twelve ancient pieces of crystal lay hidden.

"When the earth cooled beyond a certain point," he said, "the conditions for diamond formation were gone. And I mean forever. But the diamonds remained in a thin crystalline veil over the inner face of the earth."

She smiled, liking the image. "Then how do diamonds get up on top to a place where we can find them?"

"Most of the time they don't." He flicked a glance at the side mirror. "Yet every once in a while the crust shifts and a needle of magma explodes through that diamond zone so hard and fast the diamonds don't have time to melt before the rock around them cools. But most of the time, they melt. Only one in twenty pipes have diamonds."

Silently she tried to imagine a glittering diamond veil billions of years old, a fantastic crystalline residue of the birth of the planet itself.

"What a shame," she said finally, sighing.

He looked away from the mirrors. "The diamonds that are destroyed?"

"No. The ones that survive to be worn by bimbettes and loan sharks."

He smiled, but it was one of his old smiles. Bleak. The dust cloud had turned onto the Windjana road.

Everything was fucked.

22

Western Australia

Cursing steadily but too softly for Erin to hear, Cole rummaged in his kit bag on the backseat with one hand and drove with the other.

"Can I help?" she asked.

"See how fast you can put on your walking shoes," he said. "Then steer while I put on mine."

After one look at his grim expression, she didn't ask questions. She kicked off her thongs and put her shoes on quickly. Then she held the wheel with one hand while he jammed his feet into covered shoes. Inevitably the Rover slowed.

"Thanks," he said, taking the wheel again but holding the Rover to a slow pace. "Take the binoculars and see if there's anyone behind us."

She found the glasses, adjusted the focus, and scanned the road behind them carefully. "There's a white car."

"Is he overtaking?"

She waited for the space of a breath. "No."

"Shit."

"What's wrong?"

His hands flexed on the wheel. "We've been followed since we left Derby. He's a real cute one. We speed up and so does he. We slow down and he drops back. How many are in the car?"

"It's too far and too heat-wavy to tell."

Cole reached beneath the seat, pulled out the short-barreled shotgun, and handed it to Erin. "Ever use one of these?"

"Yes."

"Good. Keep it handy, but keep the safety on."

"What are we going to do?"

"Run like bloody hell."

With no more warning than that, he gunned the Rover up and over a shallow crest and dropped down into a long incline. The accelerator hit the floorboard and stayed there, held flat by his big foot. The vehicle picked up speed rapidly, its engine screaming at full revs. The speedometer needle swung across the dial.

Erin tried not to think about the assorted large wildlife that inhabited unfenced country.

The rust-red road flew beneath the Rover's wheels. The vehicle flashed past the dry ravine at the bottom of the crease and started up the long incline on the opposite side. Gradually the incline began to win. The Rover's speed dropped.

He kept the accelerator hard against the metal floor. With quick glances he kept track of the dashboard temperature and oil pressure gauges, found the smoothest part of the dirt road, watched the shoulders for wandering wildlife.

The Rover topped the second crest before the dust cloud reappeared in the rearview mirror. Cole kept the accelerator floored. The road flattened out, then ducked around a small outcropping of rock. It was the first thing Erin had seen in Australia that resembled a hill.

Cole had the Rover to the edge of its resources and held it there without mercy. The spur road to Windjana narrowed rapidly. Ruts appeared and the shoulder looked like a mixture of rust and sand. The spur snaked off into more sparse woodland and grass, but there were enough broad twists and variations in elevation that the Gibb River Road was soon out of sight.

Erin hung on to the shotgun with one hand and braced herself with the other. Like Cole, she watched the gauges on the dashboard constantly.

"How long will the Rover take it?" she asked.

"Not long enough. I'll bet he knows it, too. He's playing us like a bloody fish."

"What are we going to do?"

Cole smiled grimly. "What fish have always done—grab the line and run with it."

"What if it's all a coincidence and he's not really following us?"

"I'll shave my legs and wear a tutu."

The Rover jerked as he slammed through gears over a rough patch of road. She braced herself all over again as they rocketed along the increasingly rough route. Time after time she was sure that they were going to crash, but he pulled them through at the last instant.

The Rover hammered through dry ravines and skated eerily over sandy spots. For several miles the only sound was that of the laboring vehicle. She kept looking at the temperature gauge.

"We're overheating," she said finally.

"I know. If there are any tourists or campers around Windjana, we're going to stick to them like a bad reputation."

"Why?"

"Killing people is easy," he said flatly. "Getting away with it is a lot harder, especially when one of the corpses is the daughter of a highly placed CIA officer. ConMin won't want witnesses."

He kept one eye on the temperature gauge and the other on the landscape. Both were hot. The ground was rusty. There were more trees here than near Derby, bigger trees, but still not a forest. There were a few very low hills with small outcroppings of rock at their crests.

Nothing was big enough to hide the Rover.

They burst from the sparse open woodland onto a sandy floodplain. Beyond it a ridge of rock rose like a dark wall into the sky. After the absolute flatness of the land they had come through, the limestone ramparts seemed unreal. The Lennard River had cut a wide slice through the limestone. The river itself was invisible, but the gap of Windjana Gorge was silent evidence of the raging power of the wet.

"Can you see any vehicles ahead?" Cole asked as they raced toward the gorge.

"No, but there must be someone. It's a national park."

"In the middle of bloody nowhere."

"What about park rangers?" she asked.

"This is Western Australia, not the U.S. Out here, tourists are on their own."

Erin shaded her eyes and looked harder as they flashed by a faded sign stating they had entered Windjana National Park. The park was deserted, as empty of people as the land around it. There was nothing but an ill-defined parking lot and a few open, sun-bleached outhouses.

No place to hide. No witnesses to carry tales.

The road forked. Cole followed a track that veered away from the gorge and the park entrance. The track paralleled the south face of the ancient reef. Fingers of water-eroded limestone fringed the cliff face and created deep, very narrow canyons. Tall trees grew in a true woodland that followed the shade and runoff line of the ridge. Smaller gums and spinifex grew in cracks and crevices on the cliff, wherever the wind had deposited seeds and enough debris to create soil. Cattle trails were everywhere.

The dirt track bent slightly, following an irregularity in the cliff, cutting off the view behind. Cole swung the wheel hard to the left, sending the Rover off the track and toward the cliff. He dodged the big trees even as he down-shifted, letting the Rover skid and wallow just at the edge of going out of control. The trees closed in behind the vehicle, shielding it from the road. The ragged, deeply indented cliff face loomed with startling suddenness.

He braked sharply and shut off the ignition.

"Get a box of shells from my kit," he said, grabbing the shotgun from her as he got out. "Run along the cliff face until I catch up. Move!"

A fitful wind slowly swept away the dust thrown up by the Rover's frantic passage. Erin ran as fast as she could through the soft, sandy soil along the cliff face. Within seconds she was sweating from her scalp to the soles of her feet. After a minute she felt like she was breathing molten lead. By the time Cole caught up and pulled her into another narrow opening in the cliff, she felt wrung out and used up.

"I brushed out—tire tracks," he said, breathing hard. "Stay down—out of sight."

She handed him the shotgun shells and nodded, too winded to speak.

He turned and measured the rough, water-pitted rock that loomed around them. Without a word he hung the shotgun down his back from the leather sling and began climbing. He tested hand- and footholds carefully, pulling himself upward with the easy, unhurried rhythm of a man accustomed to climbing. In thirty seconds, he was high enough to have a view of the road. He wedged himself into a shaded crevice, unslung the shotgun, and waited.

Five minutes after he'd positioned himself, a dust cloud bloomed along the road. The erratic breeze from the gorge scattered the dust quickly. Absolutely motionless, partially concealed within the dense shade thrown by the cliff itself, Cole waited.

A vehicle shot into sight.

Cole could see only that the driver was alone and the car was a Japanese knockoff of a Jeep. Without a flicker of hesitation the boxy, enclosed vehicle roared past the point where Cole had turned the Rover into the trees.

Cole glanced at his watch and started counting. The next ten minutes would tell Cole whether his gamble had paid off, or whether he would have to stalk the man, kill him, and bury him in the sand—if the man didn't kill him first.

Erin heard the vehicle pass by even though she couldn't see it. She looked up the rock walls to the blinding blue sky and saw Cole wedged into a black slit. The predatory tension in his body was all the warning she needed. She flattened against the rough stone and waited.

And waited.

And waited some more, the land so quiet she swore she could hear herself sweat.

Finally Cole came back down the cliff. "He went by without a look."

"Thank God."

"It's not over yet. We're going back to the Gibb River Road. From there we'll have to cut overland to the Great Northern Highway again. Right now the bastard is between us and Abe's station. Assuming he has enough gas to get there—"

"Do we?" she interrupted.

"No," Cole said, and kept on talking. "When he figures

out he's lost us, he has a choice. He can go on a shitty little dirt track to Abe's station and wait for us there, or he can cut down to the paved road and hope he beats us to Fitzroy Crossing."

"What's at Fitzroy Crossing?"

"The only gas station for three hundred miles. We'll just make it."

23

Near Fitzroy Crossing

Cole and Erin found the Great Northern Highway in late afternoon, unsure whether they were ahead of or behind their pursuer. Cole ran the Rover up to its top speed and held it there. After the rough, unpaved spur road, the Great Northern's sealed surface seemed eerily quiet, almost unreal, no hissing of grit pelting over the frame and spinning away from the tires in red turmoil.

The land was flat again. Pale-barked baoboabs loomed above the much smaller gums like goblins rising from a shallow, dusty, light-green sea. The highway's single lane had more traffic than the Gibb River Road. They met an oncoming vehicle about every twenty minutes. Most of the traffic was cars or small trucks. Occasionally a diesel hauling three freight trailers behind would come howling down on the Rover.

The first time Erin saw one coming, she made a sound of disbelief. "What in God's name is that?"

"A roadtrain."

"A roadtrain," she said. "I repeat. What in God's name is that?"

"A truck hauling three trailers." He lifted his foot from the accelerator, bringing the Rover down to sixty miles an hour.

"How big is it all together?"

"Can't tell head on. Some of the rigs are a hundred feet long."

For a minute Erin was silent. The roadtrain hurtled closer and closer, filling the single-lane road to both edges, sending clouds of grit boiling up from the dirt shoulder on either side. The monster was going as fast as the Rover.

"There isn't enough room for both of us," she said.

"No worries, love," he said, smiling as he used the common Aussie reassurance. "There's plenty of verge."

With that he whipped the Rover to the left, putting two wheels off the road into the dirt. The roadtrain did the same with its left-hand wheels. The vehicles hurtled past each other. The Rover bucked and rattled with the force of the much larger roadtrain's passage.

The dust had barely settled when sunset came in a swift, slanting cataract of light that turned clouds from cream to crimson to ink with startling suddenness. No sooner had Erin started to admire the colors than they vanished.

Cole flipped on the headlights, then threw a second switch on the dashboard. A powerful spotlight mounted above the windshield cut a wide swath through the darkness ahead, reaching out half again as far as the headlights.

"Something big on the right," she said, catching a flash of light that could only come from the reflective pupil of an animal's eye. "A cow?"

"Bloody stupid animals," he muttered, braking hard and simultaneously turning off the overhead spotlight. "May they all go to those great Golden Arches in the sky."

"As in hamburgers?"

He grunted, slid the Rover past the cow in a shower of dirt, and drove on, picking up the speed he'd lost. He drove hard and fast, but he never outran his lights, for at dusk Kimberley shorthorns began wandering out from the bush's thin shade to graze along the road's edge, where water from the blacktop ran off to create relatively lush feed.

As it grew darker, spotting shadows looming at the edges of the Rover's headlights became a kind of adrenaline-filled game that distracted Erin and Cole from the clinging heat that hung on far longer than sunlight had. Overhead a carpet of stars condensed. The sky was as alien as the land had been. Except for the Southern Cross, the stars were evenly spaced and of the same brightness.

Time and again Cole braked, reached up to turn off the spotlight, and cut the headlights down to low. Dense shadows moved slowly across the road ahead. When one of the cows turned toward them, its eyes flashed eerily in the light.

"Why do you turn down the lights?" she asked finally.

"It blinds the cattle. They freeze if they're on the road, and if they're not, they're as likely to jump toward the light as away from it. I stay off the horn, too. It panics them, and a panicked cow will run right into a car."

Then, although she had promised herself she wouldn't, she heard herself asking, "Any lights behind us?"

"No."

"Could he be running without lights?"

Cole smiled coldly. "I hope so. That little Tojo he was driving doesn't weigh much more than a cow."

In the darkness ahead, what at first had seemed an extension of the star-packed southern sky resolved into a cluster of artificial lights. They were the first fixed lights Erin had seen on the landscape since leaving Derby behind.

"Fitzroy Crossing?" she asked.

"Nothing else is out here."

Fitzroy Crossing was the place where the Great Northern Highway's single lane crossed the Fitzroy River. That, and year-round water trapped in the huge billabongs gouged out by floodwaters, supported a town of a few hundred whites, a varying population of Aborigines, and uncounted crocodiles.

Cole drove into a ramshackle service station, shut off the engine, and said as he got out, "Stay in the car. If you see anything that makes you nervous, hit the horn. The shotgun is under my seat."

"I'm a lousy shot."

His teeth flashed whitely. "Doesn't matter. The barrels are just long enough to be legal and just right for close work against superior odds. The load is double-aught buckshot. Just point, pull the trigger, and watch the odds improve."

Without a word she reached under the seat and put the shotgun across her lap.

He filled the gas tank and the spare fuel cans that had been depleted by high-speed driving, added oil and water, checked various cables, hoses, and reservoirs, and finally went inside to pay.

She kept looking around but saw no one except an Aborigine with grizzled hair on top, thickly calloused feet on bottom, and a freeform castle of Black Swann beer cans piled to one side.

When Cole emerged from the combination grocery store, café, and bar, he was carrying a stack of sandwiches and lukewarm soft drinks from an overmatched refrigerator. He stopped for a moment, exchanged a few

words with the Black Swann castle builder, left a sand-
wich, and came back to the Rover.

Moments later they were on the road again. She had
the distinct feeling he was glad to be out in the darkness
once more.

"There's a roadside park thirty klicks north," he said.
"We can use the picnic tables as cots, if nobody beats us
to them. Or we can push on to the station."

"Which is safer?"

He shrugged. "Little white Japanese vehicles are common here. The town is full of them. If our bird dog got
smart and cut across the Tunnel Creek road instead of
turning around and going over his backtrail to catch us,
he's probably ahead of us. He'll assume we're going to
push for Abe's station, where we have help. It's damned
easy to set up an ambush at night out in the bush."

"I've always wanted to sleep on a picnic table."

He laughed softly. "Don't worry, honey. I've got a tarp
and sleeping bags in back. We'll hollow out a place in the
sand and sleep like babies."

They saw no other traffic until ten minutes later, when
headlights flashed into life about a half mile ahead. The
height and number of the lights told Cole that the oncoming vehicle was a roadtrain. The headlights of the rig
were a white blaze. Its searchlight reached out toward the
Rover like an accusing finger.

Automatically he lifted his foot from the accelerator
and began checking the shadows at the edge of the spotlight with unusual care, seeking the eerie flash of animal
eyes. Erin tried to look away from the oncoming lights
and concentrate on checking the shoulder for range cows,
but the cone of brilliant light nearly blinded her.

The distance between the two vehicles closed rapidly.
Cole grunted and switched off the Rover's spotlight.

The roadtrain didn't return the courtesy. It raced toward them, growing bigger and more blinding by the instant.

"Christ, must be a million candlepower on that bastard," Cole muttered. "He could jacklight deer on Jupiter."

Angrily he lifted his hand to shade his eyes from the blinding glare. At the same time he let the Rover drift farther out onto the shoulder, giving the oncoming vehicle most of the pavement. The roadtrain gave way as well but didn't slow at all. It bore down on them like a runaway freight train.

"Is he forgetful or just rude?" she asked as she slapped the spotlight switch on and off in an unsubtle reminder.

Two hundred yards away the huge, dazzling spotlight flicked off.

"About time, you stupid son of a bitch," Cole said.

No sooner had their eyes begun to adjust than the huge spotlight exploded into life again. Its brilliant blue-white beam pinned the Rover's windshield as the huge roadtrain roared straight toward them, no room to swerve, no place to hide, and the light like a knife in Cole's eyes. Blindly he yanked the wheel hard left, sending the Rover careening wildly over the savannah, dodging chest-high termite mounds and splintering small gums on the bull bar.

After a few hundred yards the Rover clipped a big termite mound, went sideways, caromed off a swollen boab trunk, climbed a smaller termite mound, and almost rolled over. The front wheels cleared the mound before the Rover stopped moving and hung canted, off center, helpless, its engine racing.

During the final moments of the wild ride, Cole's head slammed against the side window. For an instant he sat stunned. Then he killed the lights out of reflex and shook his head roughly, trying to focus. Images came in twos and fours. He shook his head again. It didn't help.

There was a screaming from the highway as the road-train's brakes locked up and burned rubber.

"Erin?" he asked hoarsely. "Are you all right, honey?"

"Shaken," she said, her voice ragged, "but nothing permanent."

"Take the shotgun and run into the bush."

"But—"

"Do it!"

Shotgun in hand, she opened her door and scrambled out into the dark. Instead of following orders, she ran around to his side of the Rover and levered the door open.

"I said—" he began.

"I'm not leaving you like a staked goat!" she cried over the sound of the road train's howling brakes. "Get out!"

He rolled out of the seat, found his feet, and staggered forward. She caught him and levered him upright with her shoulder. As soon as he was standing he broke into a ragged run, depending on her to guide him through the multiple images of night.

After a few moments, four became two and then, sometimes, one. His stride lengthened. In the back of his mind, he heard the roadtrain's brakes shrieking and rumbling, then an ominous silence as the huge mass finally ground to a stop.

A powerful spotlight began sawing back and forth through the bush like a white sword. It was off to their left, but the next sweep would catch both the Rover and them.

Without warning Cole yanked Erin off her feet, pulled her down behind a termite mound and completely covered her with his body, praying that his dusty khaki clothes would provide adequate camouflage for both of them.

Then he realized what he had done—dragged her down and overpowered her just as Hans once had.

Facedown in the dirt, Erin fought for breath, but she didn't panic, telling herself over and over again that it was Cole who was pinning her down, Cole who had never hurt her, Cole who had fought for her when she'd been helpless. Cole had never used his strength to humiliate, hurt, or violate her. He'd brought her pleasure, not pain, a wild sharing of bodies that enhanced rather than destroyed all that was human in her.

As her body relaxed, he let out a long breath and spoke in a soft, low voice. "Don't move. Don't look up. Your eyes catch light just like any other animal. Understand?"

"Yes."

Very gently he brushed his lips over her cheek and whispered, "You're quite a woman. As brave as your photos. Now I want you to be as smart. No matter what happens, stay put. I'd hate to kill you by mistake. Can I count on you not moving?"

"Yes."

She felt his weight slide slowly from her. The forgotten shotgun was eased from her grip. There was the brush of skin against skin, a whisper of cloth against spinifex. . . .

Then silence.

Cole belly-crawled away while the spotlight swept the night. An edge of the light touched the Rover, rushed by, then returned, pinning the vehicle in a tunnel of blazing white light. The Rover looked like some primeval outback beast perched on its haunches with its nose pointed into the air. Carefully not looking at the light, Cole crawled closer, knowing that the roadtrain assassin would have to get out to check his handiwork.

When the searchlight swept toward Cole, he closed his eyes completely to protect his night vision and prevent any flash of his own eyes giving away his position. The searchlight swept on, restoring darkness beyond his closed eyelids. He opened his eyes. After several minutes

he saw a shadow flicker off to his left in the pale moonlight. It could have been simply a trick of his eyes, which
were still giving him double images.

And it could have been a man.

Cole froze, then turned his head very, very slowly.
Nothing moved, yet he was certain someone was out
there. The man was a creature of the outback, sliding
from shadow to shadow, cover to cover, moving with the
silence and assurance of a king mulga.

Cole blinked his eyes, trying to clear them of extra
images.

The assassin disappeared in shadows, then reemerged
a moment later, closer to the Rover but too far for any
kind of accuracy with buckshot. Night shooting was
tricky at best. A short-barreled gun and a head that was
ringing like a savagely struck bell weren't helping Cole
at all.

Suddenly the man was silhouetted against the Rover's
window. Cole came to his feet in a silent rush, threw the
shotgun to his shoulder, and fired in one smooth motion.
A tongue of orange-white flame bloomed in the night.
The blast covered the metallic sound of the pump gun's
action. He fired again just to the right of the place the
man had been, racked in another round instantly, and
fired to the left of his first shot. As he pumped again he
leaped to the side, knowing that his muzzle flashes were a
beacon telling the assassin where to shoot.

The sound of the shots rolled through the night like
thunder. Off to the right birds cried their fear. Gradually
silence returned to the bush. There was no scream of
pain, no return fire, nothing to show whether enough of
the buckshot had found a target to make a difference.

Cole waited, neither moving nor breathing, listening
with every nerve ending. He caught the faintest suggestion of cloth against spinifex, a bare hint of boot against

soil, a blurred shadow retreating. He threw himself to one side, rolled over several times, and fired again. Then he rolled back in the other direction and waited.

Silence.

Cole eased three more fat shells into the magazine of the shotgun before he moved silently in the direction of the roadtrain. He felt a sudden flash of sensory memory— a night thick with heat and humidity and the silent jungle all around, too silent, telling of predators on the move.

Kill or be killed.

Live or die.

Nothing new.

But this time it was different, more difficult, for he was protecting more than his own life. He cocked his head, listening to make sure Erin had not betrayed her hiding place. He heard only silence.

Motionless, Erin lay and listened to the silence, fighting the urge to call out Cole's name. She'd stalked animals in the wilderness with her camera, she'd watched wolves hamstring and bring down moose, but never before had she been facedown in cover while she waited for men to kill or die. She wished she had something more deadly at her command than her own clenched fists and fraying patience, but she didn't.

A door slammed. The roadtrain's diesel growled and revved. Gears clashed violently as the train began to retreat, picking up speed with every second. The spotlight and headlights were out, as though the fleeing assassin was afraid of drawing any more fire.

Warily Cole retreated in the direction of the Rover. When he was close to where he had left Erin, he whispered her name.

"Over here," she whispered.

A moment later he slid down beside her, pulling her into his arms, holding her until she stopped shaking, being held in return. Long after the first rush of adrenaline-induced trembling passed, he continued to hold her, stroking her as he listened to the night. Slowly the small sounds of insects and nocturnal life returned, telling him that no one had been left behind on the road to sneak closer to the Rover and wait in ambush.

"You've been itching to drive all day," he said quietly. "Feel up to it now?"

She nodded.

"Stay here while I take a look around. If it's clear, try getting the Rover off the mound."

"Why wait around?" she demanded. "He could be setting up another ambush down the road."

"He was heading toward Fitzroy Crossing. We're not."

"What if there were two of them and one took off and the other one stayed behind?"

"He's not that stupid."

Her breath came in quickly. "You sound disappointed."

Cole's teeth glinted coldly in the moonlight. "There's nothing I'd like better than to put that bastard in the ground." His smile vanished. "They weren't after just me this time. You came too damn close to buying it under that roadtrain's wheels. As far as I'm concerned, it's open season from here on out."

Before she could say anything, her mouth was claimed in a swift, fierce kiss that ended as suddenly as it had begun.

"Five minutes," he said. "If I'm not back and you haven't heard anything, try to get the Rover off that hump. I'll catch up before you get to the road."

She waited until she decided five minutes had passed, then made her way to the Rover. She had to climb in at an awkward angle, but once she scrambled behind the wheel, she started the engine easily. The gear box had been designed for a man. A strong one. She wrestled the shifter into reverse gear and fed gas. The Rover dragged a few inches off its high point. She shifted into first, inched forward, then quickly went into reverse. This time the front wheels caught and held traction.

No sooner did the Rover groan and thump free of the mound than loose soil threatened to bog the wheels. She shifted into low range and tried again. The Rover eased forward. She made a very slow turn without lights, heading back toward the road.

Cole materialized from the shadows beside her door.

"I'll drive," she said quickly, stopping. "You ride shotgun."

He went around to the other side and climbed in. "You drive to the station turnoff. I'll take it from there."

"No camping out on picnic tables?"

"Not tonight. We're going to ground in the bush until I stop seeing double."

"Wouldn't we be safer at the station?"

"Safer?" He laughed, but there was no humor in the sound. He turned and looked at her with eyes that glittered like ice in the reflected light of the dashboard. "Sorry to break the news, honey. The station isn't safer—it's the hunting ground of the diamond tiger."

24

Near Abe's station

Cole came awake before the first stars began fading from the crowded southern sky. The air was humid, fragrant, filled with the subtle rush of awakening life. Erin stirred sleepily and snuggled closer to him, sharing the heat of his body in the cool of pre-dawn. He shifted until he could put both arms around her.

The headache that had plagued him last night didn't return with his movement. Nor did it return with the sudden quickening of his body when he felt the softness of the woman pressed against him. He was tempted to awaken her as he had yesterday morning, bringing her from sleep to abandoned sensuality, bypassing inhibition and fear, touching the intense passion that had been buried for years within her.

Even as he told himself all the reasons why he shouldn't, his hands were moving over her, pushing away the frail barrier of clothes, seeking the sleek center of her, finding it. He caressed her slowly, felt her body's sultry response, and wondered what her dreams were like.

Her breath broke and her eyes opened, gleaming mysteriously in the star-filled night.

"This is becoming a habit," she murmured, smiling and stretching languidly against him.

"I'll stop."

"Really?" Her hands slid down his body, finding and caressing the hard male flesh that rose eagerly to meet her. "When?"

"Whenever you want."

She looked up into the pale blaze of his eyes and knew that he meant it. He would stop right now if that was what she wanted. But she didn't. Barely awake, operating at the level of deepest instinct, she wanted him.

His hand moved and heat burst in the pit of her stomach, shaking her. His touch slid deeply inside her until the heel of his palm grazed the exquisitely sensitive nub concealed between hot folds of skin. Her lashes half lowered and her breath unraveled. Splinters of pleasure shivered through her, melting her in his hand. She looked into his eyes and knew only the truth of her love for this man.

He made a thick sound of pleasure as she urged him over on top of her and he joined their bodies as completely as he could, moving in slow counterpoint to her until pleasure overwhelmed both of them. At the last instant he covered her mouth with his own, drinking her wild cries even as he poured himself into her. Then he held her until their breathing evened out, their heartbeats slowed, and he felt the boneless relaxation of her body as she drifted into sleep once more.

"No, you don't," he said. "It's time to get up."

She murmured and separated herself from him with a slow reluctance that sent currents of passion surging through him once more. Ignoring the delicate talons of desire, he dressed quickly, rolled sleeping bags and tarp, and stuffed them in the Rover. Then he scrambled up a steep slope and stood in the moon shadow of a hilltop outcropping.

The track leading to Abe's station was below and to the right. The vague road was barely visible in moonlight. In some places, it vanished in the thin bush cover. Only someone who was familiar with the track would have been able to follow it—or someone like Cole, whose memory was remarkable.

The dusty, rutted track was deserted. The pre-dawn darkness was silent.

"I guess the bastard finally had enough," Cole said as Erin climbed up and stood beside him.

"Thank God."

His smile flashed whitely. "God had nothing to do with that one."

"How's your head?"

"Still there."

"Hold still."

He stood motionless while her fingertips searched lightly through his hair just above his right temple. His scalp prickled in elemental response as his whole body tightened.

"The bump is almost gone," she said after a moment.

His fingertip traced her cheekbone. "Come on. Back to the Rover before I do something foolish again." His voice had an unmistakable roughness to it as he added under his breath, "Woman, you have the damnedest effect on my self-control."

She followed him, picking her way carefully in the tricky light. The first few steps down the slope were steep and crumbly. She slid, caught herself, then slid again until her walking shoes found better purchase. All around her spinifex gleamed in lines of silver that shifted and rippled with the hot breeze. Somewhere in the distance an animal gave an odd, resonant cry.

"What's that?" she asked.

"Cow talking to the moon."

Another urgent cry came on the wind.

"Moon talking back to the cow?" she asked dryly.

He grinned. "You learn fast."

The two doors to the Rover closed as one, sounding loud in the stillness. He started up and eased the Rover back onto the rough, rutted track, using only moonlight until they were down on flat land again. As the Rover bumped forward, Cole could see signs where a larger vehicle had taken the track, leaving behind crushed spinifex and broken brush. There were other signs of recent traffic as well, tire tracks not yet blurred by the wind.

"Lots of traffic," Erin said.

"You have good eyes."

"Nervous eyes, after yesterday."

"So far I haven't seen anything unexpected," Cole said. "Just the sort of tracks you'd see on Abe's driveway."

"Some driveway. Must be sixty kilometers long."

"As the crow flies—or the cockatoo, since we're in the Kimberley. The narrower tread marks belong to something with a wheel base smaller than the Rover's. Probably one of the old jeeps that Abe kept around. He had three of the damn things the last time I was here. He just kept cannibalizing to keep one of them going."

"Then you don't think anyone's at the station right now?"

"Some people from BlackWing will be there. At least they damn well better be, or our prospecting won't get off the ground before the wet. Sarah might be there. Maybe some of her kids and grandkids. The men probably went walkabout after Abe died."

"Who's Sarah?"

Cole smiled strangely. "Nobody knows. She was a child when Abe and his brother first pegged out their pastoral lease. Her tribe had either been wiped out by disease and war, or they'd just gone walkabout and left her. She stayed with Abe."

The Rover lurched and wallowed. Erin braced herself on the dashboard while Cole downshifted into low gear and crawled over the deeply rutted, concrete-hard remains of a dried-out bog.

"Do you think Sarah knows about the mine?" Erin asked.

"I doubt it. If she did, she wouldn't care. Diamonds are a modern passion. The Aborigines have no use for modern things."

"Surely life changed after the English came?"

"The English haven't been here very long. The first Australians drove cattle to the Kimberley from Queensland a little more than a hundred years ago. The trek took two years. They started out with ten thousand head and lost more than half, so nobody was in a bloody great hurry to do it twice. There's been more settlement out here in the last twenty years than there was in the first hundred."

The Rover staggered and slithered over what could only have been a muddy patch of ground.

"A seep," he said when Erin made a startled sound.

"Water?"

"It happens, you know."

"You could have fooled me. That's the first free fresh water I've seen since I got to Australia."

He swerved the Rover as an animal the size of a small dog flashed across the track.

"What was that?" she asked.

"A wallaby."

She stared into the night. She couldn't see anything. She sighed and settled back again. "Did Abe ever talk about his brother?"

"Not to me. Not directly. According to local legend, after your grandfather left with Bridget McQueen, Abe went native for a time. He learned the language, lived the life, and became a kind of god or devil to the Aborigines who migrated through the station. He sat at their fires, they pledged young women to him, and saved him the choice parts of lizard and croc."

The Rover groaned and bumped along the track, taking Cole's full attention.

"Did you like Abe?" she asked when the road was less rough.

"I respected his toughness. I admired his knowledge of the land. But like him?" Cole shrugged. "No one liked Abe, least of all the people who knew him best—the Aborigines. You don't like your gods or devils. You just live with them the best way you can. He was obsessed with sex, but he hated women more than any man I've ever known."

"Then why did he leave me the station? He could have willed it to Dad or Phil."

Cole's sideways glance was a pale glitter against the dark planes of his face. "Maybe Abe didn't hate them enough."

"What do you mean?"

Softly Cole began to quote from "Chunder." " 'I'm going down alone/Where the black swan floats/O'er a dead sea's bones./Stone woman giving me hope,/Secrets blacker than-death/And truth it's death to speak./ But I will speak to you./Listen to me, child of rue./You will curse the day/As I cursed my queen lady.' "

The words spoken in a man's deep voice beneath the vast Australian night sounded very different than those same words read mockingly in an expensive Los Angeles hotel. A shiver of unease rippled through Erin.

"What had women ever done to him?" she asked.

Cole's mouth turned down in a hard smile. "Oh, probably the usual thing."

"Which is?"

"Screwed him over."

"From what you've said about Abe, being screwed was his idea of a good time."

"There's a world of difference between screwing and being screwed."

"I know," she said bleakly.

Cole remembered Hans. "Sorry, honey. I wasn't thinking." He smiled bitterly. "It's a pity Hans didn't meet Wing's sister. They were made for each other. But Justice is blind and Mercy is an unpredictable whore."

Erin wasn't about to argue that.

"I don't know what happened to sour Abe on women," Cole said. "He never talked about it. Looking at those pictures of yours, it's probably as simple as two brothers wanting the same woman and only one of them getting her."

"Grandmother?"

He nodded. "After Bridget left, one of Abe's white neighbors asked him why his brother Nate Windsor had gone to America. Abe worked the man over with a stockman's whip. If Abe hadn't been so drunk at the time, he probably would have flayed the poor bastard alive. The same thing happened every time your grandfather was mentioned. Abe went into a murderous rage. After a while, people stopped talking about Nate Windsor's sudden decision to go to America and started talking about Crazy Abe."

The track disintegrated into braided ruts climbing a hill. Cole killed the headlights before they could show over the rise. Bucking, sliding, shuddering, the Rover crabbed uphill. As soon as they were just below the top, he turned off the engine and got out. A few steps brought his head above the rise.

Down below in a windswept hollow, lights gleamed in the darkness.

Erin got out and went to stand beside him. "What is it?" she asked softly.

"The station house."

"It looks pretty busy for this early."

"During buildup, you get up before dawn if you want to get anything done. It's too damn hot otherwise."

He went back to the Rover, pulled a box of shotgun shells from his kit and dropped a dozen of them into his pocket.

She watched without a word.

"I'm going to make sure there aren't any surprises," he said softly. "If it's all right for you to come in, the house lights will flash twice. Give me an hour. If I haven't signaled by then, get back to Fitzroy Crossing, call your father, and camp with the local police until he arrives."

"What about you?"

"That's my problem. Staying alive is yours. Whatever happens, *don't come in after me*. Once I leave the Rover, I'm assuming that everything that moves out there is an enemy."

"Cole—" she began.

"Promise me you'll stay here," he interrupted urgently, leaning toward her. "I could get killed worrying about you."

She felt the heat of his breath and the gentle caress of his mouth.

"Promise me," he whispered.

She shivered as the taste of him spread like wine across her tongue. "Yes."

The sound was as much a sigh as a word, but he understood. The kiss changed for an instant, becoming less gentle, more consuming. Then he was gone.

Cole moved silently over the rise and down the slope, using natural cover to conceal his outline. It took him more than half an hour to reach the compound. When he was within ten yards of the house, he crouched near a slender gum and waited.

Nothing moved. Even the wind was still. From behind the house came the hum of a large generator. On the roof a satellite dish stood ready to receive invisible messages. Another array of electronic gear was nearby, ready to send messages.

He circled the house at a distance. Two new one-ton pickup trucks were parked in back, gleaming among the rusted carcasses of old Jeeps. Nothing stirred in the darkness except the slow expansion of cigarette smoke giving away the position of a hidden guard. Bypassing the man, Cole eased toward the kitchen window. He'd nearly reached it when the back door opened an arm's length away.

His night vision was ruined by the sudden outpouring of light. Too close to do anything except attack, he stepped forward soundlessly. As the door closed he snaked his arm around the person's throat.

"Don't talk," he said very softly. "Don't move."

Even as the words left his mouth, an exotic perfume bathed his senses. The scent was as familiar as the delicate perfection of the bones and flesh lying helplessly within his grasp.

"Hello, Lai," he said softly. "Long time no see. But not long enough."

25

Kununurra

After hours spent dodging stock along the Great Northern Highway, Jason Street reached his satellite office in Kununurra. When he parked and walked to the office door, no one questioned what he was doing out and about in bush clothes that looked as though he'd crawled on his belly like a snake over the land. No one questioned the oozing reddish burn that showed just beneath the short, ragged right sleeve of his shirt.

No one questioned him at all for the simple reason that Kununurra rolled up its few narrow streets and went to bed shortly after the sun did. The only exception to the general lifelessness was in the beer halls and on the tribal land at the edge of town, where Aborigines gathered around a huge bonfire and drank themselves into a modern version of their ancient Dreamtime.

Street's office was stale and roasting. He paused only long enough to turn on the air conditioner before he headed for the computer. He keyed in a code, lit a cigarette, and looked at the messages that had piled up while he'd chased all over the outback. The crop was about what he had expected—one of his security guards had showed up drunk for work at a mine, another client was complaining that his latest fee was too high, and a mining consortium wanted his opinion as to whether their latest decline in profits was due to a fall-off in the quality of the ore itself or to high-grading by the workers.

And Hugo van Luik had called.

Street cursed a stream of smoke, coughed, and looked at his wristwatch. Van Luik was probably still in his Antwerp office. Street picked up a phone that had a scrambler connected, entered the number, and waited.

Van Luik answered on the second ring.

"G'day, mate," Street said, his Australian intonations making the words sound a good deal more cheery than he felt.

"Is it done?"

"Next time you send me on a hunt, you might tell me I'm after a real tiger."

"Have I ever sent you after small game?"

"Jungle bunny rebels and chokie smugglers are one thing. This Blackburn-Markham bloke is another. He's too good to be just a diamond hunter. You're certain he isn't CIA?"

"Regrettably, yes. A deal might have been struck with the CIA."

Street swallowed a yawn and rubbed his scalp, where sweat had dried into a dirty crust. "Well, he's at Abe's station by now."

"Mr. Blackburn is a very lucky man."

"Lucky?" Street snarled, angry at the suggestion that he was doing less than his best work. "From where I sit, it looks more like he's one smart, tough bastard. Passport in another name, driver's license, the lot."

"What went wrong?"

"Bloody everything, that's what. He vetted the Rover

like he was looking for fleas. He found everything that could go wrong and fixed it. Took him hours. Nora wanted to hire him as a mechanic. So much for an 'accidental' breakdown."

"Go on."

"Oh, I did that, too. Chased them all over the bloody back of beyond. Blackburn spotted me once I turned onto the dirt road. He ran for Windjana. My vehicle had more legs than Nora's old Rover. I figured to catch them at the park. Rented car breaks down and two Yank tourists wander off and die in the outback, just like Crazy Abe. Bloody sad and all that, but the outback has killed better men before and will kill them again. No worries, mate. Not a one."

Van Luik's breath came in hard at the thought of the inquisition that would have followed Erin Shane Windsor's death, no matter how innocent the circumstances might have seemed. Yet even as sweat pooled along his spine, he admired the tempting, brutal simplicity of Street's plan. All problems solved in one stroke.

"What happened?" van Luik asked after a moment.

"Blackburn hid somewhere in Windjana until I went by. Then he doubled back again to the Gibb and retraced his trail until he found a spur road that connected with the Great Northern Highway. As soon as I was sure I'd lost him, I went on to Fitzroy Crossing, where he had to stop for petrol. When I got there, one of the roadtrains was parked for a bit of tucker. It was dark and no one was about except the plonkos. I decided to have a go at flattening the bastard. I jiggered the ignition and went looking for Blackburn's headlights. Thought I had him, but he's bloody quick. He went rocketing into the bush, banged about, and pranged on a termite mound." Street paused to stub out his cigarette.

Van Luik said nothing.

"Took me awhile to bring that bloody great roadtrain to a stop," Street said. "Then I had to get back to the Rover. Took me awhile to do that, too. I wasn't about to have a go at Blackburn on the rush. He's too cute by half. Bloody good thing I tiptoed. He had a sawed-off shotgun. Nearly did for me right there."

"Could he identify you?" van Luik demanded.

"Not a chance. It was dark and I didn't get that close. If I had, I'd be dead."

"The girl?"

"Never saw her."

"Could she have been hurt?"

"I checked the Rover before he tried to blow off my head. She wasn't inside. He could have carried her off somewhere in the bush. He's bloody big."

"Is there any chance that you will be connected with the stolen vehicle?"

Street laughed roughly. "The dole had just come in. Those Abos wouldn't have recognized their own mother."

"Explain," van Luik demanded.

"The Australian government pays off the Abos for being born, and the Abos take their cut of the dole to the nearest bottle shop and buy enough beer to make them forget they were ever born at all. No one white and sober saw me."

"Where are you now?"

"Kununurra. I'll go to Abe's station as soon as I'm called in to appraise the leases. Tomorrow, probably, if the file clerk pulls out her finger. Day after for certain."

Van Luik let the silence build before he said carefully, "Despite the fact that you have negotiated Abelard Windsor's contracts with ConMin and DSD for the last ten years, your government is being recalcitrant about having you officially appraise the Sleeping Dog mining leases."

"Bugger all!" Street snarled. "Has she moved on getting the will recognized yet?"

"Matthew Windsor did. He, of course, is in a position to see that matters proceed at a brisk pace."

Street lit another cigarette, blew smoke, and said, "We can't wait until I get the green light on appraising the leases. Blackburn's partner has put enough high-tech prospecting equipment at the station to make me nervous."

"We are negotiating with the Americans about the appraisals," van Luik said finally. "They are divided. I expect your permission to come through shortly."

"It better, mate. I've got some of the station Abos watching the countryside for any prospecting, but they could go walkabout at any time."

"Pay them more."

Street made an impatient sound and wondered how he could explain Australia's natives to a man as urbanized as van Luik.

"Money doesn't work real well with Abos. Fear does. So long as they think I'm Abe's shadow, they'll obey me. But if I lean too hard, they'll go walkabout."

Van Luik breathed in slowly, then he spoke with great precision. "If Erin Windsor brings that mine into production, you are a dead man. *Mazel und broche.*"

The connection went dead. Street looked at the receiver and said, "But what if I'm the one to bring the mine into production, you stupid sod?"

He laughed, then winced at the pain in his arm as he tossed the receiver into the cradle.

"Choke on your *mazel*, old man. Rack off and die."

26

Abe Windsor's station

Erin awoke disoriented, wondering where she was. The steamy heat, the lack of a mattress, and the lair-like smell of the room itself brought everything back. She was at the Windsor station, sleeping in her great-uncle's bedroom. Or what was left of it.

Cole had taken one look at the bed and thrown it into the backyard, mattress and all. He'd brought in sleeping bags and pads from the Rover. Without a word he'd set up two pallets in Abe's room and settled down to sleep next to her with his body blocking the closed door.

Lying motionless, she remembered the currents of barely controlled emotion she'd sensed in Cole when she'd walked into the station house. He'd introduced her to a Chinese woman called Lai, a woman whose hungry black glance had been all over Cole like hands. He hadn't introduced Erin to the six other men at the station who were also Chinese. They didn't understand English—or, if they did, they kept it to themselves.

Lai knew English. Erin suspected that the Chinese woman also knew Cole Blackburn. Or wanted to.

Restlessly Erin rolled over on the hard floor, tired but no longer able to sleep despite the exhaustion of her body. The sleeping bag Cole had used was pushed to the side, empty. The door was closed. She looked at the door and wondered if he was with Lai of the hungry eyes and exquisitely fragile body. The thought of him alone with the Chinese beauty made Erin's mouth flatten and turn down with a jealousy she was too honest to deny.

Cole's voice came from the other side of the closed door. "Erin? The helicopter is almost ready."

She sat up quickly, then groaned.

The door opened so fast that it banged against the wall. Cole stood in the opening looking as dangerous as a drawn gun. His gray glance flashed over the room and found nothing but the grim accommodations that Abe had always preferred. Other than the mussed, gritty tank top and shorts Erin was wearing, she seemed fine.

"What's wrong?" Cole asked, looking intently at her.

"What do you mean?"

"I heard a sound, like you were in pain."

She grimaced. "I'm just a little stiff after sleeping on the floor."

Slowly he relaxed. "The princess and the pea, huh?"

"More like a bowling ball."

He helped her to her feet, then held her close, giving her a hungry kiss that made her forget all the aches.

The sound of someone moving just beyond the open door was as startling as a shot. Although Cole's back was to the doorway, he didn't have to turn to identify the eavesdropper. He knew that Lai had followed him from the kitchen when he'd come to awaken Erin.

"What is it, Lai?" he asked without turning around.

Erin's eyes widened at the change in Cole. The difference was shocking. The sensual heat and gentleness were gone. In their place was a leashed, violent emotion that could have been anger or something close to raw desire. When she tried to ease away from the intimate embrace, he held her in place as much with his glance as with his hands.

"Chen Wing has called," Lai said. "He asks to speak with you."

Lai's voice was hushed, soft, controlled, but her eyes hungrily watched Cole's body. For just an instant she glanced at Erin as though measuring her for a shroud. Then Lai lowered her eyes and waited with the outwardly patient obedience peculiar to unemancipated women in the traditional Chinese culture.

Uneasiness moved in waves over Erin's skin. Any doubt she might have had about the currents running between Cole and Lai was gone. Cole and Lai knew each other.

Intimately.

"Tell him I'll be there in a minute," Cole said.

Lai turned and walked away, her high heels clicking on the wooden floor. Her obedience might have been that of a traditional Chinese woman, but her clothes were an elegant synthesis of West and Orient. She wore the traditional black silk slacks, but they weren't baggy. They fitted with a perfection that only personal tailoring could provide. Her blouse was also silk, also black, and unbuttoned to a fashionable depth that showed the swell of her golden breasts. Her burnished black hair hung in a smooth curtain that came to her hips.

The photographer in Erin reluctantly concluded that she'd never seen a more attractive female.

"She's stunning," Erin said finally.

"Yes."

The word was like his expression, utterly neutral. Erin had no way of knowing what emotions lay beneath his surface. She knew only that emotions were there, shielded with every bit of his considerable self-control.

"How long have you known her?" she asked before she could stop herself.

"Long enough."

"For what?"

"I'll go talk to Wing. Bring me some coffee, would you? It may take awhile." He stopped at the door and looked over his shoulder. "In any case, from now on don't be out of my sight for more than three minutes at a time. And never be out of calling distance. Understand?"

She blinked. "Don't you trust Lai and those men?"

"I don't trust anybody. That's why I'm still alive. Stay close to me. Always. If I have to come looking for you, I'll come ready to kill."

He strode through the shambles of the house to the room Wing's men had gutted and turned into a communications center. Everything Cole would need to talk to Wing or to transmit and receive computer information was already in place.

Cole picked up the phone. "Hell of a job, Wing. I was expecting to tap out my messages on a computer."

"Thank you. I regret the delay in the bedding and in the improved plumbing. Lai has promised to redouble the efforts of the men. Is everything working?"

"New generator, transmitter, receiver, modems, computers, fax, and some stuff I haven't even had a chance to play with yet," he said, looking around. "You must have had a small army for the installation."

"There were several bush pilots who were more than willing to haul people and supplies at triple rates, despite the lack of a decent landing strip. I also took the liberty of beginning the survey immediately. The findings are being processed as we speak. If you have any reason to suspect the technician's competence or the pilot's navigational integrity, the helicopter stands ready to repeat the entire sequence."

"Why did you start without me?" Cole asked bluntly.

"We learned that someone else has been quartering the Windsor station by helicopter. I have to assume they are after the same information we are. Under the circumstances I had no choice but to go ahead on the survey."

"Who was it?"

"We're still working on that. The helicopter was rented by International Mining Security Advisors Ltd. The company is owned by an Australian called Jason Street and takes contracts from various mining interests to advise on or to create security for their mines. Unfortunately, IMSA's security is quite good. We can't find who hired IMSA to do the survey. The technician simply had his orders and followed them."

"Does IMSA own any mines in Australia or any interest in an existing mine?"

"No."

"Does it do a lot of work for the diamond cartel?" Cole asked.

"A modest amount. Something less than twelve percent of its net profit. Interestingly enough, Mr. Street was formerly with ASIO."

"Formerly?" Cole said sardonically. "Once sworn, never foresworn."

"We are aware of that probability. In any case, as the Australian government finally is being brought to the point of cooperating with BlackWing on this venture, I doubt that Mr. Street is a direct threat to your operation in the long run."

"Keep after IMSA and Street," Cole said flatly.

"Agreed." Wing took a breath. "Lai said you were injured."

Cole gave Lai a narrow look. She watched him like he was a god walking among men. Once he'd trusted that look. Now he recognized it as another part of her sexual allure, an act that was as carefully constructed as the silk clothing she wore.

"A bullet burn on my thigh from Darwin," Cole said.

"Ah, yes, Darwin," Wing murmured. "You haven't mellowed, have you? Uncle Li was quite gratified. The local police are quite mystified."

"Good."

"Lai mentioned another incident . . . ?" Wing probed.

"Roadtrain tried to flatten us near Fitzroy."

"Anything that needs, er, explaining to the local authorities?"

"No. I missed the bastard."

"I see." Wing hesitated. "As you requested, I have pressed for the details of Abelard Windsor's death. Everything seems within reason. He was never a very stable man, I take it. He walked out into the bush with a can of Fosters in one hand and a shovel in the other and was never seen alive again."

"Probably the climate pushed him over the edge," Cole muttered. "Jesus, I hate buildup." He wiped sweat from his forehead. "Anything else?"

"No."

"Who looked for him?"

There was the sound of Wing rustling through papers. "It appears the people on the station who might have noticed Mr. Windsor's absence were quite drunk themselves. Finally one of the Aborigines—Sarah is her name—sobered up enough to realize that something was wrong. She called Jason Street. By the time he returned to the station, it was too late."

"Returned? Does he live here?"

"He and Mr. Windsor often drank together for extended

periods. If gossip is to be believed, they shared other tastes in common. Apparently Mr. Street is fond of women of color. He is also a redoubtable fighter. It was Mr. Street who found our people going through the station house. He killed two of them without sustaining any particular injury himself."

Cole's eyebrows went up. "Two of them, huh? Tough bastard. What did the Australian cops think of that?"

"Nothing. Mr. Street caught the people in the act of burglary, they attacked him, and he killed them. Regrettable, but they were only slants after all."

Cole heard and understood the undercurrent of rage in Wing's voice. Many Australians, especially in the outback, had little use for nonwhites. Chinese, in particular.

"What did the autopsy say about Abe?" Cole asked.

"If there was an autopsy, the results weren't included in the report. There was simply a statement that death came as the result of heat prostration. It was quite some time before the body was discovered. Considering the climate, I doubt there was a great deal left to work with."

"I don't like Street's name turning up so often."

"Noted, but not really meaningful. There are so few people in the Kimberley it is unavoidable that the same names would crop up repeatedly, particularly in that Mr. Street was as close to a friend as Mr. Windsor had. Mr. Street even negotiated the Sleeping Dog contract with DSD. Undoubtedly he will be the man designated by the Australian government to appraise the state of the various Windsor leases."

"Keep Street out of here," Cole said flatly.

"We're trying. Unfortunately, while certain members of ASIO are being reasonably cooperative with us, the Australian government itself shows every indication of being lobbied by various powerful members of the cartel."

"Are you certain Street doesn't belong to ConMin?"

"We have found no convincing proof he is ConMin's, and we are looking very diligently. I think Street's attraction for the various members of the cartel stems from the fact that he isn't our man."

"Any potential competitor of ours is a potential friend of theirs?"

"Precisely."

"I assume you're taping this," Cole said.

"As always."

"That will save faxing you the list of camera equipment Erin decoyed to London."

"Everything is already at the station. We removed it at the New York stopover and rerouted it via a private courier. It arrived while you slept." Wing chuckled softly. "ASIO was most surprised when they took apart the crates in the Darwin customs office. It seems they had erroneously concluded that Ms. Windsor was not really interested in photographing their lovely country."

Cole grunted.

"Apparently they expected to find esoteric mining supplies," Wing continued, savoring the bit of deception. "Instead they found only ordinary cameras, lenses, and film. Imagine their disappointment—"

"How did you explain all the electronic gear you installed here?" Cole cut in.

"It hasn't been installed anywhere. BlackWing's office in Darwin will be undergoing an expansion soon. We simply ordered and warehoused everything in advance to make sure all was at hand when we needed it."

Cole smiled at the satisfaction oozing from every syllable of Wing's speech. Then amusement faded from Cole's expression. "Just one more thing."

"Yes?" Wing said warily, hearing the change in the other man's tone.

"Lai is on the first transport out of here."

"That would make Uncle Li most unhappy."

"Tough shit."

"Lai is experienced in specialized communications and in computer programming with application to mineral surveys. She will be invaluable."

"Not to me."

"You sound like a man with an emotional investment in the subject. Perhaps even like a man still in love?"

Dispassionately Cole decided it was just as well Wing was on the other end of a very long communications link. Cole would probably regret delivering Wing in pieces to his too-clever Uncle Li.

"Having Lai rub up against me every time I turn around won't start the kind of fire Uncle Li has in mind," Cole said flatly. "The Chen family isn't going to get their hands on any more than half of my half of the mine. Tell Li I'm disappointed in his estimate of my intelligence."

"There is no need to irritate him. He had nothing more in mind when he sent Lai than for her to provide you with the best liaison the Chen family has to offer."

Cole laughed coldly. When he breathed in, a haunting fragrance bathed his senses, calling up buried memories of hot nights and a golden woman crying love as she climaxed beneath him.

Rooting and hooting about love./Mistresses of lies,/ Damn their hot cries.

"Liaison, huh?" Cole repeated. "Is that what you call prostitution in Hong Kong these days?"

There was no answer.

"Listen to me, Wing. Your men—and your thoroughly trained sister—had better treat Erin Windsor's welfare like it's the only hope for the survival of the Chen clan. Because it is. Tell Uncle Li to read between the lines in my file. Do you understand me?"

"I'm pained that you distrust us so much."

"Yeah, I'll just bet you are. Right in the ass. Using Lai as bait was a mistake. Good-bye, Wing. I won't call to give you progress reports. I'm sure your obedient little spy will take care of that for me."

Cole broke the connection and turned to the woman who had been standing silently behind him. His face was expressionless as he looked at her, a golden feminine statue standing in the exact center of a nimbus of light from the doorway. He wondered if she'd always been like that—every movement, every breath calculated to display her extraordinary beauty.

He didn't remember Lai as calculating. He remembered the seething violence of her sexuality, a hunger that had seemed as unforced as the sunlight pouring over her right now.

Grimly Cole measured how young he'd once been, and how old Lai had always been. Without warning his hand flashed out and closed almost gently around Lai's throat. She stood motionless but for the sudden, heavy beat of her pulse beneath his thumb.

"I trust you heard everything," Cole said.

"Yes," she said softly.

"You'll tell your men."

"Yes."

Gray eyes measured the delicate, perfectly formed woman standing before him. Once he'd dreamed of having Chen Lai in his grasp again. Wing must have known that. Certainly Uncle Li had. So the Chen family had made Cole's dream come true. As long as the diamond mine was found, Cole could do whatever he wished to Lai, punish or humiliate or rape her, take anything he wanted from her.

Even her life.

Lai knew her risk as well as Cole did. It was there in the hidden tremors that made her quiver, in the rapid pulse beating beneath his thumb, in the shallow, rapid breaths that touched him across the few inches separating their bodies, in the luminous black eyes that watched him.

But it wasn't fear Cole saw in Lai's glance. She was looking at him as though he was meat and she'd been long without food. The delicacy of her perfume was mixed with the primitive, far more heady scent of female desire. Against the thin silk of her blouse, her nipples showed as hard buttons.

She wanted him.

Cole's thumb moved against Lai's soft throat in what could have been either a caress or a threat. "Such an obedient daughter of China."

She lowered eyelashes the color of midnight. "Thank you," she said huskily, moving her chin slowly, caressing the hard hand at her throat. She shifted, easing forward, flowing against him as she lifted her hand and traced the line of his jaw with her fingertips. "We were always very good together, Cole. I have dreamed of you."

Erin came to the doorway holding two cups of coffee. She saw Lai moving against Cole and Cole's thumb caressing Lai's throat. For an instant Erin was too shocked at the intimate tableau to speak.

Then she wasn't.

"Obviously you have your hands full," Erin said sarcastically. "I'll leave your coffee in the kitchen."

"Stay."

The quality of Cole's voice was like a whip. She found herself automatically obeying. That, too, infuriated her.

"Do you keep pets?" she asked in a clipped voice.

He turned away from Lai and focused exclusively on Erin. "Pets?"

"Sit. Stay. Roll over. Pets."

He smiled crookedly, released Lai, and walked over to

take a cup of coffee from Erin. "No pets, honey. Nothing would have me."

"Really? I'll bet there's a Venus-flytrap close by with your name on it."

Cole's laughter was lost as the beat of a helicopter's rotor blades washed over the house, the sounds magnified by the humidity.

"Tell him we'll be out in a minute," Cole said.

The words were for Lai, but he didn't look away from Erin as he spoke.

Lai turned and left the room. Not once had she looked at Erin.

Over the rim of the coffee mug, Cole measured the depth of Erin's anger. He regretted it, but now wasn't the time to do anything about it. He was too angry about her lack of trust in him to be civilized on the subject. Cautiously he sipped the black coffee, found it hot but not scalding, and drank it without ceremony. The sound of the helicopter blades diminished to a lazy *whap* . . . *whap* . . . *whap* that told of a machine throttled down to idle.

"Ready to fly?" he asked her. "Maybe by the time we get back, Wing's army will have the new plumbing straightened out for a shower and a washing machine."

The casual words enraged Erin. She thought about refusing the conversational gambit but decided she would appear even more foolish than she already felt after displaying her jealousy.

"Just wear your clothes when you shower," she said, trying to sound as matter-of-fact as he had. She didn't succeed. She'd never been a very good actress. "A shower gets the clothes clean enough. I did it all the time in Alaska."

"Washing clothes with you in them, huh? Sounds like fun."

The sensual teasing was unexpected, baffling her even as it made her more angry. "It's a game for one," she said in a clipped voice. "Like solitaire."

"That doesn't sound like fun."

"Don't worry. I'm not the only woman in the Kimberley whose clothes need washing."

"You're the only one whose clothes I want to wash."

Her breath came in hard. "My God, I know I was stupid to talk about love, but even stupidity has its limits. I'm not blind. If I'd come in a few minutes later, Lai would have been all over you like a rash."

"But I wouldn't have been all over her."

"Bullshit," Erin said angrily.

The sunlight that had changed Lai into a diminutive golden statue sent streamers of fire through Erin's hair and transformed her eyes to brilliant green gems. Unlike Lai, Erin was unaware of her own allure, her color and heat and shimmering life.

Cole wasn't. He wanted Erin until he had to look away or reach for her; because if he reached for her now, she would refuse him. He didn't trust his own temper if that happened. He was never at his best during buildup and he knew it.

"Don't let Uncle Li get away with it," Cole said, when he could trust his voice not to betray his rage.

"With what?"

"Putting Lai between us."

"You should have thought of that sooner. You sure as hell didn't mind where Lai was standing a few moments ago."

He made a throttled sound. It had been a long time since he'd lost his temper, but he felt it slipping away now. His head ached, the scab on his thigh pulled with every motion, he hadn't slept more than a handful of hours since Los Angeles, the temperature at the station was well over one hundred, the humidity wasn't far behind, and now Erin was watching him like a stranger, wary and distant, like she'd never been tangled with his naked body and whispered her love.

"Look—," he began harshly.

"I did," she cut in. "Unlike you, I didn't like what I saw." Then, before she could stop herself, she asked, "Who is she?"

"Wing's communications specialist," Cole said through his teeth.

"You know what I meant. Who is she to you?"

He slammed his coffee mug down with enough force to shatter it. Before the pieces hit the floor he took a long stride forward, coming so close to Erin that she had to tilt her head back to see his eyes.

Nothing in his eyes comforted her, but she didn't back up an inch.

"To me," he said in a low, savage voice, "Lai is a living, breathing reminder of how rock stupid a man is to trust a woman's cries of love. Abe had the right idea about women. Fuck them, but don't love them."

Abruptly Cole turned and headed toward the back of the house. "Lai knows where your new camera gear is. Get it and be out back in three minutes."

27

Abe's station

Angrily Erin walked to the bedroom. *Lai knows where your new camera gear is.*

But Erin would happily roast in hell before she'd ask the gorgeous Ms. Lai for a drop of water, much less anything as important as camera equipment. Fiercely Erin grabbed her battered camera bag and went outside.

The violence of the sun brought her up short. It had been hot and sticky in the house. It was insufferable outside, a steaming sauna with no walls and no exit.

Flies flocked to her.

She waved them away automatically and walked toward the helicopter that was crouched off to the rear of the house. If the chopper had ever had doors, they had been removed.

Cole was talking with the pilot. After a moment the man climbed down and let Cole into the pilot's seat. He looked at gauges and brought up the revs. The rotors whirled more quickly, sending billows of grit into the sky. Artificial wind scoured over the ground, where Abe had made an informal dump for station trash. Beer cans went bouncing and flying out of the yard, only to become tangled in bunches of spinifex.

When Cole was finished with his preflight check, he gestured Erin over. His mouth flattened when he saw that she carried only her old camera bag. Photography was not just her profession, it was her passion—yet she wouldn't even ask Lai where to find the rest of her camera equipment.

That told Cole how angry Erin was, which told him how little she trusted him despite her whispered protestations of love. Her mistrust goaded Cole's emotions even as his mind told him not to lose his temper again.

Don't let Uncle Li get away with it, Cole told himself savagely. *Divide and conquer is the oldest game of all.*

Because it worked. Especially in the hellish climate of Western Australia in the time known as buildup.

But even knowing his opponent's tactics didn't change the emotions snaking through Cole, testing his control. Uncle Li had an uncanny instinct for the jugular, the crotch, the Achilles' heel.

Cole hadn't known that he was Erin's vulnerable point.

He'd just found out she was all three of his.

God damn Uncle Li.

"Buckle up and put on the headset," Cole said curtly over the helicopter noise. "There are sunglasses and sunscreen in the seat pocket. Use them."

She stepped up into the chopper, put on the safety harness, and began looking over the headset. There was no switch for speaking.

"Voice activated," he said loudly as he put on a pair of dark glasses.

She nodded, put on the headset, adjusted it, fished out her own sunglasses, and settled them on her nose. The relief from the intense light gave the illusion of coolness. Unfortunately, it was only an illusion. She reached for the sunscreen, which was also an industrial-strength insect repellent.

"Ready?" he asked.

His voice came clearly through the headset. She nodded again.

He cursed silently at her refusal to talk to him, but he didn't push her. His own temper was still too raw. He hadn't been this angry since Lai had aborted his child.

The realization shocked him.

He brought the revs up until the helicopter was quivering like a racing greyhound waiting to be released. He let it go.

The chopper leaped into the burning sky.

When Erin finished applying the sunscreen, she sat and stared out the window, seeing nothing of the land and too much of a delicate, extraordinarily beautiful face, eyes like black tears watching Cole, worshiping him—and his hand caressing the graceful line of Lai's neck, touching her as though she was made of fire, touching and watching her burn.

With a sense of bafflement and surging anger, Erin wondered if all males were untrustworthy or if she simply had wretched taste in men.

Don't be ridiculous, she told herself angrily. *Cole doesn't owe me anything but his expertise as a diamond prospector. He didn't make any promises, not even the implicit one of saying he loves me. He didn't talk about what would happen after we found the mine or gave up looking for it.*

Fine, it's rude of him to lust after another woman while I'm in the house, but it's hardly the first time in history something like that has happened.

Nothing new.

No big deal.

A close brush, but this time I got away intact. Once I get out of this hell-ridden climate and get a full night of sleep, I'll laugh about the whole thing.

Beneath her bracing thoughts, she sensed darkness condensing, depression growing one slow drop at a time, draining light from her. Knowing that her response was irrational didn't change it, any more than knowing she'd been the innocent victim in an undeclared war seven years ago had changed the extent of her psychic and physical injuries afterward.

At least Cole doesn't keep score with a switchblade. Any scars he leaves on me won't show.

There was little comfort in the thought, but the past had taught her to accept small comforts. Better she found out about Cole now than later. Better the dreams stop now than later.

Better if she'd had the sense never to dream at all.

"We'll fly the east edge of the station first," Cole said finally, breaking the silence. He dropped a map in her lap. "Then we'll do the north leg. Dog One is on the northern edge. I'll keep the chopper at about a thousand feet and go slow."

He paused.

She didn't say anything.

"I've never had a chance to see the station from the air," he continued, trying to keep the irritation out of his voice. "Sometimes you can pick up things you'd miss on the ground. While we fly, try to match features down there with the map."

She nodded to show that she'd heard. Deliberately she unfolded the map and forced herself to focus on it rather than on her foolish feeling of betrayal.

As the chopper bored through the sky, she looked from the map to the landscape below. The variation in the ground surface surprised her after the unrelieved flatness of the area around Derby. On Abe's station there were low ridges and blunt pinnacles of black rock. In between the ridges there were narrow grasslands and sparse trees.

At very rare intervals there were startling bits of vivid green. Cattle trails braided around the fragments of green.

"Seeps and small springs," Cole said finally, seeing her interest. "The black rocks are Triassic limestone outcroppings."

She nodded absently, absorbed in the landscape below.

When she didn't answer him, he turned and looked impatiently at her. The line of her shoulders wasn't as stiff as it had been when she'd gotten into the helicopter. Her mouth was more relaxed, too. She was wrapped up in the land rather than locked in anger at him.

He told himself that it was an improvement.

28

Over Abe's station

To Erin it seemed like a long time before the helicopter reached the edge of the station and turned north to fly the east leg of the boundary. As she watched, more ridges and shallow troughs appeared. There were red rock hills in broken array, like a rumpled blanket thrown over the land. There weren't any roads. She couldn't even see any rutted tracks. The vague, random-looking lines she saw from time to time could have been cattle trails or simply runoff channels for the few months of the year when free water existed in the land. There were no buildings, no canals, no windmills, nothing to suggest that civilized man had ever existed out here or ever would.

Occasionally Erin spotted Kimberley shorthorns or kangaroos below. Cow and kangaroo alike fled from the thunderous dark shadow of the chopper skimming over the rugged land. Once she saw a small blackened circle surrounded by a ring of something that reflected sunlight in countless small silver-white flashes.

"What's that?" she asked, forgetting that she wasn't going to talk to Cole any more than absolute survival required.

He looked away from an intriguing geologic anomaly on the landscape and glanced where her finger was pointing. "Aborigine camp. The black is where the bonfire was."

"What's the shiny halo?"

"Broken beer bottles and smashed beer cans."

She frowned and looked more closely. If people had been there last night or a week or a year ago, there wasn't any sign of them now. There wasn't anything but the chaotic, untamed land.

"Where are the natives?" she asked.

"They could have been gone since last night or since the last wet. I can't tell from up here."

"Where are their shelters?"

"In the dry, they don't need any. In the wet, they use natural stone overhangs, unless they're on reservation land. Then they'll use houses the government built for them."

The helicopter bore along its northern heading, not having completed even one leg of the Windsor station's huge rectangle. As the minutes went by, the sheer scale of the station seeped into Erin. With it came a sense of the relentless demands the land would make on anyone who dared to walk its seamed face.

The depression inside Erin slowly grew, fed by more than her own certainty that she'd once again misjudged a man's intentions. This time it was the land she had misjudged. Despite all she had been told, she hadn't believed that Australia could be as harsh, as empty, as protective of its secrets as Alaska had been. She hadn't believed that the tiny spot called the Windsor station would be physically taxing to explore. There was no ice, no untamed rivers, no jungle, no mountains, not even a real forest— nothing to hide the nature of the country itself. Surely Abe's diamond mine could not be all that well concealed.

Erin hadn't understood how sere the land was, how inhospitable to life. Alaska had the ocean and rivers full of salmon to provide a wealth of food for its natives. The Kimberley Plateau had neither ocean nor reliable rivers. It had no herds of migratory animals, no flocks of edible birds, no flora rich with berries and seeds.

Most of all, the Kimberley had no dance of clean, fresh water.

The longer Erin watched Windsor station unfold beneath the helicopter, the deeper her depression became. She'd been naïve about more than Cole Blackburn.

"My God," she said finally. "How does anyone survive down there?"

"Carefully."

She shook her head.

"It's not as hopeless as it looks," Cole said. "There are small seeps for water and big snakes for food."

The sound Erin made could hardly have been called a laugh. "When you told me how static the Aborigine culture had been until the white man came, I didn't believe it. I do now."

He gave her a questioning look.

"When you told me the natives had been walking for forty thousand years over the biggest, purest deposit of iron ore on earth but they hadn't discovered metalworking, I wondered why. When you told me they had literally walked over huge, pure gold nuggets and never hammered earrings or icons or even bracelets from the gold, I wondered why. I also wondered why they didn't domesticate any animals, invent weaving or shoes, or have any kind of written language."

He waited, watching her intently. There were shadows in her eyes that hadn't been there before, wariness and weariness combined.

"Now I don't wonder why," she said. "The Aborigines

were lucky to survive long enough to bear children who would also be lucky to survive and bear children, who would also be lucky to survive, world without end, amen."

"That's the buildup talking," he said, looking at her flushed face and sweat-slicked skin. "When it's this hot and sticky, life doesn't seem worth the trouble to live. Once it rains you'll feel different about the Kimberley."

She glanced from the ground to the sky. The odd, distinct river of clouds that poured in daily from the distant Indian Ocean had gradually become more than a dark column. It had widened at the edges until it was a hazy lid over the land. Distinct thunderheads billowed in slow motion, lazily eating the hot sky. Searing white on top, slate gray on the bottom, the clouds promised an end to the claustrophobic humidity and heat.

"I wish the clouds would quit strutting and get down to work," she said.

He smiled crookedly. "No, you don't. Once the wet sets in, we won't be able to go prospecting. We'll be grounded."

As he spoke, his gray glance went over the gauges. Frowning, he flicked his index finger against the fuel gauge. The needle wavered, rose, then fell steeply, only to rise once more, indicating a nearly full tank.

"Problems?" she asked.

"The pilot told me this gauge wasn't very reliable on the top end. If I hadn't checked the fuel level manually, we'd be heading back right now."

"What about the bottom end?"

"He didn't say." He looked at her. "Don't worry, honey. The chopper is mechanically sound."

"How do you know?" she retorted. "You didn't have time to go over it the way you did the Rover we rented."

"The pilot had just flown in from Dog Three. He topped

off the tank because he was expecting to fly us all over the station. I made sure he didn't have a chance to bugger anything after he found out he was staying behind."

Cole's casual anticipation of sabotage startled Erin. "You really don't trust anyone, do you?"

He shot her a sideways glance. "Neither do you. You don't even trust me."

"I trust you to find the diamond mine," she said evenly.

"But not to keep my hands off Lai, is that it?"

"That wouldn't be very bright of me, would it, considering the touching scene this morning?"

"Erin, for Christ's sake—"

"Forget it," she interrupted tightly. "All you promised me was your best effort at finding a diamond mine. The rest of it was just proximity and adrenaline. Subject closed."

"Shit, lady, you're really trying to make me lose my temper, aren't you? If you think—"

She yanked off her headset, cutting off his words.

He came within an inch of grabbing the earphones and slamming them down over her stubborn head. The ease that she set fire to his temper amazed him. Even as he told himself to cool off, sweat trickled into his eyes. He wiped his face on his bush shirt and his palms on his shorts. Within moments, his skin was sticky with sweat once more.

It would get worse before it got better, hours and days and nights and more days of relentless heat, stifling humidity, the sun a hammer flattening everything, the air a torpid beast suffocating whatever survived the sun's savage onslaught.

"God *damn* this weather," Cole said viciously.

Erin didn't hear him. Her headset remained in her lap, allowing the helicopter's noise to cut her off from the man she'd given too much of herself. But that was the way she'd always been—all or nothing at all, life taken at full tilt or full stop, nothing in between.

Even Hans's brutality hadn't changed that. Nothing would. It was simply the way she was.

The world shifted sharply, almost angrily, as Cole changed the heading of the helicopter, turning it onto the short north leg of the station's nearly rectangular holding.

Erin positioned the map to match the new direction and looked down at the land once more, watching for something new, something different, something to lift her spirits. She saw ground that was seamed, worn, bleached, a land lying exhausted beneath the combined weight of humid air, sunlight, and incomprehensible time.

Unhappily she admitted to herself that in many ways Crazy Abe's legacy was as bitter a disappointment as finding Cole in Lai's arms. Both Cole and the legacy had seemed to promise Erin a new world, a world where she could shed the dead weight of the past, freeing herself to explore the possibilities of life.

Both legacy and man had promised her hope.

Both had proved to be less than they seemed.

Crazy Abe's legacy was a steamy, gritty, time-ridden hell. Cole Blackburn was a man who couldn't resist the lure of one woman even while he was another woman's lover.

The dream was becoming a nightmare. She was alone and unarmed in the killing fields of the diamond tiger.

29

Over Abe's station

Broodingly Erin unfolded another panel of the map, held it against the hot air boiling through the open doors of the helicopter, and went back to the solitary game of matching land features with marks. The only useful marks on the map were the ones Cole had carefully written in. His symbols indicated the rare seeps and important geological boundaries, the dry watercourses, and the random lumps of limestone poking through the rusty surface, bringing relief to a land worn nearly flat by time.

A line of compact gum trees showed startlingly green against the landscape, catching her eye. She looked more closely, saw that the trees traced an otherwise invisible watercourse between two ragged black lines of limestone, and checked the map. Frowning, she looked down again. After a moment she picked up her headset and put it on.

"Are we still flying the northern leg?" she asked.

Cole shot her a glance. Behind the sunglasses her eyes were unreadable shadows. "Yes."

"Headed for Dog One?" she asked.

"Yes."

"Then we have a problem." She pointed to the trees below and then to the map. "The northern boundary is here.
Dog One is here. We're here."

"And right here," his finger stabbed the map, "is something I want to look at."

"What?"

"Those limestone ridges. I think they might be remnants of an ancient reef, but they could have formed in
some other way."

"What difference does it make?" she asked.

For a moment he was tempted to ignore her cool pur-
suit of geological facts and make her talk about something more personal. But he didn't. If she separated
herself from him any more, she would be brought down
and gutted as quickly as a lone lamb found by a wolf
pack.

He and she had to stand together—if not as lovers,
then as business partners.

"If the ridges were part of a reef, the coastline was
nearby," he said evenly. "Where there's coast, there's
beach. I'd love to find another Namibia. Except the beach
sands here would have been changed to sandstone, unless
the sandstone has already been eroded away a grain at a
time, making loose sand all over again."

"Is that possible?"

"Where do you think the sand in the deserts came
from, if not from rock?"

She blinked. "I never thought about it. You mean sand
becomes sandstone becomes sand becomes sandstone?"

"World without end," Cole said, echoing Erin's earlier
words. "The surface of the earth has been recycled again
and again as continental plates meet and devour each
other. Nothing survives subduction intact, not even diamonds. But the Kimberley Plateau hasn't been recycled

for a billion and a half years. It's the oldest big land surface on earth, which means the diamonds that were eroded out of their mother pipe could still be around somewhere, rounded off and gathered into placer pockets, waiting for us to find them."

He twisted the collective control, dropping the helicopter toward the ground between the ragged ranges of hills. As the chopper descended into a clearing in the gum trees, dust and grit boiled up from the ground.

As soon as the rotor settled into a lazy rhythm, she reached for her harness.

Cole's hand locked around hers. "Wait."

Eyes narrowed against the brilliant light that penetrated even the sunglasses' deep orange tint, he looked at the patches of dappled shade thrown by trees and at the thicker shadows cast by rocky knobs.

One of the shadows separated and began to move toward them.

Cole put his hand back on the controls. "See it?" he asked.

For a time she didn't. She stared intently at the dappled light and shade beneath the gum and acacia trees. Then her breath came in hard as she recognized the dusty black hide and thick curving horns of a water buffalo.

The animal lowered its head, preparing to drive off the interloper.

"My God," she said. "It's huge!"

"Mean, too."

Cole brought up the revs and held the helicopter at a hover a few feet off the ground.

The sudden sound and movement made the water buffalo cautious. It stopped and watched balefully.

"Are there any more around?" she asked.

"No. The bulls are solitary except at mating time."

"Like men," she said coolly.

The bull charged before Cole could answer.

He raised the helicopter until the skids were ten feet off the ground. The water buffalo passed beneath the hovering craft, slowed, and slewed around to face its elusive enemy.

Cole held the chopper tilted in a position that sent the maximum amount of dust and grit in the animal's eyes. After a few minutes the bull turned and trotted away in disgust.

"Reminds me of Abe," Cole said over the noise of the engine. "Angry, alone, and working hard to stay that way."

"When Abe's anger wore thin, he must have been a desperately lonely man."

"What makes you think it ever wore thin?"

"Anger always does."

He looked closely at her face, but her sunglasses still concealed any emotion. "Is that why you left Alaska?" he asked. "Did your rage at life finally wear thin and leave you lonely?"

She tilted her head, thinking about it. "I suppose that's part of it. What's your excuse, Cole? What did life do to you that turned you into a solitary rogue?"

"I trusted a woman who said she loved me."

Erin became unnaturally still. "Lai?"

"Lai," he agreed.

"What happened?"

"The usual. She didn't love me."

"Did you love her?"

He shrugged. "What's love? I wanted her."

With that Cole landed the helicopter. Instead of getting out immediately, he cut back on the revs and watched the bush where the bull had disappeared.

Nothing moved but leaves tossed by the rotor's artificial wind.

After a time he throttled down to an idle. No shadow came drifting up from among the trees to challenge the helicopter's right to land.

"Stay here," he said.

She would have argued, but without the fanning action of the rotor, the heat was unbearable. She didn't want to get out and slog over soft ground beneath the full weight of the sun for no better reason than defying Cole Blackburn.

Keeping one eye on the bush where the bull had disappeared, Cole walked toward one of the many unremarkable dark rocks that poked through the soil. The sound of steel on stone rang through the wilderness as he chipped off a sample with his rock hammer. Beneath the rough black exterior, the stone was a smooth shade of cream. He took samples from other black rock knobs before he returned to the helicopter.

By the time he climbed in, he was as wet as if he'd been swimming.

"Well?" Erin asked.

"Looks a lot like the Windjana formation, which means a reef. I won't know for sure until I look at these under a microscope."

"Do you have one?"

"Back at the station. Wing is a thorough man. What he doesn't think of, Uncle Li does."

"Anything to keep their diamond prospector happy, is that it?" she asked, trying to keep the acid from her voice.

"That's it," Cole agreed curtly. "Unlike some people, the Chens know just where their bread is buttered."

The chopper leaped into the hot, wet air and climbed to a thousand feet. Ten minutes later they descended near an irregular depression. Gradually Erin realized that the hole was man-made rather than natural. A tunnel gaped off to the side.

"Dog One," Cole said laconically.

As soon as he turned off the engine, heat wrapped around them in a thick, invisible shroud. He peeled off his bush shirt and dropped it behind the seat. She plucked at her own top, trying to create a breeze.

"Take it off," he suggested. "We're the only people in a hundred miles."

She shot him a sideways look. "I'll survive."

"Suit yourself."

He bent and reached behind her seat. She looked everywhere but at the swirling masculine patterns of hair that covered his chest. When he straightened, he was holding a large canteen. He unscrewed the top and handed it to her.

"Drink."

The water was warm and a bit stale. She quickly drank her fill and handed the canteen back to him. He shook his head.

"More," he said. "You're used to Alaska. Until your body gets used to the Kimberley, you'll have to drink much more water than you think you need."

When she'd drunk enough for his satisfaction, he took the canteen and drank. Only then did he get out and walk toward the hole in the ground that was the only sign of Sleeping Dog One's existence. He didn't look behind to see if Erin was following.

She yanked off her harness, grabbed her camera case, and dropped to the sunstruck ground. Instantly beads of sweat gathered all over her skin. She felt like she had just stepped into a pizza oven filled with wet socks.

There were no signs, no stakes, no fences to show that the land held anything but the random debris of a failed mining effort. Dog One had been worked, but never in an organized way. A rusty wheelbarrow stood on its pitted wheel beside the entrance. A pick and shovel had been discarded in the spinifex. The ore dump was so close it had eroded into the mine's entrance, threatening to seal it.

"Doesn't look like much," she said.

"It isn't."

Inside the tunnel mouth, out of the sun, the air was a bit cooler. She took off her sunglasses and let her eyes adjust to the darkness. When she turned and looked back toward the entrance, the violent contrast of sunlight and the black outlines of the roughly hewn mine fascinated her. She dug her camera out of the bag and went to work, trying to capture the elemental difference between dense velvet shade and a sun that made her believe in hell.

In Alaska light and darkness had been divided into huge, nearly seamless blocks of time. In Australia, time was shards left over from a primordial explosion. The difference fascinated her in a way she could express only through photographs.

Lost to everything else, she looked at the black and incandescent world through the camera lens.

After going farther into the tunnel Cole turned to see what was keeping Erin. When he realized what she was doing, he switched on the electric lantern he'd brought and gave his attention to the tunnel wall itself. The shoring was rude but still effective. With mining, if with nothing else, Abe had been a careful man.

Satisfied that the tunnel was reasonably safe, Cole went farther in, descending with each step. Here Abe had followed the lamproite sill to a point where it spread out in a lateral dike. There Abe had stopped.

Nothing had changed since Cole's last visit to Dog One. The walls were still dull lamproite except where Abe had misjudged the slope of the ore and had had to backtrack. The tunnel ended abruptly where Abe had lost the lamproite dike and given up, for the quality of the diamonds simply hadn't repaid the work of digging them out. Only gem diamonds repaid the cost of mining.

As Cole retreated, he studied each dead end where the tunnel strayed from the line of the lamproite intrusion. He examined the walls of these failed tunnel offshoots carefully, looking for any sign that Abe had accidentally cut across a paleo-streambed, a paleo-beach, or any stratum that might have been laid down by moving water.

Cole didn't find anything to raise his heart rate.

Erin's voice floated back through the darkness. He shined the light on his watch, saw that an hour had passed, and shook his head in amusement as it occurred to him that he'd finally found a woman who wouldn't be bored on a prospecting expedition.

"I'm coming," he called. He flashed the light back the way he'd come and walked quickly.

"Find anything?" she asked as he emerged from the darkness, pushing a perfectly shaped circle of light in front of him.

"Nothing new."

When he walked forward, the light glanced off a small pile of rubble that had been pushed against the wall. Something shimmered darkly in the little mound.

"What's that?" she asked.

Cole played the light over the mound again and said, "Diamond ore."

Erin made a startled sound and bent down to scoop up a handful of the rocks. In the yellow light of the electric lantern, the ore looked as common as mud. The few tiny crystals embedded in the ore were the color of camp coffee and nearly as opaque.

"These don't look anything like diamonds," she protested.

"You're thinking of gem diamonds. Those are bort."

For a few more moments she studied the bits of ore and minute, ugly diamonds. "I don't see any green crystals."

"If there were any, Abe would have been buried in diamond buyers. But they rarely came out here."

"Didn't Abe ever leave the station?"

"He never went beyond the store in Fitzroy Crossing. He had plenty of money for equipment and food and Fosters lager. That was as much as he needed from civilization."

"He really didn't like people, did he?"

"People hem you in and betray you," Cole said. "There's a freedom out here that's addictive."

"You and Abe were a lot alike. Once burned, forever shy."

"You should know, honey. You're backing away from the fire as fast as you can." Cole flashed the light toward the entrance. "There's nothing for us here. Let's go."

Without a word she turned and walked toward the searing sunlight that crouched at the mouth of Dog One's tunnel, waiting for prey.

30

Washington, D.C.

"No," Matthew Windsor said. "Street has worked too many sides of too many political fences. I don't trust him."

"ASIO vouches for him," Nan Faulkner said curtly, stubbing out her cigarillo. "So does MI-Six."

"MI-Six has vouched for a lot of traitors."

Faulkner swore, lit another cigarillo, and watched the man who sat opposite her broad teak desk.

"I could make it an order," she said, exhaling a stream of smoke.

"You've got my resignation. Use it."

"I'd rather use you." She drummed her fingers on the desk, then reached a decision. She opened the belly drawer, pulled out a battery-operated tape player, and set it on the desk. "Listen to this."

She punched a button and the tape began to play.

Windsor looked sharply at Faulkner, then listened intently. The first voice was male and unfamiliar. The second voice was Cole Blackburn's. The conversation made it clear that Cole had been employed to find the diamond mine regardless of whatever it cost—including Erin Windsor's life.

"I recognized Blackburn's voice," Windsor said when the tape stopped running. "I presume the other man was Chen Wing?"

"A good guess." She smiled thinly. "But then, you're good at what you do. Yes, it was Wing."

Windsor waited.

"You're not stupid, Matt," Faulkner said impatiently. "You know what this means."

"Tell me what you think it means."

"Cole Blackburn isn't the loose cannon we thought he was. He's in the pay of an ambitious Hong Kong clan run by a cunning, ruthless old bastard who happens to be Chen Wing's uncle." Faulkner waited, but no comment came from the big, impassive man who sat opposite her. She exhaled smoke and made a disgusted sound. "Your daughter's life is on the line and you've got nothing to say?"

"Erin's life has been on the line since she was named Abelard Windsor's heir."

"Shit." Faulkner sucked in hard, making the cigarillo's narrow tip glow. "We made a mistake not taking Blackburn out of the game, and you know it."

"No, I don't know it. Nothing I just heard proves he signed up as Erin's assassin."

Faulkner gave him a look of disgust. "Wing says nothing matters after the mine is found, and Blackburn doesn't say squat about it."

"That doesn't prove he—" Windsor began.

"Jesus, Matt," Faulkner cut in angrily. "I thought you'd be happy to hear we're sending a bodyguard in for your daughter. Otherwise she'll die as soon as the mine is found and the Chen clan will control half of the mine outright and you know it as well as I do."

"The Australian government—"

"No!" Faulkner said, slashing across Windsor's words. "The Aussies won't lift a finger. The boys down under would be more than happy to stick it up the cartel's ass and break it off. They're still mad as hell about the Argyle mine."

"That doesn't mean Blackburn is an assassin. He's spent his whole life avoiding being owned by anyone or anything. Why would he suddenly change his pattern?"

"Money," she said succinctly.

"He's been offered money before. Lots of it. He turned it down."

"Pull your head out of your ass. If Sleeping Dog Mines is half what we suspect it is, a whole lot of set patterns will change real quick. If Blackburn is somebody's mole, this would be the score that would bring him to the surface."

"I still don't buy it."

"I'm not selling," Faulkner said coldly, "I'm *telling*. Europe is going through the biggest economic restructuring since they scragged the czar, the Soviets are flat starved for international currency, and the cartel is the biggest cash cow they have. If the cartel goes under, so do the Soviets. We don't want that to happen, babe. We have to control that fucking mine!" She blew out a dense burst of smoke. "I've taken a lot of flak over your refusal to recommend Thomas as your daughter's diamond expert."

"Thomas is CIA."

"You bet your ass he is. That's the whole point."

"No. The point is that he would trade Erin's life for the mine any time he got an offer." Windsor watched Faulkner, seeing the new lines of strain. "Who's squeezing you?"

"You know better than to ask. I sure as hell know better than to answer."

Faulkner smoked in tight silence for a few moments before she closed her eyes and went on wearily.

"I shouldn't tell you this, but if I can't trust you I might as well cut my throat and get the waiting over with." She stubbed out her half-smoked cigarillo. "Either we give Jason Street a letter of introduction to Erin or we can forget all the strategic minerals we've been getting from Con-Min. South Africa won't sell them to us. Neither will the Soviets. Which means the U.S. will be shit out of luck real quick."

Silence was Windsor's only answer.

"Say something, Matt."

"Like what? I'm having a hard time believing that ConMin is willing to go that far over a diamond mine that may or may not exist."

"Oh, they're willing. Not eager, mind you, but willing. You know where Erin is. Call her. Use my phone."

"No."

Faulkner looked across her desk in blank disbelief. "What?"

"I was ambitious once. I came close to destroying Erin by using her as an unwitting source of disinformation for a Soviet agent known as Hans Schmidt."

Faulkner sat very still. She'd read the file and wondered about Windsor's role. Now she knew.

"I told myself it would be all right," Windsor said. "I'd gone over Schmidt's file until I had it memorized. I'd questioned other sources. If he wasn't a Soviet, he would have been everything a father could want for his daughter—intelligent, strong, ambitious, a real comer. He seemed very much in love with Erin. She was certainly in love with him."

"And if you doubled him," Faulkner said, "you'd have had a direct pipeline to the Kremlin at a time when the U.S. was spending too many days on yellow alert."

"Yes," Windsor said simply. He closed his eyes for a moment, knowing he couldn't conceal the old echoes of pain, rage, and shame from Faulkner's shrewd black eyes.

She sighed. "Don't blame yourself. You had no way of knowing Hans got off by cutting up girls."

"No, but if I'd told Erin that Hans was a Soviet agent, she would have broken the engagement. As it was . . ." Windsor's voice faded.

"As it was, your daughter ended up in the hospital. It wasn't your fault. And you got even," Faulkner pointed out with a thin, cold smile. "You got even but good."

There was silence for the space of several breaths. Faulkner waited.

Finally Windsor began talking again.

"I'm no longer sure about absolute right and absolute wrong," he said slowly. "I did what I thought was right, what was necessary, what was useful, and I got a little gold star in my file because the information Erin innocently passed on to her loving fiancé threw the Soviets off the scent of our secret negotiations with Iran for a whole three weeks."

"Every hour of that time was vital," Faulkner pointed out. "We made some real gains, Matt. We came very close to getting the moderates in power."

"Close, but no cigar. For that my daughter was beaten, raped, and tortured by a sadist. Erin hasn't trusted or loved me or any other man since that day. *Seven years*. She's not even thirty. She's got a whole lifetime of nightmares and distrust and loneliness ahead of her."

Faulkner grimaced but didn't disagree.

"Every second I stayed with her in the hospital," Windsor said quietly, "I swore that I would never knowingly use an innocent—*any* innocent—again. Ours is a game for informed, consenting adults." He met Faulkner's dark glance. "The answer is still no."

The door to Faulkner's office opened. Two men came in and stood at either side of Windsor.

With a great effort he throttled the rage that made his body rigid. If he lost his temper, there would be no chance of helping Erin at all.

"House arrest?" he asked in a clipped voice.

"I'm sorry," Faulkner said simply. "A letter went out to your daughter yesterday. Jason Street will be on the Windsor station by tomorrow. Erin will be safe."

31

Argyle mine
Australia

Hugo van Luik had forgotten how godforsaken diamond grounds and diamond mines could be. The Argyle mine was in a place so desolate and remote that workers had to be flown in, given room and board, and then flown out at regular intervals, like military personnel at a hardship post. The place was a bleak celebration of technological efficiency, an orderly assembly of barracks and mess halls, power shovels, ore crushers, conveyor belts, and X-ray tables. Argyle produced diamonds with mechanical regularity, even if it crushed some promising gemstones in the process.

Van Luik only wished the process crushed more. Diamond grit was useful. At the moment, gemstones weren't.

Sighing, he leaned back into the Otter's uncomfortable seat. He was relieved to have the obligatory visit to the Argyle mine behind him, complete with still photos of men in suits shaking hands and smiling into the camera. Van Luik no longer cared for the politically important process of pressing flesh and giving personal assurances to strangers that their lives were important in the international economic scheme.

Yet he'd played his role with all the skill of the actor he'd once wanted to be. He hadn't endured the tour out of respect for the Argyle mine and its huge output of muddy industrial bort or its modest numbers of tiny pale-pink or straw-yellow gemstones. A Japanese syndicate had recently been sniffing around Argyle, considering the purchase of the mine.

Van Luik wished them well.

Anything that would keep the Japanese from experimenting with better and cheaper ways to produce industrial diamonds was a plus for ConMin. If the Japanese purchased Argyle, it would be something of a relief. The Japanese would be more sophisticated and less impatient with the delicate balancing act among the diamond cartel's members than Australia was.

Van Luik tried to ignore the exquisite tendrils of pain infiltrating the nerves behind his eyes. The plane bucked in the torrid, seething currents of afternoon air. The buildup was on, bringing with it a wet heat that heightened van Luik's headaches and made the blinding tropical light a relentless source of pain. He closed his eyes and endured.

Not until the twin-engine Otter banked over the shimmering, man-made sprawl of Lake Argyle and lined up for a landing at Kununurra did van Luik open his eyes, mop his flushed face and sweaty neck with a handkerchief, and prepare to deal with the real reason he'd come to Australia.

Grimacing at a deep thrust of pain, he squinted out the window. River swamps, low-rising red rocks, scrubland, and a town like a crusty rash spread below him. As the plane descended, the temperature rose. The climate was as close to hell as a living man could expect to endure. It made van Luik question the sanity of the English settlers who had chosen Western Australia for their home.

The Otter touched down smoothly on the sun-softened tarmac and taxied to the mining company tiedown next to the small tin-roofed passenger terminal. The cabin steward popped the door and lowered the stairs.

"There's your flight, right on time, sir," the steward said, pointing to an aircraft that had appeared in the south and was headed straight in for a landing. "It will leave in ninety minutes."

Van Luik grunted his understanding and headed for the terminal. The real purpose of his visit would take only a few minutes, but he expected it to be no more pleasant than his tour of Argyle had been. Given a choice, he would never have taken the chance of being seen with Jason Street.

But van Luik hadn't been given a choice.

Part of the reason was that the letter he carried was too important to be entrusted to any ordinary courier. The more pressing issue was that van Luik's employers were unhappy with his handling of Abelard Windsor's legacy. Being dispatched as an errand boy without company planes and executive luxury was a sign of just how deep ConMin's displeasure went.

The message between the lines was quite simple: If the matter of the mine wasn't resolved to ConMin's satisfaction, Hugo van Luik was as expendable as Jason Street.

The Dutchman felt a damp chill as he walked into the heavily air-conditioned building. The change in temperature was welcome, but it caused an explosion of pain behind his eyes that loosened his knees. There were a half-dozen people in front of the Ansett airlines ticket counter—two barefoot Aborigines in jackaroo hats and denim pants, and an outback wife with a screaming baby and two shrill, quarrelsome children.

Van Luik headed for the louvered swinging doors beneath the sign that said PUB. The interior was mercifully dim. Jason Street sat on one of the five stools that lined the zinc bar, talking to the dumpy woman who was the bartender. Unhappily van Luik eyed the big man in his dusty khakis and unpolished boots. A broad-brimmed hat with a snakeskin band was pushed back on Street's head, revealing a sharp demarcation between his weathered face and the pale skin normally covered by the hat.

"Now there's a weary tourist if ever there was," Street said cheerily to him. "Hey, mate, might you be interested in an outback tour?"

Van Luik forced himself to smile. "Not at this time, but I'll be bringing my wife on my next trip. Perhaps we could work out an itinerary that would not be too strenuous?"

Street smiled and turned to the barmaid. "Two ales, luv, and one for yourself too."

The woman produced two cans of Castlemain ale, pulled the metal tabs on them, and slid them across the bar. Street picked both up and led van Luik to a small table in the darkest corner of the little pub. Behind him the barmaid pulled the tab on a third can and retreated to a chair behind the cash register.

"Here you go, mate," Street said.

"I am not your mate," van Luik said in a vicious tone that went no further than Street's ears.

Street slouched in a chair, took a pull from his drink, and grinned. "Bit irritable, aren't we? Heat getting us down?"

The Dutchman turned his back on the rest of the room so he couldn't be overheard. "Speak softly, *foutre*."

Street knew enough French to know he'd been insulted. He smiled more widely. "What are you going to do, mate, fire me?"

"There are dozens of security consultants in the world," van Luik said. "Are you certain I haven't already hired your replacement?"

Street's smile turned cold. "Send him on. I'll even give him the first shot. But he'd better be good, because he won't get another. When I've cut him up for the flies, I'll come for you. You understand, *mate?*"

They glared at one another for a long moment. Finally van Luik broke off the contact, picked up the can, and drank. The ale was lukewarm and bitter.

"What progress have you made?" van Luik asked.

"No progress to make until I get on the station, and you bloody well know it."

"I assume you have something more effective and deniable than a car smash in mind."

Street smiled. "I do, mate. I do."

The pain in van Luik's head was so great that his fingers tingled. He flexed his hands but didn't lift a finger to pinch the flesh at the bridge of his nose.

"Where are the subjects now?" van Luik demanded softly.

"At the station—where else? They've made some short recon trips while information is being collated."

"And?"

"The only shiny stuff they found was their own sweat."

"You're certain?"

"They have rotten radio security," Street said easily. "The scrambler on the satellite uplink is identical to one in my Darwin office. I've read every piece of mail they've sent."

Van Luik took another small sip of ale, wondering why he had the uneasy feeling that Street was lying.

"How is the woman standing up to the rigors of the climate and the land?" van Luik asked.

"The buildup got to her real quick. She's short-tempered as a cat in a bath. She and Blackburn aren't as chummy as they were."

"How close were they?"

"Fucking close."

Van Luik grimaced. "Has she made any progress on finding clues in 'Chunder'?"

"She spends a lot of time reading it."

"Good."

"Why?"

"A person does not work on a puzzle that is already solved." There was silence while van Luik fought against the impulse to squeeze the bridge of his nose. "How is Mr. Blackburn holding up?"

"Mean as a snake," Street said cheerfully. "Going on short rations will do that to a man."

"Rations? Is there a problem getting food to the station?"

"Food isn't the problem. Sex is. They're sleeping in the same room but not on the same blanket."

"Your information is quite complete."

"That's my job," Street said. "If you don't believe me, go to the station yourself."

"I will leave that dubious pleasure to you." Van Luik drew a thin parcel from his suit coat and slid it across the table. The packet was wrapped in bright yellow plastic and secured with string wrapped in a figure eight around two buttons. "Do not open it."

Street glanced down. "What is it?"

"Your entree, a letter of introduction to Miss Windsor." Van Luik reached into his pocket and withdrew a sheet of paper. "This is a photocopy."

Without a word, Street took the sheet, read quickly, and looked up.

"Genuine?" Street asked bluntly.

"Does it matter?"

"Not as long as the signature passes muster."

"There will be no difficulty with the signature."

"Bloody hell. Somebody really twisted the CIA's balls." Street shot van Luik a glance. "ConMin? Or was it their own government?"

Van Luik retrieved the copy, stood, and walked out without a word.

It wasn't until the plane was over the vast Pacific Ocean that painkillers subdued van Luik's savage headache. Just as he slid into sleep, the thought that had nagged beneath the pulses of agony surfaced.

Street had never mentioned having any satellite scrambler except the one van Luik had given him.

32

Abe's station

Dawn was a silent tidal wave of heat and savage light. The Kimberley Plateau's big birds of prey spread dark wings and leaped from their boab tree perch into the rising inferno. Erin crouched over first one tripod and then another, triggering the shutters repeatedly, refocusing, triggering again, moving quickly until the rapid *snick snick snick* of the motor drive fed the last thin strip of film and fell silent.

Even as she reached for the third camera body she'd loaded with film, she sighed and knew it was too late. The moment of the predatory kites' dark awakening was over. She stretched her back, sighed, and began removing cameras from their tripod mounts.

"That's it?" Cole asked, rising from the darkness beneath an acacia tree.

She jumped. She'd been so intent on her work that she'd forgotten he was nearby, watching her, shotgun in hand.

"Yes," she said. "I'm through for now."

She packed up her camera equipment, shouldered all

of it, and looked around at the land that was slowly, inescapably being transformed by the rising violence of the sun. She was learning new rhythms in this strange, austere country. One of them was to rise early and savor the relative coolness.

For a few minutes each morning the sun felt almost welcome.

Almost, but not quite. Despite the fact that dawn was less than five minutes old, the temperature was already in the high eighties. The heavy blanket of air simply didn't let the land cool off, even during the hours of darkness. Each day was hotter and more humid than the one before. Each day the clouds teased and muttered and didn't deliver rain.

Squinting against the early light, she looked up at the black designs made by the Kimberley kites soaring gracefully in a sky that seethed with light.

"I've always wondered," she said softly, watching the kites, "whether birds of prey spend so much time hanging in the sky because they can, or because they must."

"Probably they can because they must."

When Cole reached for the straps of the camera bags, his fingers brushed over the bare skin of Erin's arm. She flinched and stepped back, saying without words that she didn't want his touch or his help.

His mouth flattened as he turned away and started walking. She hadn't fought his order that she never be out of his sight, but she'd made it clear that theirs was now a business relationship. He hadn't liked it, but he hadn't tried to change her mind. Pushing her would only drive her further away.

As they walked the short distance to the station house, the sounds of unfamiliar birds poured from every acacia and gum. Abe's well and stock tank had created a mecca for wild animals of all kinds, making her job of photography easier. In the two days since she'd been at the station, she'd managed to capture fourteen different varieties of local animal life. She'd also learned a gut-deep appreciation of why predators waited at waterholes in dry country.

It worked.

"Which mine are we looking at today?" she asked.

"Dog Four."

"Again?"

He nodded.

"Why?" she asked.

"Because it's close to another site I want to look at."

"Isn't Dog Four where we saw the goanna?"

"Yes," he said.

"Good. I'm having trouble getting a handle on the best way to shoot one."

"With a twelve-gauge."

She smiled despite her vow to keep the relationship between them on a purely business basis. It was difficult now for the same reason it had been difficult in the beginning—Cole's intelligence and quick, deadpan humor were even greater lures for her than any regularity of face or strength of body he had.

He's even bright enough not to try to get in bed with me again, she told herself grimly. *Or maybe it's just that sweet, delicate Lai is taking care of his business.*

Yet even as the thought came, Erin knew it wasn't true. When she and Cole were at the station, he was always near her. They slept in the same room, they ate at the same table, and they flew the land in the same helicopter.

Maybe it's not just for my safety. Maybe he's afraid to be alone with Lai.

Erin's mouth turned down. He hadn't looked afraid when she'd walked into the room and seen his big hand

caressing Lai's neck. He hadn't looked particularly passionate, either. He'd looked . . . suspended, patient, curious, coiled.

Predatory.

A feeling of unease shivered through Erin. Whatever
had happened between Lai and Cole in the past had gone
deep. Love, hate, or both tangled together, it didn't matter. Cole had given Lai more than his body. She'd given
him proof that women were what Abe had called them—
mistresses of lies.

Erin stepped from the uncertain shade of the acacia
grove into the spinifex. The sun was a steaming, searing
shroud wrapping around her. Sweat stood on her skin and
gathered in rivulets between her breasts and beneath her
arms. Flies came at her in ragged squadrons but didn't
land on her. The combination of insect repellent and sunscreen the Australians used actually worked.

She only wished they had a repellent for the insufferable Kimberley climate. Already she could feel herself
becoming surly, tense, wanting to lash out at anything
within reach. She suspected Cole felt the same way, but
he disguised it better.

That, too, irritated her, making her want to pry beneath
his self-control.

"How long does the buildup last?" she asked.

"Until it rains."

She made a disgusted sound.

Cole slanted a sideways look at her. Her pale skin was
already flushed with heat and shiny with sweat. He took
off his hat and dropped it over the burning mahogany of
her hair.

"Where's your hat?" he demanded. "I told you not to—"

"And I told you I can't work with a damned hat flop-
ping and flapping in my eyes," she retorted, cutting
across his words. "Besides, I knew we wouldn't be out in

the sun for more than the time it took to walk back to the house."

She yanked the hat off and shoved it at Cole. He pushed it over her head again.

"Wear it," he said flatly. "Two weeks ago you were sitting on a glacier at the other end of the earth, getting ready for winter. Now you're sitting on a stove waiting for summer. Your body is still trying to figure out what hit it."

"Yours seems to be doing just fine," she said resentfully.

"I was in Brazil. Different stove, same temperature, same season. Stop wasting your energy trying to prove you can take the climate as well as I can. You can't. Give me the bloody camera gear."

He didn't wait for her to agree. He simply stripped the gear from her.

They finished the walk to the station in silence.

When they arrived Lai was waiting at the table that had been set in the shade of a wide white awning. The awning stretched across the back of the house, helping both to shade and to extend the living space. A big white tent had been set up fifty feet beyond the house. The eight Chinese men lived there. They serviced the array of equipment and, Erin suspected, guarded it as well.

Lai looked like golden porcelain, cool and delicate, perfectly formed within her indigo silk slacks and shirt. She nodded politely before she withdrew into the house.

"Doesn't she ever sweat?" Erin muttered beneath her breath.

"Stone doesn't sweat. Sit down. I'll get breakfast. The coffee you make is strong enough to etch stainless steel."

"So is yours."

"Yeah. We make a great team, don't we? Sit there."

Giving him a wary look, she sat down at the table in the chair he'd told her to use. He stacked her camera gear next to her and went into the kitchen. She knew without turning around that he could see her from inside the house, which was why he wanted her in that particular chair. Cursing wearily, she flapped the cloth of her tank top, trying to create breeze.

It just made her hotter.

She dropped the cloth and began rummaging in one of her camera bags for the old photos she kept there along with Abe's poetry. The envelope was becoming soft and rather fuzzy from humidity and frequent handling. The photos weren't. She held them carefully by the edges, looking at each image intently before going on to the next.

"Do you think the secret of the diamond mine is in those photographs?" Lai asked softly.

Erin's breath came in with a startled sound. She wondered whether Lai tiptoed around deliberately or if she simply didn't have enough weight to make sounds when she walked.

"No," Erin said. "But they might tell me the secret of Crazy Abe—why he lived and why he hated and why he died."

"He died of sunstroke," Lai said as she looked over Erin's shoulder at a photograph.

It was Erin's favorite, the one of her grandmother standing on a steep rise with dark, odd-looking rocks and stunted acacias all around, and a tall man standing off to the right watching with hungry eyes. With Cole's help, she'd discovered that many of the photos were taken in the same area as Bridget's Hill, but from different angles and distances. One of the shots showed only the white slash of a woman's skirt poised on the top of a ridge like a star rising over the vast land.

Erin wondered if her grandmother had amused herself climbing the rise while the photographer took other pictures.

"Who is that?" Lai asked.

"My grandmother."

"And the man is your grandfather?"

Erin shrugged. "I don't know."

"Are they still alive?"

"No."

Clear black eyes looked unflinchingly at the photo, then at Erin, then at the photo again. After the space of four breaths Lai turned away.

"Human secrets have little value unless they lead to control," Lai said as she headed back into the house. "Knowing the secrets of the dead is useless. The dead cannot be controlled."

Erin turned to give Lai a startled look, but the other woman had left as silently as she'd come.

Relieved, Erin went back to staring at the haunting picture that had been taken when people now dead were young, vivid, vital, poised on the threshold of decisions that would shape their lives and the lives of those who came after them. She turned the photo over and read again the faded lines.

> *Some love for silver, some love for gold,*
> *We love for the heat that never runs cold.*

On an impulse she bent down and sorted by touch through a camera bag, not looking away from the lines of poetry. After a moment she found the folded sheets of "Chunder." She pulled them up to the table, shook them out, and laid them next to the photograph.

A chill prickled over her skin.

33

Abe's station

When Cole came back out to the table, Erin was motionless, her eyes fixed on the lines of "Chunder."

"Feeling masochistic?" he asked, setting the coffee down.

Erin looked up.

In the light beneath the awning her eyes were a luminous green so pure he couldn't help staring. He'd seen nothing quite so beautiful to him, even the green diamond itself.

"How much does a man's handwriting change over the course of his life?" she asked.

"A lot more before he's twenty-five than after, unless he's sick, drunk, or injured. Why?"

"I think Abe wrote the lines on the back of this photo."

Cole stood close behind her, looking over her shoulder at the photo and the poetry. The longer he compared them, the more he agreed. There was a similarity about many of the letters that went beyond the careful Victorian handwriting style that both brothers would have had, because they'd both attended the same school.

•

"Could be," Cole agreed. "Does it matter?"

"I don't know. It just seems odd that Grandfather would end up with this picture if it had been written on by Abe."

Cole grunted. "Not if they were both sleeping with the same woman."

"What?"

He shrugged. "They might have been your grandparents, but they were human. Your grandmother wouldn't have been the first woman in creation to be engaged to one man and engaged *with* another."

" 'Mistress of lies . . . ' "

"Yeah."

"Well, that would explain why the two of them left for America."

"Especially if she was carrying the wrong man's child."

Erin made a sound of protest. "That's not likely."

"Why not? Birth control and abortion were hit-and-miss in those days, and lust hasn't changed much since Eve seduced Adam into eating from her hand."

"You have a rather bitter view of women."

"I could say the same about your view of men."

Ignoring him, Erin turned the photo over and looked at the glossy, faded image again.

"Is that limestone?" she asked, pointing to the oddly shaped rocks that stood knee and waist high to Bridget McQueen Windsor.

"Probably."

"And underneath the rise?"

"More of the same."

" 'A dead sea's bones.' "

Cole grunted. "When those pictures were taken, Abe was looking for water for his cattle, not diamonds."

"Still, I wonder where this was taken."

"Why?"

"It's as close to a real hill as I've found here," Erin said dryly. "I'd like to see what the world looks like from the top of it."

For an instant his crystalline gray eyes focused completely on the photos in front of her, measuring the steepness of the rise against his unusually precise memories of the land he'd seen at various times on Windsor station. After a few minutes he decided that she was right. There wasn't a hill like that on the station. He doubted that there was a hill like that on the other claims, either. Most of them were on land that was even flatter than the station itself.

"Odd," he muttered, staring at the series of photos again. "It can't be that far away from camp or from a settlement."

"Why?"

"Bridget's dress is wrinkled but not dirty. White gets dirty real fast out here."

He picked up the photo that had been taken from a distance, pulled a loupe from one of the many pockets in his bush shorts, and looked closely at the image.

"I'll be damned," he said after a moment. "That handsome jackaroo is Abe."

"Are you sure?"

"I can see a scar on his left wrist. Abe had one in the same spot, reminder of the day when he was young and foolish enough to rope a brush bull. It nearly did for him. He was lucky he didn't lose the hand."

"He's looking at Bridget with such longing."

"Poor son of a bitch. He doesn't know yet."

"What?" asked Erin.

"It's as clear as the sly, sexy little smile on her face. She wants the man behind the camera, not Abe."

"That must be Grandfather. It was a good match. She stayed with him the rest of her life."

Cole grunted, unimpressed. He moved the loupe slowly, examining the rest of the photo. "I don't see anything that looks like a seep, much less a billabong. But it was the dry when this was taken, which means they were going from waterhole to waterhole."

"Walking?"

"In those shoes? Abe used to ride everywhere before he turned the horses loose to live or die with whatever was left of his cattle. He and his brother and Bridget were probably on horseback, camping out and taking pictures and looking over the best place for the happy couple to build a home."

The savage irony beneath the surface of Cole's words made Erin uneasy. She sensed he was lumping her with her grandmother and Lai and Eve, women who had betrayed the men who loved them.

But Cole doesn't love me, so the comparison doesn't apply. Besides, I wasn't the one who was stirring through old ashes looking for sparks.

He made a sound of surprise, slanted the photo to catch the light better, and peered at a corner through the loupe.

"Find something?" she asked.

"They were camping. There's a pack saddle and dry goods in the shade of one of the distant trees. Can't see a waterhole or anything like the kind of plants a waterhole would support."

"Maybe they carried their own water."

"Doubt it. Water is heavy and horses need a lot. You reach the point of diminishing returns real fast."

She watched him study the photo with an intensity that was almost tangible. It tempted her to grab a camera and take a portrait of him.

Instead, she reached for the coffee and scones he'd brought from the kitchen. As she ate, she thumbed idly through the pages of "Chunder from Down Under." When she remembered what the title meant, she grimaced. "Vomit from Australia." Then she thought how diamonds came to the surface in a violent rush of magma from the depths of the earth.

"Did Abe have a sense of humor?" she asked.

"After a fashion. Why?"

"Would it have amused him to think of diamonds as a kind of cosmic vomit?"

Black eyebrows went up. He turned the full force of his attention on her, making her feel like she'd just been pinned by a megawatt searchlight.

"Yes," Cole said. "Any other thoughts?"

She hesitated, then pointed to the photo where Bridget McQueen stood on the windy rise. "You're going to think I'm crazy, but those rocks look kind of like black swans to me."

For an instant he was motionless. Then he picked up the photo and his loupe.

"No," she said. "Not that way. Put down the loupe and let your eyes kind of go unfocused."

"Like I was drunk?" he asked dryly.

"Why not? Abe seemed to spend most of his time soused to his widow's peak."

After a few moments Cole said, "It's possible those are swans, but the same probably could be said of any ridge capped by lumps of eroded limestone that had turned dark."

"But this isn't just any ridge. This is the ridge where Bridget McQueen stood and smiled at the man who was to become her husband, while Abe stood to one side, thinking she was his."

"McQueen . . . Queen of Lies." Cole frowned. "It fits,

but Abe didn't know diamonds from quartz in those days."

"Would you say he was obsessed with my grand-mother?"

"Probably. For revenge, if nothing else. A man who's been used like that wants his pound of flesh and then some."

Erin looked at the picture but it was Lai she saw, Lai of the flawless features and feline body.

Revenge could easily be an extension of betrayed love.

She glanced up quickly, wanting to ask Cole if it was revenge and hatred that bound him to Lai rather than love. But that would have been the kind of personal question Erin had declared off limits.

"Isn't it possible," she said carefully, looking only at the photos, "that Abe went back to this place many times, as a kind of perverse shrine?"

"It's more than possible. It would have been just like him to go there, drink, remember, and rage away the days until he was too spent to care about anything."

She barely kept herself from asking Cole if he had his own private shrine of betrayal and rage.

"How many brothers and sisters does your father have?" Cole asked absently.

She blinked. "None. He's an only child."

"If we're right about Bridget and Abe, you realize what it means, don't you?" Before Erin could speak, Cole quoted from the verses that had accompanied the dia-monds. " 'Then come to my land/Grandchild of deceit/Blood of my blood/Bone of my bone. . . . ' " Cole looked straight at her. "You're Abe's granddaughter, not his great-niece. You're the 'Descendant of deceit.' "

"Charming," she said, but her tone said the opposite. "Just what I always wanted, an ancestor who was certifi-able."

Cole smiled crookedly. "Don't worry. If there were any bad genes, they gave your father a pass. He's as hard-headed and tightly wrapped as they come."

She started searching through the poem once more. " 'Find it if you can,/If you dare to go/Where the dark swan floats/Over a dead sea's bones. . . . ' Well, that's clear enough," she muttered. "But the next part is beyond me."

"Want me to explain it again?" he offered.

"Pass," she said quickly. "I learned enough yesterday about Aussie sexual slang to last a lifetime."

"You asked."

"And you answered." She grimaced. "Talk about reducing something to its logical absurdity. . . . On the other hand, I have to admit that the man had a knack for double and triple meanings. Look at the title. It can be read as a comment on the poetry, as a comment on how diamonds are formed, and as a comment on diamonds themselves. Not bad. Not pretty, mind you, but not stupid."

Cole waited, watching her long, slender fingers tracing over the poetry. But she wasn't reading. Her eyes were unfocused. He sensed the same intense concentration in her that she normally reserved for photography—or making love.

"Are you sure there aren't any caves on the station or the mineral claims?" she asked finally.

"None that I know of."

She sighed. "Well, it was a nice idea."

"What was?"

"If there were caves or passages through the dead sea's bones, and if you had Abe's warped view of life, you might see a man's penetration of a cave in sexual terms. As for seeing the cave in feminine terms, Mother Earth is a common metaphor."

Cole shot her a surprised look.

"I was an English major in college," she said. "Words

were my passion. Then I discovered photography. Anyway, Abe was supposed to be some kind of literary scholar, wasn't he?"

"A good one, when he was sober. He used to recite Milton and Pope to me while we drank."

"Poor baby."

"Would you believe I liked it? He had an amazing voice."

Erin looked at Cole and realized that she did believe it. He was a man of unpredictable interests.

"But there's a problem with your interpretation of the poetry," he continued. "Several, actually."

"What?"

"No caves."

"We just have to find one."

"Right," he said dryly. "That leaves Abe."

"I don't understand."

" 'Crazy bloke/Drank holy' pretty well describes him."

"Wasn't he ever sober?"

"Yes. That's what I'm worried about. Remember the last lines of the poetry in the will?"

Erin shook her head and started searching through the papers in front of her.

"Don't bother," he said. " 'Goodbye, my Queen of Lies./And I am the King.' This whole thing could be Abe's gigantic joke on the world."

"But the diamonds are real."

"As real as death. 'Secrets blacker than death/And truth it's death to speak./But I will speak to you . . . child of rue.' " Cole's mouth turned down. "It's you he's speaking to, Erin. 'Child of deceit/Cleave unto me./My grave, my bones,/Hear them moan.' It's *you* he's offering death."

"You should have been an English major. You're reading more into the lines than I am." She looked at the watch on his wrist. "How much time before we go prospecting again?"

There was an electric silence before Cole accepted the change of subject. "I'll go run up the chopper."

He turned and went toward the helicopter without another word about death and poetry.

34

Abe's station

Cole checked out the helicopter and started it up. The engine ripped to life and settled down to running steadily. He waited, listening to the engine.

It missed a beat, picked up again.

He checked the gauges. Nothing unusual. He ran the revs up and down and waited.

Again, the engine missed a beat, then resumed smoothly.

He sat and listened to the engine's beat—and the times when it missed. After several minutes he shut down the helicopter and jumped out.

Erin, who was working on her second cup of coffee, looked up from the photos and poetry in time to see Cole open a panel on the chopper and probe the engine's innards.

It wasn't long before he was coming toward her, holding a round metal cylinder in one big hand. She could tell by his walk and the line of his shoulders that he was angry.

"This shoots one day all to hell, and probably two," he said to Erin, holding up the cylinder.

He looked at the sky, hazed by heat. In a few areas clouds were already forming. It was early for the wet to settle in, but the signs were there. Rain could come at any time, shutting down the possibility of finding Crazy Abe's mine until the dry returned.

"Lai," he snarled.

She appeared in response to his summons with a speed that told Erin the Chinese woman had been standing just inside the door, waiting or listening or both.

And Cole had known it.

"Yes?" Lai asked, looking only at him.

"Tell Wing to send down three complete sets of fuel filters for the helicopter. I'll keep the spares with me at all times."

Lai nodded and added a phrase in Chinese.

"Speak English," he said.

"But you understand Chinese very well," she murmured.

"Erin doesn't."

"Why don't you teach her as I taught you?"

The question was simple, but Lai's voice evoked an image of two lovers endlessly intertwined, teaching and learning things that had nothing to do with language. The same vivid sexuality ran through Lai's graceful hand, the fingers slightly curled as though to plead or to hold a man's sex in her palm.

The implied intimacy of the gesture was so great that Erin looked away.

"Call your brother," Cole said in a clipped voice.

Expressionless, Lai nodded and withdrew into the house.

"What happened?" Erin asked.

"Dirty fuel."

"What?"

He unscrewed one end of the filter assembly and pulled out a paper cone. "Feel it."

She ran her fingertip over the cone, then rubbed her fingers together. At first she felt nothing but the fuel. Gradually she became aware of a vague, almost gritty texture. She looked into his eyes, silently questioning.

"You expect some dirt to get into the fuel," he said. "That's why you have filters. But it looks like half the grit in the Oscar Range ran through the system."

"How did the fuel get that dirty?"

"I could have left the cap off," he said neutrally.

"Not bloody likely."

"Thank you."

She shrugged. "It's the truth. You've watched that helicopter like a mother hen with one chick."

"It was our best chance of finding the mine before the wet. Somebody else knew it and buggered the fuel."

"Sabotage?"

"It's what I'd do if I was trying to slow somebody down."

"Or kill him?"

"Yes."

She shivered at the certainty she saw in his eyes.

"They'll try again," he said flatly. "Walk away from it, Erin. From the mine, from the station, from Australia. Nothing is worth dying for, not even God's own diamond strike."

"The arctic taught me that walking away is another way of dying. I came here to find a new way of being alive. I'm staying."

He didn't hear any doubt in her voice. There wasn't any in her eyes. Arguing with her would be worse than useless—it would increase the distance between them, making her even more vulnerable to an assassin.

"Who did it?" Erin asked with a calm she didn't feel.

"It could have happened before the fuel was delivered to the station. More likely, somebody did it right here."

Without thinking, she turned and looked at the door where Lai had retreated.

"Possible, but I doubt it," he said. "Not that Lai wouldn't kill for her family. She would. Hell, she did. But we're the Chen family's best hope of getting a piece of the diamond tiger, and she'll do whatever her family tells her to do."

"Lai killed someone?"

"She was seven months pregnant when Uncle Li ordered her to abort my child and marry another man, a Chinese man who would solidify the Chen family's position in Kowloon. She did it and never looked back."

Erin opened her mouth, but no words came. "I'm sorry," she whispered.

"Why? It wasn't your doing."

She simply shook her head, unable to explain why Cole's past pain was hurting her now. Before she could find words, Lai appeared in the doorway.

"Wing wishes to speak with you."

Cole looked at Erin. "I can't see you from the radio room. Come with me."

Although her eyes widened, without a word she stood and followed him into the stifling rooms of the station house.

"What else has gone wrong?" Cole asked Wing as soon as he picked up the phone.

"Jason Street is on his way to the station."

Cole raked his fingers through his black hair and made a sound of disgust. "What happened?"

"We suspect the Americans threw the Australians a bone."

"Not good. Street was a lucky prospector before he took up running a mine security business."

"There is one welcome factor. Satellite photos don't

show any break in the weather. The monsoons have not materialized yet."

"Damn good thing. Prospecting by Rover is a hell of a lot slower than by chopper. Anything else?"

"No," Wing said.

"Think hard, because I won't be checking in with you tonight," Cole said. "In fact, I won't be checking in at all until we find Abe's mine or until the wet begins, whichever comes first. Erin had an idea I want to follow."

"The diamond mine?" Wing said instantly. "Are you close?"

"Not as close as we were before the fuel was buggered. Go over the files on your men, Wing. At least one of them is cashing two paychecks."

"I will look, but it is doubtful. The men were vetted with exquisite care before they were sent. Is it wise for you to be out of contact so long?"

"Erin won't abandon the hunt, so I don't have any choice. We're going to ground."

"But—"

"Don't send anyone after us you care about," Cole cut in. "Understand?"

He hung up before Wing could answer.

35

Sunlight and humidity turned the Rover into a four-wheel-drive sauna. Erin and Cole had camped the night before on a nameless patch of land beneath an acacia tree. They had awakened to heat and silence, because they were too far from water for any birds to be about. The Rover had consumed the silence. Now the vehicle was being consumed by the searing day.

On the flats some speed was possible. Dog Four had been the most productive of Abe's mines, so there was a road of sorts. Other than slamming on the brakes shortly after dawn to avoid a handful of cows, the ride had been uneventful.

"After Dog Four, where are we going?" she asked.

He flicked a sideways glance at her before he returned to watching the road—it had a tendency to vanish among termite mounds and spinifex.

"Twenty miles beyond Dog Four there's a place where the station land is joined by a mosaic of Abe's mineral claims," Cole said. "I've never been there. From the looks of the map, nobody else has either. But the satellite photo showed a highlands and what could be a karst drainage pattern. Maybe Bridget's Hill is there."

"What's a karst drainage pattern?"

"Water flows underground rather than aboveground. It's common in heavily eroded limestone areas."

"Does that mean caves?"

"Sometimes."

While he spoke, his eyes checked the gauges on the dusty dashboard of the Rover. The electrical system showed a steady charge. The oversized fuel tank was above three-quarters. He wasn't worried about petrol. With the extra cans he had lashed on the Rover, he had ample fuel to check out the most likely spots for a steep limestone outcropping, with enough gas left over to reach a neighboring station before the wet made the country impassable.

Right now he was more worried about keeping Erin alive until the wet than about finding a diamond mine. Jason Street's arrival meant that the Americans were divided about how to handle her legacy, or the rest of the cartel had ganged up and forced Street down Faulkner's throat, or both. No matter what the reason, it left Erin exposed in a way she was too inexperienced to understand.

It had been her American government connections that had prevented an outright assassination.

United we stand, divided we fall.

They were falling.

"It's running a little hot, isn't it?" Erin asked, seeing Cole's frown.

"Not surprising. It's about a hundred and ten in the sun. Close to the ground, where the engine is, the air is even hotter." He looked at her. "Don't worry. The Rover was built to take worse in Africa."

"But I wasn't." She plucked at her cotton tank top in a gesture that had become as automatic as brushing away the outback's relentless hordes of flies.

"I like the way you're built," he said. "Sleek, soft, and sweet. How much longer are you going to punish me for something that happened years before I met you?"

For a moment she didn't believe what she'd heard. Then she did. The flush on her cheeks deepened even as her heartbeat increased. She was aware of Cole with an intensity that had only increased since she'd refused to share his bed.

"If you'd been the one to walk in on a tender little scene between me and a former lover," Erin said finally, "what would you have thought?"

There was a long silence followed by a savage word. "Try trusting me."

"If I didn't trust you, I wouldn't be alone with you in this rolling oven."

"Then why the cold shoulder?"

"Cold? In this godforsaken climate?"

"You know what I mean," he said tightly.

"Call it a period of adjustment."

"Meaning?"

"Meaning I haven't had as much experience as most women my age," she said simply. "When it comes to what I should and shouldn't expect from a lover, I'm still nineteen years old with stars in my eyes. I assumed any man who was my lover would be as exclusively interested in me as I was in him. Childish of me, but there it is." She made an odd gesture that ended up with her fingers plucking at her damp top.

He glanced quickly at her, silently encouraging her to keep talking. It was the first time in days she'd been willing to discuss anything personal.

"When I catch up with my generation," she said, "I'll be able to hand my body over to an attractive man and keep my mind in reserve. But until I catch up, it's a complete package. My mind looks at you and sees an emotional attachment to Lai I can't compete with."

"You're crazy," he said flatly. "I don't love her."

"I didn't say you did. Hate binds every bit as closely as love. Either way, hate or love, Lai has a hold on you."

"Shit." Cole lifted his bush hat, wiped sweat that had been dripping into his eyes, and put the hat back in place with a yank. "Don't you see how easily you're letting the Chen family manipulate you? You're a lamb among some very experienced wolves, and I'm damned if I'll let them cut you up for a snack. If I wanted Lai, I'd be screwing her right now. I don't want her. I want you. And I know I can make you want me."

Erin's breath came in and filled her throat until she ached. "We've been around this track before. You won't rape me and we both know it."

"That leaves ninety-nine point nine percent of the sexual field wide open. Think about it, Erin. I sure as hell have."

They drove in silence through increasing heat and humidity while hot air rose in columns from the land, creating an updraft that sucked in moisture from the Indian Ocean in an endless river of clouds that would grow through the day until it slowly consumed the sky.

That was when the climate went from ugly to unbearable.

That was when the anticipation of rain hung in the air and lightning winked across distant horizons and veils of rain hung down, only to evaporate before touching the steamy land.

That was when friendships and marriages broke apart.

That was when men went troppo and killed their mates. *Divided we fall.*

And there was nothing Cole could do about it except what he'd already done—grab Erin and vanish into the lethal, sultry, unlivable outback.

36

Kimberley plateau
Same day

Cole braked just before the track twisted away from the flats and termitoriums whitewashed by bird lime. The pedal responded sluggishly. He wasn't surprised. There had been a slow leak in the system since the Rover had crashed through the brush to avoid the roadtrain.

He pumped twice and the brake pedal firmed. The Rover stopped close to a termite mound that was as tall as a man. He jumped out, took a rock hammer from the Rover, and began chipping away at the top of the mound. Beneath the white bird lime the mound was a faded rusty shade.

Erin picked up her camera, got out, and winced as the sunlight hammered down on her. She walked out among the mounds with a determined stride. Within minutes she'd forgotten the brutal heat. She was completely caught up in angles and exposures, trying to capture the alien, sun-beaten world where billions of insects built a towering mud metropolis.

When Cole finished hacking at various mounds, he looked around for Erin. She wasn't anywhere in sight.

"Erin," he called. "Where the hell are you?"

A languid, muggy breeze stirred nearby spinifex. The narrow, rasp-edged blades of grass made a secretive sound.

"Erin!"

"In a minute," she called back.

From her voice, she was several hundred feet away, hidden among the towering, broad-based mounds.

He looked at his watch. He'd spent half an hour grubbing around in the termitorium. He hoped she had more to show for the time than he did. Lifting his hat, he wiped his face on his short-sleeved khaki shirt. The cloth was already dark with sweat from collar to hem. He unbuttoned the shirt, mopped his chest with it, and tossed the damp khaki in the Rover.

"Time's up," he called.

No answer came.

"Erin!"

"I'm coming! Just give me a minute!"

Her voice was farther away than it had been before.

He went looking. It took him ten minutes, but he found her crouched amid the termite mounds with her camera at the ready. Her hat was on the ground beside her and she was staring through the viewfinder, heedless of her surroundings.

Cole picked up her hat and stood nearby, waiting until she finished the roll of film. Then he stepped in front of the lens and stuffed her hat down on her head.

Startled, she looked up, realizing for the first time that she wasn't alone.

"Wear the damned hat," he said. "When you're taking pictures you don't think about anything else. If I hadn't been here, you'd have been wonky from sunstroke before you had the faintest idea something was wrong. Get it through your stubborn head. *This isn't Alaska.* Out here, the sun is your enemy. Hear me?"

"Quite clearly." She hesitated, then asked, "How long were you standing there?"

He looked at his watch. "About seven minutes."

"But you didn't interrupt me. Why?"

"You weren't in any immediate danger. I'd rather wait than take a chance on ruining another 'Uncertain Spring.'"

For an instant she thought he was joking. When she realized he wasn't, pleasure rippled through her, disarming her. "I doubt if there's another 'Uncertain Spring' in that lot, but thank you."

"Can you always tell in advance what you'll have?"

She shook her head. "No. That's why I protect the film so carefully. Each shot is unique and unrepeatable. I could have spent the rest of my life in the arctic and never taken another shot like 'Uncertain Spring.' Just as I could spend the rest of my life in the Kimberley and never have the same reaction to it that I'm having now, take the same photos I'm taking now."

"That's what I figured." He gave her a look that was half amused and half irritated. "All the same, the next time I find you in the sun without your hat, I won't wait until you run out of film." Without warning he pressed his thumb against her upper arm and watched to see how long the pale circle remained. "When was the last time you put on sunscreen?"

"When you stood over me after dawn."

"Then you're overdue. Even inside the Rover—"

"—reflected sunlight will burn my Scots-Irish skin to toast," she finished. When the line of Cole's mouth flattened, she said, "I know it's not a joke. I won't forget again."

He let out his breath in a rush of sound and said tightly, "Sorry. I'm not usually so irritable, even during buildup. You have a way of shortening my fuse. Come on. Let's get out of the bloody sun."

"Pity we can't prospect in the dark," she said as she walked beside him to the Rover.

"For all that I've found, we might as well."

"What were you doing, anyway? A vendetta against small segmented beasties?"

Cole swiped at a nearby mound with the pick end of his rock hammer and caught the crumbling bits of earth. He smeared them across his palm and held it out to Erin.

"Dirt," she said.

"Every bit of it," he agreed, leading her toward the Rover.

"So?"

"So I know that the first forty to one hundred feet of earth around here is a fairly homogeneous layer of finely packed soil. Nothing interesting, although I'll look at it through the microscope eventually to be certain."

She blinked. "Those bugs go one hundred feet deep?"

"It's the only way to beat the climate."

"I'll keep it in mind. What were you looking for that you didn't find?"

"Indicator materials that would reveal a diamond pipe, or rounded grains of silica that would hint at old beaches or riverbanks."

Erin eyed the shapeless, ugly termitorium. "Is picking at mounds a reliable way of prospecting?"

"It's how Lamont found the Orapa diamond mine in Botswana."

"You sure he didn't just consult chicken guts in the dark of the moon?"

Smiling crookedly, Cole wiped his palm on the seat of his shorts and climbed into the Rover. "This is science, not voodoo."

She gave him a sideways glance and smiled in return. "Science, huh?" she said, opening the Rover's passenger door. "And I'm the tooth fairy."

"You can slip things under my pillow any time you're in the mood."

She tried not to respond to his retort but couldn't help it. Shaking her head, she snickered, then gasped when her bare thighs met the Rover's sun-baked seat.

"Lift up," he said.

When she did, he spread his discarded shirt on the seat. As he withdrew, she felt a breath of a caress over the back of her thighs.

"Try that," he said.

She sat down cautiously.

"Better?"

"Yes. Thanks." She looked at him. Except for dark patterns of hair, his legs were as bare as hers. "How can you stand it?"

"Same way you took the cold in Alaska. I'm used to it. That doesn't mean I like it. I'd trade buildup for a dog and shoot the dog."

Erin looked startled, then laughed aloud. "That bad, huh?"

"Worse."

He started the Rover and followed the track as it veered away from the flats, heading toward an unknown destination. Only when Erin looked back did she realize that the land was slowly rising. Just as slowly, it was becoming more uneven.

With no warning they crested a rise and found themselves driving between low, roughly parallel ridges that poked sluggishly from the ground. Stunted gum and acacia reappeared, along with an occasional bizarre boab tree. Spinifex grew more thickly, though never to a point Erin would describe as lush.

She straightened in her seat and looked longingly at the lacy skirts of shade beneath the trees.

"We'll stop up ahead," Cole said, following her glance.

"The government map doesn't show much, but the land rises about five hundred feet more. There's a gorge I want to check out. It's on the boundary between a sandstone district and a limestone district."

"Is that in the whatsit drainage?"

He smiled. "Karst. No. That's farther in."

"No caves, huh?"

"Not that I know of, but I've never explored the area. The last time I went to Dog Four, I came in another way."

She looked at him curiously. "When were you last in the Kimberley?"

"A while back."

"Why?"

"I'm a prospector."

"Did you ever find anything?"

"I've found my share," he said, dividing his attention between the increasingly rough track and a part of the Kimberley he'd never seen before.

"Any diamonds?" she asked.

"Some."

"Gold?"

"Here and there."

Her mouth flattened. "You know, each time the topic of you and the Kimberley comes up, you either change the subject or clam up."

"Look. I've got my hands full driving and at the same time trying to guess what kind of strata are beneath the surface. Is there something you really want to know about me and the Kimberley," he said, "or are you just feeling chatty?"

She slipped his khaki shirt from beneath her butt and used the hem to mop her face. "How did you get Abe's diamonds and the will?"

"A little late to be suspicious of me, isn't it?"

"Better late than—"

"—never," he interrupted sardonically. He flexed his hands on the wheel and thought of Uncle Li's thin neck. "Everybody who ever pegged out a lease in Western Australia spent some time on Abe's station. He was as close as the Kimberley came to a Renaissance man. Miner, scholar, stockman, spy. You name it, he's done it."

"Spy?" she asked in disbelief.

"Must run in the family."

She refused to be sidetracked. "If you knew that about Abe, you must have known him very well."

"Is that an accusation or a question?"

"Take your pick."

There was an electric silence before Cole spoke. "One year we sat out an early wet together."

"Why didn't you tell me before now?"

"You didn't ask." Cole gave Erin a swift, intense look. "Abe's dead. What we did or didn't do doesn't affect what I'm doing now. Nothing I did in the past affects us now. So instead of being suspicious of the one man in the Kimberley who's on your side, worry about the diamond cartel's latest entry into the sweepstakes—Jason Street."

"Are you worried about him?"

"I'd be a fool if I wasn't."

"Is that why we left the station?"

"One of the reasons." Cole shrugged. "But it will only buy us a day or two. Street knows the Kimberley better than any other white man alive. The Aborigines all but worship him the same way they did Abe. Fear, not love."

She looked out over the empty land. "Well, we've got a lot of country to get lost in."

"There are only so many waterholes. Street knows every one of them. What he doesn't know, the Aborigines will tell him. Sooner or later he'll find us. Sooner, most likely."

"Then why are we out in this bloody oven?"

"Because out here, everyone we meet is an enemy. At the station I couldn't be sure. Hesitation can kill you." He turned and looked at her. "I could have you on an airplane out of here in fourteen hours. Still want to go diamond hunting?"

"What do you think?"

"I think the ice chest full of film is in the sun."

Erin made a startled sound and turned in the seat. The reflective cloth she had put over the ice chest had slipped. She pulled the silvery cloth back in place.

"The ice will melt sooner or later," he said. "What happens to the film then?"

"Nothing, if I'm careful. The emulsion is stable even in this heat. It's just direct sun that can be a problem. The bag I carry film in when I'm shooting is insulated."

"How many rolls have you gone through since we left?"

"Not many."

He smiled slightly. "How many is not many?"

"Less than I wanted to. When I'm working, I can go through a roll of film every five minutes."

"No wonder you packed that cooler to the gills," he said. "Must be twenty pounds of film."

"Must be twenty pounds of shotgun shells, too."

"If I run out, I'll use your film."

"Wish I could say the same about your shells," she muttered. "How long are we going to be out here?"

"Until the wet."

"How long is that?"

"Until it rains."

"Gee, thanks for enlightening me."

He smiled.

"I tell myself to conserve film," she said, "but when I'm shooting I forget. Every image I see is so new. I'm afraid if I don't capture it now I'll never see it again."

Cole touched Erin lightly on the cheek. "I'm the same way when I'm prospecting. Every place is a treasure waiting to be found."

Before she could react to the brief caress, he took hold of the steering wheel again and focused on the increasingly difficult terrain.

Biting her lip, trying to ignore the leap in her pulse at such a simple thing as the brush of his fingertips over her cheek, Erin concentrated on the countryside.

"Look—kangaroos!" she said suddenly.

He glanced over to the right. "No such thing."

"What? Of course they are. Nothing else hops like that."

"Nope," he said. "Ask any Aussie. They're kangas or they're roos. Personally, I think they're roos. Kangas tend to hang out farther east."

She snickered and felt herself drifting more deeply beneath the spell of companionship that grew between them whenever she let down her guard and responded to Cole without calculation. He seemed to respond to her in the same way, without calculation.

You're a fool, Erin Shane Windsor, she told herself.

There was no argument.

37

Kimberley Plateau
Early afternoon

The Rover slowed to a stop in a patch of shade beneath an outcropping of rock. Cole got out, checked the brake fluid reservoir, and recapped it.

"Problems?" Erin asked.

"We're losing a little fluid, but not enough to worry about. There's a gallon of the stuff in the tool cabinet."

He wiped his forehead on the back of his arm, resettled his hat, and looked at the sky. Heat and moisture made it a shade of burning silver-gray peculiar to the tropics. Nothing new there.

He looked to the dry watercourse that had bitten through the earth near the road, eroding a channel for the runoff of the wet's pouring rains. There was no hint of water now. He hadn't expected any.

"I'm going to take a look at the gully walls," he said. "If you promise not to start taking pictures, you can stay in the Rover's shade. Otherwise you're coming with me."

"Why?"

"I don't want to spend half an hour tracking you

down," he said dryly. "This would be easy country to get lost in."

"I'm coming with you. So is my camera."

While Cole studied the steeply cut banks of the gully, Erin absorbed the angles, shadows, and densities of the landscape. She simply looked without expectation, opening herself to the land.

Gradually a subtle excitement tingled through her, a feeling she'd known only once before in her life, when she had accepted the arctic for what it was rather than what it wasn't.

As soon as she stopped looking for familiar lines and colors, the stark, mysterious, completely inhuman beauty of the Kimberley began to seep into her. The savage heat of the day was balanced by the seamless night, stretching from horizon to horizon without artificial light of any kind. The scarcity of vegetation was balanced by the vivid elegance of ghost gums and the fluid whisper of spinifex. The scarcity of animals was balanced by their startling shapes and unlikely means of locomotion.

And the stillness was complete, a silence more beautiful than music, a seduction greater than any easy beauty of water or grass or forest. The profound silence called to her soul.

Slowly she became aware of Cole standing next to her, watching her.

"It's getting to you, isn't it?" he asked.

"What?"

"The land."

"It's extraordinary," she said simply. "Even with its hellish climate."

"Like the arctic in winter."

She nodded slowly.

"Be careful," he said in a soft voice. "If you fall in love with this land, there's no substitute, no second best. There's a whole Arctic Circle, but there's only one Kimberley Plateau. There's nothing like it anywhere else. The Kimberley will haunt you no matter where else on earth you go."

"You love this place," she said, surprised.

"Except during buildup, yes. And sometimes even then."

"Why did you leave?"

"I was searching for diamonds the color of your eyes. Until a few weeks ago, I thought Brazil was the best place on earth to find them. I was wrong."

"Are there diamonds here?" she asked, waving her hand at the empty land.

He smiled ruefully and pulled her to her feet. "There's nothing in that gully but dirt. If there are strata made by paleo-riverbeds or beaches, they're not showing."

They walked to the Rover in an easy kind of silence.

"Would you mind driving?" Cole asked, handing her the keys. "I want to spend some time with the binoculars."

"I don't care if you want to sleep. I love driving."

"Have at it. The brake pedal is a bit soft, so leave enough time to pump once or twice."

Eagerly Erin got in, winced at the heat of the seat, and fired up the engine. The station road ascended in a leisurely fashion. The long, gently sloping ridge allowed her to take the Rover out of low range and all the way into third gear. The balky gear box gave her problems, but nothing she couldn't manage. She shifted up through the gears, bringing her speed up gradually, enjoying the temporary breeze through the window.

"Too fast for you?" she asked Cole.

"Go as fast as you want. I'm not seeing anything but sandstone."

The track continued to climb gradually until the Rover crested yet another small ridge. Abruptly the road descended into a gorge that looked more than a thousand feet deep.

"My God," she said, downshifting quickly into second gear. "We climbed to the top of a mountain and I didn't even know it."

"Actually, we just climbed the leading edge of a very minor range. In Alaska, it wouldn't even qualify as foothills."

"No problem. I've finally figured out I'm not in Alaska."

Erin looked ahead to the track snaking down in a series of long, steep switchbacks. If she didn't want to ride the brakes, she'd have to go back to low range to slow the Rover. Getting into low range meant slowing down. She touched the brake pedal with her right foot.

It went straight to the fire wall.

She tried to pump the pedal, but there wasn't enough pressure in the brake lines to make any difference.

Cole put the binoculars down.

"No brakes," Erin said tightly. "I'll try for first gear."

The Rover was going too fast for first gear and they both knew it. They also knew it was their best chance of slowing the Rover's descent.

She threw in the clutch and tried to grab first gear. In neutral the Rover picked up speed like a runaway roadtrain. There was a rending metal sound from the gear box. Quickly she double-clutched. Metal clashed against metal. She double-clutched again, and again metal screamed.

"Go back to second," he said.

She'd already reached the same conclusion. Before the words were out of his mouth, she slammed the gearshift back into second and dumped the clutch. The engine roared, the Rover lurched, then steadied.

They were still going too fast for the steeply dropping track.

A quarter mile ahead, the road turned back on itself in a tight hairpin curve. At their present speed, the Rover would overrun the curve and go flying off into the gorge to crash hundreds of feet below. Erin and Cole both realized it at the same instant.

Even as he reached for the wheel, she yanked it to the right, where ghost gums grew in elegant array among the sandstone boulders. The Rover shot off the track and broke one gum at the base. The tree went flying over the bull bar. A second gum raked along Erin's side of the Rover with a high scream. The third gum was bigger. The Rover hit it and bounced aside into a boulder.

She wrenched the wheel again and sent the battered vehicle careening between two more gums. By then she'd scrubbed off enough speed to grab first gear, slowing the Rover even more.

The last gum they hit shuddered and held. Dust, twigs, and leaves exploded around the Rover as the engine died. Erin slammed the shifter into reverse, holding the vehicle in place on the gears alone while Cole put the emergency brake on.

It became very quiet. As grit swirled through the interior, she looked at him.

"What, no cracks about women drivers?" she asked shakily.

"You can drive me anytime, anywhere," he said. "You want to get us to a level spot, or do you want me to do it?"

"It's all yours."

By the time they switched places, put the Rover in low range, and crept to the bottom of the gorge, the adrenaline had stopped running wildly through Erin's blood.

She began to feel as flat as dust. When Cole found a level place and parked, she sighed with relief.

He ran his fingertip down her nose and smiled. Then he got out, rummaged in the Rover's battered toolbox, and vanished beneath the vehicle, taking a small flashlight, a crescent wrench, a screwdriver, and several feet of small black tubing with him.

"Don't you dare wander off and start taking pictures," he said.

She jumped. His voice had come from beneath her feet. Guiltily she returned her camera to its bag. After a few moments she grabbed the binoculars, stepped on the front fender of the Rover, and from there to the platform on top. Between one of the spare tires and a cluster of fuel cans, she found a reasonably comfortable seat. Much more comfortable than the ground was, if Cole's language was any indication. She pulled her hat firmly into place and began scanning the countryside.

Nothing moved but heat spiraling up from the land. The breeze was halfhearted, as sullen as the color of the sky. The gorge and the plateau on the other side were empty of life. No cattle, no kangaroos, no birds. Nothing but rocks and trees whose stubborn will to survive had to be seen to be believed.

When she lowered the binoculars, a subdued ripple of movement caught her eye. She focused the binoculars on a spot thirty yards away.

"Cole?"

A grunt was his only answer.

"What do Australia's poisonous snakes look like?" she asked.

His head emerged from beneath the Rover, followed by his greasy, dirt-smeared torso. His shorts were the same color as the rusty earth. So were the backs of his legs. A narrow piece of tubing dangled from his right hand.

He glanced up at Erin, where she sat cross-legged on the spare tire, staring through the glasses. He followed her pointing finger and saw a snake curling across the dirt. The reptile was light brown with a faint blue blush along its belly. Shining as though every inch of its five-foot length had been recently polished, the snake moved with the languid, muscular ease of an animal supremely at home in its environment.

"Some of them look like that," he said.

"It's dangerous?"

"As hell."

"Damn. I wanted to get close enough to photograph it," she said.

"Why?"

"The contrast between the shiny scales and dust, the perfect curves against the angular land, life where there's nothing but rock and dust . . . It's beautiful."

"It's a king mulga, and it's one of the most lethal snakes on earth. Stay away from it. *Beautiful.* Christ. I suppose I should have expected it. Anyone who believes in the tooth fairy is bound to be a little weird in other ways."

Erin looked at the tubing Cole had in his hand. "Now that's ugly," she said. "No doubt about it."

"Could have been deadly, too," he said. "There's been a slow leak since we tried to climb a termite mound on the other side of Fitzroy Crossing. The clip that was holding the tube cut into the rubber. When it got weak enough, the tubing gave way and the fluid dripped out."

"Now what? More driving slow and praying fast?"

"No worries. The Kimberley is hell on vehicles. That's why extra tubing and brake fluid are standard equipment. I replaced the bad tubing and didn't find any other spots where fluid had bled through. Once I fill the reservoir again, we'll be back in business."

"Thank God. I wasn't looking forward to walking out of here."

"During buildup? Not likely, honey. You'd be lucky to get two miles before you keeled over."

He opened the supply cupboard at the rear of the Rover, removed a gallon can of brake fluid, and shook it. The can was almost full. He went to the front of the vehicle, opened the hood, and took off the cover of the brake-fluid reservoir. Remembering the helicopter's dirty fuel, he tipped a little of the liquid onto his index finger and rubbed. There was no gritty feel.

But after a few moments his finger burned. He sniffed the opening of the can. Beneath the heavy petroleum odor was something else.

"Son of a *bitch*."

He scrubbed the fluid off his fingers with dry soil, then poured the contents of the can into a shallow runoff channel at the side of the road.

"What's wrong?" she asked.

"Someone added a corrosive to the brake fluid. If I'd used this to replace what we lost, there wouldn't have been enough tubing in the Kimberley to fix the mess."

She looked at the empty can of brake fluid. "How far will we get without brakes?"

"Not as far as we will with them."

Cole began searching through the cartons of camping supplies. He pulled out several bottles, put them back, and then lifted out a big bottle of liquid soap.

She watched, horrified, as he poured soap into the empty brake reservoir. When he was finished he capped the reservoir and smiled at her.

"Fluid is fluid. This is a little heavier than the regular

stuff, but it'll do." He smiled crookedly. "Look at it this way. We'll have the cleanest brake lines in the Kimberley."

"How long will it last?"

He shrugged. "We'll be the first to know."

38

Dog Four was behind Erin and Cole. When they finally came to the area that held promise of having a karst drainage pattern where caves might be found, their progress slowed to a walking pace. Cole began inspecting the ground on foot. She went with him, because it beat sitting in the Rover's oven and baking.

The heat was, as always, stunning. Clouds towered and billowed, climbing toward a storm that never came. She watched the sky hungrily, hoping to see in its blistering turbulence the dark storm that would bring an end to the buildup's savage heat and humidity.

"Rain, damn it," she muttered.

"Not today." He stood and dumped the handful of dirt he'd been dry-panning. "Probably not for a week."

She sighed. "I wish it would rain and rain and rain."

"Tell me that in January. I've seen it start raining on one afternoon and not stop again for four months."

"Promises, promises." She flapped her tank top, sending air circulating over her breasts. "No wonder people go crazy. The buildup is just one endless striptease. Like

Abe's blasted mines, each one a little better than the last, but none of them really worth a damn."

Cole forced himself to look away as the cloth fluttered back down to conform lovingly to her breasts. Wanting Erin and not having her was making him a lot more irritable than the climate was.

"At least we're in limestone country again," he said.

"Any luck with the dry panning?"

"Enough that I want to look farther upstream."

"What stream? The only water within miles is my sweat. And yours," she added.

Shiny trails of sweat glistened through the hair on his naked chest. As she watched, a drop slid down the median line of his body and vanished behind his cotton shorts. She looked away quickly.

"Don't forget the canteens we're wearing," he said. "There's water in them."

"How could I forget? Mine weighs more than my camera bag."

"Doubt it. You must be carrying five pounds of film alone."

"And I've shot all but three rolls. I'd go back to the Rover for more," she said, sighing, "but I don't feel like walking that far."

"Is that a hint?"

She smiled wryly and shook her head while she fanned her top again. "Thanks, but it'd be a waste of energy and film. The sun is getting too high. It flattens out the shadows. By the time the light slants again, the clouds will have moved in. Maybe there will be a break at sunset. If not, there's always tomorrow."

Flapping her shirt again, she thought longingly of taking off the hot weight of the canteen, but she didn't suggest it. He'd told her to wear the canteen every time she got out of the Rover to take pictures. He was no easier on himself. Not only did he carry an even bigger canteen for his prospecting expeditions but he also carried a large rucksack of gear.

She'd been startled to discover that a shotgun and several boxes of shells were as much a part of his gear as compass, binoculars, shovel, specimen bags, labels, sheath knife, survival blanket, and large swaths of plastic sheeting whose purpose mystified her.

"Drink," Cole said. "Water weighs less in your stomach than hanging on your hip."

Dutifully Erin unscrewed the top of the canteen and drank. The water was stale and hotter than her mouth. She sighed and thought of glaciers calving into an ice-blue sea.

"Are you going to take more pictures?" he asked.

"Am I breathing?"

He glanced sideways at her and smiled slightly. "Dumb question, huh?"

The contrast between his amused smile and his powerful, nearly naked body made her breath stop. A shaft of longing went through her, making her painfully aware of her own body. Memories poured through her, hotter and more vivid than the sun, images of a sensual time before she had seen the perfect Chen Lai in Cole's embrace.

"Just keep going upstream," he said. "That way you won't get lost. Okay?"

Erin nodded. "Where are you going to be?"

"Right behind you, dry-panning as I go."

The quality of his voice made her heartbeat pick up. "Did you really find something?"

"There must be some old streambed or beach deposits up there," he said, hooking his thumb toward the two low hills that flanked either side of the dry stream course. "I'm getting stuff that's much more rounded and of a different type of rock than the rest of the recent streambed deposits. The old stuff could have been washed from layers of river or beach conglomerate."

"Diamonds?" she asked eagerly.

"Nope. But that ridge is limestone, so watch for openings where the runoff streams cut into the underlying rock. There could be caves."

"Really?"

"Wherever there's limestone and water, there's a chance of caves," he said. "Not a certainty. Just a chance. Most caves are discovered when a stream cuts down through the rock like a knife through Swiss cheese, showing all the little interior holes."

Her eyes lit up. She started to speak but ended by waving flies away impatiently.

"Time for more goo," he said, reaching into his big rucksack. "Those flies sure love you, honey."

Grimacing, she squeezed out a puddle of white, medicinal-scented lotion and began applying it. She worked swiftly, from the forehead down, covering every bit of skin that was exposed and a lot that wasn't.

"Watch for snakes," Cole said, picking up the gold pan again. "They'll be in the shadows and crevices. If you see any birds or bats, let me know. Could mean water nearby."

"Do we need it?" she asked.

"With what we've got in the Rover, we're all right for a few days, but if we can find a source of water that isn't on the maps, we can make Street's job harder."

She capped the squeeze bottle and handed it back to Cole. "Maybe Street is just what he's supposed to be, a man inspecting the Dog Mines for the Australian government."

"Maybe. Want to bet your life on it?"

When she started to answer, an abrupt gesture of Cole's hand silenced her. He stood motionless, head cocked to one side in the attitude of a man listening intently.

"What—" she began.

Another sharp gesture cut her off. Silently he pointed toward the east. She shifted her position and listened intently. After a moment she heard the far-off drone of a helicopter engine.

Cole touched her arm and pointed again. She squinted into the shimmering sky. Finally she saw a dark dot skimming above the land. The helicopter was perhaps a thousand feet high and miles away. If he continued in the same direction he was going, he would miss them by a wide margin.

"Somebody looking for Dog Four?" she asked.

"If he is, he just flew over it."

Abruptly the helicopter's direction changed.

Cole cursed, grabbed Erin's arm, and sprinted toward a clump of gums that were growing along the outer curve of the streambed.

"Get down and stay there," he said.

She didn't have any choice about obeying. He dragged her to the ground and pinned her with a forearm across her waist. Just as she opened her mouth to demand an explanation, she heard the sound of the helicopter. It was close enough to distinguish the rhythm of the rotors whipping through the air. After a minute the sound began to fade.

"No," he said when she would have gotten up. "Not until we haven't heard him for five minutes."

She lay rigid, barely feeling the textures of grit and stone and tree root beneath her, aware only of the claustrophobic stillness of the day and the coiled tension of the man stretched out beside her. The sound of a shell being jacked into the shotgun's firing chamber was like thunder to her taut nerves.

"You're certain Dog Four is off in that direction?" she asked finally.

"Yes."

"Maybe he's lost."

The drone of the engine began to strengthen once more, consuming the stillness.

"And maybe we're lying in a pool of cold water," Cole said grimly. "He's doing legs of a search pattern. When I tell you to look down and be still, do it."

A chill moved over her skin. "What if he spots the Rover?"

Cole didn't say anything. He just looked at the angle of the sun. Darkness wouldn't come in time to do any good. All he could do was hope that the trees he'd parked the Rover beneath provided enough cover. Having flown over the Kimberley himself, he knew how thin a cover the trees gave.

Like everything else that survived in the scorching land, the foliage of the gum and acacia trees was thin and grew in such a way as to minimize the amount of sunlight reaching the surface of the leaves. In the outback, leaves were narrow and hung straight down rather than broad and spread at a right angle to catch every bit of light.

The engine noise came closer, echoing off the limestone hills and between the steep walls of the ravine. Erin didn't need Cole's terse order to hug the ground. She was already there. She pressed her cheek into the hot soil and wondered how the land could seem so empty one instant and be so full of danger the next.

The sound reached a peak, then gradually fell away once more as the helicopter turned onto a different heading.

"He'll fly right over the Rover if he stays on that tack," Cole said. "If the chopper lands, I'm going to head for the Rover. If I don't come back and someone else starts calling for you, get up and walk into the open."

"But—"

"But nothing," he cut in savagely. "Your chances of surviving alone out here in the dry are the same as mine of surviving an arctic blizzard buck naked. Street might have a reason to keep you alive. The land doesn't give a damn whether you live or die."

Cole took off his hat and mopped sweat from his forehead with the back of his hand as he studied the terrain. The bed of the dry ravine was narrow and twisting. It led up a gradual slope toward a notch between two low hills half a mile away. The heat was fierce. The lid of clouds only made it worse, but the heavy air conducted sound very well.

Both of them heard the instant the helicopter changed its heading.

"Why is he concentrating here?" she asked.

"Because it's one of the few places around where the growth is thick enough and the land rough enough that a Rover could be hidden. He might even have equipment sensitive enough to pick up the Rover's metal frame."

"Or a signal hidden somewhere in the Rover?" she asked unhappily.

"Doubt it. I checked. Anyway, he's looking, not homing in."

The noise of the chopper surged suddenly. It had changed headings, approaching them once more.

Much too close.

The sound of the rotors ricocheted around them. Erin tried to drag air into her aching lungs. It was like trying to breathe through wet wool. She closed her eyes and willed the chopper to disappear.

The noise slowly abated.

She let out a sigh. Before she could speak, the sound changed, increasing steeply, then dropping abruptly to nothing as the helicopter landed.

"He spotted the Rover," Cole said.

He came to his feet in a rush, shucked off all burdens but the shotgun and a pocket full of shells, and ran down the streambed. The savage heat and bogs of sand slowed him, dragging at his feet, turning his lungs to fire and his muscles to lead. The Rover was a mile away, a distance he normally would have covered in eight minutes. Under these conditions, he would be lucky to make it in twelve.

He was still four hundred yards from the Rover when the helicopter revved and lifted into the air once more. The chopper held at one hundred feet and began spiraling out from the Rover in a clear search pattern. Dust lifted in thin billows.

Then the chopper veered and began heading straight toward Cole.

He turned and sprinted toward the thin cover of the stream-side gums. Just beyond, at the foot on a steep rise, there was a tumble of limestone boulders, legacy of a landslide during the wet. He reached the rocks while the helicopter was still a hundred yards away. With the sound of the approaching chopper filling his ears, he searched for cover. The best he could find was an undercut where an old flood had eaten away the dirt beneath some boulders, leaving them half suspended over air.

He dove toward the little cave as the chopper tipped and charged like an angry bull. The engine sound was loud, but not loud enough to cover the staccato burst of an automatic weapon. Bullets thumped in the sand and whined off the rocks.

Cole pressed his back against stone and lifted the shotgun. The sound of its blast was deafening in the enclosed space. He pumped in another shell and fired, pumped and fired, working as fast as he could, not bothering to aim because the chopper was too close to miss.

The helicopter pulled up and leaped away like a startled bird.

Cole dug shells from his pocket and fed them into the magazine one after another until it was full once more. He threw the gun to his shoulder and took slack off the trigger.

"Come closer, you son of a bitch," he said. "Just a little closer. That's it . . . that's it. Come and get it."

The helicopter hovered nervously just out of range, feinting from side to side in sudden darts, trying to draw fire.

Cole waited with the patience of a predator at a waterhole, leading his cautious adversary as the chopper swept across the front of the rock slide once more.

The pilot was either overconfident or misjudged the distance. The instant he was within range, the shotgun erupted, spewing round after round of lead shot in a pattern that must have been too close for the pilot's nerve, for the helicopter jumped upward and kept climbing until it vanished.

Automatically Cole reloaded until his pocket was empty of shells. The sound of the helicopter thinned until nothing remained but the ringing in his ears. Cautiously he rolled out of the shelter and looked around. Nothing moved between him and the Rover. He knew he should wait quietly for half an hour just in case an assassin had been dropped off, but he doubted Erin's patience would hold out that long.

Using the trees for the small shade and cover they offered, he worked his way back up toward her. He found her precisely where he had left her. When she saw him, she jumped up and ran into his arms. For a moment she clung to him fiercely. Then she took a ragged breath and stepped back.

"Are you all right?" she asked, watching him with luminous green eyes. "I thought I heard shots."

"Nobody connected."

"Who was it?"

"I didn't get close enough to see. But it was the station helicopter."

She didn't ask any more questions as she followed Cole down the baking dry wash to the place where they'd left the Rover. She was relieved to see the vehicle. Its burning interior was better than the unshielded rays of the sun.

Cole looked at the dark stains spreading out from the Rover. Even though he'd been expecting sabotage, the reality of seeing it was no less grim.

"Cole?"

"It's just what it looks like," he said roughly. "Radiator fluid."

Silently she watched while he checked the Rover's engine compartment, dashboard, and equipment cupboards.

"The son of a bitch was thorough," he said, slamming the Rover's door. "Not one bit of hose left, and no water to use in any case."

"He took our water?"

"No. He took the food. The water he poured on the ground."

She took a harsh breath. "The radio?"

"Gone. So are the maps."

Her breath came out in a rush. She looked away, not wanting to show Cole how frightened she was. "I see. Now what?"

He looked at the blazing sky and then at the woman whose skin was pale beneath the flush of tropic heat.

"Drink your fill from the canteen, honey."

"Shouldn't I save it?"

"You'd be surprised how many people have been found dead with water in their canteens. Dehydration is like hypothermia. It saps your judgment before it kills you. Drink while you can. Thirst will come soon enough."

39

Kimberley Plateau
Afternoon

Erin looked at the contents of the rucksack Cole had spread out on top of the thin survival blanket. He took the rock hammer off his belt. Without hesitating he set the hammer beside the steel pan, sample bags, and rock samples he'd collected. The thermal bag she carried film in lay nearby. The compass was beside the canteen he'd carried. So were matches, shovel, three boxes of shotgun shells, the shotgun itself, the knife in its wrist sheath, and several large, folded sheets of plastic.

As she watched, he kept pulling things from the rucksack and sorting them according to their usefulness as basic survival gear.

"How much ice is left in the chest?" he asked without looking up.

"None. It all had melted even before he ripped off the lid. He must have looked in, seen only the rack holding the film, and gone on to more important things."

Cole grunted. "Is the film all right?"

"It should be fine. The canisters are tight."

Quickly Erin sorted unexposed from exposed film. When she was finished, she began stuffing rolls of exposed film into a military-surplus hip belt. From the belt hung a variety of pouches made of camouflage cloth.

"Don't bother with the belt," Cole said. "It will just be excess weight. We can't afford an ounce more than is absolutely necessary."

"How long will it take us to get back here?" she asked, looking at the mound of exposed film.

"We can't count on getting back at all," he said evenly. "It's seventy miles to the Gibb River Road. That's if we fly. On the ground it will be farther."

"How far away is Windsor station?"

"Fifty miles, give or take, if we follow the road. Less if we don't. But there's nothing between here and the station except two limestone ridges and cracking clay flats that won't see water between now and the wet." He began packing the rucksack. "Even if we did make it to the station, the bastard in the chopper would be waiting and we'd be in no shape to outsmart, outshoot, or outrun him. There's a better chance of finding water between here and the Gibb River Road, and a hell of a lot better chance of finding help once we're there."

What Cole didn't say was that their chance of survival was slim at best. No food, little water, and mile after rugged mile of empty country, the kind of land that would demand everything from them and give back nothing but more demands on their failing strength.

Erin looked at Cole's bleak expression and knew everything he hadn't said. Without a word she turned her back on the pile of film that had recorded her first, irreplaceable perceptions of the alien landscape that was the Kimberley Plateau.

"Any water left in the ice chest?" he asked.

"Some."

"Pour it into the empty canteen that's under the front seat. If you can't do it without spilling, I'll help."

Before she finished transferring the ice chest's water to the canteen, he came up to the Rover with the heavy rucksack in one hand and the shotgun in the other. He pulled on a khaki bush shirt and stuffed another into the rucksack. Then he watched while she carefully drained the last drops into the big canteen's mouth. When she capped the canteen and handed it to him, he hefted its weight with surprise.

"Almost a half gallon," he said. "Good."

He didn't mention how little of their daily requirement that amount of water was. He simply clipped the canteen to his webbing belt opposite the other large canteen he carried. It, too, held about half a gallon of water.

"Take off your canteen and belt," he said, holding out his hand.

"I can carry it."

"Take it off."

"Cole—"

"No," he cut in. "I have three times your strength. Hand it over."

She looked into his hard gray eyes and knew arguing would be useless. Worse, it would waste energy. She gave Cole the canteen and dropped the belt in the dirt.

Automatically she turned to the Rover and pulled out her camera bag. The instant she realized what she was doing, she replaced the bag and let the strap slide from her fingers. When she turned back to him, she was empty-handed.

"I'm sorry," he said, touching her cheek briefly.

"It was just force of habit. Since we can't eat it, drink it, or kill with it, we don't need it, do we?"

"No. Wing will replace everything you lose."

She nodded.

But even if she survived to have Wing replace her camera equipment, nothing could replace the exposed film. She put the thought out of her mind, because thinking about it wouldn't help.

Cole took a reading on his compass and headed up the dry streambed with an easy, long-legged stride that was neither fast nor slow. Erin followed, trying to ignore the sweat sliding down her body and the heat rising in sheets from the parched land.

After two miles he turned and headed for a black velvet shadow that lay partway up one of the limestone hills. After a steep climb, they reached the shadow. More alcove than cave, the overhang gave shelter and a good view back down the wash. Faded pictographs showed against the rough limestone. Tongues of soot rose where campfires had burned.

"Aborigines," he said, glancing around. "A band must have camped here during the wet."

She forgot about the heat as she looked at the pictographs. By reflex she reached for her camera, remembered, and had to be satisfied with thinking about how she would have photographed the images if she could have.

"We can't be spotted from the air here," Cole said. "We'll be safe until dark." As he turned away from the drawings he saw the expression of longing on Erin's face. "If it makes you feel better, there are thousands of places like this scattered around the outback. This won't be your only chance to photograph an old Aborigine camp."

She nodded, wondering if he believed the implication of his own words—survival, not death. But she didn't ask.

Their odds of living wouldn't improve by talking about it.

"Looking at those hand designs is rather eerie," she said.

"Holy ground."

"Really?" She examined the pictographs with new interest.

"Every piece of landscape that's the least bit different is sacred to the Aborigines. Every seep, every oddly shaped rock, everything that isn't flat and spinifex or rumpled and covered with sparse gum." Cole shrugged out of the rucksack and flexed his shoulders. "But we don't need to worry about guests dropping in. This place hasn't been used since white men landed down under."

"How can you tell?"

"No broken bottles or beer cans." Cole pointed to the rucksack. "Use that for a pillow. Sleep if you can. We've got a long night of walking ahead."

"All night? Are you really that afraid of being spotted?"

"We'll need less water walking at night and sleeping by day."

She hesitated, then asked the question she'd told herself she wasn't going to ask because the answers really wouldn't change the outcome. "How long will it take to reach Gibb River Road?"

"Four days, if we're lucky. Six days, more likely. The country gets rougher than hell in the last half, and we'll be a lot weaker by then."

"How much time do we have?"

"With only the water in the canteens, we'd be dry by this time tomorrow. By the day after, we'd be staggering." He sat, leaned against the wall of the overhang, and pulled his hat down to cover his eyes. "If we get lucky, we'll find an unmarked seep. If not, there are other ways."

Before she could ask what he meant, he was asleep.

She closed her mouth and envied him that catlike ability to sleep whenever and wherever the opportunity offered. She didn't think she would be able to sleep, but her body surprised her. Even the few miles she'd walked that day had drained her strength. Her last thought before she dropped off was relief that she wouldn't have to face another hike through the brutal sunlight.

Erin didn't awaken until she felt Cole stirring beside her. The quality of the light told her it was late afternoon. Pale, almost invisible lightning stitched through the dark gray sky. The river of clouds had become a seamless, seething lid over the land, holding in heat without bringing the cool sweetness of rain.

"You're sure it rains here?" she said, swallowing to relieve the dryness in her mouth.

"Eventually. But not today. The clouds will be gone in a few hours. That's just heat lightning." He stood and held out his hand to her, pulling her to her feet. "We'll make much better time while it's still light."

When he shouldered his rucksack, she followed him out of the rock shelter into the naked land. They walked.

The sun vanished with an abruptness that Erin found startling after Alaska's long twilights. Even in darkness, heat still came up from the Kimberley's ground in tangible waves. The humidity was high enough to be suffocating, but not high enough to preserve the moisture in her own body or to prevent her sweat from evaporating.

Cole walked steadily, reading his compass by flashlight until the clouds thinned and broke to reveal the glittering massed stars of the southern sky. The Milky Way was a tidal wave of distant light washing across a third of the sky. From various quarters of the horizon, lightning stabbed upward, looking hardly brighter than the stars. The moon added its silver glow.

Erin walked in Cole's wake through spinifex and rocky scrubland. Their only rest came when he checked the compass against the stars or the black, uneven silhouette of the night horizon. More often than not, he chose to walk in dry watercourses despite the soft footing. In the dark, places where water had flowed were a lighter shade of black than the rest of the land and usually had less obstacles.

They drank the last of their water in the small, nearly cool hours of night.

By the time dawn exploded across the sky, Erin was stumbling from weariness. The land around them had changed a bit during the night. The hills tended to be steeper and separate rather than strung out in long, low ridges.

Cole took advantage of the light to walk more quickly. He kept to a hard pace through the increasing heat until he found a place where thin-leafed trees shaded a ravine at the base of a hill. He stretched the survival blanket between two tree trunks and lashed it in place, creating a canopy to shade them as they slept.

"Lie down in the shade," he said. "Don't move any more than absolutely necessary."

He dumped the rucksack on the ground for a pillow, grabbed the shovel, and walked out until he was in a place without shade. He dug a hole three feet wide by two feet deep and lined it with leaves he stripped from the acacias and gums. He put his large tin mess cup in the center of the hole, spread one of the plastic sheets over it, and anchored the sheet with rocks. He placed a rock in the center of the plastic, making it sag to a point over the cup.

Without pausing he came back to the shelter, grabbed several more plastic sheets and went to work again. These sheets he wrapped around the ends of living tree branches, then carefully gathered the edges of each sheet until it made a bag with green, living leaves inside. He tied off the neck of each bag tightly and went back to the shelter's welcome shade.

Erin looked up as Cole sank to the ground beside her. "What are they?" she asked, gesturing toward the shiny, clear bags.

"Stills. There's a lot of moisture in leaves. We'll let the sun work for us rather than against us for a change. Sleep."

She licked her lips, wondering how she could feel so dry when the air was so muggy. It was only a brief moment of curiosity. Sleep slammed down over her like a tropical sunset. Just as consciousness spun away, she felt Cole rubbing sunscreen into her skin. She tried to thank him, but the effort was too great.

The next thing she knew, she was being shaken awake.

"Erin. Wake up, honey. Breakfast is on the way."

The thought of food made her salivary glands contract painfully. She sat up and rubbed eyes that were gritty with dust and sleep.

"Breakfast?" she asked.

"You'll have to work for it."

"How?"

He pulled Erin to her feet. "See that?" he asked, pointing to a spot about fifteen feet away.

"See what?"

Then the snake moved, curling sinuously through the dry debris beneath a gum tree, hunting prey or simply a cooler place to rest.

She made an odd sound. "Breakfast, huh?"

"If we're lucky." He handed her a leafy branch as long as her arm. "Take this and keep him occupied while I circle around behind. Don't stir him up, just hold his attention. He'll be a lot harder to catch if he makes it to the rocks."

"Is the snake dangerous?" she asked as he started out from the shelter.

"Only until I kill it. Then it's food."

She shook off the last of her lethargy and walked out from the shelter to head off the snake. Though it was late afternoon, the sun beat down through the clouds with savage force. She rattled the leaves at the tip of the branch against the dusty ground. The snake turned toward the motion with a muscular twist of its body.

"I've got its attention," she said.

The reptile watched her with eyes like flakes of black glass. The snake showed no nervousness at her presence. Mulgas were the undisputed lords of the outback. For them a human being was a novelty rather than a threat.

"Don't get too close," he said.

"Look who's talking."

He didn't answer. He just eased closer to the tail of the snake while Erin made small movements that kept the mulga's attention fixed on her.

Suddenly Cole's hand shot out and fastened on the snake's tail. He jerked his arm, snapping the mulga like a bullwhip, breaking its spine and killing it instantly. He gave the snake a final snap to be certain, then waited.

Four feet of food hung limply from his hand.

Swallowing dryly, Erin reminded herself that protein was protein was protein. Her mind might know the difference between snake and sushi, but her stomach wouldn't. Certainly snake couldn't taste any worse than seal.

"There's a lot of water in snake meat," he said as he drew his knife from its sheath on his wrist. "If you don't believe me, watch me skin it out."

"No, thanks."

"Don't worry. After you cook it, the meat is white and tastes just like—"

"Chicken," she interrupted, grimacing.

He glanced up at her, surprised. "Did you eat snake in Alaska?"

"No, but I've been told the same thing about frog legs and grubs and every other so-called delicacy I've ever eaten. It's a lie. Chicken is the only thing that tastes like chicken."

"Snake is better than goanna."

"As long as it's better than seal, I won't complain. Much."

The corner of his mouth kicked up. "Have I told you that you're good company?"

Without waiting for an answer he began dressing out the snake with quick, skilled motions. She watched through narrowed eyes and decided it was about as bloody as cleaning a fish and far less gory than seal.

"Get a fire going," Cole said as he worked. "You can roast the meat while I empty the stills. If you can't eat your share now, I'll save it for you. After we've walked all night and your stomach is gnawing on your backbone, mulga will taste better than smoked salmon."

She didn't believe him but she didn't argue. When the time came to eat, she would eat, because it was the only way to survive.

By the time Erin was finished roasting chunks of protein over the eucalyptus fire, Cole had emptied the four solar stills. The result netted just under a gallon of water. While she watched, he divided the water evenly between two canteens.

"This one is yours," he said, handing it over to her. "Drink."

The water tasted as exotic as the snake meat had, for both were flavored by eucalyptus and acacia. Despite her thirst, she drank less than a third of the water in the canteen before she reached out, took the tin cup from Cole's belt, and poured in half the water remaining in her canteen.

"This is yours," she said. "Drink up."

"Don't be ridiculous."

"You're twice as big as I am. That means you need twice the water I do."

"Erin—"

"No," she said, cutting him off. "If you can carry everything because you're bigger than I am, you can damn well take your real share of the water and food."

For a long moment he looked into her clear, beautiful green eyes. "I'd rather you drank it," he said finally.

"I'd rather carry my own gear, but I'm being sensible about it. If both of us are going to survive, we both have to be sensible, right?"

He hesitated, then drank the eucalyptus-flavored water to soothe the thirst that had been tormenting him. When he was finished, he bent and brushed the last drops over her lips in a gentle kiss.

"You're quite a woman, Erin Shane Windsor."

"And you're quite a man," she said simply. "If I have to die, at least I'll have had a chance to live. Thank you for that, Cole. I wouldn't have made it alone."

His fingers caressed her cheek before he turned away and methodically began packing the rucksack. When he was finished, he consulted the compass and his memory of the map. Then he held out his hand to her.

"Ready?" he asked.

She smiled almost sadly. "As in 'Ready or not, here I come'?"

"Something like that. I know you're tired, but we do make much better progress with some daylight to help us."

She took his hand and they set off into the staggering heat and emptiness of the Kimberley Plateau.

Cole led her carefully around the area where he'd spotted fresh human tracks that morning. There was no point in letting her know their meager progress was being watched. If she knew, she'd begin wondering why they were being played with instead of being finished off in a single merciful stroke.

It was something he wondered himself.

40

Kimberley Plateau
The fourth night

Thirst was their savage companion. It was more consuming than the darkness, more suffocating than the heat, as vast as the star-strewn sky.

Erin tried not to think about water. Instead she concentrated on the need to walk steadily. Cole walked in front of her, seemingly unaffected by the grim rations and desperate thirst.

But she knew he wasn't.

She'd seen the fine trembling of his hands when he'd dressed out the goanna he'd shot. Despite the endless humidity and daily cups of exotically flavored water, their bodies were drying out hour by hour, breath by breath.

Between black shapes of clouds, cold white points of starlight gleamed. Occasional strokes of heat lightning lanced through clouds that didn't thin as much as usual as the night wore on. Despite the scattered stars, moon, and lightning, the night seemed darker than any she'd ever endured and longer than the longest winter above the Arctic Circle.

A sheet of lightning ran from top to bottom of the towering cloud formations along the horizon.

In the sudden, stark flash of light, she caught a glimpse of Cole. He'd turned and was holding out his hand to her. His expression was as dark as the clouds and the night.

When she took his hand, he drew her close. He knew if they sat down they would sleep, wasting vital hours. So they stood quietly together, holding one another, resting in the only way they trusted themselves to.

Distant lightning flickered and flashed. The fitful rumble of thunder that followed was more felt than heard.

"With a little luck," he said in a raspy voice, "it will rain in a day or two."

She nodded, because it was too much effort to talk.

After a moment he pressed his cheek against hers and released her. He checked the compass, scanned the surroundings in the uncertain illumination of lightning, and headed toward a ridge that was either near and low or distant and steep. Whichever, it lay across their path to the Gibb River Road.

The ridge seemed no closer when the sky in the east began to slide from black toward gray. Cole stood and waited for Erin to come up beside him. He pulled the canteen from his belt, took two swallows, and handed it to her.

"Last one is for you," he said.

"No."

Cole took the water himself, then pulled her close for the kind of kiss he hadn't given her since Windsor station. When her lips parted, he gently gave her the water she'd refused to take from his canteen. Startled, she had no choice but to swallow. He laughed softly and kissed her until they both forgot their thirst for a few sweet moments. Then he held her like it was the last time.

Just as he released her, dawn came up in a silent, seething violence of light. The sun exploded through half-formed clouds. Within seconds the earth was transformed into a place of startling distances, rich colors, and vivid textures.

"To hell with diamonds," she whispered slowly, looking at the glorious, timeless transformation of night into day. "I'd trade everything for a camera and some unexposed film."

He smiled slightly through dry lips. "I believe you would." He ran his palms over her tangled mahogany hair, pushing it away from her heat-flushed face. "Diamonds are to me what film is to you, the key to another world. But if I had Abe's diamond mine right now, I'd trade it for film and give it to you."

He saw the shock in her expression, felt it in the movement of her body as she pulled away to look at him.

"You mean that, don't you?" she whispered.

"I always say what I mean." He pulled Erin closer, shielding her brilliant green eyes from the sun. "Discovering *Arctic Odyssey* made me feel like I'd just found a diamond mine—full of adrenaline and awe, alive all the way to the soles of my feet."

For a few moments more he held her, then stepped back. "Keep your eyes open for birds or a clump of lush vegetation. This is karst country. Water must have collected in cracks or deep limestone potholes or even in a cave or two. All we have to do is find where—and pray that nothing found it before us."

But no water appeared.

Two hours after dawn, Erin and Cole lay in the shade of the thin blanket stretched between two spindly trees, watching waves of heat rise off the land. The water in the canteen was almost hot. It tasted strongly of the gum leaves that had given it up. Yet the liquid felt wonderful sliding down Erin's parched throat.

As she drank, he studied the dark clouds that were streaming in from the Indian Ocean, thunderheads clawing toward the sun while their massive, slate-colored bottoms dragged ever nearer to earth.

"So close and yet so damned far away," he said hoarsely.

He measured the wild, thick river of clouds that was already fanning across the sky, breaking into separate storm cells as air currents tore it apart.

Finally he forced himself to look away from the distant, taunting ghost of rain and concentrated on the land ahead. Pale gum trees were scattered haphazardly across flat red earth. Waves of heat shimmered above the dirt. Clumps of hard spinifex competed for space with weathered blocks of limestone.

The flats were surrounded by broken hills. In the distance a long, flat-topped hill or ridge rose steeply, marking one edge of the basin where runoff water must certainly collect during the wet, for there was no notch or ravine or canyon where the water could break free of the depression.

Yet no matter how carefully he looked, there wasn't any sign that the flats became a temporary lake in the rainy season.

A vague tendril of excitement uncurled in his gut, taking his mind off the hunger and thirst that had steadily eroded his strength.

"What are you looking for?" Erin asked hoarsely, studying the landscape.

"Some sign of where water runs off during the wet."

She looked around in silence for several minutes. Then she frowned and looked more closely. "Didn't we come through here yesterday?"

He gave her a sideways look and wondered if heat, hunger, and dehydration were blurring her mind.

"No," he said.

"It looks . . . familiar."

"The landscape looks pretty much the same from here to the Admiralty Gulf."

"Are you sure?" She squinted through the shimmering heat, feeling more certain with each moment that she'd been here before.

"Don't worry. I'm not wonky enough from thirst to be walking us in circles. Go to sleep," he added, pushing himself to his feet. "It will be time to walk soon enough."

"Where are you going?"

"Up there." He jerked his thumb at the small hill they'd just climbed down.

"Why?"

"I want to take a look from the top. I might be able to see a splash of green or birds flying."

When Cole left the rucksack but picked up the shotgun and stuffed extra shells in his pocket, Erin looked at him sharply.

"Is there something you aren't telling me?" she asked.

"Sleep if you can. I won't be long."

"Cole?"

"It's all right. I'll be able to see you from the top of the hill."

He was gone before she could ask any more questions that he didn't want to answer.

Sighing, she lay back in a kind of daze while the clouds thickened, reducing the hammering force of sunlight and dropping the temperature a few degrees. The air thickened too, becoming a weight that was too heavy to breathe and too thin to drink. The density of various cloud cells increased as the indigo promise of rain climbed from the base of the clouds to halfway up the towering clusters of thunderheads. One of the cells was directly overhead. Thunder echoed through it restlessly, pursuing hidden lightning.

Random drops rattled on the canopy Cole had rigged.

She shot to her feet and ran out into the open, tipping her head back and holding out her hands to catch any rain. After a moment she felt a drop fall just above her upper lip. Her tongue flicked out. Even though the raindrop was mixed with her own sweat and the fine dust that coated everything in the Kimberley, the hint of water tasted sweet and clean.

A dozen raindrops fell. Lightning winked and flirted while thunder cracked with startling force. More rain reached the thirsty earth. The drops were fat and heavy, pregnant with the possibility of life. Each drop made a dark splash pattern on the dusty ground and vanished.

"Come on," she said hoarsely, trying to coax a steady rain from the threatening cloud overhead. *"Come on."*

As quickly as the rain had started, it stopped. The storm cell moved on, driven by the sun's savage heat.

She went to her knees with the exhaustion that the promise of rain had made her forget for a few moments. Helplessly she stared up at the steamy silver sky where clouds had gathered a few minutes ago.

She didn't realize that Cole had returned until he pulled her to her feet.

"Get back in the shade," he said. "It's too hot for real rain. Almost all the drops are evaporating before they hit the ground."

Numbly she nodded and walked toward the canopy that protected them from the savage sun. She sank to the ground, no longer noticing its stones or gritty texture.

Cole stretched out next to her.

"Find anything?" she asked hoarsely.

"Any water here is underground."

"How far?"

"That's the million-dollar question, honey. I don't have an answer."

The harshness of his voice was equaled by his expression. With a hand that trembled she touched his mouth.

"Not your fault," she whispered.

His hand closed around hers, holding it close. They fell into a sleep that was restless, disturbed by thirst, hunger, and the dry groan of distant thunder.

Erin awoke in a rush, wondering what was wrong. A glance told her that she was alone. Where Cole had slept next to her there was only the shotgun and a handful of shells resting on a folded sheet of plastic. A few drops of water gleamed on the plastic, proof that it very recently had been one of the solar stills. He must have emptied a still before he left.

Heat poured down through the broken, seething lid of clouds. Sunset was hours away.

She sat up and waited for the dizziness to pass. When her eyes focused, she saw what Cole had written in the dirt just beyond the shotgun.

Gone hunting.

The other solar stills hadn't been touched. They were taking advantage of every bit of sun to draw water vapor from thin leaves.

She picked up the shotgun, checked that it was loaded, and put it down within easy reach. Then she stretched out again and wondered what was so urgent that Cole had drunk the contents of one still and gone out into the vicious afternoon. Dozing, waking, dozing again, she waited.

Just before sunset she heard a rustling from the dry scrub to the left of the shelter. She grabbed the shotgun, snapped off the safety, and waited.

"It's just me, honey."

The voice came from her right, not her left.

She spun around and saw Cole standing no more than ten feet away. With a shiver of fear, she realized all over again what a lethal enemy a man like Cole would make. She snapped the safety back into place and stood up slowly.

"You're lucky I didn't shoot you," she said.

"That's why I threw a rock into the scrub. If you were the trigger-happy type, you'd shoot the rock instead of me."

She looked at his empty hands and the sheath knife strapped to his wrist. "Find what you were hunting for?"

Absently Cole brushed dry leaves and powdery grit from his hands. "Yes."

"What?"

"An Aborigine. He's about four hundred yards in back of us."

"Right now?"

Cole nodded. "This isn't some tough young black boy who's gone walkabout for the hell of it. We've been followed since we left the Rover. I tried to catch him once before, while you slept, but he's too good."

She shook her head, trying to understand. "Why are we being followed. Is he going to kill us?"

"No. He's a Kimberley kite hanging back and waiting until we die. Then he'll call in the helicopter and our bodies will be 'found' the same way Abe's was."

Her breath came in hard.

"Too bad, how sad," Cole said sardonically, "the two Yanks died in the outback when their Rover packed it in. No bullets. No signs of violence on the bodies. Nothing but dehydration, starvation, heat prostration, and death. No unhappy questions, no international inquiries, no nasty little investigations by your father and the CIA."

"No one will believe we just wandered off and died. That Rover was sabotaged!"

Cole's smile was as bleak as his eyes. "Was it? Or did we just run out of drinking water, drain and purify what was in the radiator, and set off on foot?"

He nodded as he saw comprehension draw Erin's face into grim lines.

"They'll replace hoses," he said, "put the radio back in with a few loose connections to explain our silence, and then they'll wring their hands for the press. Everything is going as they planned except for one minor detail. They didn't know that when I'm in dry country, I always carry the means to make a solar still in my rucksack. We've lasted twice as long as they expected. That cat-footed little Aborigine they sicced on us has finally run out of water. The bastard has to hunt for it just like us. That's what he's doing now. Hunting water."

"What are we going to do?"

"Pray to God he finds it."

41

Kimberley Plateau
Late afternoon

After sunset Cole pulled down the canopy and spread it for a groundcloth.

"Too dark to track him," Cole said simply.

Erin nodded. As had become her habit despite the heat, she curled up against him and slipped into a state that was neither sleeping nor waking.

The night passed in a torment of thirst that was barely touched by the aromatic water they'd drunk from the solar stills. But unlike other nights, the clouds didn't thin and dry up as the darkness wore on. Huge sheets of lightning arced across the sky, transforming half the blackness into a blinding blue-white light. Thunder exploded. The last echoes hadn't faded before a different kind of fire came from the sky, snake tongues of lightning licking at the edges of darkness, flaring in patterns that evoked ancient pictographs drawn on coarse rock walls.

Besieged by thirst and taunted by hopes of rain, Erin and Cole slept badly. When the first light separated sky from earth, he slipped away to see if their guard had returned during the night.

He found nothing but broad, barefoot prints in the dust where the man had circled their camp before heading off into the bush.

As Cole headed back to Erin, a sprinkle of water fell. The raindrops were heavy and wet and teasing. But the promise of real water wasn't kept. Reality was the savage burning of the rising sun.

"Hurry," Cole said, gathering everything. "Sign-cutting light doesn't last long in the tropics."

She dragged herself upright. "How can I help?"

"The first slanting light of day made tracks jump out of the landscape like neon paint." He pointed to the footprints. "That's one end of our lifeline," he said, drawing a line in the dust in front of the prints. "The other end is somewhere out there at a waterhole."

Where the prints were clear, Cole walked quickly along the trail, marking tracks by drawing a circle around them in the dirt, then looking for the next track. When he lost the trail he returned to the last marked track and began again.

The tracking itself was enough of a novelty at first that Erin could push aside her thirst while she watched Cole read the land in a way that was almost eerie. But as the sun rose higher, beating down on them again like a hammer, she felt strength flowing out of her in an invisible tide.

He forged ahead without a pause, cursing the changing angle of the light that smeared and smudged signs that had formerly leaped out of the ground to his eye. Then all signs of tracks vanished on a stretch of windswept, sun-baked rock.

"Stand here," he said, pointing to the last tracks he could find.

She stood beneath the brutal sun while he checked the

entire perimeter of the slab of hard stone before he found the tracks again.

"Got it," he said. "Let's go."

She walked across the rock, wondering if the stone was truly hot enough to cook eggs. It felt like it, even through the thick soles of her walking shoes.

At a spot where the terrain presented several choices for a man walking over the land, Cole knelt and sighted along the hot ground, searching for the shadow traces of the trail the Aborigine had left.

"How far would he go for water?" Erin finally asked.

"As far as he had to. But he's moving at a good pace. He's not doubling back or casting around, and he's not climbing hills to get a look at the countryside."

"Is that good?"

"It means he knows where he's going. All we have to do is hang on to his trail."

Cole's eyes narrowed as he spotted a slight, regular disturbance in the surface of the earth. When he shifted to hands and knees, the pattern disappeared. He sat on his heels and sighted along the direction of the trail. A vague notch showed in the landscape ahead. Beyond it rose the flat-topped, steep rise that seemed little closer for the hours of walking.

When he stood up, Cole had two pebbles in his hand. He brushed them off on his shorts and offered one to Erin. The other he put in his own mouth.

"Think of it as a lemon drop," he suggested.

Her salivary glands responded instantly to the idea. For the first time in two days, her mouth was moist again.

"It only works the first time," he said, almost smiling at her startled look when saliva ran once more. "But even when it doesn't work, the pebble gives your tongue something to do besides feel dry."

"A trick, huh?"

"That's all life is," he said roughly. "A trick played on death."

She followed him through increasing heat and humidity while monsoon clouds thickened and billowed toward the instant of rain she no longer believed would come.

The trail was difficult to follow. Time and again Cole had to cast around beneath the brutal sun while Erin waited and watched.

Without warning the world began to dim and revolve slowly about an unknown center. She sank to her hands and knees, head hanging, until reality shifted back again into the dusty sun-hammered pastels of Western Australia.

Slowly she realized that Cole was standing over her, shading her with his body and the khaki shirt he held between his hands in a makeshift canopy. When she tried to stand, he put his hand on her shoulder.

"Rest. The dizziness will pass."

This time.

But he didn't say it aloud. He'd expected Erin to reach the end of her resources yesterday or the day before. Her continued endurance in the face of a climate her body was badly prepared for both amazed him and made him more determined than ever that she would survive.

"Better?" he asked finally, his voice gentle despite its dry rasp.

She nodded.

"Ready to try standing?"

"Yes," she whispered.

With his help, she pulled herself to her feet. He led her to the thin shade of an acacia and started making true shade with the survival blanket.

"No," she said hoarsely. "We've got to keep going."

"Not yet. Give yourself a chance to recover."

He put his shirt back on and studied the land from the

sanctuary of the artificial shade he'd created. The surrounding ground was still largely flat, still the floor of a basin that had no visible outlet. The only real landmark among the broken hills that surrounded the basin was the flat-topped hill that had been receding before them like a mirage.

At least the hill didn't look flat any more. Nor did it look like a hill. It was like a rough-surfaced mesa. Wind- and water-sculpted stone formations poked above the sparse vegetation.

"Cole?"

He looked away from the tortured rock shapes to the woman whose determination to survive was as great as his own.

"Are you sure we haven't been here before?" she asked.

"Yes."

She shaded her eyes and squinted, trying to see through the odd gloaming beneath the restless, opaque sky. Her breath came in with a tearing sound.

"Where are we?" she asked.

"In the Kimberley," he said gently.

"Yes, but where? Are we close to any of Abe's claims?"

He thought for a moment, reviewing his memories of the maps he had spent hundreds of hours studying. He checked the compass, glanced at his watch, did a few rough calculations, and looked back at her.

"We could be on the edge of one," he said. "Why?"

For a moment she couldn't answer. She felt like she'd been sleepwalking and had just awakened to find herself in a new world.

"Were you ever here before?" she asked.

"No. It's a small claim. Gold hunters worked it over real thoroughly forty years ago. They found just enough dust to keep them trying for years before they gave up. Too dry for placer mining."

"Did you ever hear Abe mention this claim?"

"Only when he was drunk, but he mentioned a thousand places when he was drunk. He never attached any particular importance to it. Why?"

"I think that's Bridget's Hill," Erin said simply. "I can't be sure because the angle is different. If that's the hill, the photographs were taken from somewhere off to the left and looking more north."

He narrowed his eyes and compared his memory of the photographs with the worn, eroded land.

"Be damned," he said. "You might just be right. If you are, there should be water at the base of the hill during the dry. That would explain how Abe camped there. And that's where the tracks were headed before I lost them."

She struggled to her feet.

"Easy," he said, bracing her. "There's no rush. That pile of limestone has been there a long, long time. It will be there for a few more hours."

"But will I?" she whispered as the world dimmed and brightened in time with her erratic pulse.

He tightened his hold. "You're stronger than you know."

Thunder rolled in the distance. A breeze came from the direction of the blackening clouds.

When he looked up, he saw that the clouds had thickened, dimming the sun's brutal strength. A dense, sultry wind gusted, bending spinifex and spindly gum trees alike. He sniffed the air as intently as any wild animal, and his nostrils flared at the unmistakable scent of rain.

"Cole?" she whispered, looking at the sky.

"It's coming, honey."

"When?"

Lightning arced invisibly, burning pathways through the clouds. Thunder came again. It was closer, louder.

"I don't know. I've seen it go on like this for days. And I've seen it rain an ocean within hours." He looked down at her pinched face and the green eyes whose beauty even exhaustion couldn't dull. "We'll be able to find both shade and shelter at the base of Bridget's Hill."

"And water?"

He didn't answer. He'd never lied to her. He didn't plan to start now.

Erin stared at the rugged thrust of land that was their destination. It looked very far away. She forced herself to walk forward.

For the first few steps Cole stayed beside her, ready to catch her if she fell. Watching her ragged progress tore at him, but he knew it would be stupid to carry her one step farther than he must, because his own stride was uneven, his own vision uncertain, his own body succumbing to dehydration and savage heat.

The teasing swirls of rain-scented wind lured Erin forward. Slowly she pressed on toward the hill she'd first seen in photographs that had been taken when Abelard Windsor had still been young enough to believe in a woman's love.

Bridget's Hill seemed to be retreating a step for every one Erin walked.

"Are they moving it?" she asked finally, her voice raw. "We aren't getting any closer."

"Halfway," he said. "We're halfway there. The flat ground and the heat waves fool you."

They walked on another half mile, then another. Gradually the ground fell away beneath their feet in a long decline. The hill loomed even larger above the depressed earth, crouching over the land like a demon wrapped in shimmering waves of hot air.

Erin stumbled over a bit of spinifex. Cole caught her and supported her, drawing one of her arms across his shoulders and anchoring it with one hand while his other arm locked around her waist.

"Leave me—here," she said.

He didn't bother answering.

"Damn it—*leave me*—"

"Don't talk," he said. "Walk."

Half carrying Erin, half dragging her, he pulled them toward the dark, ragged limestone formation crouching above the steamy flats. Thunder rumbled directly overhead. Neither of them noticed. Their entire beings were fixed on the darker shadow of land rising above the shimmering flats.

The closer they came, the more certain Cole was that Erin had been right. It was Bridget's Hill looming over them.

She staggered and would have fallen if he hadn't already been supporting her. He waited, breathing hard. After a minute she straightened and resumed walking, or trying to.

Two hundred yards from the base of Bridget's Hill, they stumbled across the remains of a bonfire. The charred ends of branches were partially buried in red sand. The fire had been huge. This was the gathering spot of several groups. Broken beer bottles and crumpled cans of Black Swann ringed the fire. There was no way to know the age of the tracks scattered everywhere, only that the Aborigines had visited this site since the last wet.

A shaft of lightning arced down to the top of Bridget's Hill, dimming for an instant even the savage light of the sun. Thunder followed instantly, waking Erin from her exhausted daze. Air twisted and rushed past them as though disturbed by a ghostly force. She shuddered and swallowed dryly.

"It's sacred—ground," she said.

"Everything is, to them."

"Them?"

She blinked and looked around. For the first time she realized she was standing in the midst of a huge circle of burned wood. There was a ring of packed dirt, then another ring of broken glass and discarded beer cans.

Slowly Cole and Erin walked away from the bonfire to the blocks of limestone rubble that had collected at the base of Bridget's Hill. The steeply sloping landform was more mesa than hill, more reef than either, a massive network of compressed, interlocking, water-soluble stone that had been buried in the outwash of a higher, younger Kimberley Plateau. Now the dead sea's limestone bones were slowly being resurrected by erosion.

Cole looked at the steep, eroded limestone and knew that only a fey, wild white girl would think of climbing it, and only an equally wild white man would follow her up to take her picture. The ancient limestone had been eroded in unpredictable ways. The top of the formation would be a network of deep cracks and crevices, potholes and solution channels, a tortured landscape where nothing could live but lizards or birds. There was no way of knowing whether Bridget's Hill was the last remains of a once-huge limestone mass or the tip of a stone iceberg that went deep beneath the dusty lid of soil.

No matter how carefully he looked, he didn't see any point along the ruined face of the limestone where a lush green exclamation point of foliage marked a seep or a spring.

Lightning stabbed down repeatedly, dancing across the top of the hill. Thunder followed instantly in a drumroll of sound that shook the earth. Wind sighed down the steep, ruined face of the limestone and lifted veils of grit from the dry land.

"Water?" Erin asked, her voice hoarse.

Without answering, Cole started for a notch cut in the

base of the steepest part of the hill. It was the only place where a spring or a seep might be hidden.

The approach to the notch was strewn with limestone boulders whose faces had been eroded into hollows and cups and bowls that, in the wet, would hold rain. But that water had long since evaporated, leaving behind an eerie black sculpture garden surrounded by sterile drifts of soil as fine as face powder. An empty watercourse snaked among stones like a dry, many-forked tongue whose source was the notch at the bottom of the hill.

Across the top of the limestone formation, lightning danced with lethal grace. Thunder came, hammering the ground.

Erin followed Cole to the base of the stone ravine, where the ground would be shaded much of the time. Someone had been there before them. Small mounds of dirt were scattered at random, connected by the same broad, flat footprints that Cole had been following across the empty land. He went to first one hole and then another, and in each he found the same thing—dry dirt for a few feet and then equally dry limestone bedrock.

"So far the little bastard isn't having any better luck than we are," Cole said grimly.

The footprints went from the dry watercourse to the hill itself, then vanished on the stony surface. The Aborigine had ignored the danger from lightning and climbed up to the top of the limestone formation to look for sinks or deep potholes that might hold water from one wet to the next.

Cole had no choice but to follow. Without a word he shucked out of the rucksack and began looking for the easiest way up the stone maze.

"No," she rasped urgently. "Lightning."

Even as she spoke, an incandescent sheet of lightning went from horizon to horizon in a cataract of violence that left the air itself smelling burned. Thunder exploded, shaking sky and ground alike.

The barrage of lightning continued until the hair on their bodies rippled and stood away from their flesh in response to the electrically charged air.

Between one minute and the next, the day darkened as if the sun had been ripped from the sky. The world convulsed, changing air for water. Rain hammered down as abruptly as lightning, as violently as thunder, an ocean turned inside out to flood land and sky alike.

Holding each other, Erin and Cole laughed and turned their faces up to the life-giving rain.

42

Kimberley Plateau
The next morning

An hour after dawn Erin watched the campfire flicker beneath a sky that trembled with misty light. The sky was so thick it fairly breathed water. Before yesterday's downpour had finally stopped, the sky had been black with night as well as clouds. Just before dawn a rain-scented breeze had begun blowing, bringing with it the sound of water running from every crack and crevice on Bridget's Hill.

Despite the shelter Cole had rigged from clear plastic sheets, and wearing the spare shirt he'd brought for just such an eventuality, Erin was almost chilly. The novelty of it amused her, as did the fact that she was actually looking forward to the rest of the mulga Cole had killed when the first onslaught of water had driven it from a limestone crevice.

Laughing softly, she reached for a full canteen and drank as much water as she wanted.

He looked up from the fire he was coaxing into life and smiled. "Feeling better?"

"Ridiculously good," she said, putting the canteen

aside after only a few swallows of water. "We could die tomorrow or the day after, but I'm sitting here glad to be chilly and licking my lips over the idea of snake for breakfast."

His laughter was as rich and lively as the firelight reflected in his clear eyes. "Better than seal, huh?"

"No comparison." She stretched, shivered lightly, and sat up. "What a difference water makes! Although I have to admit, for a time there I was worried about drowning."

He smiled slightly. "So was I. I still can't believe a wall of water didn't come down through that notch and wash us all the way to the Admiralty Gulf."

"Yeah." She rubbed her palms over her arms.

"Come sit by the fire while you eat," he said, stepping back from it. "In an hour you won't believe you ever wanted to."

"Eat?"

"No. Sit by a fire. It will be as hot today as it was yesterday, but it will feel even hotter. The humidity will be higher after the rain."

She shook her head. "God, what a climate. It's a wonder the Aborigines survived."

"A lot of them didn't," he said, handing her a chunk of fire-blackened meat.

"Do you think he did?"

"The one who followed us?"

She nodded, too busy chewing snake to talk.

He shrugged and bit off a chunk of mulga. "I didn't find any new tracks after the rain. If he came down off the hill, he didn't come down this side."

Before they were finished eating, the ground began to steam as the sun got hot enough to draw moisture from the earth. Cole got up and began studying Bridget's Hill with the aid of the strengthening light.

"Cole?"

He made an inquiring sound.

"What are you looking for?" she asked. "The Aborigine?"

He shook his head slowly, his whole attention on the base of the hill.

She came to her feet and went to stand by him. She stared in the same direction as him, but she saw nothing except a small, short-lived cascade coursing down rugged rock.

"I'll be damned," he said finally.

"What?"

"See that little stream?"

"Yes."

"See where it leaps down between those clumps of hard spinifex and then between those stunted bloodwood trees and then into that rubble pile at the base of the hill?"

She leaned forward. "Bloodwood, huh? Yes, I see it."

"See where the water comes out?"

She narrowed her eyes, frowned, and looked more closely. "No."

"Neither do I."

He bent, snagged the rucksack and shotgun, and walked toward the cascade. She went alongside, stretching her legs to keep up.

The answer to the mystery of the vanishing stream was no more obvious when they stood at the edge of the rubble pile. The cascade clearly washed down amid the tangle of boulders and scrubby trees. Just as clearly, the water didn't come back out.

"What—" she began, only to be cut off by an abrupt gesture from Cole.

"Hear anything?" he asked.

She listened. "All I hear is the cascade," she said after a minute.

He shrugged off the rucksack and handed her the shotgun. "I'm going to take a closer look. See if you can find any other nearby places where water runs off the hill but doesn't show up on the flats."

The longer Erin looked at Bridget's Hill, the more puzzled she became. Despite the fierce downpour, very little water was running off the huge, long rise of limestone. Even if she assumed that the pygmy trees, hard spinifex, and broken surface of the limestone concealed most rills and rivulets, she was left with the fact that only a few narrow tongues of water extended from the base of the hill to the depression beyond the big circle of charcoal left by the Aborigines. The depression itself held only a thin puddle after the heavy storm.

Cole scrambled down off the rubble pile and walked quickly to Erin.

"There's something odd about this place," she said.

"Damn little runoff," he said succinctly.

"Is that what you meant by limestone being a sponge?"

He laughed, but there was excitement burning in his eyes. "Not quite, honey. It takes time and pressure to force water into the tiny spaces between particles of limestone."

"Then where did all that water go? That's not a small hill, Cole. There must be at least four square miles of surface up top."

"Closer to ten. And we had at least an inch of rain, probably more like two."

"Did it all run off during the night?"

"If it had, we'd have been ass deep in a flash flood. I'll bet that only a fraction of the water that falls on Bridget's Hill ever sees sunlight again."

"Then where does it go?" she asked, hands on hips.

"Most of it runs down into joints and seams in the limestone and vanishes, working its way down through solution channels in the rock until it reaches the water table."

"Is that what happened to the cascade?"

He nodded. "Every drop of water that fell on top is trying to work its way to the bottom. I'll bet that limestone is rotten with solution channels."

"Caves?" she asked, her voice rising with excitement.

" 'God's own jewel box/Kept beneath stone locks.' " Cole's teeth flashed startlingly white against the black growth of his beard stubble. "Come on, honey. Let's go find the keyhole."

The first flush of excitement had plenty of time to wear off while they searched the base of Bridget's Hill for an opening that might lead to a cave. There were cracks in the stone where water went and didn't return. There were crevices where more water went in than came out.

But there was no opening big enough for a hand, much less a man, to penetrate.

It started raining again, a slow, steady, warm rain that was rather like being trapped in somebody's throttled-down shower.

After two hours Erin took off her floppy cabbage-leaf hat, mopped her face with it, and sat on the steeply sloping, stony earth beneath the thin shade of bloodwood trees. The temperature was well over one hundred degrees. Between rainstorms, the humidity was total.

"At least you have enough surplus water to sweat," Cole said.

"I wasn't complaining."

He smiled and touched her cheek. "I know. You haven't complained about anything."

"Except the goanna."

"You said it was better than seal."

"So is starvation," she retorted. "Well, almost." She sighed again, stretched her arms over her head, and made a startled sound. "A miracle."

"What?"

"The cool breeze."

"You've finally gone troppo," he said, wiping sweat from his face. "There isn't a cool breeze between here and the Snowy River."

"Sure there is." She took his hand and held it over her head. "Right here."

The instant Cole felt the cool current of air, a wave of adrenaline slammed through him. He scrambled past Erin, forced his way through a tangle of hard spinifex and scrubby trees, and stopped short. There, all but hidden by vegetation and rubble, was a dark, narrow opening in the limestone.

"Cole? Is that what I think it is?" Erin stared past him. "It's so small. How big was Abe?"

"Smaller than me."

"Who isn't?" she retorted.

With a supple movement, Cole unslung the shotgun and set it aside. The rucksack thumped to the ground.

"I'm going inside," he said. "Stay here."

"Not a chance."

"Caves are dangerous," he said flatly.

"The most interesting things in life usually are."

He slanted her a look, then smiled crookedly. "At least let me make sure there aren't any traps around the entrance, natural or otherwise."

"Good old Abe, King of Lies," she muttered.

"Something like that. Although there's no guarantee this is Abe's cave. Like I said, the entire hill could be riddled with holes."

"But this particular opening," she said, deadpan, "rather resembles a woman's 'map of Tasmania.'"

After a startled instant, Cole gave a crack of laughter, grabbed Erin, and kissed her hard.

"For luck," he said, releasing her as suddenly as he'd taken her.

He soon found that the opening wasn't as narrow as it seemed, because it was offset slightly from right to left. Between one breath and the next he pushed from tropical sun into seamless darkness.

A swift movement of his hand ignited one of the matches he'd brought with him. He shielded the fragile flame within the circle of his hand. The first thing the flickering light picked out was a mound of thick, creamy candles. The second was a row of miners' carbide helmet lamps and fuel.

The third was a rusted candy tin.

43

Bridget's Hill

With hands that trembled, Cole picked up the old tin. Something rattled inside. He stared at the tin while the match burned down to flesh. Swearing at the bite of flame, he reached for another match.

"Cole?" Erin called from outside. "Are you all right?"

He let out a long, ragged sigh and remembered to breathe. "I'm fine. Can you drag the rucksack and shotgun as far as the entrance?"

When she retrieved the shotgun and rucksack, the weight surprised her. Not the shotgun—it always felt heavy to her. It was the rucksack that felt like it was full of lead. The thought of him carrying it through the killing heat while she walked unburdened made her mouth flatten.

Carrying the shotgun and dragging the rucksack, she scrambled over rock and through brush until she could look inside the slit in the limestone hill. Cole was lighting one candle from the flame of another. He held out a candle to her with hands that had a fine tremor of excitement rippling just beneath his control.

Erin didn't notice anything but the passageway itself, a

cool darkness that absorbed light and gave it back from unexpected quarters, where wet stone reflected flame. The sound of falling water came distantly. Nearby was a steady dripping, sliding, gliding rush of rivulets that was like a tremulous sigh expanding through the cave's endless night.

The limestone was alive with water.

"What's that?" she asked, spotting the candy tin in Cole's hand for the first time.

"Something Abe left."

"Is it empty?"

"No."

"Is it diamonds?" she asked eagerly.

Cole pried the lid from the candy tin. "No. But in a cave, it's more valuable than diamonds. Matches."

There was a folded piece of paper inside, riding atop a nest of loose wooden matches and waterproof containers holding more matches.

"Take it," he said. "Like everything else that Abe left behind, it's yours."

Gently she removed the paper and opened it. The faded, elegant lines of Abe's handwriting took shape in the flickering candle flames.

Granddaughter:

If you got this far, you're more my blood than Bridget's. She hated the Kimberley. Said it was fit only for felons and black boys.

But it was me she loved, not my brother. It was my child she bore.

Mistress of lies.

Damn her.

Drink holy, child of my dreams.

Know where the black swan goes.

Touch God's own jewel box.
Feel the cold stone locks.

Goodbye, grandchild of deceit, blood of my
blood, bone of my bone. Don't stay too long. You'll
swallow black and drown.

"Looks like you were right," Erin said, glancing up from the paper. "Bridget was carrying Abe's child when she married my grandfather."

Cole grunted. Working in darkness, he bent and started sorting through the rucksack, removing everything but the small flashlight. "Like he said, 'Queen of Lies.'"

"'Damn their hot cries,'" Erin added quietly. She folded the paper and put it back in the tin. "He wasn't a forgiving sort, was he?"

"Would you have been?"

"So far, so good," she said with a shrug.

She removed a waterproof container of matches, checked its contents, and stuck the container in the pocket of her shorts.

"Does that mean you've forgiven Hans?" Cole asked as he took the shotgun and propped it against a rock near the entrance.

"It means I've forgiven myself for being stupid and trusting the wrong person." She closed the tin and set it on the floor. "I don't think old Abe got that far. I think he drank a river of beer rather than face himself."

Cole's pale eyes flashed in the candlelight as he turned toward her. "What about me? Have you forgiven me for not closing my hand and crushing Lai's throat?"

"You're asking the wrong person." Erin scooped up several fat candles and stuffed them in her other pocket.

"What does that mean?"

"You should be asking yourself, not me."

For the space of several breaths there was no sound in the cave but that of water seeping through cracks in cold stone.

Cole shrugged the rucksack into place and turned away.

The sound of his footsteps grating over stone blended with the distant murmurings of water. He worked over the familiar carbide lamps, then tried lighting one. To his surprise, it worked. A clean flame burned steadily, multiplied many times by the mirrored dish. He closed the tempered glass shield, protecting the flame.

He snuffed out his candle and tried another lamp. It didn't work. Neither did the third. The fourth one did. He took off his bush hat, strapped one of the miners' helmet lamps on, and walked over to Erin with the other helmet light burning in his hand.

She learned real fast not to look directly at either light.

"Take off your hat," he said.

She did, waited while he strapped the helmet on, and then turned her head. The helmet wobbled wildly.

"Too big," he said. He adjusted the webbing of straps. "Try again."

This time the helmet stayed in place.

"Stay at least ten feet behind me," he said. "No point in both of us falling through the same hole."

Her eyes narrowed. She hesitated before blowing out her candle. "Are you trying to frighten me into staying here?"

"No. I'm simply telling you the truth. We could be walking on limestone that's as thick as a mountain or as thin as summer ice. There's no way of knowing until the floor either gives way or it doesn't."

Uneasily she looked down at the ground beneath her feet. It was uneven and felt as solid as the stone it was.

"Maybe we should hold off exploring until we can come back with ropes and things," she said.

All Cole said was, "Wait for me at the entrance. You'll be safe there."

"No."

"Then follow me and walk where I walk. If the floor holds me, it should hold you."

She blew out her candle and started after him, leaving ten feet between them.

The passageway quickly closed down until they were forced to duck-walk. To keep her mind off the darkness and the massive weight of limestone that was between herself and the sun, she thought about Crazy Abe Windsor.

"How old did you say Abe was?" she asked, breathing heavily from the strain of the unnatural walk.

"Old enough to be your grandfather, why?" Cole retorted.

"Maybe there's more to beer and raw croc liver than I thought."

He laughed, then swore when the ceiling came down even more, forcing him onto his hands and knees. Water seeped from every surface, making the stone clammy and slick. Long horizontal stains ran the length of the smooth walls. As the floor slowly dropped, the stains rose.

"There's something wrong with this cave," she said after a time.

"Like what?"

"It's little and narrow and ugly. Caves are big and grand and gorgeous."

"Only the ones you hear about. Most caves are small muddy wormholes that never get decorated."

"Why?"

A knob of limestone stabbed Cole's kneecap. He swore again and muttered, "Conditions aren't right."

"Why?"

"Because I said so," he retorted.

She took the hint and shut up. As she crawled, she turned her head slowly, playing the lamplight over the narrow passage, trying to reason with the cold fear that was whispering to her, telling her that Bridget's Hill was going to settle on her shoulders and crush her flat. She saw several shadows in rapid succession off to her right. When she turned her head, the light couldn't penetrate their depths. The openings were big enough to hide a man. From somewhere in their darkness came the sound of falling water.

Shivering, she pressed forward. Water dripped and gathered and twisted into thin streams, pulled by gravity through cracks in the limestone. The water was cool, almost secretive, sliding away into black crevices and vanishing or flowing in thin channels along the edges of the tunnel. The stain marks on the wall had disappeared. Puddles collected in small, shallow depressions in the uneven surface. The floor looked like it had been scalloped by running water.

The passageway pitched down at an increasing angle. Erin thought about the alternate openings that had been revealed in the glare of their helmet lights.

"How do we know we're in the right wormhole?" she asked.

"Arrows."

The floor pitched downward more steeply. A limestone ripple gnawed on her kneecap, sending pain lancing through her leg.

"How far have we come?" she asked.

"Fifty feet, max."

She hissed a word beneath her breath.

"That's not shit, honey. That's cave mud. Takes a hell of a long time to collect. In fact—*don't move!*"

She froze. "What's wrong?"

"No floor," he said succinctly.

He turned his head slowly, playing the light around the roughly circular shadow that had appeared in the floor a few feet ahead. Narrow streamers of water glittered and twisted from an invisible opening in the ceiling and disappeared through a hole in the stone floor of the passage. Stretching out on his stomach, he inched forward over the slippery, scalloped surface until he could point his light straight down the narrow vertical tunnel.

Water danced and spun away into blackness. About twenty feet below, the disturbed surface of a pool returned the light in random flashes. A more orderly pattern of light came back from a pile of what looked like a tangle of flexible chain.

Cole picked up one end of a heavy aluminum ladder and shook it out over the hole. As the flexible ladder descended, water splashed and slid over the thick metal surfaces. The top end was bolted into stone a foot from the lip of the hole.

He spent a long time shining his light on the huge bolts that anchored the top of the ladder to the mouth of the shaft. There was some sign of wear on the metal, but not much.

"Is it safe up ahead?" Erin asked.

"I'm thinking about it."

Just when she was certain he wasn't going to say anything more, he did.

"Abe was a good miner. The shoring in all the Dog mines is still sound."

"So?" she muttered.

"So he probably bolted that ladder into place well enough to take my weight, not just his. Besides, those bolts could hold up the Brooklyn Bridge."

"There's a ladder?"

"After a fashion."

Cole grunted as he jackknifed his big body around and lowered his legs into the hole, supporting himself on his braced forearms. To Erin it looked as though he was trapped in stone up to his waist.

"Shine that light somewhere else than in my eyes," he said.

"Sorry." Hastily she tilted her head down.

He found one of the aluminum rungs with his right foot. Slowly he shifted more and more of his weight from his arms to his foot, ignoring the water falling on his face and shoulders.

His foot slipped.

He caught himself on his forearms.

"Cole."

"No worries. The rungs are just wet."

This time he jammed his foot all the way to the rock wall before he put on any pressure. The metal took his weight without complaining or giving way. The bolts didn't even quiver. He shifted his weight quickly, repeatedly, bouncing up and down, testing the bolts that held the ladder.

Nothing moved.

"That old bastard wasn't entirely crazy," Cole muttered. He looked up at Erin. His light made the water falling over him sparkle and shimmer. "I'd just as soon you didn't try this, honey."

"Into each life a little rain must fall."

"I'd settle for a little, but it's the wrong damn season."

He tilted his head and looked up at the black opening that was drooling thin streams of water over him. As he watched, he slowly realized that the volume of water falling down had increased just in the few minutes he had been there.

"This could be bad news," he said.

She followed the direction of his lamp, adding her own light. Despite the fugitive glitter of reflected light, the thicker streams of water appeared more black than silver or transparent.

"Right now it's running enough to be annoying," he said. "In a few hours it could be a gusher. Depends on how much of the surface water this is a collection channel for, and how long it takes for the rain to get through the limestone above us into this channel."

"When Abe talked about swallowing black and drowning," she said uneasily, "I thought he meant claustrophobia."

"Doubt it. The deeper the mine, the better he liked it. Besides, he was a literal bloke, for all his metaphors. If he said drown, he meant drown. In water."

"Black water."

"No other kind in a cave." Cole eased his left foot onto the ladder. "We're under a high-water mark right now."

"What?"

"The horizontal stains on the wall on the way in. High-water mark."

"Very comforting."

"If you want comfort, go back to the entrance."

She took a slow breath and bit her tongue.

"The scallop marks we've been crawling over are proof that water ran through the tunnel at some time in the past and could run again in the future," he added.

"Could or will?"

"Once the limestone below gets saturated, the water level will rise and rise and rise until it overflows through places like the crevice we came through. If the level rises slowly, we'll be able to get out. Or if there are enough outlets lower down for the water to escape, we'll be safe."

"And if there aren't?"

"Then we'll find out how much black water we can drink before we drown."

44

Abe's mine

Slowly Cole shifted his right hand to one of the flexible ladder's rungs. The stone was uneven enough to keep some of the rungs a few inches away from the wall of the shaft. Where the stone didn't slope, Abe had chipped out places for hands and toes.

"Cole? Are you sure we shouldn't wait?"

"I'm sure it's going to get a lot wetter down there before the dry begins. I'm damn sure our chances of surviving the ladder are a hell of a lot better than our chances of surviving ConMin's attention for the next six months with only the *possibility* of a diamond mine as a weapon."

"Be careful," she said.

"This from a woman who thinks king mulgas are beautiful?"

"Tasty, too."

His smile flashed as he shifted his left hand onto the ladder. For an instant the handle of his knife gleamed beneath the flap of the muddy leather sheath.

The ladder held his full weight.

He let out a long, silent breath and began feeling

blindly with his foot for the next rung below. The ladder flexed and twisted slightly until it crunched up against rock. He found another rung and dropped more deeply into the hole. The rucksack scraped against rock and hung up in the narrow opening.

Cole cursed and went up a rung. He wriggled out of the rucksack and slung one of the straps over his right arm. Carefully he descended again. It was still a very tight fit. If he'd put one more item in the rucksack it would have hung up.

"You're too big," she said. "Let me take it down."

"I was hoping you weren't coming down at all." But he climbed back up again and handed the rucksack to her. "Put my extra shirt back on before you get any colder."

She reached for the clammy shirt and pulled it on. "How long will it take for the limestone below to fill up with water?"

"I don't know. Maybe it hasn't filled this far for ten thousand years. Maybe it won't fill up at all." He glanced up and caught a flash of intense green from her eyes. "But I'll tell you this, honey. I wouldn't plan on making more than one trip before the next dry."

She bit her lower lip as he went back down the ladder once more. She heard the scrape of stone against cloth and flesh, followed by Cole cursing the size of the very body whose strength had gotten them this far.

"Can you make it?" she asked.

"Barely." He grunted and swore again. "Abe was built more narrow in the shoulders than I am."

Cole vanished by inches into the hole. Water hissed when it hit the glass shielding the flame in his helmet.

"Have you ever used a flexible ladder before?" he asked just before he disappeared completely below the stone lip.

"Every time I went from a cargo ship to a Zodiac. Usually in a force-five gale."

"After that, this will be a piece of cake. The wall slopes away enough so that you don't bang your hands much, but not enough to let you twist in the breeze."

When he called up from the bottom, Erin put on the rucksack, took a deep breath, and reminded herself that she'd done the same thing before under worse circumstances.

But not in the dark.

Silently Cole watched her descend the ladder while water dripped and slid and splashed all around. The rivulets had become trickles as thick as his finger. They fell harder and stayed around longer. He was standing at the bottom of the ladder in an ankle-deep pool of water. There was just enough space for two people to stand close to each another. Closer than an embrace.

A nearly circular passageway led off at an angle. The tunnel was smooth-sided and narrow.

"Watch it," Cole said, catching Erin when her foot searched for and didn't find a final rung. "The shaft is two feet longer than the ladder."

Her breath came in as cool water lapped above her ankles. "I hope we aren't going much lower."

"So do I."

Cole looked down and ran his helmet light over every bit of floor that he could. In a spot that would have been the base of a waterfall during the wet, the limestone floor was eaten away, making an irregular bowl. Small hunks of water-rounded stone lined the bowl.

"Can you go back up the ladder a few feet?" he asked.

She climbed back up several rungs. "Is this far enough?"

"One more."

Ignoring the cool shower of water, Cole sat on his heels in the space she'd opened. He started scooping out handfuls of stones, trying to find the bottom of the basin. Something in the eighth handful winked and shimmered in the light with a life of its own.

"Bingo."

"What?"

Without answering he stood up and held out his hand so that it caught the full flood of his helmet light. A rounded crystal the size of a small marble gleamed between his thumb and forefinger.

"Diamond?" Erin asked, hardly able to believe.

"As ever was. Hang onto it. I'll see if Abe missed any more."

"Missed?"

"This is the first pothole I've seen. He must have worked it over more than once on the way into the cave."

The diamond felt cool on her palm. Adrenaline swept through her. In that instant she understood why men risked their lives mining the earth. She closed her hand around the crystal until her fingers ached.

Below her came the sound of rocks rolling together, Cole searching through debris down to the stony bottom of the basin itself. There was a long crack in the bottom where water flowed out. He probed the crack. It was too narrow for his fingers.

"Oh, well," he said. "If there are any diamonds in that crack, they're not real big."

"How can you be so calm?" she demanded.

He laughed. "Calm? Honey, my hands are shaking almost as much as the first time I made love to you."

The sound she made could have been surprise or laughter or both.

He stood and absently wiped his hands on his soaked khaki shorts. "Let's not waste any more time here."

"*Waste?* We just found a diamond!"

His only answer was "Watch that last step."

Cole dropped to his hands and knees and crawled into the opening that began at a right angle to the bottom of the shaft they had just descended. The floor of the tube hadn't been pounded by falling water, so it wasn't as deeply eroded as the plunge pool had been. The surrounding limestone was damp but not under water. The floor was scalloped.

He probed the scallops at random and found one small diamond. Tucking it beneath his tongue, he went forward. He didn't bother to probe any more of the shallow scallops. Grimacing at the discomfort, he crawled deeper and deeper into the limestone formation.

Erin grubbed along right behind him, pushing the rucksack.

Gradually Cole realized that the tube was descending. Water seeped from ceilings and walls and collected into steady trickles. The trickles gathered in shallow channels on either side of the tunnel floor or found small cracks and disappeared deeper into the limestone. He wondered how high the water table was in this area of the Kimberley, and how long it would take to saturate the ancient, partially dissolved reef until the tunnel they were crawling through became full of water.

"The ceiling looks scalloped, too," she said. "Does that mean this tunnel spends a lot of time full of water?"

He grunted. It was something he'd just as soon not think about.

From ahead came the sound of rushing water. He slowed down and began searching the flickering shadows ahead very carefully, seeking any openings in the floor.

Overhead, the ceiling shed water like a sieve with a handful of uneven holes. The tunnel widened from side to side. The floor was very rough, potholed from the constant hammering of waterfalls during the height of the wet. Some of the potholes were as big as bathtubs. Others were no bigger than a fist.

Small mounds of stony debris appeared randomly, piled at either side of the tunnel.

"Abe dug out some of the potholes," Cole said.

"Can we?"

"He kept going, which means there's something better ahead."

Water showered down on Cole and Erin, drenching them while they crawled forward. The temperature of the water had gone from cool to chilly. She began shivering as soon as she stopped to probe a small pothole, but she kept at it. Even her cold hands could tell the difference in texture between fragments of limestone and the sleek texture of a water-rounded diamond.

"I found one!" she called out.

"Good for you. Put it under your tongue and keep crawling."

"But I found—"

"Abe's tailings," Cole interrupted. "See the debris shoved aside? He's already been over these potholes."

"Then why did I find a diamond?"

"Offhand, I'd guess he found something up ahead that made these potholes look like a waste of time."

While Cole talked, he kept crawling toward the throaty, increasing sound of thunder coming from up ahead. Excitement sleeted through him, taking away the pain of cuts and bruises gotten from crawling over stone. The ceiling rose until he could duck-walk and then walk almost normally. Water lapped around his feet. He ignored it as he flexed muscles that had cramped. When Erin's lamp appeared a few feet behind him, he turned and pulled her to her feet. She groaned with relief.

"This is more my idea of a cave," she said, shining her

light around. "A little cramped from top to bottom, but lots of space otherwise. Lots of puddles, too."

"Yeah. And they're getting bigger every minute."

He spat out his diamond and put it into one of the pockets of the rucksack she carried. She handed over her own diamond and watched it disappear.

To her surprise, Cole didn't immediately press further into the cave's wide horizontal opening. He simply stood and ran his lamp over everything within reach of the cone of light, memorizing his location within the larger opening. Then he turned and scanned the tunnel they had just emerged from.

A large, rough *#1* had been gouged into the limestone above the tunnel. As Cole turned away, a *#2* appeared just at the limits of his helmet light.

"See any more marked openings?" he asked.

Erin turned in the opposite direction and looked. All she noticed was a distinct cool breeze.

"No more numbers, but there's a lot of air moving."

"Probably because there's a lot of water coming in and pushing the air out of the way."

"What?"

"Listen," Cole said. "That's not thunder. Somewhere up ahead there's at least one cascade or waterfall pouring from the ceiling down to whatever passes for the floor around here."

Shivering, she stood and listened.

"You're cold," he said.

"I've been a lot colder and survived just fine."

He hesitated, then accepted her judgment of her own physical limits. "We'd better get going. I don't know how much longer we have down here."

"Which way?"

He pointed to the wall. "See that arrow? We go in the opposite direction."

"Why?"

"In a cave or a mine, all arrows point to the way *out*."

She walked closer to the arrow and made a sound of surprise. "It looks like it was just made."

"When it comes to rocks, a decade or two isn't much time."

Cole turned and began walking against the arrow. After thirty feet it was clear that somewhere ahead water was pouring in faster than it could drain out. A thin puddle appeared on the floor. Within twenty feet, the water was over his shoes.

"Don't trust the footing," he said. "There could be potholes underneath this puddle deep enough to drown in." He stopped and turned toward her. "You can swim, can't you?"

"Yes, but I'd rather not. This water isn't getting any warmer."

"Do you want—"

"No," she said, cutting across his words. "I don't want to go back. I want to see Abe's jewel box."

"We may be walking over it right now."

Instantly Erin's light flashed down to the water lapping over her feet. "Do you really think so?"

"Maybe, but not likely. I don't see any piles of rubble. Mining, even placer mining, is a messy process."

Accompanied by the steadily increasing thunder of distant water, they splashed through the broad, shallow puddle. He was careful to stay within sight of the wall and its arrows until the *#2* opening appeared. The prospect of crawling through it wasn't inviting. The opening was small. The water was at least six inches deep and flowing with a pronounced current.

"Well?" she asked as she came to stand beside Cole.

"It's flowing away from us."

"So?"

He shrugged. "So I expected it to be flowing *toward* the sound of falling water, which is behind us."

With that he dropped to his hands and knees and began to crawl, cursing steadily.

She followed without hesitating. A few minutes later she understood why he was swearing so savagely. The ceiling came to within a foot of the floor and the sides of the tube closed in until his shoulders audibly scraped both sides.

"Can you make it through?" she called.

His only answer was a grunt, followed by splashing and another round of curses as the tunnel took a hard bend to the left. He jackknifed through it and found himself in easier going. The ceiling lifted again. Soon he was standing upright, but sideways. The solution channel was so narrow that his shoulders wouldn't fit any other way.

The sound of falling water filled the narrow space, but only a few trickles showed in the lantern light. Twelve feet farther down the channel, another ladder appeared. It led up through another long narrow shaft that had been widened at one point by rushing water. The ladder was wet with runoff.

"Wait until I'm up top before you start climbing," Cole said.

He put his weight onto the first gleaming metal rung. The opening of the crack was so narrow there was no worry about the ladder twisting and banging him against stone. Water poured over an unseen lip above, drenching the ladder with an insistent shower.

Fourteen rungs later, his helmet light picked up another opening in the slowly dissolving limestone. He rolled out of the hole and called down to Erin.

"Come on up."

Her helmet light went out halfway up. Instantly he shined his own light over the rim. When her shoulders and the rucksack poked above the hole, he lifted her free, removed her helmet, and lit the flame. She gave a broken sigh of relief.

"I was afraid it wasn't going to work again," she admitted in a shaky voice.

"That might happen, honey. Too damn much water." He hesitated. "We should go back."

"We have plenty of matches and candles, if it comes to that."

For a long moment Cole looked at Erin. Her face was drawn into taut lines of unease. She was a woman who loved light, who had made it the core of her professional life. Being in the cave's total absence of light, even for a few seconds, had shaken her.

"You don't like it down here, do you?" he asked.

"I liked finding that diamond. The rest of it I can put up with for a while longer."

His grin flashed in the sidelight from her lamp. "Fifteen more minutes. If we don't find anything by then, we'll head back. It's too damn dangerous for you."

"But not for you?"

"I know the risks. You don't."

"So how risky is it?"

"If we live, I'll dream about this and wake up sweating," he said bluntly. "We're damn fools for being down here."

"Abe survived."

"God watches over fools and drunks."

"So we're half safe," she retorted.

Cole laughed. "Close your eyes, honey."

"Why?" she asked even as she closed them.

"So my light won't blind you."

She felt the smooth warmth of his lips, the rough brush of beard stubble, and the heat of his tongue as the kiss deepened suddenly, fiercely. He stripped away the weight of the rucksack, pulled her off her feet, held her hard and close.

Almost as soon as it began, the kiss ended, leaving her shivering with more than the chill of limestone and water.

He peeled off his khaki shirt and gently stuffed her into it, ignoring her protests at the third layer of clothing.

"I'll just rip it to pieces in the next narrow passage," he said calmly, handing her the rucksack.

"You'll freeze without your shirt."

"I've easily twice your mass. I retain heat much better than you do. Ask any biologist."

Before she could argue any more, he turned and began making his way along another passage. This one was tall and so narrow that walking sideways was the only way to go. This channel, too, showed signs of having been filled with water at some time in the past. It also had arrows gouged in its sides at every point where new openings occurred.

The sound of running water came from everywhere around. Erin felt like she was pushing a bubble of light and air through a maze of waterfalls and cascades. She wondered how far down they'd come into the limestone mass but didn't ask.

She really didn't want to know the exact size of the massive weight of stone pressing down overhead.

She put the thought out of her mind and concentrated on orienting herself in the three-dimensional maze. Each time she thought she'd figured it out, she found she hadn't. It was impossible to visualize their progress as they twisted and turned, crawling up and down and sideways to the sound of running water.

If it hadn't been for the arrows, she'd have been utterly lost. She wondered if it was the same for Cole.

She didn't ask.

As Cole pushed around a corner, he felt the pressure of limestone walls fall away. He walked three steps and

turned slowly in a complete circle, discovering everything within reach of his helmet light. Erin came and
stood beside him, adding her own light to his.

From all around came the sound of water rushing and
falling and cascading through unseen solution channels
in the limestone. The ceiling was beyond the reach of
their light. So was every wall but the one behind them.
Air moved faintly, stirred by countless currents of water
pouring into the space that had been dissolved by a thousand, thousand seasons of rain.

Cole looked at his watch. "Four minutes. No more."

Erin was too captivated to argue. The unmistakable
sensation of space around her was both welcome and
eerie. The opening was alive with the thousand voices of
water, water whispering, murmuring, rushing, pouring,
pounding, tumbling, seeping, dripping, sliding. There
was water everywhere she looked, a world alive with silver drops and dense blackness.

A huge, shallow pool expanded into the dark as far as
her helmet light could reach. Hidden currents caused
streaks of light to twist over the water's surface like a
ghostly silver aurora.

For the first time since she'd entered the limestone
maze, she longed for her camera. Except for her first
brush with the long arctic night, she'd encountered nothing quite so alien yet so beautiful as the underground
lake.

The roving cone of her light fell on mounds of water-
rounded chunks of limestone. The rubble piles poked up
through the sheet of water that stretched away into the
darkness.

She grabbed Cole's forearm and pointed. "Look!"

His helmet light cut a swath through the darkness until
he saw more mounds rising from the dark lake. He
walked to the edge of the lake. It quivered at his feet as

though alive, responding to unseen currents of air and water. The water in the lake was absolutely clear, having rid itself of surface grit on the long trip down through the limestone reef.

If the lake hadn't caught the light with each disturbance of air or water, it would have been invisible.

Slowly Cole turned, scanning the wall behind him, memorizing the location of the passage. Abe hadn't numbered the tunnel. As far as Cole could see, none of the other cracks and holes had numbers.

"I don't see any arrows," Erin said.

"Don't go out of sight of the tunnel mouth. You're my safety line."

Cole walked to the edge of the trembling water, then began wading along the shoreline, searching for some sign that Abe had been there before him.

"Here. Underneath the water," Cole said after a minute. He looked up. His helmet lamp easily reached to the tunnel mouth. "Come over here."

He had to repeat the words again, because the throaty roar of water filled Erin's ears. She waded toward him until she saw the arrow mark gouged out of the limestone floor.

"Does that mean it was dry when Abe was here?"

"Probably," Cole said. "He wasn't much on water. Hated it, as a matter of fact. Couldn't swim."

"It must have been awful for him to explore the cave."

"Not in the dry. The water that's coming down now is new."

Her breath came in and stayed until she forced herself to breathe out. She thought of the torrential rains of the wet and ten square miles of surface limestone covered one inch deep, and all those drops gathering together into rivulets and tiny streams, streams that flowed into crevices that also joined together, creating runoff channels that ate down and down into stone, dissolving tunnels and shafts and small rooms, water lured by gravity further and further down.

And each solution channel was the narrow end of a funnel whose mouth could be half a mile square, or a mile, or more. Tons upon tons of water sliding down and down and down. When runoff filled up all the holes, there would be nothing left but darkness and water and stone.

Don't stay too long. You'll drink black water and drown.

With an effort Erin pulled her thoughts away from the massive weight of stone and water balanced over her head. Deliberately she waded after Cole, keeping her head down and watching the silver patterns of water glittering around her feet. Overhead, long ribbons of water gushed out of darkness into the artificial light, creating random showers.

"There are potholes among the rubble mounds," Cole said. "Channels, too. At one time this whole chamber had powerful currents of water moving through it."

"During the last wet?"

He didn't answer.

Grimly she concentrated on the water that was now halfway up her ankles. There was a definite sluggish current leading into the darkness they hadn't yet explored.

While Cole knelt in the water and probed a small pothole, she looked for something to distract her from the ominous weight of darkness and the increasing thunder of water. The cone of her light probed in the water for a pothole. A circular shadow caught her attention.

At first she thought it was simply another water-rounded stone. Then she realized that it was too perfectly circular, and there were others like it, all circular, all perfect. She waded farther, then made a startled sound as she stumbled into a pothole whose depth was masked by the clarity of the water. She put her hands out to break her fall.

Her fingers closed over a candy tin.

The pothole was full of them.

"Erin?" he asked, looking up from a handful of rubble he had gathered. "Are you all right?"

She tried to answer but couldn't speak. She grabbed a tin in each hand and held them up to meet the cone of light sweeping toward her as Cole turned. Water showered down her arms, reflecting light in countless glittering points of white and green and yellow.

Then he realized that it wasn't water cascading from the rusted tins. She was standing knee deep in God's own jewel box, and diamonds were pouring from her hands.

45

Abe's mine

The ladder closest to the surface was buried in a cascade of water that was twice as heavy as it had been when they'd first descended its slippery rungs less than an hour ago.

"I'll tie the rucksack to my ankle and drag it up after me," Cole said loudly.

"Don't be silly." Erin shifted her shoulders beneath the rucksack's nylon webbing straps. "The ladder will be tough enough to keep your balance on without having the rucksack pull a foot out from under you. And I've carried packs heavier than this one. It can't weigh more than twenty pounds."

He gave her a worried look. She was shaking from the cold and from the knowledge that the lowest crawl space they had negotiated was more than half full of water and rising quickly. If they'd spent another half hour in the jewel box, they wouldn't have gotten out until the water level dropped again.

If ever.

"I'll go first," he said. "If your lamp goes out again, I'll be able to light the way for you. But don't wait long. You could drown climbing up that narrow shaft. If you get hung up, shrug your shoulders. If that doesn't work, breathe out and shrug again. If that doesn't work, back up, leave the rucksack at the bottom, and I'll bring it up. Understand me?"

She nodded, sending her light bobbing.

Turning his face to the side so that he could breathe beneath the pouring water, Cole went up the first rungs of the ladder. The runoff this close to the surface was cloudy and felt almost warm by comparison to the water down below. Ignoring the scrape of stone over bare skin, he went up the ladder on a single breath and lifted himself out onto the limestone floor. He jackknifed around and looked back into the hole.

"Up!" he called.

Taking a deep breath, Erin turned her head aside and fought her way up the ladder as water pounded over her, trying to drive her back down into the cave. Her cold hands locked around metal rungs, holding her against the water. The ladder shivered and rattled from the force of the runoff. She climbed two more rungs, driving herself upward into the narrowest part of the shaft.

When she tried to go up one more rung, she couldn't. She reached behind her back, shoving candy tins away from whatever had caught the rucksack.

Beneath her fist, a rusted tin crumpled. Diamonds poured down into the bottom of the rucksack. She lunged upward, only to be snagged again. She tried to struggle out of the straps. She couldn't.

Water beat down on her, not enough air to breathe.

Fear raced through her. Around her the shaft was filling with water. Her body and the pack were acting like a cork, keeping most of the runoff from draining.

If she didn't move, she'd drown.

She bucked against the sack, using the strength of her legs to drive her body back against the hard stone. More tins gave way, their rusted seams no match for her frightened struggles, but it wasn't enough to free her.

Shrug.

Cole's advice came back to Erin as clearly as if he was standing next to her. She drew her shoulders forward and arched her body, trying to slip past the obstruction. When that didn't work she forced herself to relax and let all the air out of her lungs. Another tin shifted, but it wasn't enough to free her.

She rolled to one side. It didn't help. She rolled the other way. The contents of the pack shifted, giving a few inches. Aching for air yet afraid to breathe, she rolled farther.

Suddenly she was free. She went up rungs in a tumbling rush.

Cole's hands clamped beneath her arms as he pulled her upper body over the lip. She lay half in, half out of the hole, gasping for air.

"Are you all right?" he asked urgently.

She nodded. No light moved at the gesture. Her lamp had gone out again. He tried to light it, couldn't, and took off his own.

"Here," he said, switching helmets with her, adjusting straps quickly. "It's just a short way to the entrance."

The passage was too small for Erin to squeeze past Cole. He jackknifed again, turned around, and crawled until he could duck-walk, using the light cast from her helmet to pick his way through the narrow cleft. His shadow loomed hugely ahead of him as it slid over and around the rough limestone, flickering with every motion he made.

That sliding, uncertain shadow saved his life.

Jason Street's blow landed on the back of Cole's skull with stunning, rather than crushing, force. Cole had just enough awareness to fall bonelessly, sprawling with his left hand underneath his body, concealing the wrist sheath he wore.

"Cole?" Erin called, scrambling forward as she saw him fall. "What's wrong?"

"No worries, Miss Windsor," Street said. "You're safe now. Did you find Abe's mine?"

The sudden white arc of an electric lantern blinded Erin just as a man's hand closed around her arm.

"Let go of me! Cole's hurt!"

"Don't worry about that bastard. He was hired to kill you."

"You're crazy!"

"Am I? Read this, luv. It's from your father."

Erin glanced at the bright yellow plastic being held out to her. She was shaking so much from cold and fear she could barely breathe. "I won't look at anything until I help Cole."

Street smiled reassuringly despite his urgent need to know about Abe's mine. If the mine hadn't been found, he would need Erin's cooperation to find it. She'd proved that she was better at unraveling Abe's secrets than anyone else.

"Check on Blackburn if you have to," Street said, letting go of her, "but you'll feel like a bloody fool after you read your father's letter."

Without looking at the man who was no more than a dark presence looming behind blinding light, Erin hurried forward and knelt at Cole's side. A quick check told her that he was breathing regularly. Blood was welling slowly from a bruise at the base of his skull.

Relief raced through her, making her almost weak. She

stroked his forehead lightly, pushing wet hair away from his face. A motion just behind her made her look around. She saw the metal gleam of a pistol.

The muzzle was trained on Cole.

"Well, Miss Windsor. How is he?"

"Out cold. Who the hell are you?"

"Jason Street. Didn't your father mention me to you?"

"No."

"Read this, luv. I'm on your side."

Erin stood and looked at the packet Street was holding out. From the corner of her eye she noticed that the pistol muzzle stayed pointed at Cole rather than following her movements. She shrugged out of the rucksack and sat down on it, ignoring the crunch and grind of ruined candy tins.

Reluctantly she looked at the packet Street was holding out to her. She really didn't want to face whatever was inside. She didn't want to know that once more she'd been just another pawn in another international game played out in bed as well as in smoke-filled rooms. At least this time no one was cutting her up with a knife.

Yet.

Silently she held out her hand. Street smiled encouragement and dropped the packet on her palm.

"That's it, luv. Read it. You're safe now."

She undid the string and folded back the bright yellow plastic to reveal a thin pouch. Inside there was an envelope with the Central Intelligence Agency logo on it and her name scrawled across the front in her father's bold, masculine handwriting. She wiped her muddy hands on her shorts and opened the sealed envelope.

It took several tries before her numb fingers managed to pull out the folded sheet of heavy ivory paper. The stationery was familiar, for it had come from her father's desk in Washington. The letter was handwritten and brief:

Erin—

I'm sorry, baby. I was a fool to let you go with Cole Blackburn. I've discovered that Blackburn is owned by the Chen family, the most powerful, ruthless, and ambitious tong in Southeast Asia.

The man who brings this to you, Jason Street, can be trusted. He works for the Australian counterpart of the agency. Do what he says. Above all, don't trust Blackburn. He's your assassin, not your bodyguard.

Be careful. I love you.

The letter was signed as her father always did in his letters to her, with an aggressive, oversized D for "Dad."

Erin closed her eyes and felt cold all the way to the center of her bones. When she opened her eyes and looked at Street, he was watching her, but the muzzle of the gun was still aimed at Cole.

Cole hadn't moved. He still lay on his stomach with one arm folded underneath his chest. His face was turned away from her.

She turned to Jason Street. "How did you find me?"

"It wasn't easy. The chokies Blackburn works for had you covered like a bloody blanket. If the black boy following you hadn't been broadcasting in the clear, I'd still be looking. As it was, I just homed in on the RDF."

"Chokies?"

"Chinamen," Street said impatiently, then reined himself in. "The Chen family. Blackburn has been in partnership with Chen Wing for years."

"Are you the one who gave that information to my father?"

"Is that what the letter said?" Street countered.

"How did you get the letter?"

"I work for the Australian government, although you won't find me on any civil service payroll form," Street said. "Sort of like your father in that. He and I do the same kind of work. That's why I'm here."

"Mistakes are made in your kind of work, Mr. Street. I believe my father made one. Cole Blackburn isn't my assassin."

"Like bloody hell," Street said. "Just because Blackburn has been in your pants doesn't mean he won't kill you. Chen Lai is his number-one woman. He's been making jig-a-jig with Lai since you were in pigtails. He's just using you until you give him the clues to Abe's mine. Then you'll be deader than tinned fish and the mine will belong to the Chen family. But I'm here to see that doesn't happen. Now, did you find that bloody mine?"

"I'm—I'm not sure."

"What do you mean?" Street demanded.

She stood up quickly, bringing the rucksack with her.

Street's eyes flashed reflected light as he followed her movements, but the muzzle of his gun remained trained on the man who lay less than two feet away.

She forced herself to go closer to Street.

"I'm no geologist," she said as she jerked at the buckles and ties on the rucksack, opening it up. "Here. Decide for yourself."

With that she stepped past Street and turned the rucksack on end. A sparkling, colorful cascade of rough stones poured through the hard white light of the electric lantern.

"Sweet Jesus and all the saints in heaven," Street said

hoarsely, staggered by the sight. For an instant the gun muzzle moved aside from Cole.

It was all Cole needed. He came off the ground in a lunge that ended only when he rammed the knife blade up underneath Street's rib cage and into his heart. Death was instant and nearly bloodless.

Cole caught the Aussie's pistol before it fell from limp fingers. He jerked the knife free and stepped back. Street slumped face first across the dancing, rolling diamonds. Automatically Cole wiped the blade on his shorts before he sheathed it. He put on the pistol's safety before he reached for the electric lantern.

Swallowing against the bile rising in her throat, Erin said raggedly, "Is he dead?"

"Pick up the diamonds."

The words were thick, almost slurred. Cole grunted as he dragged Street aside and left him facedown in dense shadow. Moving with uncharacteristic hesitation, as though he didn't completely trust his own body, Cole went back to Erin. He held out the pistol butt first.

"Can you use this?" he asked.

"Dad made sure I could shoot anything I could get my hands on," she said numbly, taking the gun.

"Smart man."

His words sounded like they came from a distance. Vaguely she realized that she was on the edge of going with shock and cold, hunger and exhaustion. She was at the end of her strength, and all she had to trust was someone who had just killed Jason Street in front of her eyes.

Street, who had been sent by her father to protect her from Cole Blackburn.

"So you believed him after all," Cole said harshly. "You're a fool, Erin Shane Windsor. I've killed men, but I'm not a hired assassin."

At first she didn't understand. Then she saw that the pistol in her hands was pointed directly at Cole . . . and she had taken the safety off. She let out a broken breath and lowered the gun.

"You're right," she said bleakly. "If you'd been hired to kill me after the mine was found, I'd be facedown in a black lake right now."

His eyes glittered with pain and fury. "Such carefully measured trust—from the head, not the heart."

"That's the way *you* trust," she shot back. "It's the way my father trusts. It's the way the whole world trusts. I'm a slow learner, but I do learn eventually. And I'm damned tired of being fucked by men on their way to more important things."

Cole turned his back on her. "If you want the bloody diamonds, pick them up and come to the entrance. I'll see if there are any more nasty surprises waiting outside."

Without a word Erin put on the safety and shoved the pistol into the rucksack. Then she knelt and began scooping handfuls of diamonds from the clammy limestone floor. The stones made secret, almost musical sounds as they clicked over one another and the cold steel of the pistol.

She ignored the diamonds that had rolled into the darkness where Street's body lay. There wasn't enough money in all of Abe's mines to make her pick up those diamonds. Street was welcome to them. He'd certainly paid enough for them.

Before she was finished, Cole came back. He was carrying the shotgun. "Leave the rest. We're getting out of here before anyone else comes."

"I don't think I can walk very far," she said with eerie calm.

"Neither can I. Street was flying the station helicopter." When Cole turned away he stumbled slightly, caught himself, and kept walking. "Move it, Erin. I loaded everything that matters into the chopper."

"Where are we going?"

"Windsor station. Now that Street's dead, it should be safe. In any case, it's the last place anyone will expect to find us."

Drawing together the shreds of her strength, she picked up the rucksack and followed Cole out of the cave.

For the first few minutes the steamy heat felt like a foretaste of heaven. By the time she'd walked to the helicopter, she was back in hell, sweating. Cole wasn't. When he handed her into the chopper, his skin felt distinctly cool.

The chopper leaped up, jittered raggedly, and finally settled.

Ten minutes later she glanced at Cole and saw his head hang, then slowly come upright. He was fighting to stay conscious.

And he was losing.

46

On the way to Abe's station

Rain fell in sheets and torrents over the bubble canopy of the helicopter, cutting visibility to a few hundred yards. Erin read the instruments for Cole as he pointed to them. Her voice was flat, as numb as her mind. She should have been terrified but she was simply too worn out to care.

She knew it must be much worse for Cole.

She sensed a great weariness in him. His coordination and his vision were erratic. He was sweating but his skin was cold. Time after time the helicopter sagged to one side or the other in gusts of wind and each time he reacted more slowly to correct their course. Concussion had sapped his strength. He was operating on nerve and reflex alone, and all around them a storm's dying fury gripped the world.

"We should set down," she said.

"Too far away. We wouldn't make it."

She didn't argue. It was the truth. She'd barely had the strength to drag herself and the rucksack to the chopper.

"You have a concussion," she said.

"No shit. Read the compass."

She focused on the compass.

A lightning bolt sizzled from cloud to earth, making the earphones Erin and Cole wore crackle violently. He flinched at the sound and turned the volume down on the radio.

They flew out of the squall as suddenly as they'd flown into it. Within minutes wind tore holes in the black line of clouds. Sun hammered through the openings with stunning force, pulling great sheets of steam from the drenched land.

Off to the left a tin roof gleamed in watery brilliance beneath the gloom of a storm cell that still had enough power to trail thick sheets of rain from its wild clouds.

"Look," she said, touching his arm and pointing to the left. "Isn't that the station?"

"'Sbout time."

The words were slurred. Cole's face was drawn in harsh lines of effort as he corrected the helicopter's course. When they flew into the trailing edge of the squall, the helicopter bucked and quivered like an unruly horse. He swore at the controls and at the reflexes that simply wouldn't respond as quickly as they should.

The chopper slewed through the rain and wind until the lights of Windsor station were a few hundred feet below them.

"Look—for—strange—vehicles," he said thickly.

He banked the helicopter and flew in a wide, ragged circle around the perimeter of the station buildings. She looked through veils of rain at the ground. Several lanterns glowed inside the large tent that had been erected as a bunkhouse for the Chinese men, but no one was out in the yard. Obviously the men had settled in to wait out the storm.

A pale flash caught her attention. "There's a white four-wheel-drive vehicle parked in back of the house."

"Street's. Any others?"

"No."

Cole let out a sigh that was almost a groan. "Thank God."

As he circled to the front of the station house, the door opened and a small figure stepped out.

"It's Lai," Erin said.

"Alone?"

"As far as I can see, yes."

Lai stepped out of the shelter of the awning and looked up into the sky, shielding her eyes against the falling rain.

Cole shook his head sharply, then winced. "Shotgun. Get it."

She leaned over and pulled the shotgun from behind his seat.

"Is it ready?" he asked.

She checked the gun, took off the safety, and said, "Yes."

Visibly he gathered the last of his strength. "Put it across my lap. Keep the pistol hidden but handy. If there's a trap down there, no one will expect you to be armed."

Without a word Erin lifted the rucksack onto her lap, dug the pistol from beneath diamonds, and slipped off the safety. She would only have to open the rucksack and grab.

Cole wheeled the helicopter and dropped into the muddy yard in front of the station. The landing was hard. One of the skids dug four inches into the red muck. The other slapped down a second later and vanished beneath mud. He shut down the engine, let the rotor free-wheel, and slumped forward.

Erin scrambled out while the blades were still slicing overhead and went around to the other door to help him.

"Get out," she said, tugging at his arm. "You can't stay here."

He didn't move.

"Get out!" she shouted. "I can't carry you to the house. Come on, Cole. *Help me.*"

Slowly his head came up. He dragged himself out of the helicopter, shotgun in hand. Clutching the rucksack, she steered him through the mud to the station house, where Lai waited.

"I'm so glad Mr. Street found you," Lai said huskily, watching Cole with luminous black eyes. "We were very worried. Wing has been beside himself." She looked beyond Erin and Cole. "Where is Mr. Street?"

"Dead," Erin said bluntly.

"Dead? I don't understand."

"He tried to kill Cole. He missed. Cole didn't."

Lai's breath came in with a soft, ripping sound.

Erin pushed past Lai and guided Cole into the house. "Cole's hurt. Get some blankets, a first-aid kit, and ice for the swelling." She looked at Lai, who was standing as though bolted to the floor. *"Move."*

"But first," Cole said thickly, "call Uncle Li and tell him to send in reinforcements. We found the mine."

For a moment longer Lai stared at Cole. He was swaying slightly on his feet, but his eyes were focused and his finger was on the trigger of the shotgun he carried. When Erin steered him toward the couch, he moved with a kind of ruined grace that spoke of willpower and muscle slowly losing control over injury and exhaustion.

Lai turned and ran toward the back of the station house.

Erin eased Cole down on the center of the couch. With a muttered curse, he slumped back and fought against closing his eyes. After a moment he pulled the shotgun across his lap. She set the rucksack at one end of the couch. As she knelt next to him to check his injury, her knee knocked against the butt of the shotgun.

"You've got a bruise half the size of my fist," she said. He grunted.

"No more bleeding," she continued. "The swelling isn't any worse. Good thing you have such strong muscles in your neck. Otherwise, I've got a bad feeling we'd still be in the cave."

"Stone dead."

"How do you feel?" she asked.

"It comes and goes."

"It?"

"Nausea, double vision, dizziness."

She shifted again. Her knee hit the shotgun. "I'll take that," she said, reaching for the shotgun. "We're safe."

"Not quite, Miss Windsor," Lai said from the doorway. "But you soon will be. Move away from Cole."

Startled, Erin looked up and saw an automatic pistol held in Lai's left hand. The muzzle was pointed directly at Cole's heart. Nothing about Lai suggested that she wasn't willing to pull the trigger. In her right hand she held a small battery-operated tape player.

"Move beyond his reach," Lai said. "Even wounded, he is still very dangerous."

Erin retreated down the couch toward the rucksack.

"Put the shotgun on the floor and shove it away with your foot," Lai said to Cole. "Move slowly or you will force me to kill you."

In slow motion he bent over, set the shotgun on the floor, and shoved it away with his foot. Black eyes and the muzzle of the gun followed him every inch of the way. Lai's attention was so fixed on Cole that she didn't notice Erin's hand coming out of the rucksack.

"Put down the gun," Erin said in raw voice. "I'm too tired to care if I kill you."

From the corner of her eye, Lai saw the gun in Erin's hands.

"Don't be foolish," Lai said quickly. "It is your life I am trying to save!"

"I'm damn tired of being called a fool—and being taken for one. If Cole wanted me dead, he could have killed me a hundred times over by now."

"You don't understand what is at stake." Lai spoke in a calm, low voice, and her attention never wavered from the man on the couch. She knew very well his strength, coordination, and intelligence. Obviously Street had underestimated Cole.

Lai never would.

"Street was playing the Chen family against ConMin," Lai said, "hoping to gain control of the mine for Australia. The Australian government wouldn't have ordered your death, Miss Windsor, but if you and Cole died in the bush and Street came to his superiors with the coordinates of the mine, the government would have registered the mine, declared you dead by accident—or by Cole's hand—and ridden out the storm of protest from the CIA."

"I'm alive," Erin said, "and planning to stay that way. Put down the gun."

"If I do, Cole will kill you. Listen to me, Erin. Your life depends on it. Cole has a forged gambling note from Abelard Windsor giving him half of the Sleeping Dog Mines."

"How do you know?"

"I oversaw the forgery," Lai said simply. "Now Cole controls half of the mine outright, plus half of your half. Don't you, Cole?"

"Whatever you say," he said. "You're the one with the gun."

Erin looked quickly at Cole. He was watching Lai with predatory focus, waiting for the least flicker of distraction on her part.

"Fascinating," Erin said, "but Cole never said one word to me about any gambling note."

Lai's mouth tightened. "He did not have to use the note. He had a much better lever against you: his body. He is a skilled, powerful lover and you are a woman of little experience. A very easy conquest. He has probably asked you to marry him already. If not, he soon would. And when you died a few months later—and you would die—Cole would have control of the mine in a way no man or government could question. You don't want to believe me," Lai said quickly, "but you will. Listen carefully, Erin Windsor. Your life depends on it."

"Cole?" Erin asked.

"Do as she says. You'll hear it all sooner or later. Divide and conquer. The oldest game of all. But whatever else you do, Erin, keep pointing that gun at Lai. The second you flinch, you're as dead as diamonds."

Lai pressed a button on the small machine. The tape started moving.

"The first speaker is my brother, Wing," Lai said. "You will recognize the second man. Cole Blackburn. The conversation took place the day before Cole came to you in Los Angeles."

After a brief silence, a voice came from the speaker.

"The Chen family didn't hire you merely because you're a brilliant prospector, although you are. We brought you into this because you have a verbal promise from Abelard Windsor of a fifty-percent interest in Sleeping Dog Mines Ltd. as a full repayment of gambling debts incurred by him during a night of playing Two Up. Do you have an IOU?"

"Old Abe wasn't that crazy."

"This was found at the station."

"Wing is referring to the IOU," Lai said in the silence that came when the men stopped speaking. "The IOU said, 'I owe Cole Blackburn half of Sleeping Dog Mines/Because I lost at 2-up one too many times!'"

After a few more moments of silence, Wing resumed speaking.

"The Chen family has taken the liberty of having two handwriting experts certify this document, so you need not fear embarrassment on that score. Even without the note, it is a legitimate gambling debt. With the note, the debt will be promptly recognized by the Australian government when you press your claim."

The tape went silent.

"There is more," Lai said.

She watched Cole with unblinking attention. He watched her in the same way.

After a few seconds of silence Wing's voice came again.

"If a woman was all that stood between you and 'God's own jewel box,' what then?"

"I learned long ago that diamonds are more enduring than women."

"And more alluring?"

There was a brief pause before Wing continued.

"Whether you seduce her or not is your choice. Your job will be to keep her from getting killed while she unravels Crazy Abe's secret or until you find the mine yourself. After that, Miss Windsor no longer matters. Only the mine itself is important. That must be protected at all costs."

"Even at the cost of Erin Windsor's life?"

"Next to that mine, nothing else is important. Nothing."

A pause, then, "All right, Wing. Tell Uncle Li he has his man."

The silence hissed with unused tape.

Lai waited, never looking away from Cole.

"I would like," Erin said hoarsely, "to hear that tape again."

Lai groped one-handed for the rewind button, then glanced aside to find it.

Cole's foot lashed out and connected with her wrist. The gun went flying. When his hand wrapped around Lai's delicate throat, she went utterly still. In a gesture that could have been a caress or a warning, he ran his thumb over the pulse beating visibly in Lai's neck.

"You're just one surprise after another," he said to Lai. "How long have you spied for Street against your own family?"

A shudder went through Erin as she heard Cole's voice. There was no hatred, no passion, no anger, no emotion of any sort, simply a ruthless patience that owed nothing to civilization or humanity. It was the same for his eyes, icy in their clarity and lack of mercy.

"I began planning my revenge the moment I was forced to abort your child and marry a man three times my age," Lai said. Her voice was low, soft, husky, the voice of a woman talking to her lover. "I was the one who approached Jason Street. I was the one who sabotaged the helicopter and the Rover. I was the one who told Jason to have one of Abe's Aborigines follow you and report the instant that you died. Then Jason and I would fly in and fix the Rover, discover the tragic deaths, and take out new leases in our own names."

Slowly Erin's hand tightened on the heavy gun.

Lai didn't even notice. Her attention was fixed on the ice-pale eyes of her former lover. She kept speaking, her voice sweetly musical, as though talking of love rather than vengeance and death.

"On the day I owned the mine, the family of Chen would count the cost of using me as a pawn," Lai said. "I am queen, not pawn. And the man by my side would be king."

Cole's strong fingers ran caressingly over Lai's neck. "Queen of lies." He glanced over at Erin. Her face was pale, her eyes so dark they looked more black than green. "I don't suppose it would do any good to say I fell in love with your photos before I ever met you."

"Love? You?" Erin made an odd sound that could have been a laugh or a sob. "Sweet God, Cole, credit me with enough sense to come in out of the rain."

"Yeah, I figured that's how you'd look at it. Congratulations, honey. You've finally learned to be a survivor. Now you'll have the same problem I had—finding something worth surviving for."

Erin looked away, unable to meet the bleakness of Cole's eyes.

"I'm going to call Chen Wing and tell him to come and get his ever-loving sister," Cole said to Erin. "If you don't like that idea, you've got a gun. Use it."

Swaying, Erin fought the slow trembling that was taking her body.

"You saved my life out there," she said raggedly, lowering the gun. "I kept Lai from killing you. We're even."

Cole's smile made ice slide down Erin's spine. "Lai wasn't going to kill me. She was going to have me sign a marriage certificate—right after she killed you."

Lai's head dipped gracefully as she brushed her chin caressingly across the powerful hand that was still holding her prisoner.

"If the baby had been male," Lai said huskily, "I would

never have aborted it. But the child was only female and you were in Brazil. It is not too late, beloved. She will not shoot you. Take the gun from her. Together we could rule the diamond tiger."

In the stretching silence, the sound of Erin's broken breathing was far too loud. Cole watched as the gun muzzle shifted to Lai's head and Erin's finger tightened on the trigger. He made no move to interfere, simply waited with inhuman patience for whatever Erin decided.

"You're better at handling snakes than I am," Erin said hoarsely, lowering the gun. "Kill her or keep her for a pet, it makes no difference to me."

Erin walked out of the room without looking back.

47

Los Angeles
Several weeks later

"It was good of you to come here," Chen Wing said to his guests.

The man nodded. The woman ignored him.

Wing closed the door of BlackWing's Los Angeles office behind Erin and Matthew Windsor. Wing's dark glance came back to Erin and stayed. She looked different from her photo. Older. More reserved. More controlled. Her hair was pulled back in a sleek chignon. Her clothes were expensive and casual.

But it was her eyes that had changed the most. There was a cool assessment in them that hadn't been there before.

"Please. Sit down," Wing said.

He smiled slightly and gestured for Erin and her father to sit at the long conference table. A closed carton sat in the center of the table.

She eyed the carton, decided it contained computer paper, and concentrated on Chen Wing. In his own way, Wing was as striking as his sister. The same perfection of physical form. The same intelligence. The same shrewd black eyes.

"How is your sister?" Windsor asked blandly as he sat down.

"The psychiatrist offers great hope for her eventual recovery," Wing said. "Until then, of course, she will have to remain medicated and under constant psychiatric observation."

"Why?" Erin asked bluntly. "Cole broke her wrist, not her skull."

"I'm afraid Lai's mind was never very strong. We have had to, ah, oversee her daily life before."

"Really?" Erin said. "Be sure her overseers have stout chairs and steel-tipped whips."

Windsor looked at his watch. "We're on a rather tight schedule, Wing."

"Of course." Wing looked directly at Erin. "Cole insists that he owns only half of Black Dog Mines, the half you gave him as a finder's fee."

"I gave him half of what I inherited," Erin said in a cool voice. "Whether I inherited all or half of Black Dog Mines depends on how well you like the signature on the IOU Lai mentioned. Unless you really subscribe to the notion that your sister is crazy."

"Cole refuses to press recognition of Abelard Windsor's gambling debt, although there is no doubt the debt exists," Wing said carefully. "Cole also refuses to make a deal with DSD for more than the half of Black Dog's output that BlackWing owns. The members of the diamond cartel are understandably . . . restless. Half a resource does not constitute a monopoly."

She shrugged. "So they'll make a little less money. So what?"

Wing looked at Windsor. "Haven't you told her?"

"My father doesn't own one carat of Black Dog's rough," she said distinctly. "Talk to me, not him."

"If the cartel is broken," Wing said, "industrial diamonds will be priced beyond the reach of emerging Third World countries such as China."

"That doesn't make sense. If the diamond monopoly is broken, the price should fall."

"The price of gem diamonds, yes," Wing said. "But not the price of bort."

"Why?"

"The cost of cleaning out a diamond pipe is staggering," Wing said simply. "Bort does not repay the cost of its own mining. For a diamond mine to make any profit, the gem diamonds must be sold at reliable, inflated prices."

"Then make industrial diamonds in your labs," she suggested indifferently.

Wing looked in silent appeal at Windsor, who sighed and began speaking.

"It's not that easy, baby," Windsor said. "Lab synthesis is coming along, but it still isn't nearly as cheap as the cartel's bort. Besides, even if lab diamonds got the job done at a low price, Japan has the best process. No one wants the Japanese to have any more international economic clout than they already have."

For a moment she was silent, weighing what had been said. And what had not.

"What you're telling me," she said finally, "is that it would be tough for Third World countries to industrialize without low-priced industrial diamonds."

A shuttered look came over Wing's face. "It would be nearly impossible. Diamonds are far more important in manufacturing than most people realize, especially in the type of manufacturing that is within reasonable reach of emerging economies." Wing spread his hands in silent appeal. "Isn't it better to let the luxury diamond trade in First World countries subsidize the cost of mining industrial diamonds for the Second and Third Worlds?"

"An industrialization the Chen family is in a position to control in China," Erin pointed out evenly, "a country that has more than a fifth of the world population and a tradition of being central to all Asian power. Whoever controls China will soon control all the Pacific Rim economies except the U.S.A. and Japan. You could, of course, ally yourself with Japan. In that case the U.S. would be driven into even stronger economic alliances with Europe. Even with Japan's help, you can't expect to succeed. Correct?"

Wing nodded slowly, understanding too late that Erin was as bright as Cole had warned him she would be.

And as hostile.

"I won't even discuss the Chen family's persistent interest in strategic minerals, which are handled through one of ConMin's many companies," Erin continued. "Nor will I dwell on the fact that if the cartel goes under, Black Dog Mines' value goes through the floor, taking with it BlackWing's half interest in a hugely lucrative chunk of real estate."

Wing shot Windsor a look.

Erin's father didn't notice. He was watching his daughter with amused admiration.

"You've done your homework, baby."

"As in opening my eyes?" She smiled coolly. "As I said to Cole, I'm a slow learner, but I do learn."

"The Chen family is already quite wealthy," Wing said neutrally. "We don't depend upon ConMin for that wealth, or upon Black Dog Mines."

Erin looked at her father.

"He's telling the truth," Windsor said. "The Chens

aren't bucking Hugo van Luik and DSD just for money. They want power."

"How does Nan Faulkner feel about that?" Erin asked.

"She'd rather give the Chen family power than sink the diamond cartel. Right now the Soviets need the cartel too much." Windsor shrugged. "Besides, the cartel is the devil we know, and we've spent forty years learning how to get a handle on it. We've turned it into a game of checks and balances. At this point no single country's interests rules. Not even ours."

Erin waited. Her father simply watched her. "No advice for me?" she asked. "That's new."

"You're too busy looking for blood to listen." Windsor smiled slightly. "Besides, you don't need my advice. You've changed, baby."

"Being hunted like an animal does that."

"Don't get me wrong," he said quickly, smiling. "I'm not complaining about the changes. You can't own half of Black Dog and be a trusting soul. And you're not planning on giving up control of your half of the mine, are you?"

"I haven't decided."

"Three choices," Windsor said, yawning. He'd spent too many sleepless nights worrying about Erin's safety and Nan Faulkner's mistakes. "One: Hand over control of your half of the mine to someone and walk away. Two: Keep control and grab a piece of the diamond tiger. Three: Kill the tiger by talking Cole into withholding his half of the rough from DSD."

She nodded, having reached the same conclusion herself in the middle of the many long nights she'd spent neither awake nor asleep, half dreaming, half remembering, regret and desire and anger clawing her soul. "As I said, I haven't decided."

With a small sound, Wing cleared his throat. "The third choice isn't a realistic option."

"What you're saying is that dear old Uncle Li won't let Cole break the cartel." It was a statement rather than a question.

The smile Wing gave Erin was as thin as the cutting edge of a knife. "Unfortunately, no one controls Cole Blackburn, not even my very clever uncle. But Cole is far from stupid. He knows it would not take much of a bomb to close off the cave or even to destroy the commercial value of the diamonds with radiation and pass it off as a mining accident."

Erin's mahogany eyebrows lifted. "Sounds rather drastic."

"Quit baiting the man," Windsor said, yawning again. "One way or another, nearly every country in the world has a stake in the cartel. No one would help you cut its throat. All of them would rather have Black Dog destroyed, and you with it, than have the cartel broken."

"Cole knows the danger," Wing said to her. "He does not want you hurt. He has made unpleasantly vivid to Uncle Li exactly what would happen to the family of Chen if any, ah, accident were to overtake you."

Windsor's eyes narrowed. "If Erin had an 'accident,' Blackburn isn't the only one who would come down on the Chen family like seven years of bad luck."

Wing nodded. "Granted, but it is Cole Blackburn we fear."

With an effort Erin kept her face impassive, revealing nothing of her inner turmoil. "You're jumping at shadows, Mr. Chen. Cole Blackburn would trade me for a bucket of diamonds. In fact, he already did."

"Bullshit, baby," Windsor said instantly.

She gave him a bleak look.

"I've talked to Cole," Windsor said, "which is more than you can say."

"When?" she asked before she could stop herself. "Is he all right?"

"His skull wasn't fractured. His brain is working just fine. As soon as he was back on his feet, he called to ask me two questions. The first was where Hans Schmidt is."

Her mouth dropped in shock. "Why in God's name would Cole want to find Hans?"

"To kill him," Windsor said impatiently. "Why else?"

"I . . . that's . . ." She shook her head, too stunned to speak.

"So I told Cole where Hans was. Name, rank, serial number, and exact address of the hospital where Hans lives in unholy matrimony with a respirator and a feeding tube sewn into his gut."

She tried to say something. She couldn't. In seven years her father had never mentioned Hans Schmidt's name.

"Seems the sorry son of a bitch had an accident about seven years ago," Windsor said with icy satisfaction. "One of those nasty little tricks of fate. A car wreck. Glass everywhere, including in every inch of good old Hans."

"An accident," she repeated hollowly.

"He's completely paralyzed," Windsor continued in a soft voice. "Well, not completely. He could still blink his eyes, if he had any eyelids. He could see, if he had any eyes. He could talk, if he had a tongue. He could come, if he had a pecker and balls. But he doesn't have any of those things. His brain waves are fairly normal, so his mind is intact. Lucky Hans."

Wing's breath went out in a stream of rapid Cantonese.

"Cole thought it over," Windsor continued calmly, "and decided that Hans would look on death as a favor, and Cole wasn't feeling particularly generous. He wishes Hans a long, long life. So do I, baby. So do I."

"An accident," Wing said in English. "How . . . convenient."

Windsor looked at him. "Nothing personal. A message had to be sent to the opposition about civilian dependents being mauled by professionals for no better reason than sadistic pleasure. I got to choose the message. It was received. Not one dependent has been touched in seven years." He looked back at his daughter. "The second thing Cole wanted to know was if the letter Jason Street had with my signature on it was a forgery."

"Why?" she asked, her voice thin.

"Probably the same reason he wanted to know where Hans was," Windsor said dryly. "You may have walked away from Cole, but he hasn't walked away from you. I'll tell you the truth, baby. I'm damned glad the note was a forgery. That's one tough man you have."

"He's not my man. All he wanted was the mine."

"I don't believe that and neither do you."

"You would if you'd heard the tape."

"I heard several versions of it," Windsor said impatiently. "All of them were true as far as they went. They just didn't go far enough. People keep forgetting that Cole Blackburn is as independent as an avalanche. He didn't just wag his tail and line up for the Chen family's diamond-studded collar and leash."

"How do you know?"

"Simple. I went up to his office to have an off-the-record chat with him before I 'met' him with Nan Faulkner. I asked Cole why he was doing it. He told me that a woman who could take photographs like you was worth more than her weight in fancy diamonds."

Erin made a small, startled sound.

"So I'll bet he took the IOU from Wing," Windsor said, "and went along with the game to prevent the Chen family from forging another IOU and cutting a deal with someone who wouldn't care if you lived or died. It's what I would have done if I'd been Cole and cared about your survival."

Wing smiled wryly. "Uncle Li recently arrived at the same conclusion. You and Cole are a lot alike, aren't you?"

"In some ways," Windsor agreed. "But not in one. I'd rather die than be down in that damned black hole right now, racing the monsoon rains for a bucketful of diamonds, watching the water level around me rise and rise and rise until there's no way out but death."

Erin's hand shot out and grabbed her father's wrist. *"What are you talking about?"*

"You heard me."

"But Cole knows how dangerous it is! He wouldn't risk his life for more diamonds, no matter how many!"

"Why not? What else does he have going for him? The woman he would have died for—and damn near did— walked away from him. That leaves him with second prize, the richest diamond strike ever made and the most expensive slice of hell ever owned by man."

"You're wrong," she whispered, forcing the words past the aching constriction of her throat. "I meant very little to Cole. I was a small affair on the way to a big strike."

"For God's sake, Erin—"

"Is that all, Mr. Chen?" she asked, cutting across her father's words.

"Except for the matter of turning your property over to you, yes."

"What property? You've already replaced the camera equipment that was destroyed when the Rover was buried in a flash flood. I took everything else I owned out of the station when I left."

"Not quite."

With quick, graceful movements, Wing opened the carton that sat in the center of the table. He tipped over the box. Eight-by-ten color photos cascaded across the surface of the polished wood. Pieces of the outback flashed and gleamed like glass in a kaleidoscope.

Termite mounds creating an alien city beneath a steamy silver sky.

Fragile, dusty, incredibly stubborn acacia trees growing out of stone.

Lightning arcing across an empty sky.

Empty stretching away to all horizons, relentlessly desolate, absolutely flat, the quintessence of loneliness.

And over all, the sun, always the sun, the blazing eye of an all powerful god.

"But . . . these are mine," she whispered.

Every single image had been taken from the rolls of film Erin had left behind in the sabotaged Rover.

"The negatives have been duplicated," Wing said. "One set is in a vault in the government casino in Darwin. The other set is in the safe here. A third is in your father's own safe. Cole did not want to take a chance on losing any of your work."

She tried to speak. She couldn't. She could only stare at images she'd been certain were lost forever.

"These are really good," Windsor said, sifting through the photos intently. "Hell, they're incredible. It's the best work I've seen you do, and that includes *Arctic Odyssey.* What do you think, baby?"

"I think—" Her voice broke. "Why did you lie about the Rover, Mr. Wing? It wasn't destroyed. These photos are taken from all the rolls of film I had to leave behind."

"The Rover and everything in it was destroyed," Wing

said. "Cole carried the exposed film in his rucksack until you went down into the cave."

"But why?" she whispered, going through the photos as though the answer was in one of the images. "After the Rover was sabotaged, we were desperate. Every ounce he carried was for our immediate survival. There were *pounds* of film. He can't have wasted his strength carrying it. That's crazy, and Cole isn't crazy."

"I pointed that out to him," Wing said dryly. "He said you had taught him there was more to life than just survival, but all he had taught you was the opposite."

Numbly, fighting emotions she couldn't even name, she sifted through photo after photo. There were hundreds of them, but only one drew her eye again and again, Cole in the dry watercourse just before the helicopter had come and sent them on a desperate hike across the Kimberley. Cole had been examining a handful of dry-panned grit when he had noticed her stalking him. He'd looked up the instant before she'd triggered the camera. Even shadowed by the brim of his hat, his eyes shone like clear crystal. The intensity in him was stunning, as was the hunger for her he'd never bothered to hide.

If I had Abe's diamond mine right now, I'd trade it for film and give it to you.

She closed her eyes. She couldn't look any longer and know that Cole had carried her film through a hell of thirst and pain and danger and had never given up so much as an ounce of his burden.

"You really didn't know, did you?" Wing asked, watching the slow, silent fall of Erin's tears.

"He never said anything about saving my film," she whispered.

"Not the film. Cole. He loves you."

A shudder went through her body. In the silence that

followed Wing's statement, she heard echoes of other words, her own accusation: *You and Abe were a lot alike. Once burned, forever shy.*

And Cole's matter-of-fact response.

You should know, honey. You're backing away from the fire as fast as you can.

Tilting her head back against the tears that wouldn't stop falling, she asked herself if what he'd said was true.

"Forgive me, Miss Windsor," Wing said, "but I must ask again. What are you going to do with your half of Black Dog Mines?"

Without a word Erin stood up and walked out of the room.

48

Like the multicolored foam of a breaking wave, a curling line of extraordinary rough stones ran the length of the DSD's conference table. Like water itself, the first impression was of transparency flushed with blue, yet there were rainbows trapped within. Rising like bubbles amid the clear foam were flashes of chrome yellow and vivid pink, and exclamation points of a green so pure it had to been seen and touched and held to be believed.

Cole shook the last stone from the battered rucksack and walked the length of the long polished table where crystal ashtrays, sparkling water, and ballpoint or fountain pens awaited the pleasure of the members of the diamond cartel. He nodded slightly to Chen Wing, who was pulling BlackWing's "prayer" from a sleek leather folder.

Saying nothing to the other people who were staring in shock at the centerpiece he'd poured down the table, Cole went to the chair that had been placed at his request along the wall rather than at the table.

A rising hum of excitement ran through the room.

Mr. Feinberg picked up a pink stone the size of his thumb, pulled a loupe from his pocket, and began muttering in reverent Dutch.

Nan Faulkner gave Cole a shuttered glance, poured a glass of ice water, drank it, and walked over to him.

"I didn't know Street was compromised," she said bluntly.

She spoke in a voice that carried no further than his ears. Not that she needed to worry about being overheard. The cartel members were still transfixed by Cole's casual display of incredible rough goods.

For a long moment Cole looked at Faulkner with eyes that were as hard and emotionless as the clear stones he had dragged from beneath the relentlessly rising black water.

"That's what Matt told me," Cole said finally. "If he believes you after the stunt you pulled with that forged letter and house arrest, I guess I can."

"Does that mean you'll extend your agreement with DSD?" Faulkner asked quickly. "Three years ain't shit in the diamond trade and you know it."

"That's up to my partner."

"Mother of God," Faulkner muttered. "Erin refuses to see me or any representative of DSD."

"Do you blame her? You nearly got her killed."

With a narrow black look, Faulkner turned away.

"Faulkner."

Warily she turned back and faced Cole, warned by the quality of his voice.

"Don't get in Erin's way again," he said.

"I hear you, babe." Faulkner grimaced. "I heard Matt, too. But both of you would make life a hell of a lot safer for everyone—especially Erin—if you'd get her off the goddamn dime!"

With ill-concealed frustration, Faulkner stalked to

the head of the conference table, lit a cigarillo, and opened a beautifully worked Moroccan leather folder. Instantly the room became still but for the soft rustle of prayers being passed up to her and the muted crystal music of stones being returned to the center of the table. Faulkner blew out a stream of smoke, set the cigarillo in a crystal ashtray, and began gathering up the prayers.

"Before I proceed to the business of the day," Faulkner said, stacking the prayers neatly in front of her, "Mrs. van Luik asked me to express her thanks for your sympathy at the tragic death of her husband. It's times like this when you find out who your friends are."

Cole didn't see the black sideways glance Faulkner threw in his direction. He was doing what he'd done many times since Erin had walked out of his life. He was staring at the green diamond she'd given him to seal their bargain. The stone had been extraordinary in the rough. Shaped, polished, and set in a brushed-platinum band, the tear-shaped diamond was a brilliant green flame burning with every dream, every secret, every hope of man.

Slowly his hand clenched around the ring until the stone's unfeeling edges bit into his flesh.

"You'll be pleased to know that a scholarship has been set up in Mr. van Luik's name," Faulkner continued. "The money will be used to train promising young geology students who wish to specialize in the discovery and utilization of diamond mines. Bringing such mines into production in an orderly, rational manner is crucial to maintaining stable prices in the diamond market. At a time when economic regimes are collapsing more quickly than we could have imagined a few years ago, maintaining DSD's stability is pivotal to the economic hopes of many nations."

She flicked her cigarillo against the crystal ashtray, opened a folder, and withdrew DSD's answers to the various prayers. After she stacked the papers next to the prayers, she poured a glass of ice water, drank it, and set it aside.

The room was silent except for the muted murmurs of men who still couldn't believe what had been set before their eyes.

"ConMin isn't bulletproof," Faulkner said baldly. "We're at a crossroads. The reason is spread down the table in front of you. I've talked privately with every member of the advisory committee. Does anyone have anything to add?"

This time the silence was complete.

"Then I would like to officially welcome the newest member of the advisory committee, Mr. Chen Wing. Mr. Chen represents the interests of BlackWing Inc., the source of the diamonds you've been admiring. Thanks to Mr. Chen's strenuous arguments with his partner, we will be handling fifty percent rather than twenty-five percent of the output of Black Dog Mines."

"For how long?" Yarakov demanded.

"Three years."

An unhappy muttering in several languages ran around the table.

"That is not enough time for short-term economic planning," Yarakov said.

The intercom began chiming with sweet insistence. Faulkner ignored it. It kept chiming.

With a sharp curse, Faulkner slapped the switch. "This better be good."

"A Miss Erin Windsor is here."

"That's real good, babe. Send her in."

The big door opened and Erin walked through. As she

walked the length of the table, she didn't notice the approving masculine looks from the various cartel members. She had eyes only for the big man who sat removed from the conference, his eyes hooded as he watched her.

Cole was dressed as he'd been when she'd first seen him—black silk sport coat, gray slacks, white shirt, no tie. She also was dressed the same as she had been then, in black shirt and slacks still rumpled from the suitcase.

"Well?" Faulkner demanded when Erin would have walked by without a word.

"What did Cole say?" she asked without stopping.

"A trial run," Faulkner said quickly. "Three years, fifty percent of the output."

"One year, one hundred percent," Erin countered as she stopped in front of Cole.

"Two years, one hundred percent," he suggested.

"Two years, one hundred percent," she agreed.

"Mazel und broche," Faulkner said quickly, sealing the bargain.

A chorus of *mazel*s went around the table, echoed by Erin and Cole.

With a look of shuttered hope, Cole watched the woman whose eyes were more beautiful than the diamond clenched in his fist.

"Two years, huh?" he asked, his voice deep, almost rough.

"Not for you." Lifting her left hand, she traced his mouth with fingertips that trembled. "You don't get off that easily. No trial run. All the years of your life. One hundred percent."

Silently Cole opened his hand, revealing the green flame of the diamond ring. "What about you?"

"The same. One hundred percent. All the years of my life."

He put the ring on her finger and pulled her onto his lap. Just before he kissed her, he whispered against her mouth.

"Welcome aboard the diamond tiger."

Author's Note

When I began writing *The Diamond Tiger* in early 1990, the world was a very different place than it is now. Updating the book in the sense of bringing plot points into the twenty-first century was impossible. Too much has happened, from huge diamond finds in Canada to wrenching political changes around the world.

I decided to leave the facts of the book intact—a snapshot of the diamond trade in the late 1980's.

Yet things other than politics change with time. Going through one of my favorite stories again gave me the chance to update some aspects of the *storytelling*. The result is a less formal, more colloquial novel.

I hope you enjoyed the reading as much as I did the creating.